DESPERATE DECEPTION

MARIA GREENE

AVON BOOKS ◆ NEW YORK

AVON BOOKS
A division of
The Hearst Corporation
105 Madison Avenue
New York, New York 10016

Copyright © 1988 by Maria Greene
Published by arrangement with the author
Library of Congress Catalog Card Number: 88–91530
ISBN: 0-380-75562-9

First Avon Books Printing: October 1988

Dear Romance Reader:

This year Avon Books is celebrating the sixth anniversary of "The Avon Romance"—six years of historical romances of the highest quality by both new and established writers. Thanks to our terrific authors, our "ribbon books" are stronger and more exciting than ever before. And thanks to you, our loyal readers, our books continue to be a spectacular success!

"The Avon Romances" are just some of the fabulous novels in Avon Books' dazzling *Year of Romance*, bringing you month after month of top-notch romantic entertainment. How wonderful it is to escape for a few hours with romances by your favorite "leading ladies"—Shirlee Busbee, Karen Robards, and Johanna Lindsey. And how satisfying it is to discover in a new writer the talent that will make her a rising star.

Every month in 1988, Avon Books' *Year of Romance*, will be special because Avon Books believes that romance—the readers, the writers, and the books—deserves it!

Sweet Reading,

Susanne Jaffe
Editor-in-Chief

Ellen Edwards
Senior Editor

For my parents,
Runar and Helmy Staffans,
and for Ingvar, Karin, and Erik

Chapter 1

West Sussex, August 1746

Bryony Shaw folded the ledgers with a sigh. "Nothing left, nothing at all." Her fingers curled around the edge of the topmost ledger. "My brother dead, and Willow Hills lost—the land, the house, everything."

"A pity the estate burned to the ground," said Mr. Holland, the Shaw family's elderly solicitor. As Bryony's face crumpled, he hurriedly continued, trying to ease her pain. "From all that we can tell, it was an accident. When the butler heard sounds of fighting coming from the study, he rushed into the room, but it was already too late. Someone had overturned a candelabra, and the curtains and papers were ablaze. The room was an inferno, and whoever had been fighting was gone." He sighed heavily. "The high winds that night carried the fire everywhere. Eventually there was nothing the servants could do but flee for their lives. Reggie's body was never found—just some ashes that were presumed to be his."

Bryony nodded and tried to smile, but failed miserably. "You were always very kind to us, Mr. Holland. I don't know what I would have done without you."

The old man placed his hand on the young woman's smooth black tresses and comforted her as he had of old. At the sight of the pale oval face before him, the slightly slanted aqua eyes blinking hard to control her tears, he was filled with sadness.

Bryony's lips trembled, and she bent her gaze to the closed ledgers to hide her sorrow.

1

Mr. Holland swore silently, then exclaimed, "I wish I had been there! I could have stopped him. Your brother always was a hothead, always was embroiled in hare-brained schemes. This time he went too far." Mr. Holland wiped his heavy jowls and watery eyes with a wildly patterned Indian handkerchief, pretending it was the heat from the fire, not grief, that brought moisture to his eyes. "It would be best for you to return to France, m'dear."

Bryony wasn't listening. "Reggie had a warm heart. He was the kindest brother anyone could want." She pressed a delicate batiste handkerchief to her eyes and dabbed at the tears that defeated her at last. "I cannot believe he is dead."

Mr. Holland wished he could tell her it was all untrue. But Reginald Shaw, the last male member of the Shaw family of Willow Hills, was gone, and his heritage with him. "What are you going to do now, Bryony?"

She lifted her gaze. The tears made her eyes brilliantly green, and it occurred to Mr. Holland that she had grown into a strikingly beautiful woman. She had been on the verge of womanhood when her father, Donald Shaw, had sent her to France to live with an aunt to gain some sophistication. Mr. Holland recalled how Bryony had scoffed at the prospect.

Life could not have been easy for her there, he reflected. The aunt was an old stick and an invalid to boot. Now there was seriousness and poise in Bryony's bearing, her throat slender and straight, her chin square and stubborn— a smaller replica of her father's, and of Reggie's, of course. There was much of Mr. Holland's old friend Donald Shaw in her. The reserve, yet also that underlying warmth and undeniable strength. And then there were the eyebrows— imperious black arches that gave her face a forceful character. Yet her manners were quiet and faultless. Donald would have been proud of his daughter, Mr. Holland thought, and tapped one stubby finger agitatedly against the bridge of his nose. How could he help her, protect her from more tragedy?

"I don't know how I can pay Reggie's outstanding debts now that the estate is gone," Bryony was saying. "What I inherited from Mama is not nearly enough." She pleated her smooth brow. "I will have to think of something. There must be no shame attached to Reggie's name."

"Reginald's debts are none of your concern," said Mr. Holland. "Go back to France and find yourself a handsome husband. It is high time you were married."

Bryony shook her head. "I cannot live with the shame, I want to clear Reggie's name first." Her lips trembled as she struggled for composure. "I just cannot accept that he's dead. Why, only last week I received a letter from him saying he was planning a lengthy stay in Paris with me."

"You know how rash Reginald was. He changed his plans at the drop of a hat."

Bryony's gaze traveled to the fire in the shallow grate. Fire had swallowed her brother's body, wantonly, without regard for the agony that her twin must have suffered during his last minutes. Mr. Holland had said Reggie had died instantly, but she had *known*, had felt the enormous tug, the shattering loneliness in her heart when he went.

Still, something did not fit. She felt as if she was suspended in a state of tension-filled nothingness. If she was ever to rest, to sever the last invisible bond with her twin, she needed answers to her question.

Still, the fact remained, she would never see her brother's carefree face and infectious grin again. Never see him riding a horse. Never see him in a setting such as this one, a book-lined and soft-carpeted study. She shivered and pressed the handkerchief to her lips.

Mr. Holland grunted something, and Bryony's attention was drawn to his massive face. "The Butterball" she and Reggie used to call him because of his yellowish complexion and inflated middle. Uncle Butterball. Reggie had invented the fitting name. He had always come up with jokes that made her laugh until her sides ached.

"You might find the labor of delving into the cause of Reginald's death a difficult and destructive pastime," the solicitor said, blinking owlishly at her above the gold rims of his glasses. "You are doomed to fail, m'dear."

"Perhaps Nigel Farnham, Lord Lippett, will know what really happened that night."

"It was in Lord Lippett's presence that Reginald gambled away the last of his inheritance that night," Mr. Holland reminded her.

"Yes, but Nigel would never do anything to ruin Reggie's life," she argued. "They were best friends at school—at Eton and then Oxford. We've known Nigel for ages." She paused, thinking, then added hesitantly. "What puzzles me is the fact that Nigel let Reggie go so far as to lose everything."

Holland shrugged his shoulders in a gesture of futility. "The rumor is that another cardplayer, Lord Bentworth of Alfriston, egged your brother on; they had some sort of wager. But these stories are often blown out of proportion when everyone is eager to find a scapegoat. No one wants to be blamed for Reginald's death."

Bryony rose awkwardly, maintaining her grip on the edge of the gleaming mahogany desk, as if the burden of her sorrow was too heavy to bear without support. "I will have to visit Lord Lippett to find out the truth," she said, her lips set in a pale, determined line.

Mr. Holland heaved himself ponderously from the chair and clasped his hands atop his well-filled satin vest. "Bryony, it pains me terribly to see you so beside yourself with grief. You should not act rashly, y'know. I don't want you to expose yourself to gamblers and rakes. A refined young lady poking her nose into business best left alone might cause unforeseen trouble."

Bryony smiled for the first time that afternoon, a pale shadow of her usual sunny grin. "Is that an order, Uncle Bu— Holland?"

He pursed his lips and looked uncomfortable. "Eh, well—yes, I suppose so. Except for the protection of your aunt, you are alone, m'dear. What can a woman and an invalid accomplish? Best return to France."

Her shoulders sagged. "Yes, I suppose you're right. But I will visit Lord Lippett before I go." She held up her hands when he began to protest. "I promise that is all I will do. You must understand that I have to talk to Nigel. He was the last person to see Reggie alive."

Holland rubbed his shining pate and dabbed at his nose with the handkerchief. "Well, if your mind is set, you must go, but I will accompany you."

Bryony pulled on her narrow tan kid gloves and stood erect as he placed her burgundy wool cloak around her shoulders. "That will not be necessary. Aunt Hortense will chaperone me, and Jules LeBijou, the coachman, will protect me." She carefully set a wide-brimmed straw hat over her ebony curls and tied the pink taffeta ribbons under her chin.

"You're not wearing white hat ribbons then," said Mr. Holland, smiling.

"White ribbons?"

"For Charles Edward Stuart. The Jacobite sympathizers wear white ribbons to show their allegiance to the Stuart cause."

Bryony shook her head. "I didn't know. I heard Charles Stuart was at court in Paris only last year, and then he disappeared."

"He landed in Scotland in July last year and is still there, a hunted man. Some call him the rightful king of England and Scotland. Others call him the 'Young Pretender.' "

Bryony eyed the old man warily. "And you, Mr. Holland, what do you call him?"

Mr. Holland shrugged. "The pretender to the throne. I don't want the Catholics to rule the country—not ever again. The Hanoverians might be extremely dull and George silly, but they are Protestants, m'dear."

Bryony finished buttoning her gloves. "Religion rules politics then? Why bother mixing the two?"

Mr. Holland threw back his head and laughed. "That is a flippant French remark, Bryony. Reinstate the fanatics, and you'll have the Inquisition on our heads. Bringing back Catholicism would mean a return to the Middle Ages. There would be no end to political plots and secret backstabbing." He shook his head so that his jowls wobbled. "The blood would never stop flowing. The old Stuart who calls himself James III was lucky to escape with his life during the rebellion in '15. Charles might not be as fortunate. Ever since his defeat, James has cowered in Rome, espousing a religion that borders on fanaticism. When there is a Stuart on the throne, violence and darkness follow. They are a cursed lot."

"Charles II was very popular, and his father was considered a martyr," she protested.

Mr. Holland patted her head, crushing the silk flowers on the crown of her hat. "You are too young to understand the intricacies of politics, my dear girl, and—"

"And I'm only a woman." Bryony smiled and righted her hat.

Avoiding her bright gaze, he cleared his throat and stepped hurriedly to the door. "Give my best to your aunt. I will write to you in France. And if you ever need anything, don't hesitate to contact me."

"Thank you, Uncle B," Bryony said, and stood on her toes to give him an affectionate hug. Blinking away a tear, she ran light-footed into the street to the waiting coach.

"Uncle B?" she heard him ponder behind her. She wanted to laugh and cry at the same time. Reggie would have chuckled and said, "Let old Butterball solve that riddle if he can, little sis." It was cruel that the world would never be blessed with Reggie's mischievous smile again.

Bryony crept into the corner of the coach and cried as she had never cried before, grateful for the twilight that shielded her red-rimmed eyes and swollen nose from the world.

It was one of those gray days that heralded autumn. The sky was pressing low to the ground, punishing the earth with a steady, listless rain and wrapping a gray mist around the trees, as if forever condemning the world to dreariness.

Bryony ordered Jules to drive to The Pig and Deer, a comfortable inn on the outskirts of Crawley, where she had already taken a room. Tomorrow she would proceed to Nigel's estate, Greymeadows, at Cuckfield.

Bryony had deceived Uncle Butterball. Saying that Aunt Hortense was accompanying her was a deliberate lie, as was her claim that she was staying with friends in East Grinstead. Had she told him the truth—that she had run away from Paris and Aunt Hortense to investigate Reggie's death—he would have had an apoplexy.

She raised her chin in defiance. However many embellishments of the truth it took, she would not return to France, not until the mystery of Reggie's death was solved.

She would never feel at peace until she knew everything about the fatal card game and fire that had so cruelly robbed her of her twin brother.

Upon arriving in England, she had gone immediately to Willow Hills, her beloved childhood home. She would always remember the bleak skeleton of the ancestral estate, now burned to the ground, the chimneys stretching black brick arms toward heaven, the chaos of charred timbers lying around the foundation. Only part of the downstairs floors was still intact. Willow Hills was a place where willows grew no more, where once-beautiful green lawns had been scarred black.

The dark image was pierced by happier memories—of ponies, sunny parties on the lawns with her dolls, her mother's smiling face bending over her. How Bryony had loved to touch Mother's silky curls, as soft as her kitten's fur. Mother's features were a blur, but her gentle blue eyes were unforgettable. Bryony would always hold dear those loving eyes.

The year following her mother's death from a wasting ailment had been bleak. Father was never himself again; he grew hard and withdrawn. It was Reggie, always Reggie, who had brightened Bryony's life. She had been his shadow, his adoring companion, until Father had sent her away with the words: "When I see you next, I hope you will act like a woman and not like Reginald's younger brother." Her proud father had sounded so bitter. She had been afraid of him, not daring to protest. She had cried and railed in her room until Reggie had climbed the lime tree outside her window, almost breaking his neck in the process, and entertained her with one of his clownish performances.

Two years had passed since then, and everything had changed. Only six months ago, Donald Shaw had died in a fall from his horse. And now Reggie was dead, too. For some unfathomable reason, Reggie had not allowed Bryony to return to Willow Hills after their father's death. If he had, would he have recognized her? More importantly, would he still be alive?

France had changed her, or rather her aunt had. Her

father's autocratic sister expected complete obedience and dedication.

Bryony shuddered. For two years she had been a slave, a lowly servant whom her aunt had drilled like a general. *Don't slouch! Sit with your knees tightly together and your back erect! Your hands! You have dirt under your thumbnail! I will never be able to shape you into a lady.*

Bryony wanted never to return to France. The knowledge sat firm in her chest, but as yet she did not dare think of the future. What would she do? What *could* she do? When she had cautiously broached the subject of balls and parties with her aunt, the old woman had snorted, saying that no true gentleman would look twice at her too-dark hair, pale features, and bat-wing eyebrows.

Bryony touched her face gingerly. Was she really so plain? Reggie's face had been full of life and laughter, and surely she looked a bit like him, didn't she? Aunt Hortense had called her a plain knobby stick with no prospects of snaring a gentleman's interest. Bryony blushed in the darkness. She wasn't sure she wanted to snare a gentleman's interest, yet in her heart there was a vague longing for companionship, for tenderness. She wanted to know what it was like to enjoy a gentleman's admiration. That was only natural, wasn't it?

Closing her eyes, she pressed featherlight fingers to her lips, trying to imagine what the touch of a man's lips would be like.

Nigel's handsome face flashed before her. She had admired him for years, but he had treated her like Reggie's little sister, without an identity of her own. Now that Reggie was gone, it was as if she didn't exist at all; the thought frightened her. Still, life was bubbling in her heart, a thirst, a curiosity as yet unidentified. Restlessness gnawed at her, and she sighed.

She would go and see Nigel tomorrow. Perhaps he could advise her on how to proceed. Perhaps he would notice that she had grown up.

Rain beat against the coach window, and a gust of wind rattled the door. The darkness was complete, punctuated by the light of only a few candles in the windows of cottages along the road. She knew they were approaching the inn, but the lights barely penetrated the murky mist.

Jules shouted at the horses. The coach took a sharp turn and skidded over the wet cobblestones. Bryony clutched the window frame as the carriage listed. "Oh, no!"

There was a crash that tossed Bryony to the opposite seat, then a grating sound, followed by silence. "Wha—?" she cried as she hit the soft upholstery. Her vision blurred momentarily before she noticed the strange angle of the coach. The sounds of running footsteps, muttered curses, and whinnying horses came to her ears. She struggled to reach the door, but shock had weakened her limbs. Helplessly she fell back against the squabs. Her shoulder ached.

The door opened slowly, the hinges creaking. Bryony saw the dark silhouette of a man's head, the bow holding his hair in a queue at the back of his neck. His nose had a prominent bridge, like that of an eagle.

"Is anyone hurt?" he asked in a deep, rough voice.

"No—no, I'm only dazed," Bryony replied, and took his outstretched hand. His warm touch made her feel safe, and she yielded to the strength of his arms as he hoisted her out of the carriage. His long fingers almost spanned her waist, and his warmth seeped through the material of her gown. He steadied her on the ground, holding her for a moment longer than necessary.

"Can you stand by yourself now?" he asked kindly, gazing into her face.

She nodded and rubbed the shoulder that had taken most of the abuse in the coach.

The man looked once more into the interior.

"I'm the only passenger," she explained.

"I see." Looming tall above her, he touched her arm gently. "Are you in pain?"

"A little, but 'tis nothing really." She rotated her shoulder, and the pain was almost gone.

"You were lucky." With a slow movement, he massaged the sore spot. For some reason she couldn't pull away.

Two ostlers bustled about. They attached torches to the outside wall of the inn, then released the fallen horses from the overturned vehicle. The animals whickered and rolled their eyes in fear.

Jules limped to Bryony's side. A farmer's son from Provence, he was a giant of a man, with a swarthy, unattractive face dominated by a misshapen blue-veined nose. Devoted to her, he followed her everywhere. Bryony felt protected by his sheer size. He had sworn to guard her with his life, ever since she had defended him the day Aunt Hortense had him whipped for picking roses in the hothouse. Roses of all forms and shapes were Jules's passion, one he shared with Bryony.

"Pardon me, mademoiselle," he said in French, since he didn't know one word of English. "I didn't see the turn in time."

The tall stranger bent over to look at the wheels. "I'm afraid your carriages will not travel again until the axle is mended. There is a clean break right at the wheel."

"Oh, no," Bryony said with a moan. Her plans would be delayed.

"At least it happened right at the inn, if that is any comfort," the stranger added.

Beside her, Jules hung his head. She patted his arm. "It wasn't your fault, Jules. Are you hurt?"

He shook his head. "No, mademoiselle, just a slight bruise on my leg. I will see to the repairs immediately."

"No, wait until tomorrow. You deserve a rest after spending hours in this miserable rain." She delved into the pocket of her cloak and retrieved her purse. Opening the drawstring, she pulled out a few coins. "Buy yourself a decent meal and a good bed. We'll find out tomorrow how long the delay will be."

He touched the floppy brim of his damp hat. "Thank you, sweet angel," he said reverently, and limped toward the lights of the inn.

The stranger was still there, leaning against one of the wheels. Bryony turned to him. "Thank you for your assistance. There is nothing else to do but to seek shelter at the inn."

"A gently bred lady should not be traveling alone. The roads are dangerous, as are some travelers."

She glanced sharply at him. She could not see the

expression on his face, but his voice was calm and sincere. She couldn't very well tell him why she was alone—because her aunt's maid, Javotte, had abandoned her in Dover and returned to Paris. "I—I live in the neighborhood," she lied.

"Then I will find you a carriage and take you straight home. This is no fit place for a lady." He stood so close that his warm breath wafted across her face as he spoke. There was no menace in his attitude, yet he had a forcefulness that was overwhelming.

"No, you have done quite enough. I have no intention of going home just yet." She hastened toward the door, eager to leave him. But he was right there, holding open the door and bowing.

"You are very foolish."

For a fleeting moment she had an impression of shiny jet-black hair waving away from a high forehead. In the dim light of the vestibule, she thought his smile had a sardonic tilt. His features were angular, as if boldly carved from pale marble by a reckless sculptor, the shadows from high cheekbones throwing dark hollows on the lean cheeks and accentuating a fierce jaw. But it was the eyes that captured her attention.

He had eyes of dusky darkness, deep-set and luminous, framed by startlingly black lashes. He regarded her with frank interest, his gaze penetrating her soul. Her heart missed a beat.

His smile widening, he presented her with another handsome bow. "Jack Newcomer at your service," he drawled.

Refusing to introduce herself, Bryony acknowledged him with only a nod. She had to remind herself to step forward, away from him, but it was easier said than done. He crossed her path to open the door to the taproom.

He was about to say something as she advanced to speak with the host, but she did not stop. She rapidly ordered a dinner on a tray and, as she ran up the stairs to her room, cast a furtive glance over her shoulder. Jack Newcomer was sitting alone in front of the fire, a tankard in his hand. Devilish humor shone in his eyes, and he had the audacity to wink.

Flushed with embarrassment, Bryony lowered her gaze and flew up the rest of the stairs. First he had the gall to tell her what to do, then he ogled her rudely. His deep laughter floated behind her as she closed and bolted her door. He had warned her about other dangers, but he had failed to warn her about himself!

It was still raining the next morning, a steady pattering on the windowpane. Bryony brushed her hair vigorously until it waved smoothly down her back, then she wound it into a loose chignon and fastened it on top of her head. Two long ringlets curled over her shoulder. The previous evening she had wound the hair at her temples in papers in order to look her best for Nigel. She missed her aunt's upstairs maid, Javotte, but she was used to caring for her own needs, since Aunt Hortense had judged the money spent on a personal maid wasted.

Bryony drew a deep breath, happy to be standing on English soil again. As far as she could see through the mist outside the window, gentle hills and meadows made a patchwork of green, brown, and red ochre, the fields bordered by trees whose leaves dripped in the rain. God knew how long she would have to wait to see golden sunlight dance among the beech leaves.

She packed two dresses in her portmanteau; the trunk with the rest of her clothes stood unopened just inside the door. Her childhood mementos had burned with Willow Hills, all except the painted porcelain miniature of Reggie that hung from a long velvet ribbon around her neck. It was all she had left of him now, a smile frozen in time.

She straightened her blue velvet dress over the stiff panniers and the quilted underdress embroidered with small sprigs of flowers. Grateful that the bodice laced up the front instead of in the back, she pulled the cords tight and arranged the wide lace around the neckline.

She viewed herself critically in the mottled mirror. Would Nigel notice the French flair of her gown? Would he notice *her?* Her heart beat uncomfortably. She lightly powdered her face, rouged her lips, and attached a black patch at the corner of her eye.

Having suddenly lost her appetite, she merely nibbled at her breakfast, warm golden buns spread liberally with honey. The hot tea scalded her tongue as she drank too fast. Grimacing, she put the cup in the saucer and gulped down a mouthful of cold water. She had to calm herself! It wouldn't do to present herself to Nigel in this state. She needed to be cool and composed.

The large inn was crowded, filled with travelers waiting for the northbound stagecoach. Fat matrons and shy girls mingled with burly craftsmen and peasants having a bite of breakfast at the rough tables in the taproom. The low ceiling was black with soot, and the fire sent out puffs of smoke that irritated Bryony's eyes. She wanted to leave behind the crowds and the pervasive odor of sour ale.

The tall stranger from the night before was nowhere in sight. The involuntary stab of disappointment Bryony felt irked her. She reluctantly admitted to herself that she had been looking for him as she stepped downstairs. She could still remember the impact of his piercing gaze. The memory made her momentarily breathless.

Jules was waiting for her below, crushing his hat between his enormous hands. "Good morning, mademoiselle. I could do nothing about the carriage." He flung out his arms in desperation. "I cannot understand a word of this strange language."

Bryony smiled. "Well, let us deal with the problem right away."

They walked past the overturned coach, which was surrounded by curious children, and down the cobblestone street to the smithy, located next to the empty livery stables. The blacksmith returned with them, passing flintstone cottages with thatched roofs and well-tended garden patches. He examined the damaged coach and shook his head, stating he could not repair it until the following day.

Bryony tried unsuccessfully to bribe him with a golden guinea. She did not want to stay at the inn one more night, but what choice did she have? She voiced the question to the blacksmith.

"M'lady could take th' stage," he suggested. "Th'

Brighton Machine to Cuckfield, an' then 'ire a wagon to 'is Lordship's estate. I'll start workin' on yer coach first thing tomorrow morn,'' he promised placidly. Bryony nodded and thanked him, wondering what evil star was throwing obstacles in her way.

She returned to the inn, followed closely by the lumbering Frenchman, who held his cloak over her head to protect her against the mist. As she waited inside the half-timbered building of The Pig and Deer to purchase their tickets, Jules disappeared behind the stables.

The host promised to store Bryony's trunk until she returned the next day. The stagecoach was due in half an hour.

Bryony scanned the taproom, but there was still no sign of the tall stranger. Restless, she walked outside. It had stopped raining, but mist lingered on the ground, and the air was heavy with the scent of rain. She smiled as Jules offered her a small posy of half-crushed asters, which she pinned to her bodice.

"Thank you," she said, and the giant blushed. She realized that Jules loved her in his simple way. He was a man with the pure feelings of a child.

Most of the London travelers were soon gone, and a deceptive peace hung over the inn yard. Bryony paced back and forth, willing the minutes to pass more quickly. She felt uneasy, as if unseen eyes were tracking her progress. As her gaze skimmed the windows on the first floor, she thought she saw a curtain move. Was it her imagination? The dark panes revealed nothing.

A horn trumpeted the arrival of the Brighton stage, and Bryony stared down the misty road. The clouds had thickened, bringing the darkness of early evening, though the clock above the inn sign indicated it was only midmorning. As Bryony stepped inside the damp and smelly vehicle, the first heavy raindrop fell.

Since the few previous passengers had all disembarked at the inn, Bryony found herself alone in the coach. Jules climbed up beside the coachman, although she had beckoned him to join her inside. As the coachman cried "Giddy-up!" and flickered the reins, she anticipated the sudden wrench of movement.

Suddenly the door flew open, and another passenger threw himself inside just as the coach jerked forward.

Bryony's eyes widened in surprise. It was Jack Newcomer.

Chapter 2

As the horses gained speed, Jack Newcomer fell against the opposite seat, his legs sprawled, his face a study of surprise.

"Oh, good morning," he said cheerfully, and dashed off his tricorne. "What a delightful surprise. I didn't know I would meet you here. Please forgive my somewhat rude entry." He shoved his portmanteau under the seat.

Shocked by his sudden entrance, Bryony sifted through her chaotic thoughts for something to say. "Good morning," she breathed.

His mercurial energy invaded the coach, and for some reason it threatened her. He was dressed in shabby if clean burgher's attire, a gray velvet coat with modest trimmings, dark knee breeches, and mud-spattered white stockings. At his side hung a sword. His jaw wore the dark shadow of day-old stubble. An unruly wave had escaped from the bow holding the hair away from his face, softening his hard features. His splendid physique carried the modest clothes well, and Bryony heaved a sigh as she studied his broad shoulders and muscular thighs. The breath was knocked out of her as his smiling eyes captured her attention.

His lips curved cynically. "Madam, your scrutiny makes me feel like a horse on market day." He opened his lips wide and clamped together a set of strong white teeth. "Would you like to examine my teeth as well?" he challenged.

Bryony blushed and lowered her gaze. His teasing reminded her of the old days, of Reggie. "No, that is not necessary.'' Mischief flying into her, she donned her haughtiest expression and continued, ''Sir, if you were a horse, I would never purchase you.''

His eyes brightened. ''I say! Tell me why.''

''Your eyes are not trustworthy, your footwork too restless, your movements unpredictable, and you have knock-kneed legs.''

''Knock-kneed?'' he exclaimed incredulously, examining that knobby part of his anatomy. ''That is a huge exaggeration.''

She shrugged. '' 'Tis the plain truth. Don't expect me to lie and give you Adonis-like attributes. *That* you can do for yourself.''

Peering at him from under lowered lashes, she decided his jaw had drooped slightly. Triumph sprouted in her chest. She had taken him down a peg or two.

But it was her turn to drop her jaw when he threw back his head and laughed. The carriage echoed with the rumbling, infectious sound. Bryony's lips twitched, but she was not about to join him—not yet, anyway.

His mirth subsided slowly; he wiped his eyes. He drew an audible breath. ''You are delightful company. May I be so bold as to ask your name?''

There could be no harm in introducing herself. ''Miss Bryony Shaw.''

She noted his strong hand as he extended it to take hers. Pale and long-fingered, persuasive hands. A small ruby glowed on his little finger. She offered her fingers to his warm clasp, and a tremor went through her as his lips barely touched her skin and his fingertips played lightly over the sensitive skin of her wrist. She didn't know how to react to his practiced homage. The loose, jet-black wave of hair fell forward again, brushing her hand. Her every nerve registered the feel of him.

His face still tilting forward over her hand, he looked up, straight into her eyes. That heart-stopping breathlessness washed over her again, and she could not tear her gaze away. It was as if he could read her past and her future, every little secret of her life. And, yes, he seemed familiar, as if he were every friend she had ever known—

and the admirer she had always secretly dreamed of meeting.

When he finally turned away, she knew one thing; his eyes held secrets she had to discover.

An urge to escape coursed through her. This was not how she had expected the day to begin. Not with this strange man who touched her soul. The route she had charted upon landing in England seemed impossible to travel alone after she had looked into his eyes.

Confused and cold, she rubbed her arms and stared out the window. He wasn't laughing anymore; silent and brooding, he too, gazed out the rain-streaked glass.

Silence stretched unbearably between them, until it was shattered by the abrupt sound of his voice. "Bryony is an unusual name. Are you black or white?"

Bryony glanced at him. Black or white? The Jacobite business? she wondered. "I'm sorry, I don't understand," she said softly. To her annoyance, her voice trembled slightly.

"Black bryony or white bryony. The black variety has poisonous red berries."

"And the white?" she probed.

"Let's just say that it is more tame."

A slow smile played over her lips. "Even though the walls of my childhood home were covered with the bryony vine, let's just say that I am Bryony, the human variety."

"And not so tame?"

"Judge for yourself. However, I don't think you'll have time to discover much about me. I'm going only as far as Cuckfield."

He whistled in surprise. "You are disappointing me."

"Where are *you* going, Mr. Newcomer?"

"Oh, well, here and there, north and south, east and west, to the ends of the earth."

"How enlightening," she commented with some irony. "This coach will take you only to Brighton."

He shrugged. "Then I will start from there."

"Oh." Itching to ask him where he was from, she opened her mouth, but warning signals went off. She heard

Aunt Hortense's voice grating in her head: *Never, never pry into strangers' business. It is both rude and vulgar.*

Bryony tried to place him. Perhaps a lawyer, a banker, or a clerk of some sort, since he spoke with a cultured tongue and had smooth hands. But he looked too disheveled. The burghers were very particular about their appearance, especially those in the city. Perhaps he was a mad artist or a poet. There was that air of danger about him.

As if he had read her thoughts, he explained. "I'm a sea captain."

"Oh," she said, feeling silly.

"Yes, north and south, y'know. My ship is at the docks of Portsmouth for an overhaul. Then I will sail to the West Indies with a shipment of iron from Sussex, which I will exchange for sugar and rum."

Bryony's interest was kindled. She leaned slightly forward. "How exciting! I have never traveled farther than Paris to the south and Oxford to the north. You must find England very provincial."

"England is the most beautiful place in the world," he said simply.

"And God bless King George," she teased.

His gaze flew to her face. "Why did you say that?"

She shrugged. "The usual comment, I guess. King and country."

He stared at her for a long moment, forcing color into her cheeks as she sought to evade his eyes. He sighed. "You're lovely when you're animated. Your smile is like sunlight on spring water. Did you know that?"

She shook her head and stared to the floor.

"You looked very sad last evening."

He was inviting her to speak about it, but she could not. She did not want to weep in front of a stranger, and yet he did not seem like a stranger anymore.

"You were very rude to stare at me last night," she countered.

"I couldn't tear my gaze away." His voice caressed her softly; a thrill traveled up her spine. "You were like an apparition."

She sensed that he was sincere, but she said, "You're

only flattering me. I can hardly believe you have seen the world. If you have, you must have met many lovely ladies much more beautiful than I.''

"It depends on what you're looking for," he replied cryptically.

"You're trying to turn my head, that's all." Struggling to conceal her confusion, Bryony pleated and unpleated the edge of her cloak.

He sighed heavily. "I'm looking for something, somebody; I have been looking for years." He leaned slightly forward, tense, expectant. "When I gaze into your sparkling, sea-hued eyes, I pretend I might have found it. What do you think? Do you trust yourself, your feelings?"

His gaze hypnotized her, and she wanted to touch him and whisper, *Yes, today I do, today is magic. You're the magician. Today is a day like no other, but tomorrow will come and shatter the spell.* Instead she said, "Feelings are volatile; they change from one moment to the next."

He took her hand and squeezed it gently. She did not resist. In a barely audible whisper, he said, "I agree. And what about love? Do you believe in love?"

Her heart cried, *Yes,* but she could not make her lips form the word. She said, "I don't know. I believe love is something serious. Love is a state that should last forever—well, at least a lifetime."

He dropped her hand and sighed. "I wish I could believe that, but I think it's romantic nonsense. Love is nothing but a temporary attraction. Love is here today and gone tomorrow—like feelings."

The magic fell apart, and Bryony flinched as if he had slapped her face. "Then you have never loved."

He gazed at her sharply, aggressively. "And you're an expert, I take it. Women are always so full of romantic blather."

Her lips trembled, but she managed to keep her voice calm. "I loved my brother, but he is dead. I must have loved my mother, but she died a long time ago. I'm the only one left."

"But you don't know about loving a man?"

Anger blossomed within her. "You have no right to ask

me that question, Captain Newcomer. I don't want to discuss it further.''

He chuckled, and it was not a kind sound. Something cold had crept into his gaze. His instant change of mood frightened her. She pulled farther into the corner of the coach.

The clouds had thickened outside, smothering what little daylight there had been. Silence hung between them, and Bryony tried to concentrate on other things, among them Nigel's face. He was a pale, elusive blur, very far away at the moment. She needed to see him, to reassure herself that there still existed a firm connection to the past. She had to get away from Jack Newcomer, the stranger who had the power to shake her world with one glance. He bewildered her and she did not need more confusion.

The day turned even murkier as the road led through a dense copse. They had to reach Cuckfield soon, Bryony prayed in desperation. She was on the verge of choking from the tension in the carriage.

The coach traveled along deep ruts of mud and gravel; the horses strained and snorted, their harnesses creaking. They slogged stolidly through the puddles. Raindrops wandered aimlessly across the windows.

Finally the horses came to a halt. A heavy stillness filled the air. Captain Newcomer pulled down the window on his side and peered outside. Rain immediately clung like diamonds to his hair. Bryony sat forward.

''Are we stuck in the mud?'' she asked.

He was waving a hand impatiently behind him, as if to quiet her.

A musket shot shattered the silence. There was a shudder and a groan as someone fell off the box.

''Jules!'' Bryony whispered, and pressed her fingertips to her lips in fear.

Then the coach shook as someone scrambled off the box and staggered behind the coach. She recognized Jules's black cloak in the window and drew a sigh of relief. Captain Newcomer was moving rapidly, tearing open his portmanteau. ''Highwaymen.''

As she gasped, he pulled out two silver-inlaid pistols and handed her one. ''Load and prime this,'' he ordered, and tossed her a horn with a silver top, then a leather pouch. Blackpowder. Her fingers shook uncontrollably as she unplugged the stopper of the horn and tilted it toward the opening of the barrel. She had watched Reggie prime his pistol hundreds of times while practicing his shooting. The sound of nervous horses pawing the ground unsettled her further, and she could barely insert the ball.

"Stand and deliver, or we'll shoot!" a man shouted. He sounded close, much too close.

Captain Newcomer had already primed and cocked his own pistol. Lithely, he heaved his torso out the window and fired. A moan sliced the air. Answering fire erupted. A ball whizzed into the coach and tore into the leather upholstery. Bryony smelled the acrid scent of sulphur as the captain pushed her to the floor and whipped the primed pistol from her hands, only to drop in her lap the smoking one that he had just fired.

Another shot sounded from behind the coach, and she burned her fingers pouring powder into the barrel and shoving a ball down the black mouth. A rivulet of cold sweat coursed along her neck; fear stiffened her fingers. She hardly dared to breathe. Her hands shook, and she spilled powder outside the flashpan.

"Shoot!" she heard the captain order through the mist of her fear. "There, through the window on your side."

Without hesitation, she cocked the pistol and crawled to her knees, sticking the barrel outside the window. The highwayman leered at her, the muzzle of a musket pointed at her face.

Without thinking, she squeezed the trigger. The pistol jerked. The sound cracked her eardrums. As if in a nightmare, she watched the highwayman's face twist into a fearful grimace. He dropped the weapon and clutched his shoulder. "Go back!" he shouted above the din of another shot echoing from behind the coach.

Three men galloped across the soggy ground and disappeared among the trees.

Bryony collapsed on the floor, exhausted with the shock. "I shot a man," she whispered.

Jack Newcomer crawled over to her, his chest heaving, his face black with soot. "It was either you or him," he said grimly. "He'll survive. But they left our driver behind, dead." He took a swipe at the upholstery. "By God, they deserve to hang!" He looked at her long and hard, then eased to her side and lifted her hands slowly, prying her numb, soot-streaked fingers from the pistol. Unable to move, she only stared at her limbs as if they were not part of her body. As he removed the hard butt, she was able to breathe again. Her arms fell limply at her sides.

His hand hovered for a moment above her head, then with the lightest of caresses, touched her hair. "You were brave."

After tossing the pistols into his portmanteau, he disappeared outside. Jules stuck his worried face inside the coach.

"Mademoiselle?"

"Yes, I'm fine. Truly." She tried to stand up but found that her legs were useless. Jules assisted her outside, a move she regretted when she saw the bloody corpse and the two wounded bandits, whom Captain Newcomer was tying up. Jules helped him hoist them and the dead man onto the roof of the coach and secure them to the baggage rack.

"At least we got two of them. There will be entertaining at the hanging tree in Cuckfield on Saturday," Captain Newcomer said.

Bryony swallowed hard, brushing away a tangle of hair from her face. "What a terrible day. I was frightened out of my wits."

"Highway robbery is a common enough occurrence. We must leave before they return with more ammunition."

She protested feebly as he lifted her back into the coach. Jules had already jumped onto the box. The horses had remained amazingly calm during the attack, and they pulled the coach slowly out of the cover of trees.

"You never considered surrendering," Bryony stated as she searched through her portmanteau for a hand mirror and a comb.

"And let them murder us in cold blood? Hardly. They were no angels." He wiped his face with a large handkerchief, then regarded her critically. "I'm afraid your careful grooming is but a memory now." He must have seen the

dismay on her face, because he added in a cold voice,
"Your beau will have to look at the *real* you and not at
all the trappings of a fashionable lady." When she gave
him a dark look, he laughed. "Perhaps he is the type who
cares only for powder and patch, and the cut of a gown."

"At least he has some manners. He would never comment on a lady's attire other than to give her compliments."

"Flowery compliments? Ah, is that what you want?
Then you're like all the rest of them."

"And you're an uncouth, crusty old salt!" she countered. She tugged at her hair, furious when the curls refused to obey her. She hated to admit it, but he was right.
Nigel would look at her with distaste. Oh, God, why did
this have to happen? The more she worked, the more chaos
she wrought, and her face was streaked with soot and dirt.
Tears of frustration stood in her eyes. She watched Captain
Newcomer upend a glass flask against a folded handkerchief, which he then extended toward her.

"Let me help you clean your face," he suggested.

She dashed away his hand. "Never."

" 'Tis only water," he chided. "Are you afraid I will
ruin your complexion?"

"Don't be silly."

He advanced slowly, handkerchief raised.

"I told you I don't need or want your help."

"And I say you do!" he almost shouted in her ear.
"You cannot show yourself like that in Cuckfield or they'll
fetch the Watch posthaste."

"Hardly likely." She fended off his arm, but he grabbed
her by the back of the neck and held her head in a fierce
grip. Despite her loud protests, he proceeded to wipe her
face, and none too gently.

"There, much better. I never liked powder on ladies.
Powder is for birds of paradise or . . . whores, if you like
that word better."

Outraged, Bryony lost her voice. In a moment of pure
fury, she sank her fingers into his hair and tugged until
the waves fell free. Raven locks framed his face, and he
looked demonlike, an untamed beast from the wild.

"How dare you liken me to a—a—"

The shock of his lips on hers made her swallow her breath. The world tilted as his tongue forced through the barrier of her teeth, a delicious sweetness coursing through her body at the demanding intrusion. Rough and soft, it carried her effortlessly to the edge of insanity. She melted, did not resist as he crushed her to his chest, as his fingers brought fiercer chaos to her hair. His passion, so unexpected, consumed her, then fulfilled her, but in the end it left her empty and longing for more.

He let go of her as abruptly as he had claimed her.

Her head lolled to his shoulder when her neck was robbed of the forceful support of his hands.

"I had to steal a kiss. Your beau must be an idiot to let you travel alone across the country."

As his chiding voice flowed over her, she plummeted from her euphoria. Hurt and disappointed, she pushed against his chest. "What do you know about me or him, my supposed beau? You are a beast without a heart," she cried, choking. "Let go of me this instant!" She aimed a tight fist at his face, but his fingers closed around her wrist and halted the movement. She was locked against his chest, his eyes flashing dark fire into her furious gaze.

"I wondered why a gently bred lady was traveling unprotected until it dawned on me that you're about to visit your lover. If I were he, I would not leave you alone and vulnerable. Don't you know what can happen to a lovely, defenseless lady?" His disgust rasped over her raw nerves.

"For your information, I have Jules."

He dropped his arms and collapsed against the squabs. "Foolish, innocent child," he uttered in defeat.

Her breath was ragged with anger. "I cannot wait to get rid of your company."

A faint smile lifted the corners of his lips. "You know as well as I do that our meeting has changed your life—and mine. I wish to God it wasn't true."

Chapter 3

More confused than ever, Bryony arrived in Cuckfield, seven miles south of Crawley. Captain Newcomer was right. The stagecoach trip had changed her life. *He* had changed it. Why was one's fate so unpredictable?

He jumped to the ground before she could step off and hurry from his disturbing presence. She never wanted to see him again, yet a part of her wanted to remain at his side forever.

He held out his arms to help her alight, but, distrusting her own feelings, she acted on impulse. Instead of allowing his hands to encircle her waist, she turned and opened the opposite door, jumping down before he had time to react. That would show him. He should not assume he could touch her whenever he liked. Such an unpredictable, dangerous, and wholly irresistible man. She ought to get away from him as fast as possible.

Lifting her skirts, she hurried across the muddy inn yard. THE BOAR, she read above the worn oak door.

The walls were made of knapped flintstone and mortar, and the thatched roof had a steep pitch. A weather vane in the shape of a cockerel swung on the roof. The mullioned windows were bordered by green shutters that needed a fresh coat of paint.

"Wait!" Jack Newcomer cried, but Bryony accelerated her pace, almost running the last few steps, and slammed the door behind her. Breathing hard, she unfurled her painted silk fan and held it in front of her face, viewing the smoky taproom. Patrons eating and drinking at every table looked up as the door clanged shut. The host stood behind the counter, serving geneva in small glasses. Five drunk men were responsible for the appalling din in the room. Catcalls and whistles greeted her as she advanced, but no one tried to interfere. There were no other ladies present. Her heart hammered in fear as the leering host waddled over to her.

"I would like to hire a private conveyance to take me to Lord Lippett at Greymeadows," she said. "I would also like a room for the night."

The host scratched his old-fashioned full-bottomed wig. Bryony recoiled as a large flea jumped to the counter. "A room is no problem, missy, and 'Oggie, me boy, can drive ye. Lord Lippett 'as a big to-do at th' Meadows ternight," he said, and winked. "M'lord 'as lovely guests, I see."

"I'm not his guest," Bryony stated coldly. "Well, thank you. Please inform your son that I want to leave right away." Recalling the prisoners, she added, "We were attacked on the road by highwaymen. Would you be so kind as to inform the law and fetch the doctor? Two of the villains are badly hurt."

The innkeeper's eyes widened in awe. "Lud's wonder! And ye survived? O' course, m'lady. I'll send someone for the magistrate, and th' doctor is 'ere already." With a chuckle he indicated a customer reeling across the floor.

Bryony recoiled and pushed a coin into the host's eager hand. "Thank you." She wanted to escape since she had spotted Jack Newcomer as he entered. She darted past him and fled outside.

She drew a deep sigh of relief. Knowing that the doctor would be useless, she inspected one of the villains whom Jules had laid out on the ground. The wound in his chest was ghastly, and a desire to retch squeezed her. Swallowing bile, she searched for a pulse in his cold wrist. Nothing. He was dead. The other villain was propped against the coach wheel, glaring at her. The magistrate would take care of him. Shaken, she turned away. There was nothing more she could do.

A young boy clad in a smock, loose breeches, and heavy clogs crossed the yard. "This way, miss. I'll 'ave th' wagon 'itched in a trice."

Jules followed Hoggie, the boy, and Bryony waited in

the muddy yard. Mist floated over a neighboring field, meeting the gray clouds that embraced the ground. How dreary, she thought, and momentarily shut her eyes.

The inn door closed behind her, and she knew Jack Newcomer had followed her. Like a pleasurable caress on her skin, she registered his presence, then fought the sensation. He had come too suddenly into her life, too overwhelmingly.

Without looking, she knew he was standing so close that he could touch her if he wanted to. She turned her thoughts inside herself.

"You forgot this," he said simply.

Her resistance broke at the sound of his voice. She turned to look at him. He was holding one of her gloves.

"Next you will say I left it on purpose," she said shakily.

He shrugged. "Why? I don't have time for games. I have more important things to consider than your gloves—two corpses and a highwayman for instance."

She lowered her gaze, humiliated. "Of course." She shot him a quick glance. He was smiling with a kindness that melted her heart. With the end of his index finger, he flicked the tip of her nose.

"Silly girl. You have nothing to fear from me. Don't run away from yourself."

"You confuse me," she said breathlessly.

He leaned closer, so close she could see the light of desire in the dusky depths of his eyes. "*I* don't confuse you, your feelings do, the feelings that my presence provokes."

Her breath rasped into her lungs. "You think very highly of your seductive powers," she burst out, her eyes stormy.

"I don't need to be a magician to read your eyes. They tell all. Your enchanting face is an open book, as yet an almost unwritten one." He traced her smooth cheek with one long finger. "I would like to write something sweet on your face."

She dashed away his hand and took a step back. "How dare you! Have you no manners at all?"

"Does my presence make you so uncomfortable?"

Anger boiled within her. "How loud do I have to shout

that I don't desire your company? You're overbearing and insufferable—''

''—and wholly intolerable.'' He laughed. ''I know, I know. You're not the first woman who has told me that.''

Bryony grimaced. ''Please stop this charade. Listen to yourself. Such arrogance! I'm not interested in hearing about your amorous conquests. I don't know you, and I don't want to know you. You only want to brag about your prowess.'' Fury blinding her, she held her arm out and pointed stiffly at the door. ''Go! Go away and brag to the men in the taproom.'' She turned her back on him. ''You bore me. Libertines always bore me. All you want to do is bask in your own glory.''

She sensed his hurt like a mist of desolation around her.

''Very well. I didn't mean to . . .'' His voice was clipped, hard. His steps echoed at staccato rhythm on the flagstones in front of the inn. He was gone.

She missed him already. Why had she lost her temper? He *made* her lose it. In his presence she just couldn't control herself.

Bryony paced the inn yard, heedless of the mud that clung to the hem of her gown. What had happened? How had this unpredicatable stranger managed to invade her life, making her acutely aware of her own limited experience? She did not know how to handle his smooth flirtation. Her stay in France, the country of famous courtesans, had taught her nothing about love. It hurt to discover that she was as inexperienced as a schoolgirl. The intensity of her emotions frightened her, and Jack Newcomer was responsible for kindling them.

The wagon pulled up. It was an unpainted farm wagon with clumsy wooden wheels, the only seat padded with a sack of straw. Bryony looked in dismay at the shabby conveyance, but she didn't have a choice. The faster she could escape and the sooner she could see Nigel, the better. He would wipe away the memory of Jack Newcomer's smiling eyes.

''Pardon me, mademoiselle, this is the only wagon they have available here,'' Jules said apologetically, spreading his large, callused hands.

''We must go now.'' Bryony accepted Jules's assistance

and glanced uneasily at the driver's leering face, which displayed a row of rotting teeth. Jules jumped up and sat cross-legged on the floor of the wagon.

"Greymeadows, miss?" asked Hoggie.

Bryony nodded, smoothing down her hair. In her agitation, she had forgotten to repair her appearance. Botheration! Now Nigel would see her at her worst, just as in the old days. He would never notice the woman she had become.

Like a river of mud, the road wound between the dripping hedges. Hoggie turned left twice and finally steered the swaybacked horse down an alley of poplars. At the very end stood two tall iron gates, open wide. The drive curved past a maze and a bare flower bed where, Bryony remembered, pinks and lavender bloomed in the summer. Nostalgia filled her, memories from the happy, carefree days of her childhood.

The house was of red brick with two wings forming the E of the Elizabethan period. Light blazed in all the windows. A formal garden of clipped yews and box hedges stretched behind the mansion. Bryony remembered how the water in the fountains used to sparkle in the summer, and how the old white folly used to be covered with climbing vines. Was it still? Now everything shimmered through a veil of rain.

Carriages were lined up in front of the wide, shallow stairs. The innkeeper at The Boar had been right; Nigel was hosting a gathering. She hoped he would have a minute to spare for her.

Bryony stepped down and ordered Hoggie to wait farther down the drive. She halted at the bottom of the steps and hastily scrawled a message that she handed to the butler standing in the doorway.

Rain was pouring down, and by the time the butler returned with an answer, Bryony's back was damp and her hair a mass of dripping curls.

"Dear Bryony," read the note, "come posthaste to the library. You remember where it is. If not, ask the butler to show you. Lippett."

Holding her head high, and ignoring the curious glances of the guests, Bryony hastened down the brightly lit corridor. The scent of roses perfumed the rooms, and the distant sound of a string orchestra came from the large ballroom on the second floor.

Voices and laughter floated on the air as she knocked and waited in front of the library door, her heart thundering. How would Nigel react to her unexpected appearance?

"Come in," ordered a male voice.

Bryony turned the doorknob with trembling fingers and stepped into the dimly lit room. Nigel rose from behind the desk, a vision in salmon silk, the wide cuffs and pocket flaps of his full-skirted coat embroidered with gold. The gold lace of his cravat gleamed in the candlelight.

"Bryony!" He came toward her with outstretched hands. "I don't believe it! Little Bryony Shaw." He took her fingers and showered them with kisses. "Let me look at you."

In dismay, Bryony waited for the smile to fade from his face as he scrutinized her. A certain stiffness crept into his lips, and his voice turned flat as he said, "Enchanting."

"You must know that I have been out in the rain and was attacked by highwaymen; otherwise, I wouldn't have turned up on your doorstep in such a disheveled state." She hated herself for apologizing for her appearance.

"Thank God you're unhurt," he said, and led her farther into the cavernous room.

Nigel had hardly changed. There was an unmistakable thickening about his waist, but it gave him a more powerful aura. His jaw was beginning to show a softening, hinting at dissipation, but just hinting. His eyes were as blue as ever. His gaze traveled openly over her figure, resting a few seconds too long on the generous decolletage. Nigel's presence was as commanding as Bryony remembered. He had always acquired what he wanted. She was sure that hadn't changed. Diamonds gleamed in his cravat, and his sandy curls were combed back and covered with a heavy layer of powder.

"Why, little Bryony has become a beauty. Reggie would have been proud of you."

Bryony smiled. "You really think so? He never saw me

after . . . after . . .'' Her voice broke, and she couldn't
hold back the tears. Facing the falling twilight outside,
she struggled silently to regain her composure.

"Reggie was a fool," Nigel said scornfully. "You are
more levelheaded than he ever was. I never thought he
would go so far as to take his own life, and I'll never
forgive him for it." He patted her shoulder apologetically.
"I know I shouldn't talk about your brother this way, but
I cannot believe Reggie's gone."

Bryony's gaze darted to Nigel's face in anguish. "Are
you saying that Reggie, th-that my brother—*killed himself*?

Nigel slammed the palm of his hand onto the desk, and
Bryony jumped. "Yes, by God! Reggie should not have
done what he did."

In the clutches of renewed agony, Bryony gripped Nigel's lapels and shook him. "Say it's a lie!" she exclaimed. *"Please*, say it's a lie."

Startled, he gently removed her hands from the delicate
satin. "Calm yourself." Studying her distressed face, he
whistled through his teeth. "Oh, my God, you didn't know
the truth, did you?"

She shook her head in misery and groped for a handkerchief in her drawstring bag. He handed her his, and she
dabbed at her eyes. "Mr. Holland only mentioned that
Reggie died in the fire."

"He did, alas, but he set the fire himself, in the study."
Nigel looked uncomfortable. "I'm sure Holland didn't tell
you because he wanted to protect you."

Bryony flew at him, pounding her fists against his chest.
"But why didn't you try to stop Reggie?" Wracked by
fury and a sense of loss, she could not help but blame
Nigel. "You were there, after all!"

Nigel grabbed her fists and held them still. As reason
returned to her, he let go and patted her arm. The gesture
was one of exasperation and didn't soothe her anguish.
"Please calm down."

Bryony whirled and reached blindly for something to
hold on to. She wanted to crash the priceless vase on the
desk against the wall. "I'm s-sorry. I'm behaving unfor-
givably." Gulping for breath, she sought to steady her

turmoil. The pain of loss and anger churned white-hot in her stomach. Reggie had killed himself without giving a single thought to her, to anyone. For a moment she hated him.

She wanted to moan, to rant and rave, but instead she dried her eyes. Slanting a glance at Nigel, she noticed the constraint that had sprung up between them. Nigel was carefully adjusting his shirt cuffs with a miffed air. His glance was veiled as it met hers.

"Egad, this must come as a terrible shock to you, my dear. But 'tis true all the same. I only wish—" He coughed and looked away.

Apprehensive, Bryony threw another glance at him. "What else do you know?"

Nigel cleared his throat and fingered the inkstand on his desk. "Well—the fact that Reggie took his life for a debt bothers me."

"He staked and lost all in one game," Bryony said. "I don't doubt he would do such a reckless thing, but that he would t-take his own life?" Bryony drew a sharp, painful breath to prevent another rush of tears. "I just don't believe it."

Nigel regarded her from under heavy lids. Without speaking, he raised a glass to his lips.

Bryony stared at him, trying to read his thoughts. "You don't share my opinion?" It was more of a statement than a question, and dread surged through her.

"I'm neglecting my duty." He ushered her to a chair, filled a glass from a gold-rimmed crystal decanter, and carried it to her on a silver tray. "Please try this—wine straight from the island of Madeira. Fruity and delicious, just as you ladies prefer."

Bryony automatically accepted the glass and sipped the ruby liquid. "Yes, it's delicious," she said. "But Reggie—"

"Reggie was more reckless than usual, Bryony. You didn't know this, but he turned to heavy gambling after your father died."

"Is that why he didn't let me come home?" she whispered, wishing she was wrong.

"Reggie talked about you all the time, but he said if

you found out about his difficulties, you'd turn against him.''

Bryony stood, her fists knotted at her sides in agitation. ''Nonsense! I'd rather die than turn against my own brother. You should know that, Nigel.''

He shrugged. ''Yes, of course, but Reggie lost his good judgment, don't you see? That's why he prevented you from coming home.''

''Yes, he told me to remain in France for another year.'' Bryony took another deep breath. Nigel reminded her of her brother and their happy past, but somehow that picture was now sullied by the fact that Nigel had failed to stop Reggie's excesses. She saw beyond the hero worship she had always felt for Nigel. The truth struck her hard. Nigel's attraction had only been part of her young girl's fantasies.

She had nothing now. No one.

Her uncertainty was returning, her fear. She had nowhere to turn because Reggie was gone.

After refilling his glass, Nigel swirled around, making the skirt of his coat flare out. ''Didn't you find it odd that Reggie failed to invite you back home?''

Bryony nodded.

''Do you know any other reason why he might have kept you away?'' When she shook her head, he continued, ''Did you know that Reggie supported the Stuart cause?''

Bryony's eyes widened. She swallowed hard and sank back onto the chair. ''You mean to say he was a Jacobite?'' she whispered.

''Yes.''

''And what are you, Nigel?''

He laughed and went to sit behind the desk. ''I shared Reggie's political views, but now that Charles Edward has lost—''

''But if you were friends, why didn't you try to dissuade my brother from supporting the—the cause, to warn him of the possible defeat?''

Nigel sighed. ''Reggie always went his own way, you ought to know that. When he was set on something, he never changed his mind. He didn't think defeat was possible.''

"Yes, that's true," Bryony said, sad that Reggie hadn't confided in her about the cause. "But Reggie never did anything unlawful," she added.

"No, he only did what he thought was right." He shrugged. "In this case he chose the wrong side."

"If he really believed in the Stuart cause, he didn't choose wrongly; he only chose the losing side."

Nigel studied her for a long moment. "France didn't ruin your loyalty to Reggie."

Bryony's lips lifted cynically. "You mean to say it ruined everything else." Now she would never have the chance to show him the sophistication she had gained, but it was just as well.

"No, no! That's not what I meant." He kept staring at her from under lowered eyelids.

Her gaze traveled over the costly art by old Flemish artists on the walls. Two paintings by Rubens, of nymphs cavorting in lush gardens, hung on either side of a William Hogarth print and a Thornhill landscape.

Marble statuettes and busts adorned pedestals. The carpet was thick, the pattern a subtle entwining of roses and vines. Brown velvet draperies framed tall French windows. Such elegance seemed a suitable setting for Nigel, an exotic bird in a luxurious cage. Yet an almost intangible air of decay clung to the splendor.

"Ah! I see you've discovered my passion, Bryony." He sighed and gazed dreamily at the masterpieces. "Art is my life. No feeling equals the joy of acquiring a coveted work of art." He smiled happily. "I have traveled extensively to find these treasures. Every room holds at least one delightful piece, but these are my favorites."

"They are impressive, and obviously costly."

He slanted an amused glance at her. "Very costly. But compared to the pleasure my art collection gives me, money is nothing. I'd rather be surrounded by beautiful things than by a heap of gold coins."

They studied the art in silence, but Bryony's thoughts strayed again to Reggie's last moments.

Laughter and the clinking of glasses floated in from the terrace outside. The guests were enjoying themselves.

"About Reggie's death," Bryony said, almost inaudibly, fearing the very words. "Did he really take his own life, or is it a cruel joke? Please, say 'tis but a joke."

Nigel stood abruptly and walked to stand behind her. "No, no joke. He really did."

The words slowly sank in, crushing her insides. Misery filled every corner of her being. As she gradually began to accept the idea, she said, "Tell me about it." She turned to look at his face, but he drew farther back into the shadows.

"It pains me to talk about it." He sighed heavily. "Reggie had set up a card game, a cover for a meeting of influential Jacobites in the area. All five of us arrived at Willow Hills at about the same time, sevenish in the evening. Reggie had been drinking."

"He got reckless when he was inebriated," Bryony commented.

Nigel nodded. "Yes, he was well over the oar that night. He kept telling us about a map he had received from a contact in France. The French had hidden two chests of gold somewhere in Scotland, he maintained. Then they sent the map to Reggie, who was expected to forward it the next man in the Jacobite link."

"Did he?"

Nigel shook his head. "No, the map burned with Willow Hills—*if* there really was one."

Bryony's eyes widened. "What do you mean? Why would he lie about that?"

Nigel shrugged. "As much as I hate to say it, Reggie was becoming overbearing, thinking that he had unlimited power. Perhaps he wanted to impress us." He paused for a moment. "Then he got into an argument with Lord Bentworth, a Jacobite from Alfriston, who wanted to see the map. In fact, Bentworth was the last to see Reggie alive. He was the one who alerted the servants to the fire and arranged a bucket brigade from the pond. But it was already too late. Most of Willow Hills burned in a very short time."

"You buried Reggie next to the chapel."

"Well, what was left of him, yes."

Bryony dragged the handkerchief back to her eyes, her

movements leaden. "I should have been there to stop him." Her gaze followed Nigel as he once again sat down behind the desk. "And what about this Lord Bentworth? Is there any chance that he had some quarrel with my brother?"

Nigel pursed his lips. " 'Tis possible, of course. I don't know for sure. Perhaps you ought to talk to him and find out what Reggie told him later that night after we all left."

Bryony nodded and stood, smoothing down the front of her gown. This was another clue she had to follow. She had to know all about Reggie's last moments on earth, and why he took his life. "Do you think . . . murder is out of the question?"

Nigel chuckled. "Your imagination is running away with you, m'dear. No, Reggie was a victim of his own folly. He took his life because he couldn't pay his gambling debts."

"That would be it, then," Bryony said. "Mr. Holland told me that Reggie mortgaged Willow Hills and sold all the valuables. The bank owns the land now."

"Yes, I'm afraid everything of value was gone. He gave it all to Stuart. Thank God, you have your mother's legacy to sustain you, Bryony, until you find a husband to take care of you."

She blushed, once more acutely aware of her rumpled appearance. "I should not keep you from your guests. It has been a pleasure seeing you again. I only wish it had been under different circumstances."

Nigel stood and bowed, a weak smile curling his lips. "My pleasure entirely. If I can help you in any way, just ask. You should know that I'm forever at your service, Bryony."

She blushed and walked to the door. "Thank you for your kindness." She hesitated. "Is there any way you could you give me the names of the other cardplayers? I assure you I wouldn't denounce anyone to the government. I only want to hear what they have to say about Reggie."

"You're obsessed, Bryony."

She folded her arms protectively over her middle, as if cradling some hidden pain. "I cannot accept the thought that Reggie killed himself."

He shrugged and rose. "You must do as you please, but I cannot give you any names."

Anger burned bright within her once more. "There must have been a way to stop Reggie from his folly. You could have found a way! I wish you had contacted me."

Nigel weighed her words for a long moment. "You make it sound as if I owe you something." Sighing, he sat down again and dipped a quill pen into the silver and ivory inkhorn. The nib rasped across the paper as he moved his hand with a wide flourish. After sprinkling sand on the paper, he folded it, but he didn't give to to her.

"Where are you staying?" he asked, tapping his fingertips on the desktop.

"I'm traveling with Aunt Hortense and staying at The Boar, for now. We will go on to a friend's house tomorrow."

He rose from the desk, moving the paper from one hand to the other. "My advice is this: Go back to France with your aunt. This is nothing here for you now." He seemed to ponder his next words, then glanced at the folded note and added, "The more I think about it, the more I hesitate to let you endanger your safety. If I give you the list and you meddle with the Jacobites, you could be called a traitor to England, and if worst comes to worst, beheaded." He frowned. "I could not live with that loss on my conscience, don't you see? Your notion that you want to find out every detail of Reggie's death is nothing but an unhealthy obsession. Why torture yourself? Return to France and start a new life."

"No." Bryony watched in disappointment as he ripped the paper to shreds and dropped it in the gilt wastebasket. But immediately she had an idea. "Very well, I will take your advice." She forced out a smile. "Please forgive my display of temper."

He smiled and kissed her hand. "It's understandable under the circumstances. I hope our next meeting will be happier."

She nodded and walked out the door as he bowed. "Good-bye."

In the brightly lit vestibule a knot of guests lingered, talking and laughing. Bryony had no desire to become the target of their rude stares; she turned toward the French doors in the back. Momentarily she thought she saw a pale face pressed to one of the windows. It frightened her, though she knew it must be one of the guests. She fled through the half-open door to the dark terrace.

There, she stood in the shadows until Nigel left the study. He joined the guests and led one of the ladies up the stairs. Bryony waited another twenty minutes before the rest of the guests followed suit. When the corridor was empty, she tiptoed back inside and over to the library door. To her relief, it was unlocked.

She gently closed the door behind her and slipped across the floor. The room was dimly lit by the fire in the fireplace, and she did not dare light a candle.

Carrying the wastebasket closer to the light, she peeped inside. There they were, bits of paper scattered among other crumpled wads of paper. She emptied the litter on the desk, sorted through it, and scooped up the fragments. She placed them on a clean sheet of paper on the desk and carefully wrapped them. Then she pushed them into her bag and cautiously opened the door. Lady Luck was with her; the corridor was empty, and she could easily slink outside.

Knowing the garden paths well, she decided to take the back way to the drive to avoid running into more guests. The rain had stopped, but the air was humid and cold. She shivered in her damp cloak. Rounding the corner of the east wing, she looked for Jules, but he was nowhere in sight.

She crossed the drive. From the shadows of the first hedge of the maze, she searched among the vehicles for Hoggie and his cart. Spotting him at the opposite end of the drive, she steered her steps there.

As she passed the entrance to the maze, a dark shadow flashed before her, the contours of a tricorne, the flapping wings of a full-length cloak. Strong hands gripped her shoulders and shook her. When she was about to scream, the hands were clamped over her mouth, stifling her. A man whispered hoarsely: " 'Tis possible your brother was murdered. Find out." Abruptly he released his grip and was gone. The only sound was the wind sighing through the trees.

Bryony moaned in distress. Lifting up her skirts, she ran as fast as she could down the drive until she spied Jules's reassuring form by the wagon.

"Let's go," she ordered breathlessly, and threw herself into the wagon. Her eyes wide with fear, she looked back as the cart lumbered down the drive. She could barely discern the outline of a man standing, with legs spread, in the middle of the drive, gazing after her.

Chapter 4

Bryony shivered, cold and shaken. The rain had been replaced by strong winds that whipped through her damp clothes. Still dazed by the latest revelation, she could not stop her churning thoughts. Reggie murdered? *No, no!* screamed her mind. It must be a cruel trick. And who was the man who had warned her?

The wagon lumbered ever so slowly toward The Boar inn. Ice-cold fear squeezed her stomach. Perhaps one of Nigel's guests had been in his cups and decided to make a joke of the first woman who happened to cross his path. But no, no matter how much she tried to deny it, she knew he had been waiting for *her*.

Your brother was murdered. The words rang repeatedly in her head until she thought she would burst. Pressing her fingers against her temples, she rocked back and forth on the straw seat.

The wagon got stuck in the mud, and Bryony feared that she would have to spend the night under some tree by the side of the road. But with Jules and Hoggie pushing at the back and the horse straining in the front, they finally managed to break the suction of the mud on the wheels, and the wagon rolled on.

Tired and hungry, they arrived at the inn. Bryony did not look forward to meeting the leering glances of the taproom patrons, but to her surprise, the smoky room was almost empty. A desultory conversation between the host and two guests at the bar was the only sound in the room. An all-pervasive scent of ale and roasted meat lingered in the air.

Exhausted and drained, Bryony longed to rest and think about Reggie and his last hour alive. She was desperate to piece together the paper with the Jacobite names.

At a small table next to the fire sat Jack Newcomer, a plate of steaming meatpie and gravy in front of him. His hair was mussed and damp, and the shoulders of his gray coat were dark with moisture. He looked up, and their gazes locked. Bryony took an involuntary step back, her heart pounding heavily. His expression was dark, his eyebrows pulled together in a fierce scowl.

As she nodded a greeting, he smiled coolly, a smile that didn't reach his eyes. He was still hurting from her earlier reprimands, she reflected as she advanced cautiously to speak with the proprietor. But her conscience stopped her before she had crossed the room.

She knew she would never have any peace of mind until she apologized to Captain Newcomer for her angry words. Holding her head high, she retraced her steps. Her heart raced as she stood beside his table, an urge to flee almost overwhelming her.

But instead of uttering the humbling words on her tongue, she was filled with suspicion as she viewed Jack Newcomer's damp hair. "Where have you been?" she demanded.

He lifted his eyebrows in surprise. "Me? Been? Well, here of course. What do you mean?"

She narrowed her eyes and steadily met his innocent, if impudent, gaze. "You're lying! You were at Greymeadows an hour ago. You spoke to me in the maze," she accused him. "And you almost frightened me to death."

He laughed and caressed her arm indulgently. "You've lost your senses, lovely one. I went out momentarily to arrange for the delivery of the remaining highwayman to the Crawley detention house. The magistrate would have nothing to do with the villain, said the crime had occurred on Crawley territory." His eyes roamed warmly over her trim form. "Not that I don't wish that you were right." He blew her a kiss. "An evening tryst with you in a maze would be a delicious experience, indeed. My senses are reeling at the thought."

"You!" she exclaimed between stiff lips. "Are you never serious? Of all the—"

"—insufferable, etcetera, etcetera," he chided gently, and unfolded his lean body from the chair. "Why don't you join me for dinner so that we can calculate the havoc an evening meeting in a maze would do to our senses." With an extravagant gesture, he proceeded to pull out a chair for her. "My appetite is growing by the minute," he whispered. "Please don't prevent my feast any longer— I'm fairly starving."

Seething and speechless, Bryony wanted to flounce out of the room in a tiff, but she wasn't going to let him have the last word. Mustering her considerable dignity and raising her chin, she gripped her skirts, sank down on the chair, and arranged the damp and muddy velvet gracefully around her.

"Very well," she said. "You have managed to evade my question. And since I cannot force you to give me a truthful answer, I will just wait until you stumble on your own lies." She gave him a dark, smoldering look. The apology she had initially intended to give him was the farthest thing from her mind at that point.

He sat down and toyed with his wineglass. "That you would think unkindly of me does not surprise me. However, creeping around at night alarming ladies is a pastime in which I never indulge."

"You could easily have returned here before me. My conveyance was not only slow, but also stuck in the mud for at least ten minutes," she challenged him.

He smiled. "If you wish to meet me in a maze at some future date, I'll be more than happy to oblige." Apparently noticing that her temper was at a boiling point, he patted her tense fist on the table. Then he waved for the host, and five minutes later Bryony had a plate of steaming pie before her and a glass of wine glowing ruby-red in her hand.

Captain Newcomer raised his own glass. "A toast to us—to our exciting future tryst. Who knows where it might lead," he added cryptically. He looked deep into her eyes, and she could not help but obey. She raised her glass, her heart beating wildly, her mind a mêlée of conflicting thoughts. They ate in silence. Bryony's temper mellowed as her hunger was satisfied. Jack Newcomer's presence was strangely soothing. She could have sat there forever drawing from his calm strength. He was a cliff bordering an unknown sea riddled with treacherous reefs.

"It distresses me to hear that your beau turned you out on an evening like this, to be assaulted in the dark," he commented, gazing into his glass. "Surely he could have found an apartment for you at his establishment, and a chaperone."

Bryony drew herself up. "I would never consider staying at the home of an unwed man. I won't compromise Nigel's reputation, or my own. However, I told him Aunt Hortense was accompanying me." She glared at him. "Besides, Nigel is *not* my beau. I don't know why you harp about it."

His eyes were veiled. "Perhaps I suffer the bottomless agonies of jealousy."

"Pshaw!" To show the depth of her frustration, she wanted to throw her plate of food at him. It frightened her to find that he could destroy her peace of mind and incite her to fury with only a few words. She gripped the wide cuff of his coat and shook his arm. "How dare you tease me like this! What have I done—"

He captured her hand and squeezed it. "How dare you accuse me of lying, Miss Shaw?" he flared. When she didn't answer, he softened his tone. "I must have touched a sore spot since you exploded so readily."

She pulled her hand away and concentrated once more on her supper. "Don't talk about Nigel again. My life is none of your business."

He shrugged, and his lips hardened momentarily. "Very well, but we're sitting together—sharing our lives, if you will—at this very moment. I ought to be allowed to say what I feel."

Bryony drew a sigh of exasperation. "How can I believe your smooth words? We've only just met. You're ungallant and rude. And evasive. You appear to be a man who takes whatever he wants, no matter what the consequences." She glowered. "And I'm not some little girl you can dazzle with a few well-chosen words, rude or otherwise!"

His lips twitched, and then he laughed, that full-throated, cheerful sound that made her skin tingle. "You may look like a fragile rose ready to snap in the first storm, Miss Shaw, but I see that I've been mistaken. There is iron under the soft petals." He whispered into her ear, "And I adore you for it."

"Oh, you never stop!" But she couldn't hide the amusement sparkling in her eyes. "Rogue."

He chuckled, a low, intimate sound. "Thank you for the compliment. My acquaintances call me a cold, heartless eccentric."

Bryony pursed her lips. "Cold? No, definitely not. Heartless? Perhaps. Eccentric? Most definitely. And I can think of some other epithets to add to the list."

"Now who is being cruel?" he chided, and gulped down the rest of his wine.

"You're as much a trickster as was my brother. He could talk for hours without saying anything. But he joked to hide a vulnerable heart."

Jack Newcomer's eyes glowed like a slowly burning fire, pulling her in. "I distinctly remember that you called me an insufferable—"

"Rogue? Perhaps 'fool' is the better word. That's what my brother was. If he hadn't been so foolish, he would be alive today."

She had Captain Newcomer's full attention. " 'Tis always easy to judge others and think you know better," he said. "You should not blame yourself; you could have done nothing to prevent the hand of fate."

His words soothed the pain that had been her constant companion since Reggie's death. She had hungered for that special comfort, just a touch of balm on her aching wounds. And it had come from this stranger. She didn't trust herself to speak; her lips trembled.

"Your brother . . . do you want to tell me about him?" Jack Newcomer asked softly.

Bryony shook her head and pinched her lips together.

"You must have loved him very much."

She nodded and traced the stem of her wineglass. "H-he loved life. 'Tis cruel that he had to go like he did. I wish I could have been there for him."

Silence filled the room, and Bryony regretted opening up the wound of her grief.

Jack Newcomer's sigh stirred the brooding stillness. "I had a Scottish uncle once whom I loved very much. He was more of a father to me than my real father. Now they are both dead. Nothing, no wrong that my father ever did, seems important today." He cleared his throat. "But it once did."

Bryony studied the closed face before her. The only animated features were his eyes, dark pools shimmering with sorrow and regret.

"Did your father treat you badly?" Bryony asked, then held her breath. Somehow his answer was very important.

He made a strange sound, a mixture of laughter and loathing. "He died. When I was three years old. The only man I remember besides my uncle is my stepfather, who didn't like children." He shrugged. "But, as I said, those days are long gone and forgotten."

His words didn't ring true. She sensed a pain in him that matched her own. A very old pain, and anger.

He leaned closer, an enigmatic smile curving his lips. "You're very lovely when your eyes are the size of saucers, darling innocent," he whispered as his gaze caressed every inch of her face. "Please hurry and decide the date for our tryst in the maze."

Forgetting everything but his suggestive voice, she felt her cheeks grow hot as some deep longing stirred within her, gathering like a warm ball in her lower belly.

All she wanted was to feel those persuasive hands on her skin. She sensed that he would be very thorough in his exploration and very . . . satisfying. She was afraid he could hear her shallow breathing, read the longing in her eyes. As that yearning sang in her veins, she looked down at her plate where the remnants of the meatpie were growing cold. "Mazes can be very chilly in late August," she forced herself to say. Was that breathless voice really hers?

"Our passion alone would transform the very air, would remind us of a sultry summer's day."

His voice created goose bumps of pleasure on her skin. She glanced at him and was startled to find his face so close to her own.

"I'm serious," he said, his eyes revealing the molten depth of his passion.

In a moment the need for self-preservation returned, and she pulled away. "You are much too bold," Captain Newcomer. We met for the first time only last night."

"Passion doesn't own a clock. It travels its own mysterious ways and in its own time."

"Well, I'm not going to become a victim of temporary folly," Bryony said resolutely, standing up. Her legs were suspiciously weak, and if she didn't break up this tête-à-tête, what was bound to happen? She would succumb to his spell and believe what she had begun to suspect ever since she had looked into his eyes—that he had the power to rule her heart.

He rose and gripped her hand, caressing it lightly. "You are alone and vulnerable, at my mercy or someone else's."

"Yes, you certainly don't hesitate to take advantage of a woman alone," she chided gently, and pulled her hand free. "Good night, Captain Newcomer. In case you will have left by the time I come down tomorrow, I wish you a pleasant journey." She gave him a final smile. "It was interesting meeting you, but I doubt I'll ever see you again."

He bowed formally, but a smile lingered in his eyes. "You have little faith in the power of Cupid."

"Cupid is aiming his arrow in vain this time," she said, hoping her eyes didn't contradict her words.

His teeth flashed in a wide grin. "Silly little fellow, isn't he? Nevertheless—"

"Good night, Captain Newcomer." As Bryony walked to the other end of the room to speak with the host, she felt Jack Newcomer's eyes on her back. She was glad he couldn't see her blushing face.

Bryony's room was on the second floor. The maid had unpacked her belongings, but a subtle disarray ruled, as if someone had sorted through them. She wandered about the chamber, touching this, touching that, sensing a sinister presence that had no name or face. A taffeta flower lay abandoned on the floor; her silk stockings were sloppily rolled up.

Bryony tried to shake off her foreboding. Perhaps the

maid had been merely curious. As far as she could see, nothing was missing.

She pulled the dusty curtains apart and peered outside. All she could see was the reflection of her own face in the flawed glass. The wind howled in the branches and slammed an open shutter back and forth. Other than that, the inn lay in a cocoon in silence. There were not many travelers this late in the year.

Undressing slowly, Bryony was reluctant to crawl under the blankets. It wasn't the lumpy mattress or the coarse blankets that held her back, but a feeling that she must stay alert. Chiding herself for her unwarranted fear, she nevertheless wedged the one and only chair in the room under the door handle. If someone tried to enter the room, she would hear.

Her lips curled sardonically. The chair would surely keep Jack Newcomer away. She wasn't afraid of him any longer; rather, she wished she could experience being crushed against him while his long-fingered hands explored her skin. He would be an expert at undoing small buttons and tight laces, she mused as she struggled with the same.

As her bodice loosened, she sighed with relief; she could breathe again. Under her shift, her skin felt hot, alive, and tingling as she slowly stroked her small breasts while imagining that her hands had miraculously turned into those of Jack Newcomer. Then she grew ashamed; she hardly knew the man! There was something about him that tempted her to abandon every ounce of decorum that Aunt Hortense had instilled in her.

Restless, she tore off the rest of her clothes except her shift and crawled between the sheets. As she closed her eyes, his face appeared on the inside of her eyelids. She remembered every shadow of his smile, every nuance of his expression. And his eyes. For the first time in weeks, Reggie wasn't the last thing on her mind before she fell asleep.

Morning arrived with an anemic sun. A lonely bird chirped on a branch outside Bryony's window. She stretched and yawned as memories of the previous evening washed over her. Jack Newcomer. And Nigel, who had been politely distant. But what more could she expect? The people one knew as a child grew up, changed into strangers altogether. If Nigel was the most handsome man she had ever met, Captain Newcomer was by far the most dangerous.

Would he still be at the inn? Her heart beat alarmingly at the thought.

Bryony got out of bed and dressed. Her flounced, quilted underdress of cream muslin showed where the rose muslin overdress parted at the front. As she was about to powder her cheeks, she recalled Captain Newcomer's forceful wiping of her face. Was he right? Would she look more attractive without a layer of paint and powder? But it was all the rage of Paris in redden one's lips and darken one's eyelashes, and there were all manner of velvet patches to affix at strategic points on the face, velvet invitations.

The Kissing, for instance, at the corner of one's lips, or *la coquette,* as it was called in Paris. Bryony giggled and placed a star-shaped patch *à la effrontée*—on her nose. That would surely make the captain raise an eyebrow!

If he was still there.

She realized she would miss him if he was gone. He had shaken her out of her numb misery and given her the strength to continue her investigation into Reggie's death. A sigh shuddered through her as she considered her loss. Sifting through the contents of her drawstring net bag, she found the folded paper with the names. After unfolding it carefully on the table by the window, she began to piece the enclosed fragments together. It was more difficult and time-consuming than she expected, but she finally succeeded. Memorizing the names, she read:

Mr. Silas Forrester of Haywards Heath
Mr. Dudley Bench of Seaford
Earl of Bentworth of Bentworth Court, Alfriston·
Reverend Augustus Cleaves of Battle

The only person she knew was Reverend Cleaves, an old friend of her father's. But Battle was the farthest distance from Cuckfield. She would visit Mr. Forrester first.

Haywards Heath were a mere hop to the east from Cuckfield.

She dreaded the meeting, reluctant to hear what the man
would say about her brother. But however much it hurt,
she needed to know the truth before she could go on with
her life.

Filled with an urgency to continue her mission, she
bound her hair with only a ribbon at the back and put on
a tiny lace cap and her cloak, which was still damp from
the previous night's rain. Without the help of a maid, her
garments would be in sad shape very soon. The realization
made her feel lonely and helpless. She wasn't used to
sponging and pressing her own clothes; how did one go
about reshaping a sagging cloak? She should have brought
her trunk. With only one portmanteau, she was stuck with
only two changes of clothes.

And she would have to rent a conveyance since she
didn't want to waste time returning to Crawley for her own
carriage.

Downstairs, the taproom was filled with travelers.
Bryony's gaze flew from face to face—old men, matrons
in mobcaps, screaming children in smocks and bonnets.
The air was redolent with the aroma of freshly fried bacon
and homemade bread. But Bryony could barely breathe
from suspense, and she heaved a deep sigh of relief when
her gaze alighted on Captain Newcomer seated at one of
the tables. His eyes lit up, and he rose in one fluid movement, waving at her. She could not stop a smile from
bursting from the depth of her heart and flooding her face.

He clasped both her hands. "You look radiant this
morning, my lovely," he murmured, and held out a chair
for her. "Please grace my table with your fair presence. I
would be honored if you would take breakfast with me
before you leave. For old times' sake," he added with a
teasing smile.

Bryony didn't hesitate. "I'm most grateful for your offer, Captain Newcomer." A feeling of pleasure coursed
through her as she gazed into his obsidian eyes, and a
wave of inexplicable recognition jolted her, just as it had
that first time.

For a moment she thought she saw bewilderment and

awe in the dusky depths of his eyes, but the moment passed as a teasing light returned to them, taunting her.

He was more disheveled than ever, wearing a clean but creased moss-green satin vest over a wrinkled shirt and a cravat tied willy-nilly around his strong neck; his fierce chin had now completely disappeared beneath the growing beard.

Did he never shave? she wondered with misgivings. But the coarse fabric of his simple gray coat could not hide the forceful span of his shoulders, nor could it conceal the authority of his bearing. The sea captain was used to commanding everyone on his ship.

A serving wench balanced a wide wooden tray against her shoulder and served them rolls and sliced bread, and a dish of bright yellow butter, freshly churned.

A man in a suit of dark brown frieze and a tricorne hat shiny with wear was sitting at the next table, staring intently as he inhaled from a long-stemmed chalk pipe. His narrow face was disfigured with a hideous red scar that stretched from his left eyebrow down to his jaw. His periwig was old and greasy, and the stock around his neck was yellow with age. His probing gaze chilled Bryony, and she spread her fan to shield her face, shifting in her seat so that her back was turned toward the rude man. "Why does he stare at me?" she whispered.

"Who?" Captain Newcomer asked, and looked behind her. "Oh, that old geezer. Like me, he's probably bowled over by your loveliness. Don't worry, he's leaving."

Bryony breathed easier. She snapped her fan shut and placed it on the table.

"Are you returning to Crawley today, my lovely?" Captain Newcomer asked.

"I had planned to, but business will take me to Haywards Heath today. I will return to Crawley tonight if possible."

"Ah! And how will you go about traveling to Haywards Heath?" he probed, spreading butter liberally on a roll.

"I will hire a conveyance, hopefully something better than the wagon I used last night." Bryony took a bite of heavy barley-rye bread. It tasted unexpectedly good, and the butter was salty and very smooth.

After taking a deep draught of ale, Jack Newcomer said, "It distresses me to inform you that there are no private conveyances to be had here. Cuckfield is too small a village and The Boar too small an inn to keep a livery stable."

Bryony's spirits plummeted. New obstacles were appearing every day. But nothing would stop her.

"Then I will ask the host to lend me his wagon and his lad. I'm sure he will not resist the gleam of gold."

"Someone else may have beaten you to it," the captain said cryptically.

She stared at him through narrowed eyes. "Where are *you* going today, Captain Newcomer?"

He shrugged and refused to meet her gaze. "I should return to Portsmouth, but my ship will not be ready to sail for another week. The Downs are much lovelier to explore than the streets of Portsmouth."

"But *where* are you going?" she insisted, tired of his evasions.

"I might remain here, or take a jaunt about the countryside."

"You sound just like my brother, full of conflicting schemes."

He shot her a glance of surprised. "You have another brother? Where? And why isn't he here taking care of you?"

"You ask too many questions," Bryony said with a strained smile. "I'm talking about the same brother as last night. He died only two weeks ago in a fire, not far from here." She sighed. "I cannot get used to it."

He stiffened. "I'm sorry," he said, his voice hoarse.

Somehow his stricken face made her want to talk. Words came tumbling out, faster and faster, as if she needed to cleanse herself of every word and thought she had had since the moment Reggie died. "I cannot accept the verdict that he took his own life," she concluded. "Reggie loved life." The only information she held back was the fact that Reggie had been part of the Jacobite cause.

Newcomer was listening intently, never once interrupting her. His hands were clenched around the tankard, his knuckles white against the gray metal.

"I will not stop until I've discovered the truth about Reggie and this infamous card game that he staged."

Jack Newcomer nodded. "That is understandable. I think you have the right idea. Who is it you're planning to visit today?"

"I cannot divulge that information. The card game was held secretly."

Leaning very close, he whispered, "Perhaps your brother was involved in the Jacobite cause—a traitor."

His words sent tendrils of icy dread down her spine; delving into Reggie's secrets might very well make her a traitor to England.

Chapter 5

Bryony scanned the busy inn yard in which traps, gigs, chaises, and frisky horses fought for space. Filled with passengers, the Brighton stage was about to leave.

The host verified her suspicion: "There are no more seats on the stage, and my wagon was hired for the day, by the gentleman over there." He pointed at Captain Newcomer's broad back as it disappeared around the stable.

Bryony seethed inside. Newcomer had done it on purpose!

"I'm afraid there aren't any wagons to be had, miss. But tomorrow—"

"—will be too late," Bryony said, trying to find a solution to her dilemma.

The host bowed apologetically and fled into the taproom.

Jules, who had spent the night in the servants' quarters, joined her on the inn's front steps. His face bore a hangdog expression, innocence mixed with worry. "Mademoiselle, what are we going to do?" he inquired, thumbing his floppy hat.

"It looks like I'll have to wait here until a wagon is available. Who knows for how long," she mumbled, frowning. She paced the path between the stables and the inn, thinking. Jules's worried gaze followed her. She halted in front of him.

"I will have to ask you to collect my carriage in Crawley. Can you handle that, Jules?" she asked. "Then we can be on our way this afternoon."

"Naturally, I'll do anything you ask. I will find some

farmer who will give me a lift," Jules assured her. He rotated his arms wildly. "I will speak with my hands and arms, make them understand me. This is a strange country," he added as an afterthought, and shook his head. "Barbarians."

Bryony smiled and patted his arm. "Yes, I know you'll manage," she said, though she harbored some misgivings. After returning inside and writing a note to the blacksmith in Crawley, she handed Jules the missive and some money to cover the cost of the repairs.

"Good luck, *mon ami*. I will look for you this evening. Be careful. There are highwaymen on the road."

Once Jules had headed north, she prepared to confront Captain Newcomer. Hoggie and the wagon had just rounded the corner, the old horse ambling toward her.

Hoggie touched the brim of his cap and called, "A good mornin' t' ye, m'lady. Are ye ready t' depart?"

Bryony stared at him in bewilderment, then spied the captain walking briskly behind the wagon. "Ah! There you are, lovely one," he shouted over the din of the departing stage.

At that moment she wanted to tear the infuriating man apart. "And where would you expect me to be? Crying in my bed? You smug, smirking, *wagon-stealing*— Ohhh!" she raged. "You *knew* I would need the cart today. You rented it just to thwart me."

He looked down at her angry face, a maddening grin on his face. "No such thing! Have you so little faith in me? I would never take advantage of a helpless lady."

"Oh, pooh!" she scoffed. "That is the very thing you *would* do. How much do you want?" Tearing open the gold-tasseled closure of her bag, she rattled the coins in her brocade purse. "How much?" Her icy gaze could have frozen his face.

He leaned nonchalantly against the cart and rubbed his chin, making his beard rasp. "In fact, I was planning on driving into the country this morning." Throwing a glance toward the pale blue sky, he added, "The weather is favorable for a little excursion, after all. Perhaps a picnic."

She shook the purse. "I'm sure the tune of gold will change your mind," she suggested.

He laughed. "Keep your coins, lovely one. I have come to offer you my escort to Haywards Heath, since I know how important you consider your visit there." He held out his arm. "May I assist you? I confess the wagon is in singularly poor taste, but we shall endeavor to stay comfortable somehow."

She presented him with a view of her back. "I'm not going anywhere with you. Why, only looking at you makes my blood boil."

"From passion, I hope," he suggested with a chuckle.

She tore away from him, lifting her bulging net bag as if to strike him. "Never! Why can't you mind your own business and let me go about mine in peace?" Tears of helpless anger stood in her eyes. "Please, go away."

"Calm yourself. All I offer is a lift to Haywards Heath. There I will take myself off for a walk and afterward collect you at the hour of your choice."

Bryony threw a longing glance at the wagon, then at Hoggie, whose smile reached from ear to ear. "Very well," she said, "but I hope that will be the last I see of you."

He held on to the cart as if stricken by a mortal blow. "Cruel, cruel woman," he lamented, and gripped her lightning-fast around the waist, lifting her into the wagon. She landed with a thud atop the straw-filled sack. Then he tossed in their portmanteaus.

Hoggie pulled out of the yard as Captain Newcomer lithely swung his legs over the side of the wagon.

Through the maple leaves, the sunlight dotted the lane with golden patches. A light breeze caressed the dry grass lining the ditches. Two squirrels chased each other around the trunk of an old oak tree.

But Bryony didn't pay much attention to the serenity around her. She fumed in silence, inventing and discarding ways to punish Jack Newcomer for this latest trick. Why did he want to accompany her? It just couldn't be a coincidence that he had hired Hoggie and the wagon. She couldn't believe he enjoyed her company enough to waste an entire morning with her.

"Do you know where you're going?" he asked, and leaned back against the end of the sack. His shabby tricorne slid across his eyes as he propped his head against her shoulder. She tried to move away, but the side of the wagon was already jarring her hip. His curly, dark hair gleamed richly in the sunlight, and Bryony had to quell an urge to touch the unruly wave that insisted on escaping the confines of the narrow leather thong at the nape of his neck.

She ought to tear the wave out by its roots!

Pushing ineffectually against his shoulder, she tried to show her disapproval, but he only settled himself more comfortably against her. "Well?" he reminded her.

"You can let me off in the village," she answered evasively. "I can take care of myself."

He shrugged, the back of his arm rubbing against her breast. "If you insist."

Spellbound by the sensation caused by his movement, Bryony could think of nothing else. There was something about this maddening man that touched a place inside her that no one had ever touched before. Why him? Why not Nigel, or some Frenchman of Aunt Hortense's circle of friends?

Nigel definitely aroused something within her, but she could not find words to explain it. Perhaps exasperation, disappointment.

Jack Newcomer's presence was both calming and exciting at the same time. But when he opened his mouth, he was arrogant, infuriating, and so sure of himself and of . . . *her* that her anger was fanned to a steadily burning glow. Somehow she would get back at him for his insufferable remarks and careless caresses.

"You are silent, my lovely," he mused, and turned his head, tilting back his tricorne. "A penny for your thoughts."

She had difficulty returning his warm gaze, feeling color rush to her cheeks. "My thoughts are worth a lot more than a penny."

He laughed, and Bryony had to join him. "This is ridiculous," she exclaimed between laughs.

His hand rested on her knee. Possessively.

She could not bring herself to push him away.

Without warning, the wagon slowed down, but Bryony

didn't notice anything except the sensation of Jack New-comer's hand on her leg. She flinched as Hoggie's broad voice broke the spell.

"I'll be gormed! Th' poor 'oss 'as gone lame. A pebble in 'er 'oof, most likely. Whoa, Daisy ol' girl, lemme see." He jumped down, and the captain followed suit. They lifted up the fetlock and bent over the hoof.

"Yep, an outright nasty piece o' rock that is. She'll likely 'ave a bad bruise," Hoggie said, shaking his head. "Can't go on now, can we?"

Jack Newcomer swore and threw his tricorne on the ground. "Hellish bad luck! Why does everything keep going wrong?"

Bryony climbed down. "What are we going to do?" she inquired, pondering Newcomer's unexpected display of anger.

"Walk, dammit," he swore, and glared at her as if the accident was all her fault. "I take it you're wearing useless satin slippers, like all silly women do."

Bryony jabbed a finger into his chest and, her voice harsh with wrath, said, "You walk that way." She pointed down the road behind them. "I'll walk in the opposite direction." Her eyes spewed fire. "And as for silly women, you have no knowledge of our strength. What abuse from arrogant men like you do we endure in silence! But I will tell you once and never again, *I* will never take another ounce of abuse from you!"

Twisting the tricorne that she had initially picked up in a desire to comfort him in his disappointment, she flung it back on the ground. Then she hitched up her skirts so that he could clearly see her low-heeled kid shoes, and ground her heel into the rounded crown.

"There!" she exclaimed, and stalked off toward Hay-wards Heath.

"Wait!"

She walked faster.

She walked until her side ached and her hair stuck to her forehead and neck. Fury fueled her until she couldn't take another step. Panting, she leaned against a tree trunk and pressed a hand to her side.

"What got into you?" Captain Newcomer chided as he reached her. He was carrying his portmanteau and hers.

"I'm only a silly woman in satin slippers," she hurled at him. "I'm expected to act like an idiot."

"You're a keg of gunpowder, my lovely. It's extremely difficult to keep abreast of your whims."

"So don't!" she exploded. "Didn't I order you not to follow me?" She stumbled back onto the road and continued to walk. Why did he always get her goat?

The sounds of creaking wheels and trotting horses reached her. She would try to get a lift to Haywards Heath, but before she could move, Captain Newcomer was already standing in the middle of the road, waving his arms.

A coach painted black with gold ornamentation on the corners and a crest on the door came into view. Four chestnut horses pulled the carriage, and two lackeys stood on the box in the back. The owners must be people of some means.

The coachman pulled in the reins, and the carriage came to a halt. Jack Newcomer hurried forward and spoke through the open window, but Bryony couldn't discern the words that were exchanged. Still, when the captain beckoned her, she reluctantly acquiesced.

The coach was dark inside, the curtains drawn, but Bryony saw the outlines of two old men and a woman.

"Step forward, child, so that I can look at you," invited the old woman in a quavering voice.

Bryony stepped closer. "I'd be eternally grateful if you'd give me a lift to the next village," she said.

"Only you, child? Your husband here told us about your accident. In fact, we met the unfortunate horse and boy on the road, I believe."

Bryony lost her voice and whipped her head around to glare at Jack Newcomer. Husband? she mouthed. The gall!

He took her elbow and maneuvered her forcefully into the coach. "We're, of course, extremely grateful for your hospitality, Lady Fitzbourne."

The old lady jabbed her cane in the roof of the coach, and a moment later they were jerked forward. "Young man, usually we don't take up strangers, especially a stranger with a *beard,* but this delicate young lady cannot

be left exposed to the elements.'' She waved her fan slowly
in front of her face. ''Algernon! Say how-de-do to the
young newlywed couple, Captain Newcomer and his little
wife.''

The old man directed an ear trumpet toward her voice.
''Whaddayasay?'' he shouted, and blinked.

Bryony had an impression of two heads of wispy white
hair and two pairs of round, blue, blinking eyes. The other
old man was taller and darker. He remained silent during
the introductions.

''That's brother Algie for you. Can't hear a cat wink,''
Lady Fitzbourne said with a hearty if trembling laugh. She
peered at them in the gloom. ''Ah, to be young again and
so romantically in love.'' She sighed and fluttered her fan.
''I have only to look at you two to see that you're lost in
love.''

Bryony forced out a smile, and her ''husband'' placed
his arm around her shoulders with a proprietary air, pulling her close. She gave him a look that said he might have
won this time, but it would never happen again.

''I don't understand why you allow such rough com-
moners to ride in your coach, Augusta,'' said the dark
gentleman with a chilling smile.

Jack Newcomer stiffened, and Bryony sensed his
mounting anger.

''Oh, humbug!'' scoffed the birdlike Lady Fitzbourne.
''They are just harmless young people, Malvin.''

The haughty Malvin Fitzbourne *harrumphed.* ''Raff and
scaff all the same. I don't see why we should have to—''

''Enough vinegar, Malvin! You should be grateful that
you're one of the chosen few who can afford an elegantly
cut coat on your scrawny back.'' Lady Fitzbourne leaned
forward eagerly and addressed Bryony. ''Now, you have
to tell me every delicious detail of your wedding party,
m'dear. I can see that you found a very manly husband,
but I warn you,'' she cautioned with a wink, ''other
women will fight you for his favors.''

Let them have him, Bryony thought with a silent sniff.
''Ah . . . well—'' she begun.

''I wouldn't trust him for a moment, young lady. You
have acted thoughtlessly in choosing him,'' grumbled

Malvin, while Algernon directed his trumpet toward his brother and repeated "Whaddayasay."

Jack Newcomer had tensed into tightly coiled fury, ready to attack. "I will not have my wife insulted," he ground out between clenched teeth.

Bryony placed a calming hand on his arm. "Why shouldn't I trust my husband?" she queried, then sensed Captain Newcomer's fury turning against her.

Malvin shrugged and smirked. "*I* would never trust a sea captain. Too fickle. Always traveling."

Bryony leaned back, disappointed that he had no other reason. "I have my fears," she said dryly, and met the captain's angry glare measure for measure.

"And especially one who cannot afford to have his coat sponged and pressed," Malvin went on. "Or his beard shaved. The worst kind."

Captain Newcomer rose halfway out of his seat. "That is quite enough! If you say one more word, your advanced age might not prevent me from calling you out."

"Calm yourself," Bryony urged, pulling him down. His face had paled, and a muscle worked in his jaw. Why couldn't he see the humor in the situation? An old man's ravings meant nothing, after all. Closed inside his cocoon of anger, Captain Newcomer stared stiffly out the window.

Lady Fitzbourne rattled on about old memories, and Bryony was grateful that she had forgotten to probe about the wedding party. Bryony had never dreamed she would spend the day in the company of three eccentric septuagenarians and the bold stranger who had turned her life upside down.

The lane widened, and a few cottages appeared on either side.

"Haywards Heath has nothing to recommend itself," Lady Fitzbourne said, "except a small inn that serves exceptional fare. Now Lindfield, right next to it, that is a pretty village, with its beautiful pond and swans. The annual sheep fair is held on the common across from the pond. The church is quite old, as is Tudor House beside it. I can't imagine what business you have in a tiny hamlet like Haywards Heath."

"I—ahem—we will visit an old acquaintance," Bryony

explained. She would have to ask someone in Haywards
Heath for directions to Mr. Forrester's house.

"We will halt for luncheon here," said the old lady. "I
take it our paths will part, unless you want a lift to Tun-
bridge Wells. We're going to take the waters there."

"No, but thank you for offering," Bryony said, and
looked out the window. The inn, an old stone building
with few windows, was surrounded by lime trees and unkempt box hedges. The stable had a sagging thatched roof,
and weeds grew along the walls. The inn yard was empty
except for a rooster scratching in the mud.

The horses came to a halt. Captain Newcomer jumped
from the coach and offered his assistance to the ladies,
although Bryony chose to ignore him. Algernon needed a
steadying hand, and Bryony linked her arm with his. He
tottered across the muddy yard and up the two stone steps
into the taproom. The captain had already ordered a private room for Lady Fitzbourne and was assisting her into
a parlor behind the taproom.

Bryony returned outside and considered escaping before
Captain Newcomer returned, but her thoughts were abruptly interrupted when she heard a cry from inside the
coach. She hurried around the horses and found Malvin
still there.

"Child, come here!" he ordered impatiently.

As Bryony looked inside, he demanded that she find the
coachman for him. "My dratted legs are useless."

Bryony noticed his two canes and hurried to oblige. But
the coachman was nowhere in sight, and the lackeys had
disappeared. The captain was standing on the steps, and
she waved to him.

"The gentleman needs to be carried inside," she explained, and watched the captain's face darken.

"He can crawl for all that I care," he grated, and
marched toward the lane. "My day has been ruined, and
I will return to Cuckfield on foot if necessary."

Bryony ran after him and gripped his arm, halting him
in midstride. "How can you be so callous and selfish!"
she berated him.

"I've had enough of overbearing old men," he snarled
savagely, and tore his arm free.

"And you're turning into one yourself! You bragged about how you eventually forgave the wrongs your stepfather did to you, but now I can see that you were only pretending. You're as filled with hatred as ever. Any man with a censorious tongue has the power to ignite that hatred as easily as wind tosses a dry leaf." Holding on to both his arms, she forced him to stop. His eyes were inscrutable obsidian pools, and his face was as hard as chiseled marble. He avoided her eyes.

"Look at me," she demanded, and shook him. "Help the poor man and help yourself. Hatred will eat at you until there is nothing left. Don't you see? Your stepfather will have won in the end, even though he's dead."

Newcomer trembled with the effort to keep his temper. His breath hissed through his nostrils, and he looked as if he would explode at any moment. "No!"

Then he turned abruptly and stalked across the yard without glancing at the carriage. Malvin was watching their movements with great curiosity. At the same time one of the lackeys arrived and lifted the protesting old man, carrying him inside.

Jack Newcomer was a fool. Bryony knew she had done the right thing in scolding him, even if it meant he would be angry with her for the rest of the day. But she would be better off without his company. She was going to speak with Mr. Forrester alone, as she had planned from the beginning.

When Bryony returned to the inn to thank Lady Fitzbourne for her hospitality, Jack Newcomer was nowhere in sight. She kindly declined the older woman's invitation to lunch. Then she spoke with the host, who gave her directions to Mr. Forrester's house: " 'Tis Potter House by Lindfield, th' old place near th' church—cannot miss it, m'lady. Now what's odd is that 'e seems to 'ave left in a 'urry. 'Asn't been seen in nary a fortnight. Yer visit'll be in vain."

Bryony's spirits fell. Just her luck! Everything had gone wrong since the moment she set foot in England.

"Since I'm here, I might as well take a look at Potter House," she said with a sigh of disappointment.

" 'Tis but a short trip from here, miss. Haywards Heath

ends where Lindfield starts,'' he explained, his belly bouncing as if he had told a joke.

Lady Fitzbourne, who had overheard the conversation, instantly offered her carriage. ''We will not continue until Algernon has had his afternoon rest, and the coachman will be better if he works this afternoon than if he imbibes tankards of ale.''

Potter House was a square brick building with latticed windows and clematis vine framing the front entrance. Bryony jumped out of the carriage and looked in vain for a knocker. Gone. It meant that Mr. Forrester was definitely absent. Where could he be? It became imperative that she find him and hear his account of Reggie's last hour.

She told the coachman to wait for her at the local alehouse down the road while she explored the back of the building. He complied with alacrity.

As soon as he was gone, Bryony looked first right, then left. She didn't want someone to cry ''Thief!'' while she was trespassing. There was nobody in sight, however, although she could not tell if someone was staring at her from behind the curtains of the neighboring cottages. She walked around the tall lilac hedge at the corner of the house, toward the back entrance.

The garden was shrouded in profound stillness, and the tall oaks cast deep shadows over the damp grass and the wilting flower beds. Bryony shaded her eyes with her hand and studied the windows of the back wall. There was no movement behind the dark panes. Fear rolled along her spine. The silence was brooding, sinister, reaching out as if with invisible hands that would suffocate her.

Bryony pushed away the sensation and banged on the back door. She waited, nervously fingering the tasseled drawstring of her handbag. It was as quiet as death inside. She knocked hard once more, although she knew it would be futile. Mr. Forrester wasn't there, and she had wasted a day trying to locate him.

Sinking down on the stone step, she pulled her knees up to her chin and tried to form a plan. There was no use waiting; she knew he wasn't going to return. As she considered several ideas, she heard a faint rustling coming from the side of the house.

Tensing, she listened. Was someone spying on her, or was it just a squirrel or a cat moving under the unkempt bushes? Holding her breath, she strained her ears.

Silence.

Then came the call of a robin. The bird jumped across the grass, head cocked first one way, then the other, in search of worms. Bryony let her breath out, but she noticed that her hands were trembling, and cold sweat glued her bodice to her back.

Then her body stiffened in shock as a disheveled and filthy boy catapulted through the hedge and halted at her feet.

"Who—" she croaked.

"Shhh," the urchin whispered, and pulled her behind a clump of lilacs. "Ye've been spotted."

Bryony calculated that the boy was about ten years old, although he had the experienced look of an older child. His peppercorn eyes were sly and quick, and his blond hair was a mop of dirty curls. "What's going on?" Bryony demanded. "I'm looking for Mr. Forrester. Do you know him?"

"O' course I know 'im! Ever'body round 'ere knows 'im. Traitor they calls 'im—th' redcoats that came round to arrest 'im." The urchin wiped his runny nose. " 'E's one of 'em Jakkerbites. That's why 'e's 'idin' out down at th' ol' ruins."

Bryony's interest was awakened. "Can you show me where?"

The boy regarded her scornfully. "O' course I can! I bain't no wee babe." Eagerly he held out a grubby palm.

Sighing in exasperation, Bryony pulled out her purse and handed over a shilling. The money might be well spent if the boy led her to Mr. Forrester. Besides, the child's family probably needed what little extra money they could get.

"How did you find me here?" Bryony asked.

"Was lookin' fer redcoats. They're thick round 'ere nowadays."

Bryony tried to see the lane beyond the hedge. "I haven't seen any."

"They're 'ere all th' same. 'Urry up, lady." He gripped her hand and pulled her through a hole in the hedge without paying any attention to her full-skirted dress. As she muttered a protest, he urged, "C'mon, then."

As she disappeared among the dense lilacs, a flurry of movements erupted behind her and three musket shots exploded in her ears. Charred leaves rained down on her head, and a musket ball grazed her cloak.

Fear drained all the blood from her head and the world tilted. She clung to a slender lilac branch for support. The urchin was shaking her sleeve furiously. " 'Urry then, 'urry!"

Chapter 6

Throwing a terrified glance over her shoulder, Bryony saw the flash of a gray coat among the trees and the silhouette of a tall man. Fire flared from the same spot, and another ball whizzed through the leaves right above her head.

Driven by fear, she managed to pull herself through the hedge. It was a miracle that her legs still functioned. All she could think of was escaping the terror that pursued her. She pinned her gaze to the urchin's thin back and ran, faster than she had ever run before. Blood pounded at her temples, and she dragged air painfully into her lungs. She glanced back, but nobody was following her.

The urchin led the way down a hill, past a row of sheds and dilapidated stables, through a small spinney, and across a glittering brook. Bryony had to stop once to get her breath. She peeped through the trees. The village was concealed from their view.

"Quick! In here," the boy cried, and circled a huge boulder. Bryony followed suit. A building almost completely hidden by vegetation was barely visible.

The boy hurtled through the door of the tumbledown cottage. He waved frantically at her. "C'mon!"

Bryony followed him inside. She was ready to collapse on the dirty floor, but the boy beckoned her toward a wide crack in the back wall. He slunk through easily, but she had difficulty pulling the stiff hoops of her dress through the opening. The urchin tugged at the other side and finally tilted the hoops unceremoniously upward until they flattened and she could slide through.

''What are you doing?'' Bryony snapped, and pulled down her skirts and hoops, which had risen to her thighs. Looking around, she saw that they were standing in the overgrown backyard.

The urchin shrugged, unperturbed. ''Would ye rather be caught in th' crack like a mouse in a mousetrap, silly mort?''

Bryony glared. ''Where are we going, anyway?''

The boy walked a few yards along the wall and pulled away the heavy curtain of ivy. A hole in the ground opened before her. A rotted ladder led down under the house, into the cellars.

''They won't find us 'ere,'' the boy said confidently, and scuttled down the rungs. ''Careful, these bain't none too safe.''

Bryony stepped gingerly onto the topmost rung, expecting it to collapse under her weight. It held, and by some magic, she descended into the damp cellar without breaking her leg. The cavelike room smelled of mold and earth and rotting wood. A grave would smell like this, she thought with a shiver.

She held her breath as slow, leaden steps clumped above her head.

She listened tensely for more footsteps, but there was only one pair of legs, the massive steps shaking the disintegrating floor joists. The boy streaked past her up the ladder and pulled the ivy back across the hole. His movement disturbed a loose brick, which tumbled onto the floor.

''Oh, daggers!'' swore the urchin under his breath.

The footsteps above them stopped abruptly.

''What now?'' Bryony breathed. ''He'll find us for sure.'' Her gaze darted around the dim chamber in search of cover. A large overturned crate stood in one corner, and a broken wooden bucket lay in the middle.

In silent agreement, they slunk behind the crate and crouched, praying the man with the deadly musket would not discover their hiding place.

As Bryony listened to the steps coming ever closer, she realized that, by prying into Reggie's death, she had become involved in the cause that had claimed his life—and might claim hers.

If the pursuer was a British soldier, he wouldn't hesitate to kill her if he thought she was a Jacobite. The possibility was very real and terrifying to her. How could Englishmen kill their brothers in cold blood just because they wanted different sovereign?

It was too tragic, Bryony thought as the steps above moved outside the cottage, nearing the ivy curtain.

She gripped a brick and hid it behind her back, and the urchin instantly imitated her. She wished the earth would open up and swallow her. Rather that than experience a musket ball tearing into her flesh.

Sunlight seeped into the cellar as the ivy moved. Bryony heard twigs breaking outside, then there came a sudden crash and a rattling sound as a heavy body fell through the hole. A man groaned. Mortar and bricks rained down into the hole and covered the man, who lay sprawled on the floor. The air grew dim and gritty with dust.

"Blast and damned!" he swore, and Bryony shot to her feet, throwing the brick in her hand to the ground in disgust.

"Captain Newcomer! I should have known it would be you," she stormed, and ran around the crate to kneel at his side. "Are you badly hurt?"

The captain swore again, sat up, and shook mortar out of his hair. "Why did you have to rush off in such a hurry? I had to walk all the way from the inn," he challenged, brushing off his coat.

Her jaw fell in surprise and indignation. "How come you didn't hear the muskets, sirrah? Mayhap you fired one yourself. Come to think of it, one of our pursuers wore a gray coat just like yours." Her gaze rested on his portmanteau. "And I know what you have in your bag that you won't leave out of your sight."

He paled, and his dark eyes seemed to probe her very soul. She squirmed and had to look away. *Could he really be the one who'd shot at her? No. No!*

"What, pray tell?" he asked.

"Pistols, of course," she reminded him. "Have you

already forgotten the highwaymen who almost killed us on the Brighton stage?''

He relaxed, stood, and brushed off his legs. The honed muscles of his thighs strained against his knee breeches, captivating Bryony's imagination. For a short moment the recent horrors faded as she felt an irresistible urge to touch those thighs, to slide her palms the length of those fascinating forms, and—

''You shouldn't have gone alone to Mr. Forrester's house,'' he continued in a stern voice.

Jerked back to reality, Bryony blushed. ''You've been meddling in my affairs. I didn't ask for your company. I'm not alone,'' she said, and called to the boy.

He came out of hiding, nonchalantly dropping his brick and shoving his hands deep in his pockets.

The captain raised his hand to shove back the unruly curl that had escaped the boy's queue, and the urchin flinched, protecting his face as if in anticipation of a blow.

''What's this?'' Captain Newcomer said in surprise, and gripped the thin shoulder hard. ''What's your name, boy?''

''Cl-Clover, guv,'' said the boy, cringing.

''A dirty, sniveling pickpocket, are you?'' the captain said tersely, and shook the boy. Bryony's eyes flew wide. ''If you've pinched Miss Shaw's purse, I'll spank your bottom.''

Clover's face was pale and distrustful, the button nose almost comical as he thrust it defiantly in the air. He aimed a kick at the captain's shin. ''I did not! A silly mort, she is! Goin' to visit that Forrester fellow in broad daylight. Ever'body knows 'e's a traitor.''

''Now, listen here—'' Bryony began, but Captain Newcomer halted her with a gesture.

Holding Clover out of kicking range, he said, ''Do you live around here?''

''O' course I do,'' Clover said, hedging.

''Where?'' Captain Newcomer pressed.

''Ar—well, down—er—by th' pond.''

As Bryony listened in growing amazement, she inched closer to the captain's portmanteau, which lay overturned next to the broken ladder. He was addressing her while keeping his concentration directed at the boy. "What we have here is a fugitive. A starving, dirty fugitive."

With her eyes on the captain, she said in distracted tones, "I see." She righted the portmanteau, unlatched the clasp, and took a quick glance inside. The pistols were there. She touched one. The barrel was warm.

"And what are we going to do with you?" Captain Newcomer's voice boomed, startling Bryony. She pulled her hand away as if it had been burned and pinned an innocent look on her face. When she realized that he was talking to Clover, she drew a breath of relief.

Taking another hasty glance into the portmanteau, she saw a wad of papers, some sort of documents, a wrinkled shirt, a folded waistcoat, and some cravats. And a thin stack of letters bound with a white satin ribbon.

Love letters. Misery welled up within her. Everything Captain Newcomer had said to her about love was just a hoax. Oh, how taken in she had been! Until now.

"What are you doing?" the captain demanded, and yanked the portmanteau away from her. He slammed it shut and set it on top of the crate. "Snooping?"

Red roses of guilt blossomed on her cheeks. "I—I was looking for a handkerchief," she said feebly.

He glared at her, a sardonic smile curling his lips. "And the sun is blue."

"Oh, very well," she retorted hotly. "I wanted to see if your pistols were warm, and they are." She thrust her chin defiantly upward, her eyes challenging him.

He lifted his shoulders and spread his hands in a gesture of innocence. "I was shooting at your pursuers, lovely one. But they got away."

"Redcoats, bain't they, guv?" asked Clover.

"No, I didn't notice any soldiers. There were three men dressed in dark cloaks and spurred boots. I heard the spurs jingling and followed the sound, but they rode off before I caught up with them."

Bryony's glance was full of suspicion. "We have only your word for it. Clover says he saw soldiers at Potter House."

Captain Newcomer smoothed back his hair. "They were at the alehouse beyond the green."

"I take it you stopped in there," Bryony scoffed.

"Naturally! Running behind your coach was exhausting work. I arrived with a raving desire for a tankard of ale."

"One thing I have learned," Bryony said. "You are never at a loss for words."

"And one thing I have learned; never trust a woman," he retorted.

Bryony held her head high, but her eyes glittered with unshed tears. He had the power to hurt her so. "What does that have to do with this issue? Though daring and flirtatious, you're astoundingly bereft in certain areas—grace, for one. Tact, for another. And trust."

She turned to Clover. "Will you take me to Mr. Forrester's hiding place now? Please."

The boy thrust out his palm. "That'll cost ye another shillin', ma'am."

"No such thing! You will take me to Mr. Forrester this instant, or I'll report you to the Watch."

Clover hunched over in fear, hiding his face in his hands. Bryony relented. "Well, I would never do that. But you're a greedy little boy, and you're wearing my patience thin."

"Promise?" Clover muttered.

"I promise." Bryony patted his shoulder. "But why are you so afraid?"

"I'm an—er—orphan. They'll send me back to th' workhouse. I'll *die* if I 'ave t' go back there. I'd sooner starve t' death." Clover dragged a too-long, grimy sleeve across his eyes and sniffed miserably. He darted up the remaining rungs of the ladder. "C'mon then, stir yer trotters."

Captain Newcomer heaved himself out of the hole and stretched a hand down to help her up. Though she resented it, she had to accept his assistance. She knew that when his fingers touched hers, she would be at an instant disadvantage, spellbound by the sensations he aroused in her. When it came to Jack Newcomer, her heart betrayed her time and time again.

Chapter 7

"Where are *you* going now?" she asked the captain as he hoisted her out of the cellar.

Resting his hands on her shoulders, he let his gaze rove slowly over her trim figure and linger on the agitated pulse at the base of her throat. With breathless intensity she stared into his enigmatic dark eyes as his thumb gently caressed the delicate skin of her throat.

"After what happened at Potter House, I'm not about to leave you alone," he said, tracing the outline of her jaw. He touched her lips. "Oh, how I'd like to kiss you!"

Remembering the letters in his portmanteau, Bryony swore she wasn't going to fall for his smooth charm again. She was about to quell his ardor, but Clover did it for her by peeking around the side of the cottage and exclaiming, "Crikey! C'mon, ye cod's 'eads."

He led them down a narrow path in the woods behind the cottage. Sunlight streaked between the branches, creating a pattern of light and shadow among the trees. Birds chirped and hopped from one branch to another, studying the small procession with unrestrained curiosity. The air was soft, saturated with the scents of moss and warm, spicy bark. It was a rare afternoon, reminding Bryony of the balmy summer that had passed.

They crossed a meadow and some bare fields, reached a wild-grown hedge. Clover put a finger to his lips in warning and disappeared through the hedge, but only after Bryony had stuck one of her calling cards into his hands and explained that she *must* see Mr. Forrester.

Captain Newcomer said he would keep watch while

73

Bryony met with Mr. Forrester. "I will hoot like an owl if there is mischief afoot." He faded into the dense shade of a huge oak tree. Bryony stood silent, feeling inexplicably nervous.

A bee buzzed past her toward a clump of blue bachelor's buttons, and a chickadee clung to a twig close by, investigating her.

"Pssst, c'mon then, m'lady," came Clover's harsh whisper. He motioned toward her from the side of the hedge, and Bryony was grateful that she didn't have to crawl through another mesh of clinging branches.

Silas Forrester was crouching next to a meager fire in the ruin of a small cottage. He was a tall, burly man in his middle years. His coat hung in wrinkled folds to his knees, his waistcoat was spotted, his face was unshaven and dirty.

He rose as Bryony entered the cottage. "What d'you want?" he demanded harshly.

Uncertain, she remained in the doorway and looked into his hostile, haunted eyes. Bryony sensed instinctivley that he was not a man whom Reggie would have chosen as a friend.

"Are you here to gloat, Miss Shaw?" he chided. "Well, you arrived in the nick of time. I'm leaving the country tonight." He took a threatening step toward her. "What business do we have?"

"Can you tell me anything about my brother, about his last night alive?" Her voice trembled with emotion, and she clasped her hands tightly together. His answer shocked her.

"Yes. Reggie Shaw was an idiot. He's to blame for everything. I'm not surprised he died. Actually, I now believe he deserved to die for endangering all our lives." He laughed wildly and pointed accusingly at her. " 'Tis your brother's fault that I have to escape from England tonight in a tiny French fishing vessel that will surely perish at sea."

Bryony swallowed convulsively, guilt washing over her. "Why? You cannot blame Reggie. Y-you were in it together."

"I didn't trust Dudley Bench, never liked the fellow.

He was always thinking of his own safety first. He was a Judas. And Reggie should never have let Lord Bentworth in on the secrets. I never trusted Bentworth. He's the man who informed the militia.''

"Bentworth." Bryony furrowed her brow. What had Nigel said about him? The name was on the list.

"Yes, Lord Bentworth was a new member, though Reggie insisted he had worked behind the scenes for some time. Aided Stuart into Scotland last year—or so Reggie maintained. But we other members knew nothing about this Bentworth, other than that he was a peer of the realm and supposedly a Jacobite. Shaw was foolish, too green to be a member of our select group."

Forrester clenched and unclenched his hands, barely holding his anger in check. He let out another wild laugh. "Are you here to pay for your brother's sins? If not, you're wasting your time, and mine, Miss Shaw. If you're not careful, you might be mistaken for a Jacobite and murdered outright, no questions asked." He pretended to be pointing a pistol at her head and squeezed an imaginary trigger. "Bang!"

Startled, Bryony took a step backward. He came closer, staring at her, a crazed look in his eyes. She wanted to rush away from the gloom and bitterness that pervaded the cottage.

Had Reggie been so careless as to endanger this man's life? No, Silas Forrester had chosen to follow Charles Stuart of his own accord, and now that Stuart had lost, he had to pay the price by fleeing his country. Had Reggie been about to escape when he announced he was planning to join her in Paris? She would never know now.

"I have nothing to do with the Jacobite cause," she said.

He mimicked her voice. "Silly girl, you have now. You're talking to a traitor, and you're the sister of a traitor." He clutched his balding head, tore heedlessly at the limp strands of hair. "Oh, God, why is there no justice in this world? The Hanoverians are imposters! Why is the rightful king of England hunted like a rabbit across the Highlands?"

Bryony tried to find an explanation, hoping it would

calm the raving man. "Not sufficient Englishmen share
your beliefs. If they did, Prince Charles Edwards would
be on the throne now. The wind of change is blowing
through England, through the rest of Europe." Bryony
stared into the distance. "There was a whisper of unrest
among the poor in Paris this summer, due to the costly
war. We are being pushed toward inevitable upheavals.
Neither time, nor the changes brought by time, can be
stopped."

Glancing repeatedly in her direction, Silas Forrester's
eyes took on a strange gleam. He paced the floor, muttering to himself.

"Please, Mr. Forrester, do you think Reggie took his
own life or was he . . . murdered?"

"That coward would take his life and leave us all in the
lurch," he cried savagely. "And for the silly reason of
being unable to honor his debts. As if they mattered now!
Stuart is the one who matters, but Shaw chose to ignore
that."

"Reggie wasn't a coward," Bryony defended staunchly.

Silas Forrester looked as if he wanted to strike her.
"There wasn't any damn map, either. If we had found it,
the true king would be marching toward London today.
According to Reggie, there was enough smuggled French
gold hidden on Scottish soil to maintain an army large
enough to throw out the Hanoverians for good."

"He never mentioned the map to me."

Forrester laughed insanely. "Why would he? You were
not part of our group. Besides, it was a secret. But that
didn't stop your brother from babbling about it to Lord
Bentworth. God knows where the map is now, if it ever
existed."

Bryony could find nothing to say. Mr. Forrester was
getting more agitated by the minute. He suddenly lurched
forward, grabbed her arms, and shook her.

"I'm glad your brother got his, and if you don't leave,
you'll go the same way he did." He spat at her with a
wild light in his eyes.

Bryony wanted to scream, but no sound left her lips.
He pushed her out of the cottage. "Go! You remind me
too much of your brother, and I cannot be responsible for

my actions. I just might take the law into my own hands.''
He disappeared behind the cottage, sobbing hysterically.

Bryony fell backward onto the moss-covered flagstones
and scraped her hands. Hot tears flooded her eyes.

Clover appeared at her side as she scrambled to her feet.
To hide her tears, she dusted off her skirts and rubbed the
dirt off her hands with a wad of grass.

"Rough treatment, what? Fella's a looby," Clover commented, unperturbed, and tore a handful of yellowing maple leaves off a branch and tossed them in the air.

"You could have warned me," she complained.

Clover giggled as the leaves rained over Bryony's head
and clung to her untidy curls. "Ye look like a witch,
m'lady," he said happily.

"And you look like a—a nightmare," Bryony said, taking a firm hold of Clover's earlobe. "You need to learn
some manners."

Clover squirmed as she pulled him down the path. "I
meant ye looked like a *white* witch, m'lady," Clover
wailed. "Let me go."

"You *knew* Mr. Forrester had lost his mind, and you
didn't tell me."

"Ye wanted t' see 'im at all cost, ma'am," Clover
whined, and squirmed to get away from her punishing grip.

"You enjoyed every minute, didn't you, you miserable
little imp." She let him go, and he hid his face in his
sleeve and sobbed.

Bryony was wracked with guilt. What had come over
her? She wanted to cry, too. She swallowed hard, her
throat dry and aching.

Taking a deep breath, she gently touched Clover's
shoulder. "I'm sorry. I shouldn't have involved you in my
problems."

He surprised her by throwing himself against her and
curling his arms around her waist. He sobbed against her
middle. "Don't send me away. Please, don't send me
away," he kept repeating.

Bryony touched the dirty head, and something soft as
cotton wound around her heart. She caressed the bony
shoulder. "Don't you have any family or friends who can
take care of you?"

"I-I don't know," the urchin stammered. "Th' parish beadle said I was—am—a-a bastard, a cove no one wants."

Clover's hopeless life added another layer of misery to her own. "And how have you survived since you fled the workhouse?"

He glanced at her darkly, tears clinging to his long lashes. "Stealin', miss, an' odd jobs, runnin' errands an' such."

Bryony smiled through a film of tears. The urchin's soulful gaze tugged at her heartstrings. "I wager you're very hungry," she said.

Clover nodded, and his thin features lit up with anticipation.

"Then a plentiful dinner you shall have. But first we should find Captain Newcomer." She glanced toward the oak tree where he had been on the lookout, but there was no sign of him.

The urchin's eyes were as round as saucers. "An' ye bain't th' Missus Newcomer?"

Bryony blushed and was about to say that, thank God, she wasn't, but instead she said, "No, he is a-a friend." *I think,* she added silently. "A traveling companion," she explained to the curious boy.

"A fine gent 'e be."

Bryony nodded and wondered what the boy saw in the rascally captain. Takes one to know one, she thought wryly. But where was Captain Newcomer? Remembering the deadly musket fire, she hesitated before investigating the deep shadows under the trees.

Still, there was no sign of the man. A movement among the bushes, a rustle and a sigh sent fear crawling along her flesh. She stiffened and called out, "Captain Newcomer? Mr. Forrester?"

Nothing.

A twig snapped, brittle foliage crackled, branches swayed ghostlike.

Bryony didn't stop to find out what the bushes contained. She retraced her steps at a run, gripped Clover's hand, and dragged him with her. "Hurry! Let's return to the village. There's no time to waste," she cried, panting.

The boy caught her fear and ran as fast as his short legs could.

Exhausted, they reached the old church, and there, at the end of the lane, stood Lady Fitzbourne's carriage. Bryony let out a sigh of relief when she saw Captain Newcomer running toward her. "Is something wrong?" he called out.

"Why did you leave?" Bryony demanded as he joined them.

"I saw the coachman driving up the lane looking for you. He thought you were lost. Now we can return to the inn without delay." Jack Newcomer touched her hot face. "You look as if you just saw a ghost."

"Perhaps I did. A malevolent one at that."

He wrinkled his brow in concern. "Did you see who it was?"

"No, I didn't wait to stare into a musket barrel," she scoffed, and righted her slipping coiffure. Holding on to Clover's hand, she proceeded to the carriage.

"Perhaps it was a deer or a fox," the captain suggested, his expression worried. He held the door open for Bryony and offered his hand in assistance. She ignored him and lifted Clover onto the seat.

"What about the boy?" Captain Newcomer queried in baffled tones.

"I'm taking him with me."

Chapter 8

Clover ate a plate of thick ham slices spread with mustard, three sturdy rye rolls liberally covered with butter and honey, two slices of golden Yorkshire pudding, and an apple. Then he laid his head on the table, burped, and promptly fell asleep.

Amused, Bryony stared at him, shaking her head. She had never seen a child eat so much. He had eaten twice as much as she. Standing, she rubbed her arms against the chill in the air. The host of The Fox and Gander in Haywards Heath was stingy with his fuel, if not with his food. At least he could have made a fire for the old people dozing in front of the empty grate.

Bryony ran outside and fetched a fur rug from the carriage. She spread it gently over Lady Fitzbourne's legs. What now? She wanted to return to Cuckfield, but how could she abandon Clover? He had begun to look at her as if she were an angel of mercy. She certainly didn't feel like one; she felt like a lost and grieving workhouse orphan herself.

The meeting with Silas Forrester had only confused her more, so much so that she almost suspected him of being responsible for her brother's death. But why would he have done it? They had been working toward the same goal.

She wished she knew more about the mysterious map that Mr. Forrester had mentioned. And what about the French gold? It sounded preposterous, but it would be like Reggie to chase after some hidden treasure in Scotland.

Captain Newcomer entered the parlor, gave the nodding

Malvin Fitzbourne an acid stare, and joined Bryony by the window.

"My lovely, you look tired and distressed."

"I would like to return to Cuckfield, but what shall I do with Clover? I cannot send him back to the workhouse."

Jack Newcomer's smile completely transformed his hard features. Bryony read awe and tenderness in his eyes.

"Your continued kindness and consideration baffle me," he said candidly. "I must say, I've never met a woman with a heart before, at least never one with a heart the size of yours."

Bryony smiled, a wave of warmth flooding her. This was a compliment that came straight from his soul, and it delighted her more than any of his usual glib remarks.

He traced her cheek with a gentle finger, and she tingled all over with pleasure. "I took the liberty of speaking with the proprietor about Clover's future. He needs a stableboy and has promised to care for the child as if he were a son."

Bryony stared unseeing out the window. "I hope Clover is happy with that solution. He's a restless soul, a very unhappy little boy."

"Did he say where he's from?" Newcomer asked.

"No, I never asked. Perhaps he doesn't know. He's a child born on the wrong side of the blanket."

Newcomer was lost in thought, and Bryony stretched, longing to take a nap, but she had not procured a room for the night.

Dark clouds were gathering on the horizon. "Looks like this perfect day will be ruined," she commented. "Rain, rain, and more rain. All my clothes are still damp from last night's downpour."

"You could always take them off to dry," the captain responded cryptically.

"Ah, there you go again. You have oiled your tongue. If I don't leave you now, I will have no peace of mind." But before Bryony could depart, Lady Fitzbourne's quavering voice halted her, and she was forced to sit down to half an hour of conversation.

Bryony sensed Captain Newcomer's eyes on her. When

she returned his stare, the look in his eyes almost knocked the breath out of her. She found herself drowning, helplessly melting in a maelstrom of emotion. She couldn't deny the attraction, the combustible passion, and—love? that flowed between them, an invisible river.

She barely noticed the rain lashing the windows or the wind buffeting the walls.

"Oh, dear me!" wailed Lady Fitzbourne, "we'll have to stay here until the rain stops. I do not cherish the thought."

Bryony realized that if the rain continued, the roads would be impassable, preventing her return to Cuckfield.

"Botheration!" she said between her teeth. She ran to the window and looked outside. The clouds were hanging low in the sky, and rain beat like drumsticks against the flagstones near the door.

"I have to return to Cuckfield. To my carriage, and Jules . . ." she moaned. "Why did this have to happen on top of everything else?"

"Write a complaint to Him Above," Captain Newcomer said with a chuckle. "You'd better prepare yourself to spend a night here, my lovely."

Bryony let her gaze stray to the horizon and prayed for the lighter band of clouds that would herald the end of the storm. But the clouds were a uniform leaden mass. "Oh, this endless rain! Sometimes I wish I were back in France."

"But then I would never have met you," the captain whispered close to her ear. He brushed against her on his way to the table, where he bent over Clover. "This stripling needs a bed, that much is clear. He won't disturb us during the rest of the evening, or night for that matter."

Bryony studied Newcomer's expression as he lifted the sleeping child. He moved brusquely, but could not hide his wonder as he studied the boy's innocent face.

Every time she saw a glimpse of Jack Newcomer's closely guarded heart, she softened further toward him. Still, she knew very little about him. . . .

He left with his small burden, and Bryony heaved a preoccupied sigh. There were so many questions she wanted to ask him.

Lady Fitzbourne summoned the proprietor to reserve lodgings for the night. Since there weren't any other travelers, her request should not raise an objection.

"But, m'lady, there are only two chambers available," he explained.

"No problem, surely," Lady Fitzbourne said.

"They are connected, only one door."

The old lady pondered the situation for a moment. "Well, the young couple can use the inner room, and my brothers and I will share the outer room. Brother Algernon always takes a little walk in the night, y'see," she explained with a creaky laugh.

"But—" Bryony began.

"That will suit us fine," Captain Newcomer interjected as he reentered the parlor. "My wife and I don't mind." His stern gaze silenced Bryony's protests. "I have deposited the boy on a cot in the kitchen next to the fire, where he will be warm and comfortable." He stood close to Bryony and placed an arm around her shoulders.

"We cannot sleep in the same room," she whispered.

"Do you want to tell the lady that we lied about our marital status?" he whispered back.

She glared at him. "*You* lied about it, and now I'm forced to go along with it. 'Tisn't fair."

"Are you so adverse to spending the night with me?" he asked softly, his eyes glittering suggestively.

She blushed hotly. "It depends on what you're planning to do with me. If you as much as lay a hand on me, I will scream. That is a promise."

"Woe is me," he said playfully, and pinched her nose. Bryony wanted to—well, she didn't know *what* she wanted. He was such an unpredictable man.

She had to force a smile to her lips and go along with him, pretending to be his adoring wife. Clearly he loved every minute of the charade, the rascal.

The rain was still pouring down as they were closeted in one of the two bedchambers on the first floor. From the other room came the droning voice of Lady Fitzbourne as she prepared for bed. Her brothers punctuated the conversation with "Whaddayasays" and querulous complaints. Newcomer chuckled.

"Don't laugh at them. There will come a day when you'll be just like Malvin Fitzbourne, old and grouchy," Bryony admonished him as he divested himself of his coat.

"Hardly likely! The problem with them is that they are puppets manipulated by their headstrong sister. Always have been, I wager." He stretched his arms above his head and grunted in pleasure. The powerful muscles of his shoulders played under the thin layers of his waistcoat and shirt. "I will never become the puppet of any woman," he continued and raked his gaze over her.

"A puppet of your desire—which you are already," Bryony chided. "Any woman can see that and use it against you—against any man, that is. Men are all the same in that quarter."

He growled deep in his chest, a dangerous light flaring in his eyes. "Shameless hussy," he grated, and stepped toward her meaningfully. Everyone of his steps sent a thrill up her spine, and she had an urge to goad him further.

"It will be a pleasure cutting out your tongue for you," he threatened.

"Tit for tat! You've spouted incessant abuse over my innocent head, and only because I happen to be a member of the fair sex." She retreated behind the sagging narrow bed, grasped the pillow, and held it in front of her. "Don't come any closer," she warned.

"I'll come as far as I please," he said, and advanced until she was backed up into a corner.

Bryony gasped when the rough-timbered walls halted her retreat. Like an eagle concentrating on an attack, Captain Newcomer tilted his head slightly forward, his far-seeing gaze tense, alert. He lifted his arms, and Bryony remembered the strength of those honed muscles, which were now covered with only the shirt. Nothing would protect her against his strength, his onslaught.

He stopped mere inches from her, his arms trapping her against the wall. She both cringed away from him and longed for him. She yearned for the slow-burning embers within him to erupt, to sweep her up into that fierce, hot blaze that raged under the surface of his skin.

She longed to find out if the fire would scorch her, hurt

her, or if she would join him, become fire, too, and be consumed by his love. Oh, yes, she wanted to know. . . .

The only problem—it wasn't love.

Instinctly she knew this for a fact. Though passion had never been part of her life, she recognized the age-old tempting flame that leaped and danced in his eyes. And she had to give in to it, just a little bit. Just to taste it. Wasn't that why she had taunted him in the first place?

"Which one of us will sleep in the bed?" Was that thick, hazy voice really hers?

"I'm willing to share it with you. We would fit very comfortably together on it, don't you agree?" Was that his voice, so husky and deep?

His words released a heavy molten flow of feeling through her body that settled in her lower abdomen. "I have no idea," she said dreamily, her rapid heartbeat making it difficult to talk.

"We ought to find out," he urged, never taking his eyes from her face.

Her whole body started throbbing, as if every nerve ending was directed outward, toward him, seeking to extract as much of his closeness as possible.

She traced her lips slowly with her tongue, a gesture she was forced to do to soothe the yearning for his kiss.

Still, he didn't slake her longing. His eyes gleamed like mystical onyxes in the light from the fire as he followed the progress of her tongue.

His words came out in a hoarse whisper. "When I make love to you, lovely one, I want you to be consumed with desperation for my embrace. Only then will me meet, though I might go insane in the meantime."

With a soft groan he leaned forward and captured her lips with his, a gentle but demanding touch that sapped all of her strength.

Bryony shivered as a fire flared to life within her. Her hands wandered of their own volition to his neck, where they explored the hard muscles there. Her legs grew weak as she touched the smooth curls at his nape, and she moaned softly against his lips.

He took her arms and slid them entirely around him so that she was leaning against him. Her palms found the firm surface of his back, and she discovered that she loved the feel of his taut muscles. She traced the column of his spine, explored the heady expanse of his shoulders.

What would it feel like to have no barriers between them?

Her breasts ached with a need to rub against his skin, to be fondled.

He took her lips over and over, but his hands lay quietly on her back. His tongue mated savagely with hers, but he held his loins chastely apart from her, refusing the contact with her soft body.

She knew then that she would never be satisfied until she learned all the secrets of his sorcery. It was magic, what he did to her lips, and magic the response he conjured up in her body.

"I want our first time together to be perfect, a night to remember all our lives, my lovely," he said against her forehead. Then he laughed wryly and cradled her face between his large hands. "And I don't want to shock our irascible neighbors with the sounds of our love. Do you?"

Her heart pounded so hard she couldn't answer. She leaned her head against his chest and breathed deeply, delighting in the spicy scent of his warm skin and the raspy feel of his beard on top of her head.

"I don't know what you are, or who you are, but you've put a spell on me," he said, and his words sent jolts of pleasure through her body. "I knew that the very first time I laid eyes on you. No woman has ever intrigued me the way you do."

Despite her desire, she pushed away from him, grateful that he had broken the spell between them. What if she had given herself to him, awakened in bed tomorrow with this stranger—

She wanted it, but at least she had some control over her raging emotions. And she was grateful for the restraint he displayed.

"I'm afraid," she said simply, and slid away from him. "You once said that love is here today and gone tomorrow.'' She gazed at him, a shimmer of sorrow in her eyes. ''I cannot live by those words. I will give myself only when I know that the man who desires me cherishes me as well.''

''And how can you be sure when a man cherishes you?'' he asked with raised eyebrows, and sauntered over to the fireplace. Taking the poker, he rearranged the logs.

Bryony thought for a moment, realizing that it was a difficult question to answer. ''Perhaps when he's willing to consider a future with me,'' she explained, feeling foolish.

''You think a ring on your finger will ensure undying love?'' he asked with a sneer.

She folded her arms across her chest. ''It would be a good start,'' she retorted. ''And I wouldn't want any child of mine to end up like Clover, nameless and unloved, scorned by everybody.''

He sent her a guarded glance. ''You're wise for your tender years.''

''Practical is more the word. *I* would be part of the public's scorn as well, don't forget that.'' She slanted a veiled glance at him. ''A man can go on his merry way, never worrying about the future.''

He was very quiet.

Uneasiness crept over her. Had she sounded like a preacher? She sighed and traced the pattern of raindrops on the windowpane. He moved, but she didn't turn around. She jumped as his warm hands closed around her shoulders.

''You're such a fierce, serious woman, lovely one. I've never before met anyone like you.'' His lips brushed the tender skin on her neck.

''You don't consider me a prig then?'' she whispered. Somehow his opinion mattered terribly.

Silent laughter shook him. ''You remind me of my Scottish grandmother, a stern lady whom I loved dearly. I respect your opinions, my lovely, as I always respected hers.'' With his lips, he pulled the curl at the base of her neck. ''Do you know why?''

Bryony shook her head and stared tensely out the window.

"She was always right." He chuckled and turned her around. "You fear that I would ravish you and sail off to the West Indies, leaving you behind?"

"Yes."

He smiled crookedly, a guilty flash creeping into his face. "I suppose I would."

Bryony didn't bother to take off her clothes, except her hoops. That she did hiding behind the tall-backed armchair by the fire.

She lay on the narrow bed and pulled the two rough blankets up to her chin. Her body still ached for Jack Newcomer, but she was proud of herself for withstanding his advances. Yet he had claimed he didn't want to make love to her until she begged for it. The nerve!

She heard him settle in the chair by the fire. She would never beg, no matter how much he tempted her. Then the truth dawned on her. Her eyes flew wide, and she jerked upright in bed.

"Our roads separate tomorrow morning, so how do you expect me to have the time to beg for your love?" she challenged.

He gave her a cheerful wink. "The night isn't over yet. Good night, lovely one." He pulled his coat over his head and yawned loudly. "Wake me when the time is ripe," came his muffled voice. She settled back against the pillow, seething.

"Oh, you!" she retorted.

She tossed and turned, unable to sleep as her thoughts meandered like a murky stream through her head.

Jack Newcomer didn't move, but there was a tension to his body that betrayed his sleepless state.

Toward dawn, she must have slumbered for a while, a kaleidoscope of dreams haunting her. A particularly vivid dream that included Jack Newcomer awakened her. She opened her eyes and noticed instantly that the fire burned with renewed vigor. Newcomer's dark form was silhouetted against the window. He was staring outside. The whisper of a slow rain filled the air, and gray light crept across the horizon.

"You can't sleep," Bryony pointed out.

''Nor can you.''

'' 'Tis cold,'' she lied.

"Chairs were never my favorite place to sleep." He sounded so glum that Bryony could not help smiling.

He crossed the floor to stand by the bed and look down at her, his face a study of woe. "I don't see any humor in the situation."

Giggling, Bryony swept away the blankets and moved over to the edge of the mattress. "If you promise to behave, you may share my bed," she said.

"At this point, I'd promise anything," he said, the gloom disappearing miraculously from his face. With a growl of contentment, he slid between the sheets and confiscated most of the blanket.

He gave her a long, questioning look, which she met squarely, then he turned his back on her with a deep sigh. She curled up against him, finally at peace. Warmth stole into her, and she dozed off, her arm nestled around his chest.

A warm, tingling sensation awakened her. She was lying with her face outward, her back to Captain Newcomer. Light streamed through the windows, but she had no desire to rise.

She tensed as she became aware of his hand sliding gently along her stomach, back and forth. She was about to protest, but his touch drew an overwhelming response from deep inside her. Her skin burned under his fingers. She moaned and turned over, wanting to tell him to stop, but his hand closed over her breast and squeezed gently through her bodice.

Before she could protest, he had released her breast from the confines of the material. As his lips closed around one taut nipple, she arched against him momentarily, taking enormous pleasure in his tender wooing. Yet something within her panicked, and she made an effort to wiggle away.

"You're beautiful," he whispered against her, and fondled her breast until she wanted to cry out in pleasure. All her nerve endings strove toward his touch, her flesh suddenly parched and compulsively hungry for more.

His tongue made circles around her nipple, and she

held her breath, afraid that the magic would shatter if she dared to breathe. His hand slid down her stomach, under the loose waistband, under the two skirts, and beneath the shift that was bunched up to her thighs. His fingers lit a trail of tiny fires along her silky skin. As sure as a bee is drawn to nectar, so were his fingers drawn to the most sensitive spot on her body. His touch became sweet agony.

"This is the alluring place I'm dying to explore," he muttered, and caressed her lightly. Then he drew back, returning to her stomach. "Your rose-petal skin intoxicates me."

She sighed deeply. There was no haste in his caresses; he made her feel so good about herself.

He held her chin and kissed her lips. She melted against him, wanting more. His eyes danced. "You're soft and delicious. I almost broke my promise. You've truly spellbound me," he muttered hoarsely.

"No, you're the magician here." She sought his lips with her own and gave a little sound of satisfaction as his mouth closed over hers. She pressed closer to him as he pushed his tongue deep into her mouth and groaned.

He pulled away slowly and whispered, "Inviting me to your bed was a mistake." He gently released her arms and slid out of bed. "I'm sorry. I could not help myself. One more kiss and I will violate my promise."

Bryony wanted to ask him to come back, but she could not make herself do it. She was deeply shocked by her wanton body. She had acted as if she had been dying for his lovemaking and, yes, she had been. There was no use lying to herself. Blushing from shame, she hid her face under the blanket.

He left the room after dragging on his coat and boots. He had promised not to touch her, yet he had. But he had not demanded anything in return. Was it possible to be fulfilled and bereft at the same time? She already missed him. She wanted to give him something in return, but could she give what he wanted most?

A kiss would never be enough.

And how could she be sure that the man loved *her,* not just her body? She had no answer to that puzzle, but at least she had discovered she wasn't wholly undesirable, as Aunt Hortense had claimed.

A rogue desired her, but what gentleman would love her?

Chapter 9

Bryony washed in the cold water from the pitcher on a stand. The washbasin was chipped and the porcelain covered with a web of cracks. When she glanced at herself in the mirror, she gasped in despair. Her hair was a bird's nest with wisps standing out on all sides. Her bodice was stained with last night's dinner sauce, the lace torn in places. Her skirts looked as if she had crawled through *ten* hedges, and her face belonged to some bedraggled hag who had not washed for a fortnight. Her skin was pale, her eyes hollow and red-rimmed from lack of sleep.

Nevertheless, she was alive inside, her heart racing, butterflies fluttering in her stomach. Would she ever dare face Jack Newcomer again after what had happened that morning? Awed, she touched her full bottom lip. Her body felt languorous and warm, yearning for more pleasure.

You betray me, she chided her body, which instinctively relished a man's touch.

She brushed her hair and braided it, coiled it into a simple bun, and covered it with her wisp of a muslin cap. Then she tried to rearrange her clothes to her satisfaction, an effort in futility. What wouldn't she do for a bath and a set of clean clothes.

She swept her cloak around her in an effort to conceal her torn and stained dress, and her guilt.

Downstairs, Lady Fitzbourne was preparing to depart. The brothers were already seated in the carriage.

"Sweet child," she greeted. "You slept for a very long time." The old eyes searched her face, and Bryony blushed. "Ah, to be young again," Lady Fitzbourne sighed, shaking her head in wonder. Laughing, she patted Bryony's hand. "Take good care of your husband. That one has a wicked twinkle in his eye."

Tenderness spread through Bryony. She smiled and hugged the petite lady. "I know it well," she said. "But he hides his true heart."

"Hah! All men are like that, y'know. Most of them anyway. 'Tis for you to make him reveal his feelings, m'dear." She waved her fan as one of the lackeys lifted her into the coach, then laughed. "He was kind to Malvin. Carried him to and from the breakfast table this morning, though his look could have killed. . . . Good luck, sweet child," she called out. "You will need every ounce of it."

Bryony ate breakfast. There was no sign of Captain Newcomer, and she wondered what had become of him. Had he left? She couldn't bear the thought.

Clover scuttled into the room, wiping sleep from his eyes and yawning hugely. "A good mornin' t' ye, m'lady," he greeted cheerfully. He clamped a much too large tricorne on his head and sat down at the table. "Where's th' food?"

Bryony moaned and directed her gaze heavenward. "You have to learn some manners, Clover. First, I want to teach you a new word. It's called "Please." Repeat, please."

He repeated dutifully in a singsong voice, then added "please" to everything he said. Bryony could not help but laugh. "What a pretty day, please. Th' lovely lady says please."

As Clover bent to retrieve a bit of ham that had slid from his fork to the floor, she noticed the hole in the crown of his tricorne. She snatched it off his head.

"Where did you get this hat?"

"Th' guv give it t' me, please. 'E told me ye stepped on it." He snatched it back and crammed it atop his dirty curls. "I've niver owned such a nice 'at afore."

"Hmm. What you need is a long hot bath with plenty of soap."

The boy cringed at her words. "Naw, I don't need it. I'm clean an' white as God's lily."

Bryony wrinkled her nose and smiled. "That pure shade I have yet to see on you." She finished her eggs. "When you have eaten, we will go out and buy some soap."

"Aw, lady, why?" The boy grimaced, then sulked.

"Because you're a rapscallion, that's why. And a dirty one at that."

They walked—or, rather, Bryony walked and Clover skipped—the length of the village street to the one and only shop. HIGGINS & SONS, MERCHANTS read the sign above the door.

The interior was dark and musty. Boots, wooden buckets, rakes, and pewter mugs hung from the walls. Hams and sausages were suspended from hooks in the ceiling. A wooden wheelbarrow held used ladies' hats.

The obsequious clerk stepped forward, bowing to Bryony but giving Clover an angry glare. "This nipper stole a pie from me windowsill th' other day," he scolded.

"Ye can't prove it, Mr. 'Iggins," said Clover, unperturbed, and fingered a sausage on the counter. He instantly had his hand slapped. Glaring at the proprietor from under his fringe of blond curls, he reached into a barrel and touched as many apples as he could until Mr. Higgins howled in anger.

Bryony, who thought it best not to become involved in the argument, ordered a cake of Higgins's best soap. While he wrapped it, she looked at hair ribbons, finally choosing one of royal-blue taffeta. It would go well with her dark hair and blue-green eyes. She discovered a stack of secondhand black felt tricornes of the Dettingen Cock style, the large upturned brims trimmed with gold braid. Tentatively, she touched one. It was far from the best quality, but it would replace the hat she had ruined for Captain Newcomer.

After she had compared the size of the hat with the one Clover was wearing, she asked the clerk to wrap it up. She was surprised to notice a great difference in quality. Under all the dust on the original hat there was an expensive silk lining, and the hat had once been exquisitely trimmed with the tips of ostrich feathers. Could the captain afford such an elegant article of clothing? She had no idea how much sea captains earned, but if he owned his own ship, surely . . .

Near the hats was a row of used boys' coats, clean if somewhat worn. Anything would be better than the coat Clover was wearing. Bryony decided to buy him a set of clean clothes. Who knew when the proprietor at the inn would supply some fresh attire for his young employee?

She still hadn't told Clover the news about his future home, The Fox and Gander. She measured a few coats against Clover's back. The boy squirmed and grimaced, but she didn't give up until she found one that fit. She selected breeches, shirts, wool stockings, and a new pair of boots. Winter was coming.

Her thoughts were interrupted when the bell on the door tinkled. Another customer entered, bowed, and murmured something to the clerk.

Bryony watched them from the corner of her eye. Something about the man was faintly familiar. Was it the brown, full-skirted coat, dark knee breeches, and white stockings? Then she remembered: she had seen him at the inn in Cuckfield, the man who had given her the rude stare. He turned toward her, and she saw the long red scar on his face.

A cold shiver traveled the length of her spine, and she had a sudden urge to turn and run. She counted out the money for her purchases and, laden with packages, prepared to leave the store.

But the man was blocking her way to the door and refused to move for what seemed like an eternity. She stared into his stony face as terror seeped into her blood. The scar appeared to glow, and his blue eyes were cold and wary. Then he bowed stiffly and stepped aside.

Clover tugged at her hand. "C'mon then, snail lady."

Bryony's legs were pokers of lead, and the distance to the door interminable. Why did the man inspire such fear in her?

The thought went around and around in her head, and she couldn't shake the terror until they had reached the inn. The presence of other people in the taproom broke the horrible spell.

Bryony leaned against the door and breathed hard, trying to still the wild pounding of her heart.

"That evil-faced cove at th' shop," panted Clover, his cheeks bulging with candy that he hadn't had before they entered the shop. "I saw 'im at Potter 'Ouse, yesterday."

The boy's words confirmed her suspicions. The man was after *her*. Had he also fired one of the muskets? There had been more than one shot. Perhaps Captain Newcomer and the man were in league. . . . She swallowed convulsively, refusing to follow that awful thought, and chided herself for becoming hysterical about nothing. Most likely it was merely a coincidence that the man had entered the village shop when she did.

She looked for the captain, but he wasn't in the taproom. When she had calmed down, she summoned the host and ordered a bath for Clover. She explained that she couldn't leave him without giving him a fair start in his new home. She couldn't very well tell the kind host that she had certain misgivings about Cover's future.

"Naw, m'lady, I don't want no bath," the urchin whined, his lips trembling and his peppercorn eyes pleading. "Please."

"This time I will not give in, Master Clover," Bryony said, and pushed him toward the scullery, where the host had promised to set up hip bath.

"Ye can't watch me take a bath, m'lady. I will die o' shame, I will."

Bryony's lips twitched. "I promise not to look, but you have to promise not to neglect your scrubbing. When you're done, I want to see you as shiny as a gold sovereign, and dressed in these clothes." She placed the packages in his arms. "And don't forget to wash behind your ears. And wash your hair at least thrice! With the soap."

She watched him depart, grumbling and despondent. Before she left, she would inspect him. Yet, as she stood alone in the narrow path between the kitchen and the taproom, she wanted to flee from Haywards Heath and never lay eyes on the village again.

Chapter 10

As Bryony waited patiently for Clover to finish his bath, she kept an eye on the front door. Where had Captain Newcomer gone? She couldn't bear the thought that he might have left without saying good-bye to her. He *had* sounded as if he expected theirs to be a continuing friendship.

Oh, how she let her hopes, her longings, run away with her!

The portly proprietor delivered a note. Puzzled, she broke the seal. She glanced at the signature, S. Forrester, a bold scrawl across the page.

She read: "Please meet me at Potter House. I have some important information about your brother. Don't ask me how I got it, just come!"

The note bothered her. Mr. Forrester was supposed to have sailed for France last night. Surely he wouldn't have delayed his trip just to tell her something. But she had no choice; she had to find out what he wanted. Please God, don't let him be involved with the frightful man at Higgins's shop, she prayed as she rushed down the lane once more. She could not shake the memory of his sinister face, and according to Clover, he had been at Potter House the day of the attack.

The wind tore off her hood and cap. Her smoothly coiled hair was shaken loose as she ran. The air was cool, and rain threatened.

She managed to intercept a cart full of cabbages going toward Lindfield, and the kindly farmer gave her a lift. She chafed against the cart's slow pace, but there was nothing she could do to speed it up. The farmer let her off near the pond.

After running the length of the high street, she stopped abruptly outside the open gate of Potter House. The brick building looked closed up and deserted and Bryony remembered the horrors she had experienced in the overgrown garden.

"Mr. Forrester?" Her voice sounded raspy, and her rapid breaths seared her throat.

There was no answer, not a sound. A hushed stillness surrounded the house. Cold sweat broke out on her forehead, and her fingers were stiff and trembling as they clutched the topmost rail of the gate.

She took one step, then another. A few seconds later she rattled the front door, but all was quiet. The silence wrapped itself around her. She had no choice; she had to go to the back door and seek entrance to the house.

If she dared.

For a long moment she contemplated returning to the inn, but she knew she must go on. She could never live with herself if something happened to Mr. Forrester because of her. No one was ever going to call her irresponsible or craven.

Licking her dry lips, she advanced around the corner of the house and squeezed past the overgrown bushes. Having resided in a large house like Potter House, Mr. Forrester must have been a man of some standing. But he had let the property deteriorate. Some shutters were warped and rotting, their slats missing, and a board at the corner of the eave swung drunkenly in the wind.

Bryony steadied her turbulent heartbeat by taking a deep breath. Then she forced herself to plunge around the last corner.

The back door stood ajar, as if someone had just left in a hurry. With her fingertips, she gently pushed it fully open. It creaked, and her hand flew to her heart in sudden panic. Perhaps someone was waiting for her in the shadowy interior. At this very moment Mr. Forrester might be— She dared not finish the thought.

He might not even be there.

Hesitantly, she took one step inside. The floorboards

squeaked, and her gaze darted to each object in the room, from the tall carved mirror on the wall to the two high-backed chairs and the oak chest covered with a multitude of garments thrown haphazardly over the top. She was standing in a drab and untidy hallway. Three closed doors led into the interior of the house. As she advanced toward the first, the door seemed to take on a sinister air, warning her not to enter.

Her hand was icy as she turned the knob. She drew a ragged breath, but she'd opened only a closet. She almost collapsed with relief. Layers upon layers of cloaks, shawls, and coats hung from pegs on walls.

A sound came from behind her. She slammed the door and swung around, almost choking on fear.

There was nobody there. Before she completely lost her nerve, she hurried to the next door and pulled it open. Bleak light trickled through yellowed curtains and illuminated a study or an office of some sort. The walls were lined with books arranged haphazardly on sagging shelves. Dark, heavy furniture dwarfed the wide floor.

And on the worn, faded carpet lay Jack Newcomer, spread-eagled.

Bryony whimpered and flew across the floor. His face was deathly pale, and a trickle of blood had dried at the hairline below his ear.

"Captain . . . Jack! Please, wake up!" She touched his shoulder, then his hair. Water. She needed water—or brandy.

A water carafe and a tray of glasses stood on the huge oak desk. Dashing her hand into her pocket, she dragged out a handkerchief and drenched it in water. Her fingers trembled so much that she overturned the carafe, sloshing water all over the papers strewn across the dusty surface of the desk.

Sobbing, she returned to kneel beside Newcomer. Placing the wet, folded handkerchief on his forehead, she prayed that he would recover.

His eyelids fluttered, and he made a floundering movement with his hand, as if to push away the handkerchief. "Wh-what?" He groaned, clutching his head. "Dammit.'' As he faced her, Bryony noticed the rising lump on the side of his head.

"What happened?" she asked, and gingerly touched the purple mound. She pulled the cloth from his forehead and spread it over the lump.

"Ah—ouch," erupted from between his clenched teeth. "The damnedest—"

"Did you fall?" Bryony asked.

He struggled to sit up. With her help he leaned against the side of the desk. He grimaced and braced his head against his updrawn knees. Motionless for a long moment, he at last lifted his head to peer at her. His eyes were bright, almost wild with panic.

"You're here at last, and late. Did you hit me over the head?" he demanded.

Bryony's eyes widened. "Of course not! How can you ask such an idiotic question?"

"You begged me to come here, posthaste," he said, pausing at every word as if speaking caused him awful pain.

Bryony's jaw fell. "*I* did? No. Mr. Forrester sent me a note ordering me to meet him here."

Newcomer turned his head slowly and stared at her. "A note? He sent a note to you?"

Bryony's anger momentarily overshadowed her dread. "Then who sent me this?" she asked, and extracted the crumpled message from her cloak pocket. "Who is playing games with me?"

Bleary-eyed, he stared at the paper, holding it between his fingers while trying valiantly to stop them from shaking. With slow, painful movements, he delved into the voluminous pocket of his waistcoat. His hand returned with a folded note.

She snatched it from him and read the unfamiliar handwriting. "Come to Potter House. Urgent. Bryony Shaw." It was the same handwriting as on the message she had received. Her dread intensified, pouring through her veins.

Crumpling the paper, she tossed it across the room. She looked automatically toward the door, almost expecting someone to enter. The rustle of tiny feet sounded above their heads, and she heard the gnawing on wood.

Captain Newcomer sensed her fear and placed his arm across her shoulders. "Someone was playing a cruel trick on us. I went for a walk this morning, and when I returned to the inn, you were gone."

"I took Clover to the village shop," she explained, her eyebrows furrowed in thought.

He struggled against his pain, his breath coming in shallow gasps. Misery flowed from him in waves. "Your brother must have known something extremely important." His fingers closed convulsively around her shoulder. "Do you know any of his secrets?"

Bryony nodded. "Mr. Forrester spoke about a map and a hidden treasure, but the map was destroyed in the fire that killed Reggie. And I found it odd that Reggie wanted to join me in Paris. It was almost as if he was fleeing from something. He never liked France very much." Tears of sorrow and exhaustion stood in her eyes. The unsettling threats were taking their toll on her. Who wanted to do her harm?

The rustling in the ceiling intensified, seeming to move toward the door. Captain Newcomer stood on unsteady legs. He closed his eyes, holding one hand against his head and steadying himself with the other on the desk. Byrony wanted to assist him, but he waved her away. He walked around the desk and sank down on the chair behind it. With a jerky movement he touched the wet papers on the desk.

"Did you pour water on these?" he thundered, then grimaced and clutched his head.

"Well, they surely aren't yours," she scolded, nonetheless awash with guilt. "It's extremely rude to read Mr. Forrester's personal letters."

"Don't you see?" he asked tiredly, his voice tinged with desperation. "Perhaps there's some sort of clue about the gold in Mr. Forrester's correspondence. But it's too late to find out now." He held up a sodden document smeared with ink.

Bryony narrowed her gaze. "When did you start taking such an interest in my brother's and Mr. Forrester's affairs?

Worry bored deep groves from his nostrils to his chin.

"You were shot at, and your brother obviously died under mysterious circumstances." He paused before adding, "Besides, I feel close to you, responsible for you."

Bryony blushed upon recalling her display of ardor earlier that morning. At this point that beautiful experience seemed remote, as if it had never happened. This stranger was taking over her life, bit by bit, and she could only stand and watch, speechless.

"I suppose I have some say about the directions of my investigation into Reggie's death," she said uncertainly. "You cannot come in and take over."

"I'm not stopping you, only lending a helping hand." He pulled out every drawer in the desk. "Look at this disorder. Did you—?"

Bryony bristled. "I didn't touch Mr. Forrester's desk. I wouldn't dream of it."

The captain shrugged. "I suppose the man who hit me over the head did it and left when he didn't find what he was looking for. You didn't see anyone when you arrived?"

"No." Bryony paced the floor, throwing a series of suspicious glances at the captain. She accepted that he attracted her immensely, but that shouldn't cloud her judgment. The fact glared at her: she didn't trust the rascally sea captain.

"We should leave," she said with finality. She made a show of assisting him to stand, but he stopped her by holding a finger to his lips. He was listening intently, and suddenly she heard it, too. A door slamming, and the sound of something scraping against the outside wall.

"Someone is coming!" she whispered. In self-defense she grabbed the first thing she saw—the water carafe.

The captain struggled to his feet, his face hard. "No, someone is leaving," he said grimly. "Do you smell something?" He staggered toward the door leading to the back vestibule. Resting for a short moment with his hand on the doorknob, he took a deep breath, his shoulders heaving, then pointed to the floor. Tendrils of smoke curled between the door and the floor.

He tore open the door.

Bryony gasped as a cloud of smoke billowed into the

room. But it did not stop the captain. "No!" she screamed as he placed a handkerchief over his face and disappeared into the smoke. She rushed after him, but he returned immediately. "Get back," he croaked, coughing. "The back door is locked."

They were soon enfolded in smoke. Flames licked along the floor, grasping at anything that would burn. In an instant the musty curtains were transformed into writhing orange tongues of fire. The heat intensified, and the smoke thickened, invading the room completely. It had crept up on them with little warning. Bryony held on to Captain Newcomer's coat as he tottered across the floor to the door on the other side of the room.

She was blinded by the smoke, her eyes streaming and aching. Her throat was raw, and her lungs protested against each harsh breath. A wracking cough sapped her of all strength.

The door was locked.

The captain swore and was instantly overcome by a violent coughing fit. Bryony pulled him with her toward one of the windows that wasn't yet framed in flames. She knew that by opening the window, the fire would explode into an inferno, but the window was their only escape route now.

They stumbled over a footstool, and Captain Newcomer crashed to the floor. He lay motionless, and she feared he had lost consciousness. She shook his shoulder.

"Hurry! There's no time to lose," she cried. Was that hoarse whisper her voice? Dizzily, she tried to focus on the pale square of the window.

She could have sobbed with relief when he shifted and rose to his feet in agonizingly slow movements. She held him around the waist and propelled him forward. He cradled her close, and together they reached the window.

Captain Newcomer managed to undo the latch with sluggish fingers, and they pulled the lower sash upward. It didn't move.

Bryony sobbed in desperation. The heat at her back was excruciating. It seemed that the very material of her gown was smoking now. With the last ounce of her strength, she attacked the recalcitrant window.

It wouldn't budge.

"Stand back," Captain Newcomer croaked. He was holding the footstool that had tripped him. Without preamble he smashed it through the latticed glass. The shards rained onto the floor and the flower bed outside. He cleared the lower frame of the remaining jagged glass and ordered Bryony to crawl through the opening.

She couldn't think, couldn't breathe, couldn't hear as she obeyed. That a bush of wild roses would receive her bothered her not. She let go.

Her hands, arms, and face were scratched by the unfriendly thorns. Thank God she wasn't wearing her hoops. They would never have fit through the window. Not caring about the scratches, she scrambled away from the bush and peered upward. The entire upper floor was glowing orange, as were the rooms adjoining the study downstairs. A mighty roar rose as the fire broke through the roof, and an immense crash reached her tormented ears as part of the structure collapsed.

"Jack," she whispered, and extended her trembling hand toward the window. There was still no sign of him.

Sounds of running footsteps and raised voices sounded at the front of the house. The villagers were forming a bucket brigade down to the pond. Bryony wanted to beg for help, but her legs would not carry her around the corner.

"Please, God, let him live. Let him come through that window . . . alive," she prayed, and stared in breathless agony toward the black hole where flames were consuming the window frame.

Then, just when she had given up hope, his hand gripped the sill convulsively. His head appeared, soot-streaked and tortured, then his torso as he heaved himself ever so slowly over the edge. He held out his arms toward her as he let go. Helplessly, he slammed into the bush, which cracked under his weight. Thorns slashed his hands and face, just as they had hers. He lay there for the longest time, motionless, and Bryony thought he had died. His eyebrows were singed, and his beard was smoking.

She pulled on his arm, trying to release him from the

rosebush's hostile embrace. He came to, his red-rimmed eyes focusing on her face.

"Lovely . . . one," he forced out, and labored to his feet. Swaying, he leaned heavily on Bryony. She led him in among the dense lilacs.

He tensed and listened to the agitated voices of the village people. "We should not be seen here," he breathed with difficulty into her ear. "We'll be blamed for the fire. If the militia catches us, we're done for."

Bryony nodded and slapped the smoking tail of his coat with a corner of her cloak until the smoldering fire died. She showed him the hole in the hedge that Clover had used, and as silently as possible they crawled through. As they stood on the path, an explosion shook the earth. The rest of the roof and upper floor caved in. Sparks and soot shot in every direction.

They took refuge in the woods behind the once-proud Potter House. Holding hands, they gazed into each other's eyes and shared a long moment of profound gratefulness. They had escaped with their lives.

" 'Twas a trap y'know," Captain Newcomer said, and sank onto a rock.

"Someone was in the house while we were there. We were lured there to be victims of the fire." She regarded him uneasily.

He did not reply. He stretched his limbs in slow deliberation and rotated his neck. "I need a brandy to dull the pain in my head. It's a miracle I'm still alive."

The lump behind his ear was black with soot, and Bryony realized the agony he must be going through. "We should return to the Fox and Gander."

He laughed, a slow, pain-cracked sound. "You look like a chimney sweep."

"Then we could pass for twins," she retorted. Suddenly, it dawned on her that if it hadn't been for this mysterious man she might have shared her brother's fate. Had someone purposely set fire to Willow Hills, her ancestral home? She shuddered at the thought and realized that she doubted more and more that Reggie had taken his own life. The words of the wild man in the maze might be true after all. Reggie might have been murdered.

"We'll have to steal a set of clothes and seek a secluded spot on the river to wash off the soot," said Captain Newcomer."

Bryony sighed. "I don't know why I am suddenly acting like a person wanted by the law. I have done nothing illegal."

"Even talking to a man like Mr. Forrester automatically makes you a lawbreaker," Newcomer explained, and brushed some soot from his hands.

"No one except Clover and you saw me in the ruined cottage."

"I wouldn't be so sure of that," he said. "Someone obviously doesn't like that you're talking to your brother's friends—or fellow traitors, rather. Perhaps your brother had mysterious secrets, ones that you don't know anything about."

Bryony rubbed her hands against her sooty skirts. "I'm not sure I want to know his secrets. But I would dearly like to know how he died. If it was accident or—"

"Then you may have to uncover his secrets as well." He held out his hand. "Come, let us find some new clothes."

"I will not steal them," she said stubbornly.

"There is no question of what you will or won't do. You might have to steal if you expect to continue investigating your brother's death. Or you can always choose the militia and the detention house, and beyond that the axe block."

"I have done nothing against the law," she repeated heatedly as they walked through the woods.

"Convince the law of that, if you can."

They followed a different path than the one they had used on the previous day. Tall linden and elm trees shaded the path and sang softly in the wind.

"I do hope the wind will not carry the fire to the entire village," Bryony said. "We ought to have stayed and helped." Captain Newcomer did not respond, and she drew a heavy sigh. "Everything has gone wrong since the moment I landed in England," she said to herself.

"There!" he exclaimed, and halted her with a grip on her arm. "Our new wardrobe."

They were standing behind a small flintstone cottage with a well-tended garden from which most of the vegetables had been harvested. Bright red apples lay on the ground under gnarled apple trees. Between two beech trees was strung a clothesline from which hung knee breeches, coarse work shirts, a drab brown peasant skirt with matching short jacket, a blouse, darned petticoats, wool stockings, and a huge white mobcap.

"All we need," Captain Newcomer said, and rubbed his hands.

A dog barked inside the cottage.

"We'll be detected," Bryony warned. "And hanged as thieves."

"We have no choice; we'll wait for the perfect moment."

Bryony grimaced, knowing he was right. She brought out her purse from her pocket. The brocade was charred and smelled of smoke. "At least we can pay for the clothes," she said, and fished out a crown. "We'll put it on their doorstep."

He smiled. "Little Miss Justice."

Bryony glowered at him. "Well, it's good one of us is law-abiding!" she retorted.

They waited for a whole hour under a yew tree, leaning against the trunk. Nobody stirred in the cottage or in the vicinity.

"I don't think anyone is home," the captain mused aloud. "This is as good a time as any to attempt our little strategy."

Bryony wanted to tell him not to, but she kept her lips sealed. He was right, they couldn't very well show themselves looking like chimney sweeps. Not without raising a lot of questions.

Jack Newcomer's rest had restored his strength, but his face was still pale, and pain clouded his eyes. Bryony's heart ached for him, but there was nothing she could do.

He climbed over the low fence and sneaked from bush to bush so as to stay out of sight of curious eyes. Bryony's heartbeat escalated as she followed his progress. She had never stolen anything before, and it was an uncomfortable feeling. Clutching the crown in her hand until the metal rim bit into her palm, she swore she was going to pay for the clothes. When she had suggested earlier that they knock on the door and buy the clothes, the captain had refused, emphasizing that they didn't want to be seen. Gossip would reach the ears of the militia before they had a chance to escape the village.

As Newcomer slipped the clothes from the line, no one came running out of the cottage, but the dog barked furiously inside.

Captain Newcomer returned, laden with the dry, sweet-smelling garments. Bryony looked at the lovingly sewn clothes and felt a twinge of guilt. "We have to pay for them before we go."

He didn't protest but sank down against the tree, his head obviously hurting. "Very well, you go and apologize," he said with heavy irony.

Bryony sent him a dark look. She took out a black lead pencil and a scrap of paper from her pocket. She wrote a short apology and rolled the coin inside the paper. With her heart in her throat, she hurried to the garden path and placed the message on the stone doorstep. Momentarily paralyzed by fear, she heard the front door slam. The dog's claws were scratching wildly against the back door, and his barking was so close she thought he might burst through the door at any second.

She threw a glance over her shoulder. Captain Newcomer was waving frantically at her, and she whirled looking for a hiding place. She could clearly hear voices coming from inside now. "What's that big looby barkin' at now? Better go an' see. A cat, I'll lay."

Bryony dashed behind a lattice covered with climbing roses whose yellowing leaves still clung to the branches. Her heart almost stopped with fear as the door opened a crack. She looked for the captain, but he had disappeared among the trees. They would surely let the dog out after him now, and it would track and attack her first. But to her surprise, the dog was held back.

A man whistled in surprise. "By all thass sacred," she heard him say. "Shut yer gob, ye great 'ulk!"

The dog squealed in pain and was silent. A long, sinewy arm reached out and took her message. The man still hadn't discovered the empty clothesline at the side of the house.

The door slammed shut, and Bryony immediately crawled on all fours behind a line of tall sunflower stalks until she reached the fence. Taking a deep breath, and fully expecting a shout of outrage from the cottage, she darted through the gate. She tripped on a root and fell face-forward into the tall grass. With closed eyes, she imagined she felt the dog's hot breath on her neck, but nothing happened. Stillness reigned; only a bird chirped in the tree above her.

She crawled farther away from the gate. Unease fluttered through her as she dared to stand up and take refuge among the trees.

There was Newcomer, leaning against a tree, holding the clothes in his arms.

"Do you see the danger in insisting on justice at every turn?" he chided gently.

"We didn't get caught, did we?" Bryony retorted with an angry glare. She wiped perspiration from her brow and struggled for breath.

To her surprise, he dropped the clothes and pulled her into his arms. "Oh, little one, your tender heart will bring ruin to you one day. Someone will take everything that is yours and destroy you."

His words brought sadness to her. It was as if for a moment she glimpsed the world through his eyes, a world of bitterness and deceit.

Chapter 11

The River Ouse flowed with eternal calmness through the woods, under the bridge spanning the road that meandered into Lindfield. Newcomer cautioned against going too close to the bridge; he found a spot on the river guarded by tall weeping willows whose fronds swept the ground. The silent woods behind them and the meadows on the far side of the trees belied the recent horror they'd suffered in the village.

Captain Newcomer handed Bryony the woman's garments he'd taken and a flannel cloth with which to dry herself. "I know 'tis cold, but you have to wash off every trace of soot on your face, neck, and arms."

"We don't have any soap," Bryony reminded him.

He pulled a small yellow cake out of his pocket. "Yes, we do. This was lying next to the well."

She smiled wryly. "You think of everything."

He scanned her hair. "I'm afraid you may have to wash your hair. Part of it is singed at the back."

Bryony had thought he looked comical with scarcely any eyebrows left and his singed hair plastered to his forehead, but she had forgotten her own appearance. Her hair hung in a loose braid down her back, and when she pulled it forward, she found that a good three inches had been burned off the end. She wanted to cry out in despair, but pinched her lips together.

"All you need to do is to cut some off the end," he soothed her. "I will do it for you once we find a pair of scissors." He was standing in a patch of sunlight, stripping off his waistcoat and shirt. Bryony could not help but stare in fascination as his smooth muscles were revealed, lightly tanned planes and ridges. Whorls of black hair curled on his chest.

"Burrr, it's dashed cold. Autumn already," he complained, but a smile lurked in his eyes. "I suppose 'tis extremely uncouth of me to undress in a lady's presence, but then again, I can see that the spectacle amuses you."

She jerked her gaze away, her cheeks hot.

"Can't be helped, etcetera," he went on, unperturbed. "Aren't you going to change your clothes? We don't have all day, y'know."

She half-heartedly undid the ribbons holding the waistband of her skirt together.

"If you're shy, you can undress behind that willow sweeping across the water. I promise not to look."

Bryony hid behind the generous tree. She discarded her cloak, noticing with dismay the many small holes that flying embers had made in the material. Still, she would need the cloak in the future.

Stripping down to her shift, she knelt in the grass on the soggy riverbank. Her skin was covered with goosebumps, and she shivered. Bracing herself, she washed her face, neck, and hair with the harsh soap. Half blinded by the suds and water streaming down her face, she was surprised to see Captain Newcomer's face floating only inches from hers. He had slid into the water without a sound and swam under the willow's floating fronds. "This does wonders for my aching head," he said.

"You must be so cold," was all she could think to say, realizing he had a full view of her breasts in the deep neckline of her shift. Her wet hair streaming around her, she folded her arms protectively across her chest to shield herself from his laughing gaze.

"It's cold enough, but the sight of a woodland fairy with starlight in her hair warms my heart—and other areas as well." He swam closer. "Do you know how lovely you are, Bryony?"

"What are you doing here? I thought—"

"Spell-crusher!" he chided. His head disappeared under the water, then he came up with a great snort, shaking his hair wildly. His voice became brisk. "I need the soap.

It's damn cold, I say. I'm going to turn into a log of ice if you don't share some of that soap soon.'' In his cap of flattened curls, he looked like a defenseless boy. So attractive. "Shall I come up and collect it?'' he suggested.

Jerked out of her sweet reverie, Bryony tossed him the soap. It almost got lost in the water, but he managed to catch it at the last moment. ''That feint was uncalled for,'' he admonished. With the soap between his teeth, he returned to his side of the tree.

Bryony dried herself with the flannel cloth. Greatly refreshed, she pulled on the simple petticoats, the skirt, the blouse, and the jacket.

There was a splash as Newcomer heaved himself onto the bank, as naked as God had made him. Bryony peered through an opening in the fronds, and her breath caught in her throat. Her heart lurched helplessly. Unable to tear her gaze away, she watched him stretch languorously and gently examine the lump behind his ear. Then he began soaping himself with slow, deliberate movements. His hand made circular movements over his chest and powerful neck and arms, then traveled the hard, flat surface of his stomach to his buttocks and as far up his back as he could reach. He soaped one muscular thigh and one strongly shaped foot, then repeated the action on the other leg. At last he reached the nest of black curls that Bryony's gaze had avoided the longest. He threw his head back, sighed, and rubbed the core of his virility liberally with soap. Still the suds weren't enough to hide the tempting sight from her eyes.

When he moved to the less seductive areas of his armpits, Bryony could finally let out her breath. His teeth chattering, he soaped his hands once more. Then he dove into the water, hardly making a splash—a pagan forest god. All that he lacked was a wreath of leaves on his head.

Bryony braced herself against the tree to calm her thundering heart and tumultuous emotions. Her longing for his embrace almost suffocated her. He was the most exasperating, but also the most exciting, man she had ever met. And she had to admit it—she desired him madly. The realization brought a new wave of color to her cheeks, and she hurriedly pulled on the coarse stockings and her badly scuffed shoes.

Newcomer's head popped out of the water on her side of the tree. "Ahhh, that felt good, and if I could but ease the fire in my blood for you, everything would be perfect. But even this icy water cannot quench that fire."

Not daring to meet his gaze, she hid her flaming cheeks behind the curtain of her hair. "You'll become ill if you stay in the water any longer," she answered, and combed her hair with her fingertips, then braided it.

"Cruel, cruel woman," he chided, and she had to look at him.

His eyes were dancing.

"Oh, you! You will wait until eternity if you want me to beg for your favors," she threatened, and stuffed the braid into the enormous mobcap on her head.

"A pity," he said without sounding very put out. "You seem to have pulled on the farmer's wife's stuffy personality along with her clothes," he teased, and ducked beneath the surface as she was about to splash water on his face.

"I hate that mobcap," he added from the safety of the opposite side of the willow fronds.

"And I hate you," she blurted out through she instantly regretted the angry words.

She heard him dress as she swept the cloak closely around her and waited. Remembering his naked splendor, she trembled with longing to touch him, failing to still the tumultuous images of his flesh against hers. Blushing with shame, she steeled herself.

"Now we look like sturdy farmers," he said cheerfully as he joined her. "We can mingle without being noticed."

She watched as he smoothed back and bound his damp hair with a piece of string.

"Except for that lump on your head, and your—er—naked face," she observed.

"Naked face?"

"You look naked without eyebrows, and your skin is reddish from the fire, or is it from embarrassment?"

He rubbed his beard. "Am I so disgusting that you're loath to look at me?" He gingerly probed his abused face.

She could not help but smile. "Who is being vain now?"

"Vain? I hope a face isn't the only thing I have to offer the world. Besides, my face was never something to brag about."

Bryony disagreed. He was the most attractive man she had ever met. Not handsome like Nigel, perhaps, but immensely more alive. She patted his arm, her lips curving. "Let's return to Haywards Heath and then Cuckfield. Jules must think he has lost me forever."

Newcomer gripped her arm and swung her around, and his gaze burned into her. "I can't stand it when you tease me."

Her eyes widened with innocence. "I wasn't teasing."

"Then what do you call that unholy amusement on your face?" He pulled her savagely into his arms. "Oh, sweet wood nymph, don't reject our passion. I can feel your skin grow hot under my hands."

She pushed against his chest. "Oh, how silly you are! My skin is hot because you're warming it with your hands."

A predatory expression came into his face. "Well! Let me warm your lovely lips as well."

Before she could protest, he had captured her cool lips with his own. She forgot the brisk air and her cold feet. All that existed was the sweet sensation that flowed through her as he enfolded her in his embrace.

As they approached The Fox and Gander on the back of a farmer's cart, it dawned on them that they couldn't very well show themselves in farmer's attire at the inn without raising questions. They decided to return to Cuckfield and collect Bryony's carriage, but Newcomer insisted on collecting their portmanteaus. Bryony waited nervously at the roadside while he sneaked into the inn. When he returned with their belongings, he told her he had left a note and some coins in payment for their room and board.

"I'm sad that I didn't have the time to say good-bye to Clover," Bryony said as they walked west toward Cuckfield. "Did you see him, Captain Newcomer?"

"Bryony, isn't it about time you called me Jack? No, I

didn't see Clover. He has most likely run away. I don't think he'd be able to hold a position for very long, anyway. Stealing for survival is easier."

"Until he gets caught and hanged," Bryony countered grimly.

Carts of all shapes and sizes rumbled by, but no one stopped to offer them a lift. They had walked for an hour, Bryony's arm aching from carrying her portmanteau, when a gig slowed. As Jack talked to the driver, Bryony stared at some rustling bushes by the wayside, expecting a deer to emerge, but the movements stopped.

After tossing their portmanteaus in the back of the gig, they squeezed themselves onto the seat with the driver, a large, garrulous man with a rumbling laugh. He took his time introducing himself as Dr. Cook and reciting a list of errands he had to accomplish in Cuckfield.

As the horse finally set off, he said, "I live hard by Lindfield. A terrible fire ruined one of our most beautiful buildings in the village and some adjacent barns."

Bryony recalled the dilapidated shutters and the overgrown garden of Potter House. "An accident?" she probed cautiously.

"We don't know. The house belonged to a known traitor, a Jacobite by the name of Forrester." He snorted. "To think that we had such a villain among us in our peaceful village, a person we have lived with and trusted for years. I say, the Jacobites should be hunted down and killed, every one of them."

Bryony glanced at Jack, surprised that he was not adding to the conversation. He was pale and pinch-lipped, staring straight ahead. The bath must have been too much for him—or was he just playing another game? She hardly dared speak, realizing that her voice would contrast sharply with her clothes if she didn't contort it.

"Them Jakkerbites are a sad lot," she said, praying Dr. Cook wouldn't find her dialect odd.

"What do you know about them?" he asked curiously.

"Nuffin', sir. But they 'ad 'igh 'opes, an all, dreamin' an' 'opin' that th' Stuart cove would be th' king o' England."

The doctor laughed. "Madcaps the lot! Romantics."

He peered at her. "You know a great deal. What is your opinion on this issue that divides our country?"

She gave him a vacuous stare and shook her head. "I don't know nuffin', sir." She shrugged. "I don't care who's th' king o' England. Same garbage, all. I do care when me cabbages are eaten by beetles."

Dr. Cook laughed so hard that the whole gig shook. "And your husband, what are his views?"

Bryony slanted a glance at Jack and realized he was struggling to stay upright. What was he up to? He obviously didn't want to talk with the doctor.

"Me mate isn't feelin' 'is best. Took a bad spill in th' barn this morn." She smiled at the doctor. "Mayhap th' good doctor could look at th' lump on 'is 'ead, I'll send ye a few cabbages as payment later. Me cabbages be o' prize-winnin' stock, y'know." She was enjoying the charade immensely. This was the kind of game Reggie would have loved, the kind she had liked, too, before she had been packed off to France.

Jack pinched her thigh and gave her a sharp glance in warning.

The doctor studied Jack's face. "He looks like he's been in a fire, and that nasty contusion will give him blurred eyesight for days to come."

Bryony thought rapidly. " 'E like as fell against th' anvil an' a flyin' coal from th' pit put the fire t' 'is beard."

"Hmm. With that kind of bad luck, he should have stayed home. The planets are conspiring against him." The doctor patted her knee in a fatherly manner. "I dabble in astrology, y'see." He pulled in the reins and rummaged under the seat. Bringing out a black cloth bag, he searched through its contents and extracted a flat metal tin. "This ointment should help heal the bruise. It's horse fat and some herbs I picked myself. Rub it on the lump twice a day until 'tis gone. He should rest in bed for at least two full days."

Jack peered at her from under half-closed eyelids. His black eyes were unfathomable, but she thought she saw the ghost of a smile flit across his face.

They arrived at The Boar in Cuckfield in time for the midday meal. Bryony prayed the good doctor wouldn't stay; he'd no doubt find it odd if Jules addressed her as "ma'am" while bowing from the waist. She complained loudly about the inn's fare, but that only made the doctor eager to prove her wrong, since he confessed he liked the food at The Boar.

Bryony realized her mistake. Thinking of ways to get out of the doctor's invitation to join him, she jumped down in the busy inn yard. There stood her carriage, with Jules lounging beside it. She pulled the mobcap closer around her face.

The doctor stepped down and walked to the back of the gig. He reached into the boot, and his eyes popped wide as he hauled out something that looked like a bundle of clothes. Suddenly the inn yard echoed with his terrible bellow and he stepped forward with Clover squirming in his sturdy grip.

Chapter 12

Bryony stared from Dr. Cook's angry face to the face of the squirming boy. *"What* are you doing, Clover?" Instantly realizing that he could jeopardize her whole act, she seized his collar and took over. "Ye li'l ruffian! Didn't I tell ye t' stay at 'ome?" She gave the doctor an apologetic smile while Clover stared at her, mouth agape."

"But—" he began, trying to wiggle out of her grip.

"Ye keep yer mouth shut, ye' li'l varmint."

The doctor shook his grizzly head and ambled off toward the inn.

"I'm sorry 'bout this, doctor. I'll send ye a giant cabbage," she cried after him. He only nodded and waved.

Relieved, Bryony found she could breathe again. She turned to address Jack in the gig, but there was no sign of him. As usual he had disappeared mysteriously when she most needed his help.

"That bain't no doctor," Clover scoffed as he managed to tear himself free. " 'E be a witch-doctor, if anythin'. Bet 'e put a curse on ye. Yer 'air will turn green, an' yer fore'ead will gown 'orns."

Bryony pulled her eyebrows together in a scowl. "Bibble-babble! What are you doing, following us like this?"

Clover's lips trembled. "I bain't no stableboy, m'lady. Th' 'osses don't like me an' nip me in th' 'ead, an' 'ay makes me sneeze." The fat tear quivering on his eyelashes was Bryony's undoing.

"Very well, we'll find something else for you." She tilted up his face and was delighted to see that the grime had given way to a pink complexion, but there was nothing she could do to wipe away the look in his peppercorn eyes that said he had seen too much in his young life. His hair gleamed like gold guineas, and he was wearing every garment she had purchased for him.

"I see that you obeyed my orders," she said, and smiled. "You're clean now, if still a scamp. That trait water cannot wash away."

Clover's scowl indicated he wasn't entirely pleased with her judgment. "M'lady 'as changed, too, jabberin' eggsackly like th' fishmonger's wife in Lindfield."

" 'Tis only a little game I'm playing," she explained lamely. "Now, have you ever traveled in a big coach before?"

His eyes grew round as saucers. "Naw, ma'am, niver!"

"I'll show you one, a French traveling chaise." Taking Clover by the hand, she hurried toward her coach. But where was Jack? Worry nagged at her. She couldn't linger at the inn lest someone recognize her and begin asking questions. But why did she feel the need to hide? She had done absolutely nothing unlawful. Jack had instilled caution in her only because he believed someone was out to harm her.

Was he right? There was no reason for anyone to harm her. She had no enemies.

She alerted Jules with a loud "Pssst."

Startled, he automatically wiped his hat from his head. His eyes grew wide, and his lips worked convulsively as he recognized her.

"Mademoiselle!" he blurted out. "I thought you were dead." He looked so miserable that Bryony's heart twisted. "I fetched your trunk, like you asked me."

"Thank you. I'll explain everything later."

"The host said you had disappeared. I didn't know what to do."

"Thank you for waiting," Bryony said, and opened the door. Stretched out on one of the seats lay Jack, one arm flung over his face.

"Jack?" she whispered, but he remained motionless. His display of weakness in the gig had not been a ruse.

Bryony helped Clover into the coach and climbed in

behind him. The boy gingerly touched the velvet squabs and traced the gilt molding around the door. "Blimey! Pure gold." He made a lame effort to pull it off. " 'Twould fetch a goodly sum at th' 'oss fair," he calculated. "Could I sell it fer ye? Ye be a rich mort, m'lady."

"Absolutely not! What a preposterous idea. Besides 'tis not gold." After throwing a worried glance at Jack's still form, she stuck her head outside the window and ordered, "Jules, transfer our portmanteaus from the gig and drive south, toward Seaford. And make haste, *s'il vous plaît.*"

The sooner they left Cuckfield, the better. She didn't know why, but she felt that speed was of the essence. And she was anxious to visit the next man on the list—Mr. Dudley Bench.

At the last moment, Clover decided that he preferred to ride on the box with Jules. "The bloomin' Frog speaks a queer tongue," was his only comment after he tried to ask Jules's permission.

Once he'd scrambled to his high perch outside and the coach pulled out of the inn, Bryony knelt on the floor beside Jack's prostrate body. Clasping his cold hand and holding it to her cheek, she prayed that he would recover.

A few minutes later his fingers curled around hers. "You're praying for a blackguard like me?"

She blushed and was glad that the muted light in the coach concealed her confusion.

He groaned as he turned his head toward her. "What a nuisance. My head took greater abuse than I thought. I'm weak as a kitten." His eyes grew warm as he studied her. "But that doesn't change one fact."

"What fact?"

"I know I have no right to say this, but I believe I'm falling in love with you."

The words hung fragilely between them. Bryony savored every word, wishing he really meant them.

"I-I didn't think you believed in love."

He laughed. "I don't, but how do I explain the wonder I feel every time I look at you?"

"Please—don't say this to me unless you really mean it. I cannot take it lightly."

"Most likely the wonder will disappear if I sneeze," he said dryly.

Bryony gazed momentarily down at her hands in her lap. "I don't know," she murmured.

He looked at her, his eyes vulnerable, full of questions. "How will we know if it's love?"

"Time will tell. If the wonder is still there, say, the day after tomorrow, then 'tis love."

He flicked her nose with his thumb. "Don't be flippant. I'm serious."

Bryony gulped and looked away. What did she know about this man, other than that he attracted her immensely?

"I think we're birds of a feather," he said softly. "You have two adorable sides to your character, one that is fierce and serious, and one that is a mischievous little imp."

"What makes us alike?" Bryony asked, her curiosity aroused.

"We're both lonely, I think."

"Perhaps. 'Tis true in my case, but 'tis difficult to picture you alone."

"Well, you're not married, and neither am I."

Her eyes twinkled. "You're probably difficult to live with, a fact the poor ladies discovered before it was too late. And not every lady would be tempted to travel the seven seas with you, or become a sailor's widow for months on end."

She wondered if he would ask her if *she* was tempted, but he was silent, looking at her hard and long.

"I almost married once, but my fiancée found the love of another man more to her liking." He grimaced. "She just discarded the undying love she had pledged to me."

Bryony sensed the angry turmoil within him. "Did you know the man?"

He hesitated, his hand clenching convulsively into a fist. "He was my stepfather. He had a way with women—made them his slaves. He set her up as his mistress in London and visited her regularly. Mother said nothing, but I think she died a bit when she found out the truth."

Jack smiled flippantly, but he could not hide the pain in his eyes. " 'Twas a long time ago. They are all dead now, though the vile memories live on in the minds of neighbors and friends.''

She caressed his bearded cheek. ''And you cannot forget, or forgive, your stepfather.''

He gripped her fingers and kissed them. ''I want to, but my hatred is very old. I might as well admit it, it is a canker eating my insides.''

Bryony was grateful for his confession, his trust. She loved him more for it. ''I wish I could take that hatred away,'' she whispered.

His eyes were shimmering with unshed tears. ''You really mean that, don't you? That's what I love about you, Bryony.'' He took a deep breath. ''Yesterday when you tried to make me carry that peevish old Fitzbourne from the carriage, I was forced to face my terrible anger.''

''You'll have to confront it. Only when you accept yourself and your hatred, only then will your anger go away.''

He touched her face tenderly. ''How come such a young lady is so very wise?''

'' 'Tis very simple. I hated my aunt because she always prodded and pinched the parts inside of me that I most wanted to forget, my shyness for one.'' Bryony peered into the distance. ''At first I thought it was my aunt that I hated, but in reality I hated my own weakness. Now that I'm alone, I'm forced to test my strength.'' She smiled, a sad, lopsided twist of her lips. ''Before, someone was always making the decisions for me, y'see. Even telling me who and what I was. Reggie's death has forced me to take stock of my own life, so he has actually helped me—even from beyond the grave.''

She gripped Jack's hand. ''I wish you could have met him. I know you would have liked him.''

He squeezed her fingers. ''Yes, I'm sure I would have liked him, very much.'' They shared a moment of silence fraught with emotion. It was only natural that she should lean over and place a gentle kiss on his lips. There was no mistaking the ardor that surged between them, and Bryony savored the special sweetness his closeness evoked.

''Today your eyes are the color of a cool Scottish loch. My grandmother on my mother's side had eyes like yours, the color shifting from green to blue.''

"Do you miss her?"

He sighed. "Yes, I do. I was very fond of her. I have nothing but happy memories of the Scottish side of my family. My closest friend, Carey McLendon, is also my cousin. I hope you'll get to meet him someday." Jack chuckled. "Carey is the black sheep of the family, and very reckless."

"Then you are two of a feather," Bryony said wryly. "Does he fight for Stuart since he's Scottish?"

He hesitated for a moment. "I think so. I haven't heard from him lately."

She could tell that the contusion on his head was giving him increasing misery. He pulled a flash from his waist-coat pocket and took a deep draught. "Ah, just what I needed."

"I have something for you." She stuck her hand inside the side opening of her skirt and pulled out the tin of ointment. "Dr. Cook gave me some salve for your poor head."

She glanced at the writing on the lid, but could not decipher the strange signs. Perhaps they were hieroglyphs, or some foreign language, but she recalled Clover's earlier warning, and shuddered. She cautiously opened the lid, almost expecting a lizard or something equally vile to jump out at her, but there was only smooth unguent smelling faintly of lavender.

Jack protested, but she overruled his groans and rapidly applied a heavy layer of ointment to the lump on his head.

"It tingles. What torture I stoically accept at your hands," he said with a wry smile. "My angel of mercy."

"The doctor ordered rest."

"I'm resting now. Looking at you is rest for my eyes."

"It seems that some ointment has slipped onto your tongue."

He drifted off to sleep, and she sat on the seat gazing out the window at the gentle farmlands rolling by. Green, yellow, and brown fields were separated by stone walls, here and there punctuated by clumps of trees clad in early autumn colors. Toward the south, the land rose into the more undulating patterns of the Downs. They would pass through Lewes in the very lap of the Downs. On the other side, the sea would be only ten miles away.

But to reach the village of Seaford, on the banks of the English Channel, they first had to cross the salt marshes. It would take them the rest of today and part of tomorrow to get there.

Bryony hoped that Mr. Dudley Bench would have more detailed answers to her questions about Reggie's death.

Gazing dreamily at Jack, she pondered the fact that if he had asked her to marry him, to follow him on his travels, she would gladly have said yes. But the rascally sea captain didn't want a wife. Did she dare give him what he *did* want?

Chapter 13

The room was dark, lit by only two guttering candles. One tall man, wearing a simple black satin coat and a neat wig, sat in a sagging wingchair in front of a smoking fire. The dreary building held little allure, but the decanter at the man's side was full, and the brandy was of the best quality.

Before the fire stood three rough-looking men. One had a red scar from eyebrow to jaw and wore a brown coat. His tall, burly companion had a scraggly mop of white hair, and the third man was thin and hobbled on a wooden leg. Despite his impediment, he could move with amazing speed.

The man with the wig set down his glass so hard that the stem broke and brandy splattered the table. Anger glittered in his eyes, and his breath came in wheezing gusts through his nostrils. Twirling the ring on his little finger, he pinned the ruffians with a paralyzing stare.

"She is still in England?"

They nodded miserably. The crippled fellow finally dared to speak. "She 'as protection, sir, from some bearded, rough-lookin' fellow. We was sure they'd be frightened away from Sussex by now."

The man with the wig laughed evilly. "I asked you not to kill Miss Shaw, only frighten her! That fire almost finished her off, due to your stupidity. You weren't supposed to set fire to the house." He paced the room like a caged animal.

"We—I—overturned an oil lamp," said the man in the brown coat, cringing. "It was so dark on the second floor that I stumbled and fell, setting fire to the gauze bed hangings.''

The man with the wig stopped before him and gripped his lapels savagely. ''We have to make sure she returns to France. Do you realize what might happen if she finds out the truth?'' he asked in a condescending voice.

''Aye, 'twill cost you yer life, guv,'' said the man with the mop of white hair.

The bewigged man laughed, a cold, contemptuous sound. ''And you most certainly will lose yours—before I do. If you bungle your assignment one more time, I will *personally* see to your execution.'' He sank down on his chair, his restless fingers tapping the armrest. ''She's been making a nuisance of herself, asking questions, snooping around Lindfield. 'Tis imperative that she be stopped. Is that understood?'' He raised his eyebrows.

The three ruffians looked at him in horror. As his satanic gaze lit into them, they were frightened for their lives. They thumbed the rims of their hats and took several steps back. ''Yes, sir, we understand,'' said the man with the white hair. ''We'll put th' fear o' God into th' lady. Th' fella travelin' wi' 'er will get a knife in 'is back.''

''Leave him alone. I don't plan to have strangers murdered. Only complicates matters. But try to find out his identity.''

The ruffians exchanged uneasy glances. ''Whatever ye say, guv,'' said the crippled man. ''If she finds out that you killed 'er brother—''

''Enough!'' The man with the wig laughed harshly. ''Reggie Shaw was a fool, and fools die young. Go! Get to work. Threaten her, promise her death, but get her out of Sussex.''

Mr. Dudley Bench was not what Bryony had expected. Although he was a partner in a successful law firm, he wasn't portly like Mr. Holland in Crawley. In fact, he was emaciated to the point of starvation. He wore ill-fitting clothes, a dark coat of indefinable color, and a similarly nondescript waistcoat and knee breeches. His old pigtail wig was motheaten and untidy. He gave Bryony a wary glance, and she feared she would have to pry every ounce of information out of him.

"You must know, Miss Shaw, that I'm a family man and a man of some distinction in the village—yes, even in Lewes where my business is located. If any of this scandal should come out, I would be ruined."

You should have thought of that before you became involved with the Jacobites, Bryony thought uncharitably.

"I'm not here to threaten you in any way, Mr. Bench, and your secret is safe with me. A friend of yours gave me your name and address."

He had received her in the study of his home while Jack took Clover to the fish market. Bryony had insisted on going alone, and Jack had not protested. Jules was waiting down at the docks with the carriage, perhaps staring across the Channel, longing for France.

Dudley Bench gave her a cold glance. "I did not know your brother well. He was a likable young man, if somewhat foolhardy. Charles Stuart wouldn't be fleeing for his life at this very moment if we had been able to deliver that gold. Your brother wrecked that chance, mayhap ruined the true king's entire mission."

Bryony swallowed hard to suppress the angry comment on her lips.

"Will you take a glass of wine with me?" he asked, and stood with precise, economical movements. He paused next to her chair and stared down at her. "You know, I'd go to any lengths to protect my family. They shall never know the truth unless Charles Edward gains the throne of England."

"No, thank you, I don't drink wine," Bryony lied, suddenly afraid of what he might *add* to the wine if he felt threatened. He made the hair at the nape of her neck stand on end. Everywhere she went with her questions, she was met with hostility.

"Can you tell me anything about the night Reggie died?" she went on, unwilling to accept defeat.

Dudley Bench filled a glass etched with a full-blown rose twisting around a stem. The design reminded her of another set of glasses she had seen earlier, at Nigel's. The carafe had the same pattern.

"You're staring at my glass," Bench commented. "If you're a Jacobite, you know that these are the glasses with which we drink the true king's health. All across England glasses like these are raised."

Bryony found it prudent to refrain from mentioning that she was not a Jacobite. "I—er—have just returned from France and am not familiar with the customs here. Of course, I met His Royal Highness at court in Paris."

"A ladies' man, they say." He raised questioning eyebrows.

"Yes, a very likable young man with the most courteous manners." Bryony couldn't very well tell him that she had only viewed the young prince across a huge ballroom at Versailles.

Bench seemed to mellow at her statement. "Ah! How true." He sipped the wine, then turned his attention to the business at hand. "Yes, the fatal card game . . . I arrived late. Reginald was in his cups when the game started." He inserted a thin finger under his wig and scratched his head. "What I don't understand is why we had to endure the elaborate charade of a card game when all of us in the room were Jacobites."

"The servants. Lord knows, they were always loyal to my brother, but perhaps he didn't want to take any chances," Bryony suggested.

Bench nodded. "True, but why the game turned so serious, I don't know. It was wrong of Bentworth to claim his payment so brusquely."

"Bentworth?"

"Yes, by the end of the evening Reginald owed him a large sum. Your brother played a very reckless game that night, and I must say, Bentworth egged him on."

"Mr. Forrester hinted at some other bet. Do you know anything about that?"

Bench shook his head. "That is a ridiculous assumption. They were only quarreling about the gambling debt."

"I will have to visit Lord Bentworth," she stated with a sigh.

"It may not be as easy to see him as it was to see me. He's a very arrogant fellow. Won't speak with the likes of you." He indicated her simple clothes with a contemptuous twist of his hand.

She was about to explain her adventures but realized she did not owe him any explanation. "Please tell me a little more about Lord Bentworth."

He shrugged. "He's an earl, the wealthy owner of Bentworth Court and a score of other estates. A grouchy, unlikable man." He laughed unpleasantly.

"Well, no wonder he is a Stuart sympathizer if his reputation is that of an arrogant curmudgeon."

Bench stiffened in offended righteousness. "Only the most upstanding of citizens, like myself, support Stuart. Bentworth must have done something worthwhile once to become one of our circle."

Bryony hastened to change the subject. "Is there anything else you recall about that night?"

He pursed his lips. "Well, there was that matter of the map. The French should have known better than to send the map to Reginald." He snorted. "It was inevitable that he would ruin the mission."

"Why are you not fleeing from the country like Mr. Forrester?" she asked. "I have heard that the militia is ferreting out all the sympathizers in the country." She glanced suspiciously at the paneled walls, as if they had ears.

Bench laughed, a derisive sound that made Bryony ball her fists and grind her teeth. "As I told you, I'm an upstanding citizen. I did my stint in the British army at Flanders. Fortunately, a wound prevented any participation against Stuart in Scotland. You might say I worked behind the scenes, carried information to the Scots so that Stuart could win the Battle of Prestonpans." He made a movement of impatience with his hand. "In the eyes of the public, I'm a British war hero. Yet, after the terrible Battle of Culloden, I could have wept with Stuart, and I did."

"I see." *But he would only weep for himself.* Bryony could not feel any pity for the boastful gentleman. She felt sorry her brother and the Scots were working with such a despicable man. No wonder Stuart had lost his throne!

And no wonder Reggie was dead.

She would visit Lord Bentworth next. If he had been in

any way responsible for Reggie's death, she didn't know what she would do. A resolution had hardened in her heart; she wanted to blame someone for her twin's death. She knew revenge was wrong, but she couldn't help herself. She had never loved anyone as much as her brother. She barely listened to Mr. Bench's next words, but the meaning slowly trickled into her consciousness.

"We were sitting around the dining room table at Willow Hills," he explained.

Bryony could easily picture every detail of that dear room where she had eaten so many meals, the huge oak table, the carved high-backed chairs, the sideboard, the cheerful yellow walls with matching brocade curtains.

"Your brother had mixed a huge bowl for our delectation. Wine, rum, geneva—everything—and he had obviously sampled it repeatedly before we arrived. But he was a splended host. I give him that." Mr. Bench cleared his throat. "Then he explained the reason for the card game. We all like a hand of cards now and then, so no one demurred." Bench stared for a moment out the window, his elbows on the arms of the chair and his hands steepled before him.

"Then, right in the middle of the game, Reginald stood up, his legs unsteady. He claimed that he had received a map from France. He argued in whispers with Bentworth, beside him, then said that he wanted us to know about the map if something happened to him before he could leave for Scotland."

Bryony dabbed at her eyes with a handkerchief. Dudley Bench's description brought it all so vividly to life. Reggie, always the trusting innocent, had made a mistake that night, but she could not put the puzzle pieces together.

Bench continued. "I was one of the last to leave. Your brother had gone off to his sleeping quarters, I believe. He was in no condition to continue playing, especially after Bentworth started dunning him. As I left, I saw Bentworth enter Reginald's study without even saying goodbye to me. He was skulking around in a odd sort of way." Bench sighed. "I didn't think about it at the time, but Bentworth might well be responsible for Reginald's death. Most likely they had a fight in the study after the rest of

us left and accidently overturned the candelabra that set
fire to the draperies.''

He leaned forward and pinned his cold gaze on Bryony.
''But there is no way you could prove Bentworth guilty of
murder. He's a peer, has extremely powerful friends. No
one would ever believe he was involved in our cause.'' As
if to himself, he added, ''No wonder he can be of such
tremendous help to Stuart. He has connections everywhere, bound to have—even though he's an old stick in
the mud.''

He stood abruptly. ''I'm sorry about Reginald, but I
really don't believe he was a victim of foul play, as you
imply. More likely than not, you're wasting your time.''

Bryony rose, stuffing her handkerchief back into her
pocket. ''I just cannot stop until I know the whole truth.
Thank you for your time. You may rest assured I won't
breathe a word to anyone.''

Bench gave her a wintry smile and ushered her to the
door. ''You wouldn't get very far if you tried some tom-
foolery behind my back, Miss Shaw. I would track you
down and make you pay.''

A dark cloud of depression settled over Bryony as she
left the house. The encounter with Mr. Bench had not
given her the answers she sought.

Chapter 14

As Bryony walked along the brick path to the gate, she pondered her next step. She would have to go and see Lord Bentworth, however much she abhorred the idea. What if he had really killed Reggie? What would she do then? The trick was to find some proof; naturally the man wouldn't confess to so hideous a crime. And who knew what he would do to her once he discovered her identity?

The Bench family lived at the top of a narrow, sloping road that wound through the village. Rustic cottages rubbed shoulders with flintstone houses with roofs of thatch or slate. Roses grew in profusion along and over the stone fences, a few late flowers making a last stand against the approaching cold. A finch warbled from the arrow of a sundial, and seagulls cried harshly overhead, gliding on the wind with effortless grace.

Beyond the cliffs, glittered the sea, a dazzling silver sheet in the sun. The roar of the breakers filled Byony's ears, and the salt-laden air pounded into her lungs, wiping away the cobwebs in her mind. Her problems seemed smaller when confronted by the majesty of the sea, even if it was only the Channel. She imagined she could see the hazy outline of France in the distance, but that was impossible.

Ready to join Jack and Clover at the fish market, she walked down the steep street, enjoying her solitary walk in the sun. As soon as she reached the carriage, she would ask Jules to drive to Alfriston. If she didn't find the answers she needed from Lord Bentworth, she would have to pursue other avenues to the truth.

132

Scores of children and fat matrons were clustered around the market stalls. Jack's tall form and raven curls should have been easily visible in the crowd, but he was nowhere in sight. She grimaced. Captain Elusive—where had he vanished to now?

A tall chestnut tree cast its shade over part of the street, and the green, softly spined chestnut shells crunched under her shoes. Deep in thought, she passed the old smithy, a tumbledown shed with weeds growing in every crevice and grass knee-deep around it. Then, from the corner of her eye, Bryony registered a movement beside her.

The attack came so fast and so unexpectedly that she had no time to scream. A shaft of sunlight blinded her as her head was pulled back and a large, sweaty hand was clamped over her mouth. Her arms were twisted back so furiously that tears stood in her eyes. Within seconds, she had been pulled into the shed, her feet dragging on the ground.

Her eyes adjusted to the gloom inside and filled with terror as she recognized the scar-faced man dressed in a brown coat, who had apparently followed her all the way from Crawley. Her instinct to fear him had not been wrong.

"I will take my hand off your mouth if you promise not to scream," he breathed into her ear.

She was startled when another man spoke behind her. "If ye let go o' 'er gob, she'll scream, ye great mutton 'ead! No talkin'! Let's 'ave some en'ertainment 'ere. I start pullin' out 'er nails an' ye can saw orf 'er ear. I can't wait t' begin."

Bryony moaned and tried to squeeze out of her attacker's painful grip. Twisting sideways, she had a fleeting impression of a dirty stocking cap, a rough beard, and a wooden leg. She trembled uncontrollably, and her gaze flittered around the shed in hope of finding help or some way to escape. The lane outside was silent. Only the muted sounds of the market and the sea penetrated the sagging walls. No one would find her.

"But before we do away with her, she ought to tell us the identity of her traveling companion," said the man with the scar. He loosened his hold slightly, but still she had to fight for every breath.

''Naw, we'd better do as th' gent said. She's a threat t' us all.''

The man with the scar stared at her as if in deliberation. His blue eyes were somewhat protruding and shone with avarice. ''For the last time, will you keep silent if I take my hand away?''

She nodded; she had no other choice if she wanted to keep breathing. Her head was swimming, her eyes blurring. As he released the grip on her mouth, she staggered forward, but the pressure on her arms at her back intensified. She gasped and closed her mind against the pain. Nevertheless, she could not stop the throbbing, searing agony in her shoulders.

The scarred man in the brown coat hovered over her. ''Well, where is he?''

''Where is who?'' she asked, stalling for time.

The arm went higher, and she whimpered. ''I don't know where he is.'' She had to think! *Help! Jack!*

The man at her back gave her a shove, and she fell to her knees. ''Jest let's finish 'er orf. She bain't goin' t' talk. We don't have much time.''

Bryony's legs trembled so much she could not stand, and her throat was dry with fear. Pressing a hand to her throat, she swallowed convulsively. ''Who—who are you working for?'' she whispered. ''Why do you want to harm me?''

''Jest shut yer pretty li'l gob!'' the one-legged man savaging her arm cried. '' 'Twill be over in a minute.''

''But why?'' she dared ask.

He didn't reply, just twisted her arm even higher. Tears of pain burned in her eyes.

''Tell me your companion's name!''

She would have to think of a way to escape. ''I don't know.'' First she had to get out of the building; perhaps Jack was already looking for her. The chance was slim, but she had to keep hoping. She ought to have known something like this would happen. First, she had been shot at. Second, someone had tried to burn her alive. It was as if none of it had been real until this moment when pain was her prime concern.

"Let me go, please," she pleaded, unable to stand further abuse. "I have done nothing wrong."

Loosening his grip, the one-legged man laughed and hauled her to her feet. Waves of dizziness surged through her, and the scene took on strange colors, as if she was about to lose consciousness.

Somehow she managed to stumble toward the warped door opening, but the scarred man grabbed her again, halting her. She drew great gulps of air into her lungs.

"If you don't tell me now, wench, I'll shove this knife into your gut," the scarred man threatened. The deadly glitter of a wide blade flashed before her eyes, and she felt a light prickling sensation at the base of her throat. "Is that understood?"

She nodded and swallowed to ease the bitter taste of terror in her mouth. "I'll tell you." Then, before she could blink, everything changed before her eyes.

With the scream of a banshee, Clover jumped from the cottage roof onto the back of the one-legged man. The attack came so suddenly that the man with the dagger let go of Bryony for a moment. She convulsed in agony as her arm regained its normal position, but biting her teeth together, she aimed a kick at the man's shin and looked frantically for something to use as a weapon.

He yelped and threw himself at her. She screamed as his large hand clasped around her thigh and pinned her to the ground. Scratching frantically in the unkempt grass beside her, she located a midsized stone. Without hesitation she raised it and crashed it onto the man's head.

He grunted like an angry bear and began clawing for her throat. She sputtered and tossed her head from side to side while groping for a hold on his hair.

In the middle of the struggle she sense the ground vibrating under her as running footsteps approached.

"Help!" she croaked, laboring to pry the ruffian's fingers from her neck. In the background, she heard Clover's hair-raising guttersnipe epithets. Then her attacker was pulled off by the scruff of his neck. She fought for air and scrambled to her knees.

In front of her eyes appeared a pair of very fine white silk stockings encasing a pair of sturdy calves. The square gold buckles on the high-heeled shoes shone in the sunlight. She jerked her head back and stared in utter surprise into the eyes of Nigel, Lord Lippett.

Then there came the sounds of more running footsteps up the lane and voices raised in alarm.

The ruffians did not linger. With bounding leaps they took off through the high grass, rounded the cottage, and disappeared among the hodgepodge of cottages on the terraced street below.

Bryony could only stare after them in confusion. Clover broke the silence. "Cove's got a bleedin' right 'ook," he complained, massaging his shoulder. "Fairly knocked th' breath out o' me."

Nigel helped Bryony to her feet. Four sturdy fishermen rushed up to the trio, carrying cudgels and clubs. The first one to arrive said, "We saw th' fight. Are ye hurt?"

Bryony shook her head numbly and pointed toward where her attackers had disappeared. A roar went up as the villagers ran in hot pursuit of the villains. "We'll catch 'em, miss, don't ye worry," the last one cried as he turned the corner.

"Dearest Bryony, did they beat you badly?" Nigel asked, holding her close.

"No—no." She still couldn't calm down enough to speak coherently.

"Cor, them coves were arter us in Lindfield, could 'ave sworn it," Clover said, shaking Bryony's skirt.

She pulled away from Nigel's embrace and cradled Clover's head against her. "How brave you were," she whispered.

" 'Tis really amazing that I happened by at this very moment." Nigel said, dashing off his hat. "I couldn't believe my eyes when I recognized you. I was on my way to visit Mr. Bench, a lawyer with whom I have business, when I looked out the window of my carriage and saw you."

For the first time Bryony noticed the carriage parked under the chestnut tree. She smiled tiredly. "If it hadn't been for you, I would have been dead by now."

"What did they want? To rob you?"

Bryony laughed bitterly. "No. Do I look like someone

who has something worth stealing?'' She caressed Clover's head as he clung to her. Looking steadily into Nigel's eyes, she said, ''They wanted to kill me.''

Horror dawned on his face. ''Kill you? But why?''

''I don't know. But perhaps someone doesn't want me to find out the truth about Reggie's death, or murder.''

Nigel sighed heavily. ''You believe that Reggie was murdered? Bryony! That is nonsense.''

''I'm not so sure.'' She wiped her face with a handkerchief. ''Somebody does not want me to discover the truth about that terrible night.''

Nigel kneaded his chin, and studied her long and hard. ''By the way, what are you doing here, Bryony?''

She glanced away, suddenly embarrassed. She would have to confess now. ''I saw Mr. Bench. I went back into your study and stole the bits of paper with the names. See here.'' Reaching into her pocket, she hauled out the list of names that she had glued onto another paper. She grabbed his arm impulsively. ''You must understand that I cannot stop until I have turned every stone, especially if Reggie met with foul play.''

''I see. How foolhardy of you,'' Nigel said with a frown. ''But dashed plucky all the same.'' He clasped her hands and smiled. ''I'm glad you came to no harm. But this time I will accompany you on all the other visits you have planned. 'Twill not do, you know, a lady traveling alone and unprotected. Where are you staying? I'll endeavor to find some answers by this evening.'' He looked deeply into her eyes. ''Perhaps we can have dinner together, if your aunt permits.''

Bryony frowned. Nigel would bundle her off for France if he found out that she was traveling with a stranger. ''I have my carriage here; Aunt Hortense and I are, in fact, planning to go to Alfriston to visit Lord Bentworth. She was an old friend of his mother,'' she invented without batting an eyelid.

Nigel nodded. ''I see. Well, you may encounter difficulties there. The man is an eccentric with a thundering temper.'' He warmed her cold hand between his own. ''Do you want me to accompany you? Surely Bentworth cannot refuse to see *me*.''

Bryony shook her head. "It is very kind of you to offer, but I don't want to ruin your trip. Besides, no one has ever refused Aunt Hortense entrance to hut or palace."

Where was Jack all this time? she wondered, and glanced toward the empty lane. There was no sign of his tall form anywhere. He had done one of his mysterious disappearing acts again. "Where is Jules?" she asked Clover.

"Jules?" Nigel asked with a frown.

"My French coachman."

"Don't rightly know," Clover said. "Last I saw o' 'im, 'e was 'eadin' down t' th' 'arbor. Said 'e wanted t' ogle th' ocean."

"I'll start out for Bentworth Court this afternoon," she said, almost to herself.

"How will I be able to reach you?" In a sudden display of temper, Nigel slapped his fist against his open palm. "I'll stop at nothing to find the men who mauled you! They should hang from the first available tree."

Bryony smiled. "Thank you. You don't know how much your support means to me. If you need me, send a note to Mr. Holland's office in Crawley. I'll contact him after I've been to Alfriston."

"Very well." Nigel sighed. "I'd better be off to deal with my own affairs."

"Mr. Bench wasn't very happy to see me," she explained lamely, and instantly regretted her words. What had transpired between her and Mr. Bench was her private concern.

A glimmer of interest flared in Nigel's eyes. "Did he tell you something that leads you to believe Reggie was—er—murdered?"

She shook her head. "No, the attempts on my life gave me that idea. Again, I'm extremely grateful for what you did, Nigel. I know Reggie would have been, too."

The horrifying experience she had just undergone was beginning to take its toll, and she excused herself as tears threatened to overcome her. She hurried down the lane, followed closely by Clover.

Chapter 15

As Bryony approached the carriage, she saw Jack leaning against the shafts, talking to Jules. The Frenchman was gesticulating wildly in his Gallic way. Bryony could have sworn that Jack was speaking French, which, she supposed, wasn't strange, since he was a sea captain. Another piece of the puzzle that was Jack, she mused.

"How come you were at the ruin in time to help me?" she asked Clover who was clinging to her hand.

"I was lookin' fer ye, m'lady, so that ye couldn't run away from me again."

Bryony rolled her eyes heavenward. "And who says you have any right to follow me around?" She regretted the chastising words as soon as they were out of her mouth. She berated herself as his bottom lip trembled.

"I jest thought I could meet ye." His grimy hand sifted through the contents of one bulging pocket. "I wanted t' give ye this." He held a shiny red and yellow apple toward her. "I stealed it specially fer ye."

Bryony knelt before him, her eyes filling with tears. "That was very kind of you, but from now on you don't need to steal anything. I'll give you a few farthings to buy your gifts."

Clover's head was still hanging low, and her heart ached. How could she explain? "I have enough money in my purse to pay for an apple or two," she said. "Promise you won't steal again?"

He shoved the apple into her hand and ran to the carriage, where he clung to Jack, hiding his face against his full-skirted coat.

Feeling like an arch-villain, Bryony approached the carriage. Jules immediately jumped to attention.

"Mademoiselle! A long conversation with Monsieur Bench, yes?" he commented, sweeping off his hat.

Bryony smiled wryly, not daring to look at Jack. "Indeed it was." She asked Jules to transfer her portmanteau from the baggage rack to the interior of the coach and climbed inside. Her legs were stiff, and the rest of her body was begging for rest. As she closed the door, she heard Clover say:

"She would be dead if it wasn't fer me—an' that other cove, o' course."

"What? Dead? And what other cove?" boomed Jack. He lifted Clover into the carriage and climbed in after him, his face a dark scowl.

Jules stuck his head through the open window. "Where to?" he inquired, his misshapen face creased with concern.

Suddenly Bryony had an urge to push them all outside and drive the coach away herself—away from her problems, away from her companions. Where could she turn to get answers about Reggie, about her confusing emotions? Certainly not these two rascals, one big, one small, her self-appointed guardians. She was just too tired to deal with any more today.

"Take the road west of Cuckmere River and head for Alfriston, Jules. Al-fris-ton," she repeated to the befuddled Frenchman. She would confront Lord Bentworth and then return to Crawley and speak with Uncle Butterball. He would know what to do if she found out that Lord Bentworth was guilty of taking Reggie's life.

She tried to avoid Jack's penetrating stare, but as usual, his presence overwhelmed her and she couldn't think clearly. "What happened?" he asked as the carriage lurched forward.

Clover was more than eager to tell the tale, embroidering liberally. Jack's face grew darker and darker. "Who was the man who came to your aid?"

"Lord Lip Spit, or somebody. I don't remember rightly."

"Lord Lippett," Bryony said with a weighty sigh and a glare at Clover. "The friend I visited in Cuckfield when it rained so hard."

Jack's lips curved upward. "The man who owns a maze?"

Color surged into her cheeks, and she had to hide her embarrassment by pretending to look into her drawstring purse. "Yes, that's him."

"But what about the attack today? I know I shouldn't have let you go alone!"

Bryony shrugged, trying to make light of the fact that she had almost been abducted, or even killed. " 'Tis all over now."

"And what were you doing there?" he asked Clover. "You should have fetched me immediately." He took the boy's shoulder in a hard grip, and Clover's head hung low. Bryony laid a calming hand on Jack's arm, shaking her head in warning.

Jack scowled and let go of the boy. Knocking on the roof, he ordered Jules to halt the coach. The Frenchman opened the door and peered curiously at them.

"Clover, sit with Jules for a few minutes," Jack demanded. His eyes challenged Bryony to protest, but she remained quiet. "You have been very naughty. We will discuss your involvement in the attack later," he added ominously. Looking thoroughly crestfallen, Clover slunk out of the carriage. Bryony heard him mutter glumly to Jules, who responded in voluble French.

As soon as they were alone, Bryony said, "You shouldn't be so hard on the boy. He was very brave, and he really admires you."

Jack's laugh was jarring. "Some idol, eh? That little varmint needs a good spanking."

"Is that the way your stepfather treated you? With a good spanking?" Bryony asked gently.

Jack paled and glanced out the window, refusing to look at her for a long moment. She was beginning to think she had angered him irrevocably, but there was no trace of emotion in his voice when he finally confronted her.

"Someone is trying to kill you, don't you see? You have to stop dashing madly about Sussex on a mission that is destined to fail. And why return the same way we came? France can very easily be reached from here. We will hire a vessel—"

"You have no right to tell me what to do," Bryony declared, twisting the cord of her bag. "I will let you off somewhere where you can catch the westbound stagecoach." She flung out her arm in a gesture of exasperation. "I'm so tired. Do we have to go into the problems now? Why are you scolding me?"

"Because I'm concerned, dammit. I care what happens to you, you stubborn woman!"

A tired smile crept across her face, and warmth stole into her heart. "Thank you," she said simply. "I'm surprised you care, since you barely know me."

He moved over to her seat and clasped her hand. "These few days have changed my life. I know you better than I know myself." His fingertips traveled up her arm, over the coarse material of her peasant jacket.

"I confess that I've always been at odds with the world, but for the first time, I dare to open up, dare to speak from my heart," he continued. His hand had reached her throat, and he cradled her face between his palms. "It's all because of you, Bryony, my darling." His thumbs moved carefully across her face.

"You always find something flattering to say," Bryony whispered, transfixed by his touch. Her blood sang every time he looked into her eyes, every time he touched her.

"Only with you," he breathed.

"A vast exaggeration." Bryony tilted her head slightly forward, lured by his sensitive lips. It seemed so long since he had kissed her. Had it been only yesterday? When he didn't touch her she yearned for him. When he wasn't present, she longed for him. But when he did touch her, she panicked, wanted to escape. From herself. Reason had no place in their relationship.

His lips tasted of apples and tenderness. As his mouth

moved slowly over hers, she sensed the depth of his caring. Her arms crept around him, and she found herself enfolded in his warm embrace. The horrors she had experienced earlier slowly faded to the background as she opened up to him. This kiss was nothing like his previous advances. He was neither savage nor cynical.

"I need you," he whispered into her hair. "And I want you."

Bryony could not respond as he showed just how much he wanted her. His lips drained all willpower from her; she was an empty receptacle that needed to be filled by him.

As his hands moved up and down her back, she couldn't find a single reason to stop him. He pulled off her jacket, and she waited patiently as he sought the tie strings of the coarse blouse. She breathed deeply in contentment as he removed the scratchy material from her skin.

His hands were warm, soft and rough, soothing yet unspeakably exciting.

"Let me show you what I've been wanting to repeat ever since we shared that cot. I've wanted to do this." He pushed away the long, midnight curls that had worked loose from the chignon at the top of her head. Her fingertips dug into his hair as he bent and took one of her nipples between his lips. His breath caressed her, a sweet gust that warmed every inch of her. Fiery sensations flowed through her blood, accumulating in the hard crest that his tongue was worshipping until she arched against him, moaning with pleasure.

"You skin is as silky and pliable as the finest mother-of-pearl tinted satin; touching it is like running my fingers through the softest spring water. To drink from your skin satisfies a man's thirst," he said as he studied her breast. "But also drives him to desperation." He claimed her other breast, covering it with kisses.

"Please don't stop," Bryony said breathlessly, thrilling to his taste as she kissed his throat where his pulse pounded. Somehow she had worked open his peasant shirt, and somehow her hands had found their way underneath to explore the hard planes of his chest. She felt no shame as her fingers traveled the length of his spine, across his hip to one strong thigh and the hard ridge straining against the simple peasant culottes.

Her heart missed a beat, and her breath clogged in her throat. He chuckled against her navel as she jerked her hand away and covered her embarrassment in a fit of coughing.

"Took you by surprise, didn't it?" he taunted gently, his eyes dancing as he gazed into her scarlet face. "Don't worry, it won't bite." He took her hand possessively and made her explore him without shame.

"Oh, how I've waited for this," he said with a groan, fire surging into his eyes and color tinging his lean cheeks. "Don't stop now, Brye darling. Don't leave me in agony," he begged as his hand was wandering up one of her legs, under her petticoats. His bold caress sent tendrils of delicious sensation all through her body, and she wanted to melt. When he found the hot center at the joining of her thighs, she felt as if she would die of pleasure.

Nothing could feel more right, yet a tiny part of her hesitated. Her doubt was like a thorn in her flesh.

Jack sighed against her throat as she tried to move away. "What's wrong?" he asked.

"What about Clover and Jules?" she whispered.

"You cannot stop now," he urged, pressing against her. "They won't notice."

She shook his head. "They aren't the only reason. This is not the perfect place, and—"

He placed his fingers over her lips. "Shhh. You're afraid I will take your love and leave. Just as you accused earlier." He removed his hand and let it hover for a moment before he caressed her hair. "I love you, Bryony. I cannot ravish you. There was a time—up until the moment I met you, to be exact—when I would have done just that. Now all that matters is your feelings. We don't have to go on."

She curled closer to him, holding him in a suffocating grip around his chest. "The passion I feel bewilders me; I don't know if I dare go all the way," she whispered. "I'm afraid of failure."

He looked deeply into her eyes and grimaced. "I'll never hurt you."

"You cannot hurt me if I give myself voluntarily. But I cannot."

He groaned and pressed her head to his heart. "I know you would make me very happy, but perhaps the time isn't right yet." He sighed. "I never thought I would say this, but I'm . . . afraid, too. You see, I don't know if I'm ready to surrender to a life with you. I cannot but be honest with you. And you said once you would give yourself only—"

She silenced him. "I know you would never deliberately hurt me." She gathered up her courage. "I'm longing to know what 'tis like to be loved by a man."

"Oh, lovely one, with you 'twould be heaven," he said with a tenderness that came from deep within his heart. And she knew he was telling the truth.

"I regret starting this. When I'm with you, Brye, I forget myself. We should wait until the perfect moment. 'Twill come, and we'll recognize it. We'll be ready."

Every inch of her was on fire, resisting his words, but in her heart she knew he was right. And she loved him all the more for it.

But he hadn't mentioned marriage. He probably never would. The other side of the coin was: would she be happy traveling the seven seas with him? She could not answer that.

His embrace gave her security, his presence gave her happiness, his smile made her heart dissolve.

"I have a present for you," she said, and disentangled his arms. Leaning down, she opened her portmanteau and pulled out an oddly shaped brown package. "Here, open it."

Curious, he unwrapped the tricorne hat she had purchased in Haywards Heath. "Ah! Just what I need," he said with a wry smile. He placed it on his jet black curls, and the wide upturned brim gave him a lordly air. His forceful virility made her heart constrict in sudden agony.

"I'm sorry I stepped on the other one," she said.

"Darling Brye, Clover was more than happy to wear it. He carries it around like a talisman, the silly boy!"

She nodded. "But I'm glad I bought this one for you. It fits you as well as it would any prince." She flapped her hand across the brim. " 'Tis a bit dusty."

"The fact that you bought it for me makes it the most wonderful thing I've ever owned."

Bryony savored the precious moment and stored it in her heart, to take out and relive whenever she needed strength.

Chapter 16

Bentworth Court lay like a shimmering gem in a valley carved eons ago by the flowing river. The property was guarded by the rolling Downs at its back and beautiful golden beeches at its front. It was one of the most impressive estates Bryony had ever seen. The vast, three-storied pink brick mansion displayed glittering windows interspersed with marble statues mounted in niches. Two side-wings arched back at a slight angle from the main building. The stately white columns of a portico adorned the middle of the central building, framing two huge front doors. A terrace marched the length of the house, lined by a graceful balustrade of white marble. There were paved paths and pleasure gardens, and even a pond where swans glided serenely.

Bryony's courage threatened to give out in the face of such splendor, and she wished Jack was with her. He had received an urgent message at the inn in Alfriston saying that he was needed in Portsmouth. Having hired a boat to take him down the Cuckmere River, he had gone off to inspect his ship. Most likely he had met some smuggler captain who had promised, at an inflated price, to take him from Alfriston to Portsmouth, Bryony thought angrily. She missed him; she resented every minute away from him even though he had promised to meet her in Alfriston three days hence.

Alfriston, located three miles north of Seaford, had the reputation of being a veritable beehive of smuggling activities. The small town was a market cross, a meeting point where half the county met for bustling commerce, legal and otherwise.

Jules was at this very moment drinking ale with French smugglers at The Star, the old medieval cross-timbered inn on the high street of the village. Not wanting to draw attention to herself by asking questions, Bryony had hired one of the local stablehands to drive her to Bentworth Court.

But, as it turned out, asking questions could have saved her a trip.

She descended the carriage in the wide, circular drive, climbed the long, shallow steps to the enormous double oak doors, and lifted the brass knocker. After what seemed a very long time, one of the doors opened, and she stood face to face with an impressive butler. He stared down his nose at her and lifted one disconcerting eyebrow.

"Yes?"

"I would like to see Lord Bentworth on a very urgent matter." She handed her calling card into his white-gloved hand. He took and inordinate amount of time studying the card, then his gaze traveled over her creased gown of green velvet, partly concealed by her cloak. She had changed into the second, cleaner, gown of the two she had packed before leaving Crawley.

The butler's nose rose disdainfully. "Lord Bentworth is away. The servants' entrance is at the back." He was about to close the door in her face.

Bryony drew herself up, angered by his insolence. "You show Bentworth my card. When he sees my name, he will be extremely put out if you refuse my request."

"Miss—er—Shaw, as I said before, Lord Bentworth is not at home. He is in Paris on business and is not expected back until next month. You could reach him at the palace of Versailles." He drew a majestic breath. "And that's God's truth."

Bryony had no choice but to believe him. There was a somnolent stillness about the estate as if all activity had been curbed to a minimum. No servants were in evidence. No horses clattered along the flagstone path curving around the main house. Even the smoke in the chimneys curled lazily. Early autumn darkness was falling over the trees.

"Is there a Lady Bentworth?" she asked.

The butler shook his head and closed the door. There was nothing else to do but return to Alfriston, Bryony decided with a sigh. She pondered whether she ought to go to France and trace Lord Bentworth right away.

Her spirits low, she returned to the carriage. Clover might have cheered her up, but he was asleep on the seat. She spread a rug over him and ordered the stablehand to drive back to The Star. All she could do now was wait for Jack to rejoin her.

A hot dinner and a mug of mulled wine in front of the fire was what she needed to boost her spirits. When they reached the inn, it was growing dark. She let Clover sleep in the carriage and ordered the stablehand to take care of the horses. As she passed the latticed windows of the common room of the inn, she happened to look inside.

Her heart lurched in fear as she recognized the ruffians from Seaford standing near the fireplace. Nigel had been unable to apprehend them! And they had obviously followed her here. If they found her, there was no way they would let her escape this time.

A thousand thoughts crowded her mind at once as she tried to form a plan. She could not stay there, but where could she go? Her entire body was stiff with terror, and only with difficulty could she tear her gaze away from the window. The men were at that very moment interrogating the proprietor. She had no reason to doubt the nature of their questions.

Groping along the wall, she retraced her steps. The carriage. She had to use her carriage to get away.

Somehow she managed to cross the inn yard, though her legs were shaking so much she could barely walk. Luckily the stablehand had not yet released the horses from the carriage. He was filling two feedbags with oats.

"I have changed my mind," she told him, wondering if that pitiful voice she heard was really hers. "I would like you to give my coachman a message." She pulled out her purse, which had grown distressingly thin since she had arrived in England, and, pushing a coin into his hand, ordered, "Please go now and be discreet. I don't want the entire taproom to hear the message. And when Captain

Newcomer returns, I want you to tell him to meet me at Mr. Holland's office in Crawley.''

The stablehand bowed politely and hurried off. Bryony paced the yard, throwing nervous glances at the door. Where was Jules? Why was he taking so long? Just when she was ready to give up, he struggled through the door. For a few moments he stood unsteadily without support, singing a French ditty at the top of his lungs.

Mustering all her strength, she dragged her inebriated coachman across the cobblestones. He protested loudly, but did not try to stop her.

Suddenly the door opened again, and two silhouettes filled the doorway. There was no mistaking the two ruffians, the burly, scar-faced man and the thin, limber fellow with the wooden leg. They were already in hot pursuit as she bundled Jules into the carriage and slammed the door. Her skirts held high, she leaped onto the box and grabbed the reins.

In sheer desperation she lashed the whip in the air above the horses' heads and, frightened, they sprang forward, almost ripping Bryony's arms from her shoulders as she fought to control the reins. The carriage lurched and swayed along the narrow, winding lane.

All at once her heart lodged in her throat. It was a nasty shock to realize that the man with the wooden leg had managed to cling to the back of the carriage. She heard him curse and pant as he slowly worked his way along the side of the coach. Bryony knew that if he managed to reach her, she would be dead.

Dusk was rapidly approaching, making it difficult to see where she was going. As if sensing her terror, the horses increased their pace until she could barely control them. The carriage rattled and bounced. The harnesses creaked and jingled. She fought to hold the reins and drew a sigh of relief as they left the village behind, entering an open country lane, bordered by hedges on both sides. Here, at least, the horses would be forced to stay on the road. Her only prayer was that no other vehicle appeared to bar her reckless progress. The lane was empty as far as she could see.

She angled a quick glance over the side of the carriage.

The ruffian had already advanced past the door and was clinging to the side like a monkey to a tree. If only she could shake him off! But he had already survived the jostling across the cobblestones and clearly intended to hang on until he could overpower her and snatch the reins.

On an impulse she flicked the whip toward him, but she could not control her weapon and the horses at the same time.

"Ye . . . shouldn't 'ave done . . . that, missy. I'll pay ye back in a . . . trice," he choked out as he labored to remain on the coach.

Bryony held her breath, her teeth clamped together in concentration as the horses bolted along a tight curve. Her two years in France had not diminished her skill with horses, something Reggie had encouraged her to develop.

His dear features flashed before her inner eye, and her determination hardened. She was not going to be a victim, not ever! She'd fight until her very last breath. She was doing it for Reggie, but most of all for herself. This would be her ultimate test of strength; if she could survive this, nothing would ever frighten her again.

Each thought flashed with brilliant lucidity through her mind just as the horses changed pace, winded at last. As they slowed to a trot, the villain made a final lunge toward the front. His fingers clawed around the edge of the box seat, and Bryony screamed. She jabbed the leather-wrapped handle of the whip repeatedly against his fingers, but they kept inching forward. His shoulders were level with the seat, and all he needed to reach her was one forceful push.

As he gathered his last reserves of strength, Bryony searched frantically under the seat. There must be a weapon somewhere. To her relief, her fingers closed around the cold barrel of a musket. With one hand holding on to the reins with all her might, she pulled out the musket with the other. She had just managed to turn it, butt directed toward the villain's face, as he heaved himself up, groping for her throat.

In mindless self-defense, she shoved the musket into his middle with all her strength. With a bellow, he crashed backward, fell from the carriage, and landed hard in the hedge below. She craned her head back to see if he was still alive. He lay motionless, his legs dangling above the lane.

She might have killed him.

She couldn't go on without knowing for sure. She drew in the reins and cautiously waited to see if he would move. He didn't.

She found a horn of blackpowder and a pouch of lead balls under the seat. Before she investigated the man's fate, she would load the musket—just in case.

As she climbed off the box, the door opened and Clover jumped down. "I thought we'd entered an 'oss race, m'lady," he said, glancing curiously at the musket. "What's afoot?"

"Come with me and bring a piece of rope," she demanded, advancing cautiously toward the still body, the musket trained on the man's heart.

As she came closer, she heard him groan. Jubilation sprouted in her chest; she wouldn't have to carry the loss of his life on her conscience.

Clover joined her as she was poking the wooden leg with one toe. "Oh, daggers, a bleedin' corpse! What 'ave ye done, m'lady?"

"He's still alive. You will help me turn him over and bind his hands. Then we'll take him to the nearest gaol."

The villain made no effort to resist as they dragged him from the hedge and turned him over. He moaned and swore, but none of his bones seemed to be broken.

A silvery moon had crept over the treetops and bathed the lane in an pale, eerie light. Sniveling and snorting from the effort, Clover bound the man's hands. "There! Trussed up like a maimed sausage," he commented proudly. "They'll need a saw t' cut 'im loose, I'll lay."

Bryony lowered the musket, and together they managed to set the man to his feet. Swearing, he stumbled toward the carriage, and Bryony checked the rope around his wrists before she ordered him to step inside. He spat in her face and hurled virulent epithets at her before succumbing to their insistent pushes.

Jules, whose strength would have been invaluable, was snoring in happy ignorance. As the villain half sat, half sprawled on the seat, Bryony shoved the barrel of her musket into his belly.

"I swear I will kill you if you don't tell me who hired you to kill me," she threatened, at that moment believing her own threat.

He laughed evilly and aimed another stream of spittle at her face. She sidestepped neatly and jabbed him harder. "There will be no witnesses to your death, only these loyal friends of mine. Your carcass will be found by the wayside, another poor victim of murderous highwaymen."

The villain muttered and glowered at her from under bushy eyebrows. "I don't know 'is name. A fancy cull, 'e is, but I don't know 'is name. Thass all I know—an' stop maulin' me insides wi' that thing!" He tried to shove aside the barrel.

"Better tie up his legs as well," Bryony said grimly to Clover, who hastened to comply. He wound a thick layer of rope from knees to feet, including the wooden leg, then slipped some rope through the leather loops in the ceiling.

"Th' cove bain't nuffin' but a bound-up pile o' kindlin' now."

"That reminds me," Bryony said. "Did you set fire to Mr. Forrester's house?" She glared at the villain, challenging him to defy her.

His gave a wheezy chuckle. "Are ye daft, missy? Why would I set an 'ouse afire?"

"You were going to kill me," she reminded him coolly. "If you didn't set the fire, who did? The scar-faced man?"

"Yer alive, bain't ye?" he retorted. "I don't know nuffin' 'bout a fire, and I've niver met th' Forrester cove."

"I don't believe you. You were one of the men at Potter House."

The villain shrugged. "Believe what ye want. I'm tellin' th' truth."

It was useless to try to make him change his story, and her bravado was rapidly seeping away. Her efforts to find the truth about Reggie's death were growing increasingly difficult and confusing. Her invisible enemy was very powerful. And who had been the most powerful member of Reggie's Jacobite society? Lord Bentworth, without a doubt.

She had no choice. She had to confront him in Paris, even if meant further endangering her own life. But first she would deal with the captive.

Night stillness had fallen, and an owl hooted in the distance. Some nocturnal animal crashed through the undergrowth as she got the horses moving. They obeyed listlessly, and she realized they could not continue without some rest and sustenance. In the sharp moonlight she discovered a dense copse of trees not far from the lane. A grass-covered path just wide enough for a coach led between the trees, and it took some clever maneuvering to reach the copse. Bryony was pleased, especially when she saw that the trees shielded a bend in the river. There was water for the horses, and Jules would have a way to slake his thirst in the morning.

She climbed down, her shoulders slumping, her arms aching. Still, she made sure the carriage was well concealed from the lane and from highway robbers' greedy eyes. It took her last reserve of strength to release the horses from their shackles. Tears of frustration stood in her eyes before she could push out the metal pins and release the pole chains, and then the pole landed painfully on her foot.

She led the horses to the river and was overwhelmed by the beauty of the silver moonlight on the water. The animals drank deeply while she wished that Jack was there to share the view. He was probably at this very moment sailing past Brighton in a boat brimming with illegal French brandy and Chinese tea. That would suit the carefree fellow just fine, she realized, and kicked a boulder.

"Ouch!" she snapped, the pain giving her an excuse to let her tears flow freely. All the fear and tension that had piled up within her came pouring out. She had never felt more lonely and desperate than at that moment.

Nevertheless, something kept pushing her to go on. If the roles had been reversed and Reggie had been in her shoes, he would never have hesitated. She pressed the enameled miniature of his face to her tear-soaked cheek.

Sitting down on the ground, her back propped up against

a tree, she dozed on and off. Every night sound made her bolt upright in fear, and she was happy when morning arrived.

When the carriage reached Crawley at the end of the following day, they were all tired and hungry. After eating a hot meal of roast joint smothered in fragrant gravy, and stewed parsnips, at the tavern next door to Mr. Holland's law offices, Bryony left Clover to watch the horses and Jules to guard the prisoner. Then she walked straight to Mr. Holland's office. He would know what to do with the captive inside the carriage.

She knew she looked tired and disheveled, but there was no time to do anything about it. She applied the knocker. The Butterball would worry about the state of affairs, of course, but she could handle him.

The office was silent, and she had to knock a second time before someone opened the door. She recognized Mr. Grimes, Butterball's secretary.

"Good evening, Mr. Grimes, I would like to see Mr. Holland on an important business matter," she said.

Mr. Grimes was a short, dapper man wearing a perfectly curled and pomaded pigtail wig. His brown eyes deeply embedded in fat mirrored a kindly disposition. "Miss Shaw! Come in, come in." He eyed her clothes with clear misgivings. "We thought you had returned to France. I'm sorry to tell you that Mr. Holland is away on business. He had to execute a will at a distant estate in Yorkshire."

Bryony's spirits sank. She explained that she had caught a thief, though she left out the details. Mr. Grimes promised to take the villain to the gaol. "The magistrate will question you about this, Miss Shaw." He glanced once more at her clothes. "I—er—pray no other calamity has befallen you. Is your aunt, perchance, awaiting in the coach?"

She was force to invent another lie, and it weighed heavily on her conscience. "She's with friends in East Grinstead." She hesitated. "Since I'm here, I would like to see once more before I leave the ledgers and the papers concerning Willow Hills. When I was here the first time, I was too upset to go through the estate papers."

"Of course!" Mr. Grimes was eager to comply, and soon she was ensconced in Uncle Butterball's chair with a stack of ledgers and legal documents in front of her. "Mr. Holland has taken care of your father's affairs for many years. I'm sure you'll find all the accounts in order, Miss Shaw," Mr. Grimes added before closing the door. "Just call me if you need any help."

Time passed quickly as she scanned the accounts. There had been a steady loss of revenue over the last thirty years. After her father's death, the decline had become an avalanche. Reggie had sold off art, furniture, and land. He had finally mortgaged what remained of the estate. But why? To support his cause, or his gambling? Bryony furrowed her brows grimly. It had to be the cause. He had never been a serious gambler—or had he changed in the two years she had been away? She wished she had never gone to France.

She flipped through a stack of personal letters, yellowed sheets covered with her father's handwriting. There was a stack bearing Reggie's signature, and she read them. Mr. Holland must have been distressed by Reggie's constant demands to liquidate more funds. A sigh fluttered deeply in her chest as she read the last letter, written shortly before her twin's death.

Her gaze flew over the few lines telling about the harvest, the weather, the latest horse races. It was the postscript at the bottom of the page that captured her attention. Her heart constricted in pain and sorrow as she read her own name in his crabbed hand: "Ask Bryony if she remembers one hundred steps to the north, five steps to the east, ten steps to the west. Tell her it's imperative that she remembers!"

Thoughtfully she stared at the crackling flames in the marble fireplace. She vaguely recalled a game they used to play as children, but what was it? Had he hidden something that she needed to find? The message eluded her. The fact that it was a secret message to her was clear. Obviously Mr. Holland had forgotten to tell her.

Mr. Grimes broke off her thoughts by entering the room and introducing the magistrate, Mr. Willoughby. Leaving out her suspicions that someone was determined to kill her, she spent half an hour answering his questions about the villain with the wooden leg. Stating that the man had tried to steal her purse, she steered the magistrate away from questions about her business in the area. Under no circumstances did she want to talk about her meetings with Jacobite sympathizers.

When the magistrate finally left, she addressed Mr. Grimes. "I cannot thank you enough. You've been most helpful."

After placing Reggie's letter in her handbag, she left the law offices. Walking to her carriage, she pondered Reggie's message to her. What did the words mean? What could he have hidden? The map to the gold? No, it had burned in the fire.

To jog her memory, she would have to return to her ancestral home located outside East Grinstead, five miles east of Crawley.

Chapter 17

The man shoved back his brocade-covered armchair in anger and shouted, "You failed?" He stalked to the window, pushed the curtain aside, and looked outside. The day was the best autumn could offer, golden warm sunshine, piercing blue skies, colorful leaves winking in the light breeze. He turned to the scar-faced man in the brown coat and the man with a mop of white hair. "And where is Woody?" he asked ominously.

"We don't know, guv. He clung to Miss Shaw's carriage as she escaped and hasn't been seen since.

"You had explicit orders to deal with her before returning here," he spat, and pointed a sharply honed paper knife at the villains' perspiring faces. "How could you fail to put fear in one defenseless woman?" he raged.

"There were only two of us—Woody and me," explained the scar-faced man. He pointed a thumb at his companion. "He tried unsuccessfully to locate her protector."

Mumbling and swearing, their employer paced the floor, the sausage curls of his wig losing their starched precision. He jabbed the knife-edge against the scar-faced man's throat. A thin line of blood showed on the man's doughlike skin.

"Miss Shaw has a friend, sir." He wrung his hands in distress and dared to add, "She has that mysterious protector. It might be important to eliminate him, if you're going to get rid of Miss Shaw."

The man with the wig tested the edge of the knife with

his thumb. "I hired you because you're supposed to know how to deal with a situation like this. You're an experienced hunter."

He shook his head and mopped his brow. "I've never met a more determined lady. To get her, you'll have to use other means, sir."

Cold eyes bored into him, and he cringed. "Dare you give me advice?" the bewigged man snarled.

"In this case, yes, sir. Miss Shaw will stop at nothing now to find out the truth. You might have to take stronger measures to stop her." He pointed significantly at the paper knife.

Even the warm morning sunlight could not hide the devastation of Bryony's home. Willow Hills was just as depressing as she remembered it from her first visit after it burned. Soaked with rain, the charred timbers looked blacker than ever. The collapsed walls and sprouting weeds around the foundation were a bleak reminder that, once nature had taken over completely, her ancestral home would be nothing but a memory. And then the memory, too, would be lost in the hazy recesses of time.

"Stay with the carriage until I return," she ordered Jules and Clover.

"I can't speak wi' th' bloomin' Frog," Clover said, peeved.

"To pass the time, Jules can teach you French."

"Aw, m'lady, 'tis worse than death!"

Death. Reggie had died here. Bryony swallowed hard against her tears, her throat dry with an ache that would not subside.

"No more complaints, please," she said as she headed toward the ruins.

Shards of porcelain cracked under her shoes, and she bent to pick up the base of a figurine, a Dresden shepherdess her mother had cherished. The bits and pieces of Bryony's life strewn haphazardly about and buried in the deep grass were all that was left. If Reggie had had a secret, it was buried with the rest.

After taking one last look for familiar objects in the rubble, she hurried off to the chapel, unable to stem her sorrow. The chapel roof had caved in, and fallen timbers barred the entrance. The grass stood tall around the head-stones of the family. There was Father's austere iron cross, his name painted in fresh white letters, while her mother's name on her own cross had faded with time.

And there was Reggie's marker. The last time she was here, Bryony had had erected a marble angel with spread wings. Tears swam in her eyes. The grave was too bleak a reminder of her loss, and she failed to suppress her sorrow. Sobbing wildly, she fell to her knees on the slight mound.

Had Reggie really been murdered? The suspicion assailed her until she thought she would burst. As if sleep-walking, she stumbled among the mossy tombstones of her grandparents and great-grandfather. With shaking fingers, she picked a few of the asters and late-blooming roses that grew wild against the chapel wall.

She tucked them and the shattered Dresden figurine at the head of Reggie's grave. "If there is a way, I swear I will find out what really happened the night of your death," she said in a thready voice, staring into the distance as if expecting to see Reggie himself among the trees. She clasped her hands and prayed, "Dear God, if there is any justice in this world, please let me find Reggie's murderer."

Yet she did not feel any easing of the pain in her heart. It was as if she had died. Her hands were icy, her breath coming in short, shallow gasps, but she noticed nothing as numbness spread through her body.

Her vision blurred with tears, she stared emptily at the singed trees behind the graveyard. Something moved there, among the trees.

She had to rub her eyes to comprehend that she wasn't seeing a vision. A man in a gray coat and a black cloak was walking slowly toward her, a large tricorne shading his face.

Fear gripped her, and she stumbled backward, a cry of terror bursting forth.

"Bryony! What is the matter?" came Jack's warm voice.

Her legs gave way, and she crumpled, but before hitting the ground, she sensed Jack's arms catching her. The familiar scent of him, of virility and fresh air, enfolded her and she could relax. In silence she lay in his arms with closed eyes, letting his presence seep into her consciousness. Gradually she grew calm, his gentle hand on her hair soothing her frayed nerves.

"Dearest Brye, what has happened to you? You look like a shadow of yourself," he whispered. When she couldn't answer, he continued, "I got your message from the stableboy at The Star in Alfriston and rode all night to Crawley, all the while wondering why you had left without me." Pressing his cheek against her hair, he whispered, "I was frightened as I've never been frightened before. I thought you had left me for good." He groaned and held her closer.

She wished she could wipe the scowl off his dear face. Dark circles surrounded his eyes, and his beard was unkempt, in desperate need of a trimming. "I worried you might sail off to the West Indies, once you got back to Plymouth," was all she could think to say.

"So little faith! I followed you to Mr. Holland's law office in Crawley, and the clerk told me you had traveled here to visit your brother's grave one last time before returning to France."

"He was telling the truth." She had regained her strength but was loath to leave the haven of his embrace. "I will return to France shortly, to trace Lord Bentworth. He must be responsible for Reggie's death. There is another man who might give me some answers, the Reverend Augustus Cleaves, but I don't suspect him. He's an old friend of the family and would never have killed Reggie.' Then she told Jack everything that had transpired from the moment they had separated in Alfriston.

When he heard about the villains' most recent attempt on her life, his rage knew no bounds. "I would not have hesitated to finish them off," he said savagely.

"I don't think I could live with a man's life on my conscience," said Bryony. "We rendered one of the villains harmless and sent him to the gaol."

Jack frowned darkly. "I shiver when I imagine what could have happened to you. I should never have left you alone."

"I was sure Nigel had apprehended the villains in Seaford, but they must have slipped away. I'm certain he tried." She traced the sharp bridge of Jack's nose. "And your ship, is it ready to sail?" She waited nervously for his answer.

He had a far away look on his face and answered automatically. "A few more days. Some of the sails needed to be replaced. And the tarring of the hull wasn't completed."

"A few precious days," she repeated, and struggled out of his arms. "What will you do now? Explore the country further?"

He studied her thoughtfully. "Would you mind if I follow you? Your road is a dangerous one, and I would be unable to relax not knowing what was happening to you. I'll be your unofficial guardian angel, if you'll let me."

A warm glow of happiness suffused her. "You will accompany me to France then? We could reach the coast by tonight if we ride hard."

He seemed to ponder the words. "Is it really necessary to go to France? The answers you're seeking must be found in England."

"I have to confront Lord Bentworth. He was the last one to see Reggie alive, and he had enough reason to kill my brother. With Willow Hills mortgaged and worthless, he might have realized that Reggie would be unable to pay his gambling debt."

"Still, why would he want the estate to burn down? There surely were antiques and art worth a great deal inside," Jack argued.

"Reggie sold them all. And the fire could have been an accident." Stepping away from him to think, she snapped off a twig from a fallen branch and whipped the knee-high grass with it. She could find no solutions, nothing but frustration.

"I wish I knew what kind of person Lord Bentworth really is," she said with a heavy sigh. "I suppose I must believe the description I received from the innkeeper at Alfriston. It coincides with what Mr. Forrester and Mr. Bench told me. Lord Bentworth is supposed to be a cold, overbearing sort of fellow whom people avoid. It as almost as if the local people were afraid to talk about him.''

''You shouldn't listen to the gossips. They love to exaggerate,'' he said, standing closely behind her. ''Lovely one, I wish you would forget this whole idea. Your desire for vengeance is destroying you, don't you see?''

She studied him, her eyes dark with pain. ''Put yourself in my situation. If you had a twin brother whom you loved more than life itself, and he died under strange circumstances, wouldn't you want to know what happened to him?''

He nodded an smiled wryly. ''You're right, of course. But it pains me to look into your face and see such sorrow, and such—well, determination to seek revenge. You're worn to a shade. And I don't like the idea of you racing off to France just to confront some aristocrat who will only deny that he ever knew your brother.'' He caressed her cheek. ''I don't want to see your face ravaged with more despair.''

She flung herself into his arms and he held her tightly. ''Jack, I'm so happy that you're here,'' she said, her voice muffled against his coat. ''I was frightened.'' She tilted her head back and glanced into his face. His deep-set eyes were warm, hypnotic, and for the first time she could meet his gaze without feeling like a trapped rabbit longing to escape.

They melted into each other, their love so precious and so full that neither dared to breathe lest the perfection should evaporate.

He gripped her hand convulsively and held it so tight she almost had to protest. Glancing up into the glittering sunlight playing in the leaves, he said, ''With the soul of your brother as my witness, I hereby pledge you my love, and maybe one day . . .'' He paused and swallowed hard. ''Maybe one day I can pledge you my life.''

He looked so solemn that Bryony wanted to giggle. Laughter bubbled through her from a well deep within her heart, a happiness that spread like a shimmering rainbow until her entire being was deliciously weightless.

''Come, I want to show you my favorite spot in the garden. Fortunately, it wasn't touched by the fire,'' she explained, and took him by the hand. "As a child, I would invite only my very best friends to my secret hideout."

He smiled and followed her. "I'm honored," he said, and kissed her hand.

She led him through the charred park on the south side of the estate, through the spinney behind the burned-down stables. The lawn on the west side sloped down to a stream swollen with rainwater. The sunshine seemed to cast handfuls of diamonds on the rushing water, and mallards squawked in a lagoon where the stream made a sudden turn. The woods opened up to reveal a circular, white-painted folly, entirely overgrown by hops, the leaves brilliantly red against the walls. On the upper part of the walls, glass panes glinted through the leaves. Slate shingles formed a cone-shaped roof.

Bryony spread her arms. "Look, isn't it just like a fairy-tale house with the carved ornamentation of the eaves and the golden ball on the roof?"

Jack smiled and placed his arm around her shoulders. " 'Tis lovely. Can we go inside?"

Fueled by her happiness, she ran before him along the flagstone path, reliving the sweet days of her childhood.

The air in the folly was slightly musty, but the worn cushions lining the benches were dry. An old wooden box still contained two of her old dolls, and she touched them reverently. "Minnie and Mrs. Jones." She laughed at her feelings of nostalgia. "This was my happy place, and my dolls are still waiting for me."

"Well, I suppose they're delighted that you're here at last." He held out his arms. "Come here, lovely one. You're too old to play with dolls." He flicked the tip of her nose. "You're old enough to play with a life-sized male doll now."

It was the most natural thing in the world to float into his arms. "Is it really possible to be both truly happy and filled with sorrow at the same time?"

He stroked her hair. "Is that what you feel?"

She nodded. "I miss Reggie terribly, but I'm so happy that I met you. If the awful things hadn't happened, I wouldn't—"

"Shhh, let's not analyze what happened. You have to learn to live with your sorrow as well as with your joy."

"Please make love to me," she whispered, standing on tiptoe and clasping his face between her hands. "Now." Her lips quirked upward in a teasing smile. "See, I'm begging you. You said I had to beg before you'd make love to me."

He groaned. "What an idiot I was then."

"It wasn't very long ago," she reminded him, "but it seems like a lifetime."

"It *is* a lifetime. I was only half alive until I met you."

"Strange, but I was just about to say the same thing," she said, her face suffused with pleasure.

The next moment he had claimed her lips. She boldly let him worship the soft recesses of her mouth, then every inch of her face, ears, and neck. She sensed when the fire ignited within him, and this time she could respond measure for measure. Luxuriating in the erotic current that pulsed at the touch of his lips on her skin, she arched back so that he could cover the exposed skin above her decolletage with a trail of intoxicating kisses.

The air was still and warm outside, but their love stirred up a storm within them, so strong that Bryony thought the whole world must be swept into the maelstrom of their emotions.

Jack's hands moved to the laces of her bodice. In what appeared to be one single caress he undid them, and her bodice fell open. As tenderly as he would hold a newborn child, he cupped her breasts and stroked his thumbs over each crest until she thought she would burst with enchantment.

"To touch you is better than to drink the headiest of champagnes," he whispered, his eyes dark and hot. "The very essence of you is flowing through my veins at this very moment."

"Your magician's hands play havoc with every inch of my skin," she breathed, finally daring to return his compliment. The words fell easily from her tongue, and she thought of many more compliments she wanted to give him, precious pearls strung on a solid thread of love. But not now; now, she had to discover every nuance of his love, gather memories into her heart, and give back caress for caress.

She undid the buttons of his waistcoat, opened the plain white shirt, and buried her fingers in the thick curls on his chest. To touch his springy hair made her feel warm and heavy inside. Her heartbeat accelerated until she could scarcely breathe.

Then her legs wanted to give out for the sheer joy of feeling his strong arms around her.

He managed to unfasten the waistband of her panniers, and they fell down around her ankles, as did her rumpled velvet overskirt, her underskirt, and the triple layers of petticoats. She stood before him clad only in her thin shift.

Nibbling at her earlobe, he slid his hands from her breasts down to her waist, over her slim hips to her firm buttocks.

"Ah, I've longed so much to touch you here. But had I as much as dared to pinch your erotic backside, you would have knocked me out with your portmanteau—or worse still, your net bag."

His eyes danced as he lifted the heavy bag from the bench and dropped it to the floor. "What do you have in here? Boulders?"

"You—you Mr. Glib!" she admonished, gripping the lapels of his coat. "Much worse than that—a keg of blackpowder."

He made a show of fright. "Blackpowder? We don't need it. Our love will blow us to smithereens." He swept his cloak across the cushions of the bench, and before she knew what was happening, he lifted her up and laid her down on the cloak. Her shift had slid up over her thighs to reveal the core of her femininity to his eyes. He drew in his breath sharply, feasting on the sight. "Ahhh," he sighed as he unbuckled his sword and dragged off his clothes. He pulled the shift over her head and threw himself on top of her, skin pressed to skin.

"Oh, Bryony, I need you. You don't know how much," he rasped against her neck. "Without you, I'm the loneliest man in the world.'

She had seen him splendidly naked once beside the river, but the feel of his skin covering hers came as a sweet shock. It was hot and covered with hair; he was like a blanket of forceful energy that wrapped around her soft body, demanding her complete surrender.

It must have been the moment his legs curled around hers and his arms trapped her against him that she ceased to think coherently. His fingers traced the outline of her face, and his tongue explored her neck, sending the sweetest, most intoxicating sensations through her. She sighed in delight as his lips found her nipples, teasing them until they grew turgid and sensitive. Pleasure swirled through her as he sucked gently. His hands fanned every flame to life, making her open to the enchantment he was conjuring up from the depths of her body. He cautiously ran a finger in the nest between her legs, as if testing the potential for pleasure in this uncharted spot. As she moaned against his neck, he chuckled and readied her for his entry by making slow circular movements, until she could do nothing but beg him for release. His eyes glowed with a consuming fire as he was absorbed in her mounting ecstasy.

As he thrust slowly into her, tears quivered in the corners of his eyes. "I never dreamed love could be so sweet, so healing," he forced out between gasps of pleasure.

She reached up and took his lips between her own, and prayed that the perfect moment would last forever. His heavy thrusts churned up a roaring tidal wave of rapture that started at the mysterious depths of her being and were amplified with every thrust, until she could breathe no more. Every fiber of her body quivered in his arms as his last frenzied thrusts pushed her across the sea of ecstasy to the opposite shore, where peace filled her.

When she opened her eyes, she found him on the same peaceful shore, and they laughed together.

Chapter 18

They spent the rest of the day blissfully exploring each other's bodies, bringing each other to new heights of ecstasy. When evening came, they decided to stay overnight in the folly. Jack went to collect the rugs from Bryony's carriage. He awakened Jules and Clover, gave them money for a hot meal and a bed, and sent them off to East Grinstead.

Jack made a mattress by putting the cushions side by side on the floor of the folly. He spread his cloak over the cushions and used the rugs as blankets. Their love nest was cozy and warm.

The night was a wonder of starlight and soft breezes.

And love.

For the first time Bryony felt whole, satisfied with happiness. Their love was right. They could bathe in each other's souls as easily as they found ecstasy in each other's arms. Jack knew exactly how to please her, and she obviously made him very happy. That knowledge gave her immense pleasure. Little Bryony Shaw, Reggie Shaw's shadow, had the power to please and fulfill another human being. She had never dreamed that she would meet a man who would suit her so perfectly, who would match her every mood, who would understand her every thought. No matter where Jack had come from, who he was or where he was going, the knowledge that he was right for her had been firmly etched into her mind.

After a night of lovemaking, they fell into exhausted sleep at the darkest hour, just before dawn.

* * *

When Bryony awakened the following morning, she stretched blissfully, every inch of her bursting with love. Drowsily, she reached for Jack beside her, but her hand touched only air. Aghast, she turned over to look for him. He was gone.

His cloak was still beneath her and was heavily creased where he had slept. Where had he gone without telling her? The agony of uncertainty gripped her, and, wrapping one of the rugs around her nakedness, she opened the door to the folly and stepped outside.

The park was shrouded in dense fog, the trees' ghostly arms reaching out to her in the milky light. She shuddered and tried to locate Jack's familiar form in the silently floating veils. "Jack?" she called, her voice barely more than a croak.

The silence was oppressive, closing in on her when she realized that she was completely alone. Returning inside, she found that Jack's clothes were all gone. Except for her sweetly aching body, there was no sign that he had spent the night with her.

Her happiness was being destroyed by a nagging doubt, a creeping fear. Why had he left her? She dragged on her clothes; with every garment she put on, she felt as if she was gliding farther away from Jack and what they had shared. She did not regret one minute of the night she had spent in his arms, but now it seemed to have had happened in another lifetime.

She dragged her cloak around her and, sweeping Jack's cloak over her arm, left the folly. She had no reason to fear the fog since she knew every path and stone of the park, yet she hesitated before letting the mist devour her.

Wet, cold air was creeping across the ground, swirling around her ankles. She called Jack's name as she walked. Burned tree stumps, rising abruptly from the fog along the path, were a ghastly reminder of past terrors.

She made her way across the overgrown graveyard, stopping momentarily to touch her brother's tombstone. The asters she had placed at its base on the previous day were already wilting. She knelt on the soggy ground and prayed, her eyes closed and her head bent as she emptied the sorrow from her heart. As her concentration on the prayer slowly evaporated, she became aware of something moving through the grass behind her, a sudden grind of metal against rock, wheezy breathing . . .

A blinding pain struck her from behind.

Her head exploded in a kaleidoscope of colors, and pain echoed like a gong in her ears until merciful darkness closed in.

Her throat rasped with thirst, her head ached like an open wound, her body was heavier than lead and icy cold. She didn't want to open her eyes, but something prodded her to do so. Urgency nibbled at her mind like a tireless rodent.

Groping for support, she encountered bare earth. She dug her nails into it and heaved herself up to lean on her elbows. Her eyes were gritty, but the dim light in the building did not hurt them.

Where was she? Spears of red-hot pain shot up from her neck as she turned her head. Almost immediately she recognized the woodshed, one of the few buildings that had not been totally demolished in the fire. The roof would soon cave in, though, if the lopsided angle of the beams was any indication. Bending her knees, she managed to push herself into a sitting position. With her forehead pressed against her knees, she waited until her nausea had subsided before she looked around.

She had no idea what she was doing in the woodshed at Willow Hills, but she knew something terrible was lurking outside. She feared the very air which was filled with a foul stench, still and foreboding.

As her head cleared, her determination and anger grew: she would face, and fight, whatever danger threatened her.

But her terror was so strong it made every nerve in her shiver so that she could barley function. Her heart seemed to have lodged in her throat, preventing her from breathing.

Ever so slowly, she gained some control over her fear and dared to examine her surroundings. Some horror surely awaited her, but the shock almost knocked her over when she saw the man stretched out beside her.

He was dead, his eyes staring vacantly at her, an echo of unspeakable fear in the empty depths.

She recognized the Reverend Augustus Cleaves of Battle, an old man of whom, as a child, she had been very fond. An old friend of her father's, and a godfather to her older brother, August, who had died in infancy, Reverend Cleaves had always brought her sweets.

The reverend had been the last name on her list of Jacobite sympathizers. Had his political views brought about his death?

Bryony could not bring herself to touch the corpse, which was fully dressed in a dark coat, a starched collar, and an austere horsehair wig that was now tilted over his ear. The black cloth of his coat showed darker stains in several places, and Bryony didn't have to look closer to know it was blood.

Silent tears coursed down her cheeks, and she began to crawl toward the exit, inch by inch. She had to get away. When she reached the door, she extended her trembling hand toward the knob. As she struggled to turn it, she found that the door was locked.

Moaning in defeat, she slumped against the wall. From the perimeter of her vision, she saw that a folded and sealed note was clamped between the dead man's fingers.

Indecisively, she stared at the note for several minutes before she gathered the nerve to crawl back and pull the paper from his stiff grip. It came away easily enough, as if it had been placed there long after the reverend was dead. With shaking hands, she unfolded the note and read: "If you want to stay alive, stop your investigation into your brother's death immediately, or there will be witnesses to swear that you killed this man. Do you want to hang like a common murderer?"

A cold shiver rustled along her spine. Her teeth chattered with shock and misery, and she couldn't seem to control the trembling of her limbs. Frozen with shock and fear, she stared emptily into the gloom of the shed. She had no idea how much time passed, but gradually the light slanting through the square, windowless holes in the walls changed angle and grew stronger.

The sound was low at first. A few minutes later it came

again, closer now. Someone was shouting among the trees.
"Bryony? Where are you?"

Her name echoed in her empty mind and stirred her out
of her shock long enough to make her reach trembling
fingers toward the locked door. "Help," she uttered in a
weak whisper.

"Bryony, answer me!" The sound was closer, stronger.
She recognized Jack's voice, and something in her heart
wiggled, struggling to get free. It jogged her out of her
state of numb horror, and she crawled toward the door.
"Here!" she cried.

The door crashed open, and there stood Jack, filling the
shed with life. Tears streaming down her face, Bryony
held out her arms, and he swept her up, holding her fiercely
against his chest.

"Darling Bryony, you frightened me! Why did you leave
the folly?" His voice was gravelly with worry and anger.

"You left without saying a word," she breathed, and
pounded weakly on his chest. "Why? I've never been more
hurt."

His eyes were dark and mercurial. "I rode into East
Grinstead for some food. There I met with Jules and Clover. I wanted to serve you breakfast in bed. I even bought
a bottle of champagne to celebrate our first morning together."

Without answering, she pointed at the corpse. She could
not bear to look at the dead man again, so she buried her
face in her hands. Jack swore and hurried to examine the
sad remains of the Reverend Cleaves.

"He has been dead for days, I'd say," he muttered.
"How did you come across him?"

Bryony told him, and he immediately inspected the lump
on the back of her head, the note in her hand. "This is
terrible! I wish I had the blackguard's throat between my
fingers," he exclaimed after reading the note.

Two red spots of anger glowed on his cheeks, and there
was deep worry in his eyes as he said, "I won't sleep a
wink until you've ended your investigation. Your precious
life is in danger, and I don't know what I'd do if something
happened to you."

Bryony took a deep breath and pulled her sleeve across

her wet eyes. "This man used to be an old friend of the family."

"We'll have to notify the authorities," he said, rubbing his beard thoughtfully. He took one hard look at Bryony and added, "I take it nothing will stop you from continuing your investigation?"

She shook her head. "I will never know a moment's peace until I discover the truth."

"Then I will help you. By God, if it came to that, I'd give my life for yours. But we must catch the villain before he makes another attempt." With a groan, he pulled her to him. "I cannot bear to see you so distraught."

"We have to deal with the body."

"Of course, but if you contact the law in person, they'll keep you as main suspect in this murder, little one." He sighed. "No, I'll handle it somehow. Let's get Clover."

She had forgotten her rascally young companion. "Did he come back with you?"

"Yes, I left him at the stream feeding bread to the mallards. If I know the varmint right, he'd fed our entire ration to the birds," Jack added, in a feeble attempt to lighten the mood.

'Let's find him." Bryony staggered outside and drew great gulps of fresh air into her lungs. But she could not wipe away the indelible memories of the man on the floor inside. She crumpled the note she had found in the reverend's hand and tossed it into the bushes beside the shed. "Where is Jules?"

"At the smithy in East Grinstead. One of your horses needed a new shoe."

"I hope it'll be ready for my trip to France." As she turned to Jack, determination hardened her eyes. "Will you accompany me to Paris? I cannot rest until I have confronted Lord Bentworth. I have a feeling that once I find Reggie's murderer, I will also find the reverend's killer."

Jack held her arm as they traversed the park, his grip slowing her progress. "How can you be so sure that Bentworth is the culprit?"

"It's the most likely possibility I have."

"Any one of the other cardplayers could have killed your brother," he argued, sounding tired.

"What was their motive? Lord Bentworth wanted the debt paid, and when Reggie could not comply, he killed him."

Jack laughed. "That reasoning is very thin, and you know it."

Overcome by anger and frustration, Bryony wanted to slap him. "Why do you argue at every turn? You can't stop me from going to Paris."

He gave her a long measuring glance and shook his head. "Stubborn girl!"

His resistance sparked a new suspicion in her. Was *he* somehow involved? Tendrils of fear floated through her as she recalled everything that had happened between them since the first day they met.

Jack had been nearby during every attack on her life. And she had to admit it, she didn't know much about his past. Yet her heart trusted him, always had, even at his most evasive turns.

Nevertheless, doubt poisoned her blood, tainting her love. Perhaps their night of passion had been too good to be true. She had never met anyone who lived in a perfectly loving relationship. Why should she be any exception?

As they left Willow Hills, Bryony realized she had completely forgotten her original reason for coming—to search for a clue to the riddle in Reggie's last letter to Uncle Butterball.

Chapter 19

At least Jack had told the truth about his trip into East Grinstead. Beside Clover at the stream waited a well-filled basket. There was a cured ham; cheese; half a loaf of bread; and kedgeree, a dish of fish, boiled rice, and eggs. The neck of a bottle of champagne rose above the rim of the basket.

Clover munched on a piece of bread and threw crumbs to the ducks. "Yer takin' yer good ol' time, lettin' a good cove starve t' death," he admonished them.

"I thought this would be a romantic breakfast *a deux,*" Bryony said in an undertone to Jack, but the teasing words lay brittle on her tongue.

"This isn't the right moment to celebrate," Jack said as he hoisted the bottle, "but you need a nip of something to thaw the chill out of your limbs."

Guilt nagged at her for suspecting Jack of treachery. Worry etched his features, as if he were under some great strain. He concentrated on pouring the champagne, but his gaze had penetrated her soul only moments before, and doubtlessly he'd read her suspicions.

"How is your head?" he inquired.

"Much better." She clasped her hands tightly together, aiming to still the turmoil within her. "I cannot comprehend how 'tis possible to travel from the extreme of happiness to the pits of terror in a matter of seconds."

He held the glass toward her. "Drink up. 'Twill dull the ache. Only time will soften the horrible blow." He smiled and dragged his knuckles lightly across her cheek.

"You're the bravest woman I've ever met, and the most fascinating."

"Twaddle! Don't embarrass me," Bryony chided, but she could not help smiling. Already his presence was beginning to soothe her pain.

"I could go on for days telling you just how much you please me."

Bryony drank the cool champagne. "We don't have time for that. France awaits us."

"I still don't see why you want to travel to France on what must be a mission of futility and sheer pigheadedness."

She returned the glass to the basket with unnecessary force. "I don't expect you to share my beliefs, but after talking to all the cardplayers, except the Reverend Cleaves, I have formed the opinion that perhaps Lord Bentworth is guilty of murdering Reggie. It's highly likely."

Jack pointed toward the shed beyond the woods. "How do you explain this murder? Did Bentworth commit this long-range?"

" 'Tis easy for you to be flippant," Bryony snapped. "You did not speak with any of the cardplayers, so you don't know what they told me."

He pinched his lips together, and a scowl darkened his brow.

As if sensing the mounting tension, Clover studied them. "When are we goin' t' France?" he asked.

Bryony realized she had no choice but to take the boy with her. "Today. But first we have to fetch Jules and the carriage." She turned to Jack. "If the carriage is at the smithy, how do we get back to East Grinstead?"

"I hired two horses. I hope you know how to ride."

"Crikey, guv!" said Clover. "Ye shoulda seen 'er drivin' th' team. She 'as a dab 'and wi' 'osses."

"A lady to her fingertips," Jack commented, and Bryony couldn't tell whether he meant it as a compliment or a slur. She was sensitive and overwrought. Regretting her uncharitable thoughts, she touched Jack's cheek. Sweetness edged with doubt swelled within her. He looked pale and tired suddenly, all animation gone from his eyes.

Jack lifted Clover up behind Bryony on her horse, a

dappled gray, then stepped into the stirrup of his own mount. "Let's go," he said with an audible sigh.

As they rode into East Grinstead and up its high street, Bryony noticed her large black carriage parked outside the smithy. She slid from her horse and asked Jack to wait while she rushed inside to inquire about the horse.

Jack offered to inform the authorities about the reverend's corpse. "You'd better stay out of sight," he warned.

After much arguing, he finally obeyed Clover's loud demand that they ride together to the square at the end of the street, where a group of puppeteers had set up their Punch and Judy show, which was part of the autumn fair.

Bryony hesitated on the steps of the smithy, glancing at their retreating forms, the proud man and the ragamuffin boy. More often than not, there was a strain between the two, and she wished Jack would fully accept the boy. She suspected that Clover reminded Jack of his own difficult childhood. Bittersweet love squeezed her heart. She had begun to think about Jack and Clover as her new family. But Jack had not promised her a future. And where did Clover belong in this world?

She entered the smithy. The soot-streaked walls resembled a dark cave. The blacksmith's sledge hammer shot sparks in all directions as it connected with the red-hot iron on the anvil. The clanging was deafening.

Bryony glanced around the dim room. There was no sign of Jules. To her surprise, she found herself standing eye to eye with Dudley Bench.

"Oh, good morning," she greeted him, confused. Under his close scrutiny, fear stirred in the pit of her stomach, and her muscles tensed. "I need to speak with the blacksmith."

"Yes, yes indeed," Bench said distractedly. "My horse lost a shoe. Business as usual."

"I see. Well, I didn't know you had business in East Grinstead." She wished she had her fan to hide her face from his rude stare.

"I'm visiting a solicitor. We're working on the same case." He took a step closer to her, looking like a large crow in his charcoal-gray cloak with black frogging.

Bryony took a step back.

"Don't be afraid," he murmured. "Perhaps I chastised you too harshly the other day, but you must understand that I worry about my family. In this situation—"

"Please say no more. Your secret is safe with me." Bryony felt a wild urge to run. She turned and lifted her skirts to walk down the steps, but his next words halted her.

"I arrived here two nights ago and stayed at The Swan. Nice hostelry, that. Anyway, I was surprised to run into Lord Bentworth. He was in France for several weeks, and when I asked his errand in East Grinstead, he stated a pressing business matter." Bench rubbed his hollow cheek. "Had I but known that you were going to arrive here today, I would have asked him to meet you. Perhaps you could have found the clues you need." He arched an eyebrow meaningfully. "However, he said he was returning to France today. He's there in a diplomatic capacity, trying to negotiate peace." Mr. Bench laughed evilly. "The government should know his *true* leanings."

Bryony nodded automatically. If she made haste, she might catch up with Lord Bentworth before he left English soil. "When exactly did he leave East Grinstead?" she asked.

"Oh, perhaps yesterday. He said he had one more matter to see to before he left the country."

Killing the reverend! Bryony thought. Or perhaps Lord Bentworth's last business matter was to snuff out someone else's life, Nigel's, perhaps. Or this fellow Bench's. Cold shivers of fear rippled through her. She had to warn them. None of them was safe now. She was about to tell Mr. Bench of the reverend's fate when the blacksmith stopped hammering and greeted her.

"Are ye Miss Shaw? That blasted Frenchie said ye'd be comin' 'ere, if I understood his gibberish rightly."

"Yes, is my horse shod?"

"O' course." He ushered her into the adjoining stable to her horses. "They're eatin' all me oats an' 'ay, missy."

"Where is my coachman?"

"Th' Frog? I don't know. Disappeared shortly arter 'e dropped orf th' 'oss. At th' fair, I'll lay. Ever' body's at th' fair."

"Very well, I will find him before I settle with you."

"Don't delay, missy," he said darkly. "Yer 'osses eat too much."

As she left the smithy, she again ran into Mr. Bench outside.

"I didn't have a chance to say good-bye," he said, and swept off his hat.

Bryony hesitated and glanced along the empty street. Mr. Bench's presence made her stomach heave with unease. "I—I ought to warn you," she said, "but I'm afraid you might not believe me."

"Believe what, Miss Shaw?"

"This morning I found a corpse at the ruins of Willow Hills. It was the remains of Reverend Cleaves." She dragged air into her lungs. "Someone murdered him and placed him there with a warning note that I should cease my investigation into Reginald's death, or else I would be blamed for Cleaves's death."

She studied Mr. Bench's face for any change of expression, but he didn't even lift an eyebrow. "That is the most harebrained story I've ever heard. What are you implying, Miss Shaw?"

"Don't you see? You may be the next victim. The reverend was a friend of yours, and a"—she lowered her voice—"a Jacobite."

He laughed, a dry, raspy sound. "Your imagination is running amok, m'dear. It's unfortunate that Cleaves died. He must have been attacked by highwaymen."

Bryony stared at him in disbelief. "Highwaymen wouldn't warn me to stay away. They wouldn't know me."

He paled. "This is nonsense." He jumped into his carriage and ordered the coachman to wield the whip.

"I warned you," Bryony called after him, then heaved a great sigh. She'd done her best.

East Grinstead, the town nearest to Bryony's ancestral home, was located at the top of a hill, with buildings spreading downward on all sides. At the crest, Bryony gazed at Ashdown Forest below, an impenetrable thicket of ancient trees. She remembered her governess telling her that in ancient times East Grinstead would have been called a clearing, a *green stede* in the forest.

Turning slowly, she observed the familiar buildings of her childhood—the church dedicated to St. Swithin; Sackville College, a fine Jacobean house; and the many timber-framed shops and offices that lined the streets.

At the square she looked for Jack and Clover in the crowd, but they were nowhere to be seen. She walked among farmers dressed in dark frieze, matrons in washed and starched aprons, colorful kerchiefs tied around their necks. Children clustered around a dancing pony with a monkey on its back. Delight radiated from the their faces, and they cheered as the monkey made a somersault. Clover was not among them. Neither could Bryony see Jules or Jack. She sauntered along a row of horses for sale, and passed the stalls of fruit and sweets, but the men were still nowhere in sight.

The sunlight was beginning to slant as the afternoon wore on. Fatigued and angry, she circled the square once more. Where were they? She was already beginning to tire of the clamor of the fair and the young men's lewd suggestions. She had to get away, but where could she go? She had no desire to return to Willow Hills.

She glanced at her watch, which she pulled out of her net bag. Two o'clock. She would not catch up with Lord Bentworth before he left England after all, and it was all Jack's fault! What was keeping him? To get away from the rude stares at the fair, she could go and see Nigel once more, and warn him of the danger. He might be next on the murderer's list.

Either she could ride off to Greymeadows by herself or she could wait for Jack to return. She knew he would argue about her decision to speak with Nigel, just as he had argued about her trip to France, and she had no desire to cross swords with Jack again.

On horseback, she could make a shortcut across the fields and reach Nigel's estate much faster than by carriage. She might even be back before Jack knew she had gone.

Tired of waiting, she set off. After fetching one of the horses at the smithy, she rode down a side street and onto a country lane leading southwest toward Cuckfield. As she entered a band of trees, she regretted her decision to leave

Jack behind. He would storm at her when she returned, and who knew what danger lurked about. She almost turned around, but instead set her lips in a determined line. Shilly-shallying would only weaken her resolve.

The landscape was bathed in a watery light, a sorrowful shimmer, as if the sun was mourning the loss of summer. Dry leaves rattled across the lane, making Bryony's mare dance skittishly. On the horizon loomed a dense bank of pewter-tinted clouds.

Rain was on the way. Bryony set her heels into the flanks of the horse, who took the rapidly approaching stone wall with a flying leap. Nothing had changed much in the two years since she had been gone. She had ridden this road so many times, she could have done it in the dark. Still, this time was different. Or, rather, she was different.

She was no longer an innocent girl who had learned to ride at neck or nothing to keep up with her brother.

She was a woman now. With Jack she had discovered the deepest secret of love, and found there was much more to discover. She was on the brink of life, and now she worried that if her road and Jack's road parted, she would remain forever on the brink.

Important though it was to find out the truth about Reggie, even more urgently she wanted to discover how far Jack was willing to go with her in their burgeoning love.

As the horse sped through woodland and across fields, she breathed the fresh scent of damp earth and decaying leaves. From the crest of a hill, about three miles southwest of East Grinstead, she saw the wrought-iron gates of Greymeadows at a distance, and beyond the alley of poplars, the tall chimneys.

The view spurred her on. A mile later, she rode up the alley. Had it really been only a short time ago that she had driven up this same path, so very concerned about her appearance?

Nigel was home, preparing for a ride. Standing on the impressive front steps of his mansion, he looked splendid in a red riding coat striped across the front with gold braid. White knee breeches hugged his slightly stocky thighs, and the surface of his riding boots vied with the gleam of the diamond in his cravat. Ostrich tips waved in the light breeze along the rim of his tricorne's upturned brim. Powder dusted his tie wig as delicately as confectioner's sugar on a cake.

Bryony looked down at her velvet dress, for the first time noticing the stains, tears, and wrinkles in the fabric. She had been so occupied solving the puzzle of Reggie's death that she had neglected her appearance. The fine wool of her cloak was dull with dust and riddled with tiny holes, and her hair resembled a crow's nest.

Pushing those thoughts away, she waved at Nigel as she let the mare charge all the way up to the steps.

"Bryony, my sweet! What in the world are you doing here? I thought you had returned to France. Have you had an accident?"

"No—no."

"How every lucky I am to see your vibrant face again. Will you ride with me and tell me why you're still in England?"

She nodded. It would be difficult to convince Nigel not to escort her posthaste to Dover and the packet to France. She watched him mount a magnificent black that the groom held at the bottom of the steps. The prospect of riding with him reminded Bryony of the old days, when Reggie had been part of their threesome.

"How are you?" Nigel continued as they cantered side by side down the lane. "You look pale. Why?"

"Because of a blow to my head, I have a thundering headache, but it's bound to subside." She gingerly patted the already receding lump at the back of her head. "I'm here to warn you," she added, then told him about her misfortunes since they had last met in Seaford, deciding at the last moment not to mention her relationship with Jack. Nigel would be shocked and angry if he knew she was traveling alone with a stranger, and she had no desire to argue with him about the impropriety of the situation. "I have, of course, informed the authorities about the reverend's corpse." By keeping Jack a secret, she had to make it sound as if she had taken care of all the details herself. She waved her hand impatiently. "It makes me so angry that the villain had the nerve to kill a kind gentleman like the reverend."

Nigel nodded gravely. "What an awful experience! Had I but known that the ruffians would get away from my men in Seaford, I would not have slept a wink for worrying about you."

"Your men didn't report to you?"

"As far as I know, they are still looking for the villains." His horse shied at the appearance of a rabbit in the lane, and for a moment Nigel lost control of the animal. The black reared and flailed its hooves, frightening the mare.

Bryony had to use all her skill to prevent her horse from bolting before Nigel could calm the stallion.

He mopped his brow with a handkerchief. "That was unforgivable! I'm so sorry."

"Not your fault. I'm followed by a curse. Everywhere I go, accidents are drawn to me like iron filaments to a magnet. By the way, I delivered one of the villains to the gaol in Crawley." She went on to tell him about that episode.

His face darkened further, just like the sky. "I ought to tear those villains limb for limb."

"How hideous! The law will deal with the one we caught." She glanced cautiously at Nigel. "You look overly tired, Nigel. How are you, really?"

"Thank you for your concern, sweet Bryony." He sighed. "I've been having financial difficulties. My ironworks aren't producing the way they used to, and the crops were smaller than expected."

"I'm sorry to hear that. Reggie must have been in the same predicament."

"Yes, I believe he was. The management of Willow Hills was too much for him, unfortunately." His voice took on a cheerful tone as he changed the subject. "I've had my eyes on a wonderful Rubens painting." His face was miraculously transformed as he spoke about it. "The colors are so clear and translucent, like pure light." He gave her a sly look. "The subject matter of the painting is a trifle risqué for gently bred ladies like yourself, but the artistry is outstanding."

"Sounds interesting," Bryony murmured, "but I can't say I have as burning an interest in art as you do."

"I'm about to go up to London and purchase it. I have to add it to my collection." He smiled indulgently. "If you weren't about to return to France, I would ask you to accompany me."

"Thank you, but 'tisn't possible. I still haven't found the truth about Reggie's death, so I will spend my remaining days in England investigating."

"You're a very determined young lady." His voice held an edge of disapproval.

She considered showing Nigel Reggie's letter with the cryptic message, but refrained since the clue might mean nothing to him. Instead she asked, "Did you and Reggie ever have some sort of secret hiding place when you were children?"

He rubbed his chin thoughtfully. "As a matter of fact, we often played in the stables at Willow Hills and stashed a treasure trove behind one of the feed bins." He shrugged. "But the stables were burned to the ground." He rode closer and patted her arm. "I think you should abandon your quest, m'dear. You'll only become more depressed. Reggie will not arise from the dead. I know 'tis thoughtless of me to ruin your hopes like this, but sometimes the stark truth is better than lies wrapped in cotton."

Bryony smiled. "I know you're speaking from common sense, but please advise me; if, against all odds, I find that Reggie was murdered, what should I do?"

He shrugged. "Go to the authorities, I suppose, but you will have to have solid evidence to put before them, or else they will not be able to apprehend the murderer. And if they start delving into Reggie's past, they might discover that he was a Jacobite, and you would be beheaded for treason as an accessory," he explained seriously. "Bryony, please let this wild investigation go! You will bring yourself nothing but heartache."

She nodded and sighed. "You're right, Nigel. There is nothing to do now but return to France. But I will do one more thing—find Lord Bentworth and try to discover how deeply involved he was in Reggie's affairs. Perhaps Reggie owed him more than the gambling debt."

"I have no idea what business they had."

They had stopped the horses on a hill with an expansive

view of the patchwork of fields and across the rolling hills of the Downs. Nigel took her hand and squeezed it gently. "I promise to do everything in my power to capture the men who attacked you in Seaford. I'll even help you further. In fact, I will send my men to Alfriston to see what they can learn at the Bentworth estate. They have ways of finding out secrets that a well-bred lady like yourself could not apply."

Bryony gently pulled away her hand. "Thank you. You don't know how much it means to me, knowing that you stand behind me, protecting me. I know Reggie would have thanked you, too." She flashed a lopsided smile. "The strange thing is that I came here to warn you. Since two of the cardplayers have died, you may be the next on the murderer's list. But instead of cautioning you, I find myself being reassured and pampered." She touched his arm impulsively. "Thank you, again."

He chuckled. "I guess I'm about the only friend you have left in England now," he said, and looked up at the roiling clouds. "Better return to Greymeadows before the downpour overtakes us."

Chapter 20

While it rained, Bryony was forced to stay at Greymeadows. Nigel spoke of old times, and Bryony threw worried glances at the ormulu-framed clock on the sideboard. Where was Jack now? He would be furious with her.

Explaining that Aunt Hortense was waiting for her at the home of their old friends, the Billingslys in East Grinstead, Bryony finally said she must go. Although she vehemently declined Nigel's escort, he insisted on sending her in his carriage, with Mrs. Dawson, the housekeeper, as her chaperone and Mr. Dawson, the steward, riding beside the carriage.

By the time Bryony returned to East Grinstead, it was dark. She ordered the coachman to halt in front of the smithy for a moment. Pale moonlight was reflected in the rain puddles.

Standing in the recessed doorway of the smithy, Jack waited for her, his hat crushed down low over his eyes and his cloak swept closely about his face.

Bryony jumped down as he emerged from the shadows. "Where have you been?" he demanded, his voice icy.

Bryony's heart leaped in fright. His anger washed over her as he glared down at her from the top step. "Jack, I'm sorry—" she began feebly.

Mr. Dawson rode up and slid from the saddle. "Who is this man? Is he accosting you?" he demanded in clipped tones. "Stay away from Miss Shaw."

Bryony placed a hand on Mr. Dawson's sleeve. "This is a friend of mine. He's a sea captain who has been very kind to me in my difficulties."

"I see," Mr. Dawson said ominously. "But where is your aunt, Miss Shaw? My orders were to escort you to the Billingslys, and I don't take my orders lightly."

The two men measured each other silently in the dark, barely more than two silhouettes against the silvery moonlight. Hostility infested the air. "She's going with me," Jack stated angrily.

"I don't like strangers accosting defenseless young ladies," Mr. Dawson said, and placed his hand on the hilt of his sword. "I promised to protect Miss Shaw with my life."

"I'm not exactly a stranger," Jack drawled with a sideways glance at her. He pulled her possessively toward him, and Mr. Dawson took a step closer.

"If you have taken liberties with Miss Shaw, I will have to challenge you, in the name of my employer," Mr. Dawson threatened.

"I have taken nothing she didn't offer freely," Jack said insolently. The cloak muffled his voice, but there was no mistaking the controlled fury in his posture. "Come, Bryony, let's go."

Mr. Dawson jumped back and whipped out his sword. "I have orders to escort Miss Shaw elsewhere. Defend yourself, sir."

"No, please, don't fight," Bryony begged, stepping between them.

"Don't listen to him, Miss Shaw," Mr. Dawson commanded, and shoved her away. "I'll protect you and take you safely to the Billingslys in a minute."

"No!" Bryony cried as she heard the clang of a sword being pulled from its scabbard. She whirled around, facing Jack. "Don't do it! I can explain."

"*En garde,*" Jack growled to Nigel's steward, ignoring her, and swung his weapon.

The two swords came together with a jarring clash.

"Please, don't." Bryony pressed her fingertips to her lips. "No!" She flinched as the swords collided once more. The thrusts came fast and furious now. The two men, cloaks swirling around them, danced a deadly jig on the cobblestones, the blades of their swords glittering in the moonlight. They panted with exertion, expelling muffled oaths. Jack grunted as Mr. Dawson made a mad forward lunge.

Jack stubbed his toe and fell sideways. Bracing himself on one hand, he leaped to his feet in one fluid movement and sprang backward, thus evading a thrust meant to pierce his heart.

Mr. Dawson swore profusely as Jack retaliated with a series of swift lunges which the steward parried with difficulty. The parrying led to a lock. For a long tense moment, they stood eye to eye. Only after a series of grinding wrenches, did they manage to disengage each other.

Mr. Dawson jumped back, and his sword sliced the air in a lightning-fast jab. Jack sidestepped neatly, and instead of retreating, advanced while deflecting another blow of Mr. Dawson's sword. He made one surprising feint forward and pierced the steward's upper arm.

Mr. Dawson screeched and aimed a wavering swing at Jack's throat.

"Stop!" Bryony whimpered. "The constable is coming."

Candlelights now shone in the windowpanes of the houses lining the street, and shouts reverberated farther down the road.

Jack jerked his sword up, the flat side hitting Mr. Dawson's sword close to the handle and wrenching it from his hand. The sword flew five or six yards up in the air and then clattered to the ground.

Mr. Dawson staggered toward it, clutching his lacerated arm.

"Don't touch it," Jack warned, and stepped away from the steward.

Mrs. Dawson was having hysterics inside the carriage, while the elderly coachman was trying to calm her.

Bryony had watched the fight in silent agony with her hand pressed to her heart. When Jack gripped her shoulder and propelled her forward, she could barely move.

"No time to lose now, lovely one. The bloodhounds are after us." He shoved his sword into it scabbard and led her around the carriage, where he released Bryony's horse tied to the back. He tossed Bryony into the saddle and led her horse to his stallion, which was tethered to the slender trunk of a tree. "We'd better hide somewhere fast," he whispered angrily as he swung into the saddle.

"How could you be so stupid as to meet with some stranger alone!" he berated her as he maneuvered the horse into a narrow alley that led to a soggy field.

The horror thawed from Bryony, and she finally found her voice. "Stranger! That was Mr. Dawson, Nigel's steward. Why did you have to fight when you saw that I was safe and sound? You could have killed him."

"Yes, slinking away to meet with your beau as soon as my back was turned," he spat. He sounded hurt.

"How insubstantial is your trust in me!" she reiterated, suffused with anger.

"After what we shared—"

She glared at him in the darkness. "You—you *idiot!* Nothing has changed. I went to warn Lord Lippett of the dangers that may be shadowing him right now."

"So Lippett's another of your brother's cohorts."

"That is none of your business, sir! I have no idea why you harbor a grudge against Nigel. He's nothing if not a gentleman."

"I don't trust him," he hurled at her.

"You have no reason to distrust him."

Jack snorted. "I know his kind. Always an eye for the ladies, just like my stepfather."

"Balderdash! I will not discuss this matter further until you can see reason." Bryony set her lips in a stubborn line.

Jack was obviously struggling to control his anger. She sensed his every muscle tighten with implacable wrath. "You're just like other women," he grated. "When you're sure of having manipulated one man's heart to your satisfaction, you move on to the next." He made a sound of disgust. "All of you are brightly painted peacocks and nothing more," he threw in for good measure, as if searching for words that would hurt her most.

She could not maintain her precarious hold on her temper. "How dare you throw such cruel accusations at me!" she said on a sob of anger. "I have done absolutely nothing to justify your ire."

"You slunk away without warning me."

His breath came in short, angry snorts, but he said nothing more. The horses slogged across the wet turf, and when they halted before a gate, Jack jumped down, opened the gate, and led the mounts forward. On the other side lay a thin band of trees.

"You disappeared," she defended herself. "I looked everywhere for you."

Her anger had sapped her of her strength, and her eyelids were growing heavier by the minute as Jack led the horses along a dark, narrow path in the woods. How he could see where to place his feet was a wonder. She was so tired.

"The magistrate kept asking me questions about the Reverend Cleaves all afternoon," he said. "That's where I was."

Bryony could not remember a time when she had felt more guilty.

"I will take you to the small inn where I left Clover and Jules," he said.

"Very well."

"Then I will leave."

Panic set in; he couldn't leave her now. Bryony sought frantically for something to say, but no suitable words came to mind. All she could think of was that he was behaving like a vengeful and jealous husband. In the right circumstances she might have found it amusing.

"Of course. Here today and gone tomorrow," she murmured scathingly. "You're no better than your stepfather."

He whipped around and glared at her. The darkness shielded his expression, but she read the tension and the silent accusations.

"You say that love is flighty," she continued relentlessly. "I say that *you* are flighty. No wonder you've never found a woman to marry. She'd find a new mistress in your bed every week, the poor soul."

"You should talk!" he accused her. "You're fickleness personified."

Hysterical laughter bubbled up within her. "Listen to us. Have we lost all perspective?"

He stopped and stared at her. The only sounds were the

horse pawing the soft ground and the churr of a frog. Then he was at her side.

He lifted her from the saddle and cradled her against his chest. "Lovely one, tell me you didn't let that *friend* of yours touch you." He sounded so desperate, her heart was wrung.

"He did not touch me other than to kiss my hand once."

Jack covered her face with kisses. "You don't know what hell I went through waiting for you outside the smithy. I thought you had been abducted and killed." He kissed her savagely, "How could you leave me? Don't you understand what terrible accidents I conjured—"

She placed her fingers on his lips. "Shhh. I was wrong not to tell you of my plans, but I didn't want to argue. Besides, you would have forbidden me to go." She pushed her fingers through his thick hair. "Don't you see? I couldn't live with myself if I didn't warn Nigel. He could be the next man on the murderer's list."

He groaned and almost crushed her in his embrace. "You know I would have accompanied you."

"But not without argument."

He sighed. "Bryony, sometimes you drive me out of my mind. You're never thinking of the danger. You're headstrong and foolhardy. I'll never have any peace until this business with your brother is settled."

"I pray you'll keep better control of your temper in the future."

He kissed both her cheeks passionately. "Ohhh, Brye, I see red when other men paw you."

"But Nigel didn't *paw* me. He never has!"

Jack was silent for a long moment, gently caressing her hair. Then he said, "I'm sorry for being such an idiot."

"I want you to trust me," she whispered into his cravat.

"If I had known that loving someone would be such torture, I would never have given you a chance to sneak into my heart." He sounded so agonized that Bryony could not stop a chuckle from bubbling over her lips.

"That is the most wonderful compliment I've ever received," she said softly. "I love you—no one else."

He held her so hard she could scarcely breathe. "I don't know what it is, but it must be love that overcomes me every time I look at you. And when you're not there, I think I will expire with longing.''

She trembled exquisitely in his arms as his lips closed gently over hers. He made her life exciting, rich, and wholly enchanting. She refused to believe that someday—soon—he would leave her to sail away on his ship.

As she returned his kiss with mounting ardor, she wondered if she would be with him on that ship.

Chapter 21

It was wet and cold and very dark outside, yet Jack managed to locate a barn filled with dry and fragrant hay. He attached the reins to a tree whose leaves would provide ample cover for the horses. Bryony grabbed a load of hay and dropped it on the ground in front of the animals.

Longing escalated between them as Bryony turned to Jack, and then she was in his arms. He crushed her to him, and wonder filled her. Their bond of love was to be forged anew.

Like a flood, Bryony's desire for Jack swept through her, breaking all the barriers between them.

"I want you, Bryony," he whispered, and lifted her into his arms, carrying her inside the barn. After spreading his cloak, he carefully laid her down in the hay.

If the first time they made love had been a river of delight, this was a volcano of passion exploding. Heedless of the havoc wrought to buttons and ribbons, they tore off their clothes until there was nothing between them.

Bryony felt the heat of his skin, the fire in his blood as he pressed her so close that she lost awareness of everything but his presence.

She sighed blissfully as his hand found her rose-tipped breasts and caressed them until she lay limp in his arms. He explored her every hollow and curve, and she reacquainted herself with his rippling muscles, the taut, sinewy cords along his hard thighs, and the curly hair on his chest. Her fingers traveled up and down his spine, playing with the long, crisp hair at the nape of his neck.

The sensation of skin against skin and his magic ca-

resses emboldened her. She slid her fingers up and down
the hard shaft of his desire until he groaned in pleasure.
He spread her legs, pulled the palm of his hand forcefully
from the sole of her foot up along her calf, her thigh, to
halt at the throbbing center of her yearning. Ministering
in the same way to her other leg, he whispered in her ear.

"Your skin intoxicates me. I could go on all night exploring every inch of you, but I don't know if I can contain
myself much longer." He chuckled. "Do you want me as
much as I want you?"

"I'm bursting!" She gasped, and guided his hand to the
ache between her thighs. She whimpered with pleasure as
his fingers made their slow journey back and forth until
she writhed in his arms.

"Do you want this?" he moaned against her neck and
slipped his fingers deeply into her.

She was rushing toward a precipice. "Yes, don't . . .
stop."

"This will do it for you," he whispered, and slid across
her and thrust deeply into her. He shivered with the effort
of controlling himself. Inexorably he moved against her,
slowly, deeply, until she dug her fingernails into his back
in agonized pleasure. Then he rode her as he would a wild
horse, and together they hurtled over the precipice.

Healing languor enfolded them and they slept, still
joined together, forged ever closer in their love.

It was still dark when Jack awakened Bryony. Her feet
were icy cold, and she shivered in the damp air.

"We'd better leave before the farmer finds us here."

"We're close to a farm?" Bryony scrambled to her feet,
searching for her clothes; her teeth chattered in the raw
air.

"Regrets?" he whispered as he held out her shift for
her.

She shook her head. "You're a wizard," she joked.
"You've truly bewitched me."

He laughed as he helped her on with her petticoats.
" 'Tis the other way around. You have ruined my life.
From now on, I'll be in misery when we're not together."

Bryony held her breath in expectation. Was he going to

propose to her? If he did, she would say yes without a moment's hesitation. He didn't ask.

He was buttoning his waistcoat. "What are you going to do after you find the answers to Reggie's death—if you ever do?"

She thought for a while, then said, "Your question is difficult to answer. When I returned to England, I had no thought of my future, only of the disaster that had befallen." On her hands and knees, she searched the ground for her garters. "I really don't know what I'll do. Jules and I share a passion for roses. Aunt Hortense employed an old man who experimented with new strains. I found it fascinating. Nature is so . . . well, so generous. It gives and gives without asking anything in return."

Jack pulled her to her feet and pressed her close. "You're just like Mother Nature, giving and warm. I'm tempted to drown myself in your sweetness and never surface again."

"That sounds uncomfortable," she said, and kissed his lips lightly. "About the roses—I don't have a place left to grow them." She chuckled. "I suppose I could build a large greenhouse somewhere with a small lean-to where I could live."

"I thought you would return to France and partake of the social whirl."

"Aunt Hortense would only force me to wed some doddering, toad-faced gentleman. No, thank you! I will not return to France to let her bully me again. And London holds no allure to me. Most likely I'll end up in a genteel boardinghouse for young ladies in one of the watering places." She shuddered at the awful thought. "And I will hire a sour-faced companion."

He chuckled, and she waited expectantly for him to offer her the shelter of his name and life, but he was silent, brooding. This would have been the perfect moment, but he kept quiet. Her spirits plummeted, and new doubts assailed her. Had she been a fool to trust him, after all? Due to her practical nature, she could not help worrying that she would bring a child into the world, another wretch born on the wrong side of the blanket. She felt frozen in apprehension, then resolutely pushed her fears away. She had decided to surrender to her desire, and the fact could not be changed now.

She regretted nothing. Her love for Jack could not be destroyed so easily. Still, she realized that this very love might cause her agonizing heartache—when he sailed.

They rode into the gray dawn in silence. After settling Jules and Clover somewhere safe, they would continue to the coast. Bryony hoped this would be the last leg of her journey to discovery.

Jack mentioned that he had friends at a small estate not far from Alfriston where Jules and Clover could stay. They would leave the carriage and Bryony's trunk there.

They decided to ride all the way since they could travel faster on horseback and leave fewer tracks behind, if Bryony's enemies were still in pursuit.

Bryony took pleasure in the hot breakfast served at the small roadside tavern. While eating fried golden cakes made from flour, milk, and eggs, and spread liberally with butter and strawberry preserves, she watched Jack talk to Jules. She was too hungry and tired to pay much attention. In fact, it was a relief that Jack wanted to take charge of the practical details.

Clover was turning cartwheels in the yard, his loose shirttails flapping in the wind. He looked expectant and glanced at Jack with much respect. She realized the urchin had grown fond of the sea captain. Jack was having a more difficult time accepting the unruly boy, but he was struggling valiantly. She knew Clover would surely have a future on Jack's ship. The thought cheered her, yet she knew she would miss the imp. Jack spoke to him, and suddenly Clover's face crumpled and he ran off toward the stables. Jack looked very angry.

He joined Bryony at her table and drank deeply from a tankard of ale. "That boy is too impertinent," he complained.

"He's just a boy."

"Hah! A varmint, rather. Since we're sending Jules to my friends's estate along the Cuckmere River, outside Alfriston, Clover ought to accompany him."

"What did you say to the boy?"

"I told him about our plans and, said that he could not ride with us."

"Perhaps he should. I can't bear to see his sorrow. He has known nothing but unhappiness."

Jack sighed. "He will only be in the way." He took Bryony's hand and kissed the tender skin on her wrist. "Your dedication to him makes me jealous."

"You have no reason to be." She smiled mischievously. "He isn't exactly competing against you. My heart is big enough for both of you."

Jack's eyes lit up. "Looking at you, I sometimes believe that you're an apparition, and that the lightest breeze will carry you away."

She touched his cheek. "Are you saying you're afraid that I might leave?"

His eyes clouded over. "I wish you would change your mind about going to France. I assure you, we will accomplish nothing there. But you might decide to remain, abandoning me."

She sighed. "We've talked too much about this already. I'm not changing my mind." Their gazes clashed as she slid one more cake onto her plate.

He shrugged. "Very well. 'Twill be my pleasure to say I told you so when we return here, mission failed." Then he smiled. "But at least I'll be close to you until then—that's what matters most."

Bryony's lips curled. "You know exactly what to tell a lady to make her warm inside," she whispered, and swallowed the last of her ale.

"And a smile from your lips makes my knees turn to jelly." He caressed her with his eyes, forcing color into her cheeks. "On this trip, I will show you just how much you mean to me—if we can keep that varmint Clover from spying."

She rose. "We'd better prepare ourselves then."

As Jack went outside to see to their horses, Bryony ordered a bath, which she had to take in an old, weathered wooden tub in the freezing scullery. At least she had her trunk now and could discard the dresses that had been ruined in the course of her adventures.

She donned a clean silk shift, two cotton petticoats del-

icately embroidered with rosebuds and trimmed with wide
Mechlin lace, white silk stockings, and her riding habit.
It consisted of a royal-blue wool skirt trimmed with wide
bands of black velvet. The jacket was snug, the lapels and
cuffs trimmed with the same black velvet as the skirt. She
tied her flowing hair at the back of her neck with a velvet
ribbon, shaping it into a bow. When she had acquired her
little tricorne hat with gold edging in France, she had
thought it was the height of fashion, but Aunt Hortense
had laughed at her, claiming that caps and hoods were the
only headwear suitable for a lady. Yet the hat, a replica of
a gentleman's tricorne, suited her to perfection. The black
felt accentuated her pale skin and her jet eyebrows.

Clean from head to toe, she was in excellent spirits and
eager to continue their journey. Her riding habit had a
matching cloak for warmth. With it wrapped around her,
she might never be cold again.

Jack whistled in appreciation as she stepped out on the
front steps. "Next to you, I must look like a vagabond,"
he commented, and stared ruefully at his dusty and torn
clothes. "Unfortunately, I have nothing to change into except a clean shirt. I never calculated that I would be involved in hair-raising and *dirty* adventures when I set out
to explore Sussex."

She regarded him critically. "In those peasant rags you
look like my servant."

He swept his hat to the ground in a deep bow. "I'm
forever at your service, ma'am. Day and night." He
winked, and she was reminded of that first night she had
encountered him.

"Rogue," she whispered, and swept past him with a
sly grin. "You could do with a shave, if anything."

He clutched at his beard in mock despair. "Cut off my
sole source of pride? You must be pulling my leg."

"I've forgotten how you really look under all that hair,
that's all."

He hoisted her up on her horse. "One day, I'll show
you.'Tis a promise."

Jules held the bridle, glancing at Bryony with longing.
"I'll miss you, mademoiselle."

"We'll meet again soon," Bryony consoled him, and

leaned forward to pat his sturdy shoulder. "Good-bye, and try to learn some English words while I'm gone."

He bowed deeply, crushing the brim of his hat between his large hands. *"Au revoir."*

Clover came running from the stables, tears streaming down his grimy cheeks. "Please, l-let m-me go wi' ye," he stammered, and pulled a dirty sleeve across his eyes. The clean clothes that Bryony had given him were nothing but a memory now. Buttons were missing, and one of the legs had a tear along the entire length of the seam. Jack's old hat was crushing his ears and hanging low over his eyes. As usual, the sight of the little urchin wrung her heart. "I cannot un'erstand that strange Frenchie.'E speaks as if 'e 'as 'ot porridge in 'is gob. Let me go wi' ye. Please."

Bryony and Jack exchanged glances. She read the silent resignation in his eyes and smiled.

"Very well, you may accompany us. But from now on you will obey our every command. Is that clear?" she said. Clover's smile was like the sun breaking out from behind a raincloud.

He made an exact replica of Jack's extravagant bow and said, "Yes, ma'am, I will obey yer commands."

Bryony sent her gaze heavenward. Jack lifted the boy up behind her. "We'll take turns," he said.

Clover clung to her waist and began singing a lewd ditty at the top of his lungs. Bryony silenced him with a sharp elbow in his ribs. "I'll teach you some decent songs and a psalm or two." In her clear voice she sang as they rode down the shady lane. Soon both Jack and Clover had joined in, and the trees sent back the echo of their happiness.

Chapter 22

As exhilarating as the most potent tonic, the salty, humid air of the sea flowed into Bryony's lungs. Behind her rose the cliffs of a secluded cove near Seaford, and in front churned the dark waters of the Channel.

Soon she would stand eye to eye with Lord Bentworth. She hoped the trip would not be in vain.

The moon was a thin sliver of light in the sky. Waiting impatiently to board the boat, a few travelers paced the shore, bending against the gusting southerly wind. Bryony watched the silhouettes of burly French sailors dressed in stocking caps and leather jerkins cart sacks and crates to a rowboat, and row out to the French *chasse-marée*, a three-masted lugger anchored in the bay. The vessel smuggled brandy and silk from France, and transported people for a high fee when wartime activities between France and England made normal movement impossible. To keep the operation secret, the lugger sailed only at night.

Standing at the waterline, Jack was talking to the captain. They glanced up and pointed toward a bank of clouds forming to the south. Bryony realized that rain and stronger winds threatened, but she did not fear the prospect. She had never been seasick. Jules had been pitifully sick on the crossing from France, and she smiled at the memory. He had called on all the saints, believing he was about to die.

The clouds were covering the pitiful moon even as she stood there. Three stone buildings lined the shore—abandoned fishermen's huts. In the weak light from a lantern beside one of the doors, she thought she recognized the

scar-faced man in the brown coat. Her heartbeat accelerated in fear, and she took a step toward Jack.

She pointed toward the hut. "He's—"

"There is room for three people in the rowboat this
time," the captain called out as the dinghy returned to
shore. The passengers whispered in French, and Bryony
wondered what they were—spies or fugitives.

With a strained smile, Jack assisted her into the boat.
A cold had taken hold in his throat and lungs. He coughed
and wound the woolly scarf that he had purchased closer
around his neck.

As the boat pushed away from shore, Bryony twisted
her head to see if there was any sign of the man in the
brown coat, but she saw no one. Perhaps her imagination
had been playing tricks on her. At least this time Jack was
there to protect her.

"You don't look well," she commented, and threw him
a sharp glance.

"I'm deuced tired, so if you don't mind, as soon as we
reach the ship, I'd like to find a spot to lie down. Clover
will entertain you."

"Where *is* Clover?"

Jack chuckled. "He managed to wangle an invitation to
visit the captain at the wheel. He was rowed over to the
lugger on another trip."

"Have you noticed that he always gets what he wants,
the little rapscallion?"

"Yes. He should be pressed into diplomatic services."
Jack gripped her shoulders and looked into her eyes. "You
understand there may be difficulties in France because of
the war."

"I have French papers," she explained. "And you and
Clover can act as my servants."

Jack made a feeble attempt to brush the dust off his
coat. "I do look the part, which is all for the best."

She gazed at him through narrowed eyes. "Besides, I
believe you're proficient in French. I take it a sea captain
knows all kinds of languages."

He didn't meet her gaze, and Bryony felt a twinge of
uneasiness. She dearly wanted to know what he was hid-

ing, and she was slowly working up her courage to confront him.

Once on board the lugger, they found a heap of blankets on some planks among coils of sour-smelling rope. Thick canvas stretched over poles formed a roof from one side of the lugger to the other. Jack folded himself on top of the blankets and tipped his hat over his eyes. "Awake me in time for dinner. We'll have a picnic with Clover, unless we drown in the approaching storm."

Bryony enjoyed the invigorating air at the bow as the lugger hoisted anchor. The wind whipped her hair across her face, and she had to hold on to her hat. Pestering the captain at the wheel, Clover waved to her, and she returned the gesture. The man in the brown coat was nowhere in sight. Fear, and the strain on her nerves, must have made her conjure up the vision of his sinister form.

The English coastline was soon a faint blur, but the lugger had not traveled far before the waves increased in strength. Bryony clung to the railing as a particularly tall wave tossed the boat up, then flung it down as if preparing to devour the vessel whole. Water drenched her, and she realized she'd better get under the shelter of the canvas.

Frightened and cold, she struggled across the deck. The French travelers were huddled around one of the masts. Jets of water found their way under the makeshift roof, soaking everything. The timbers groaned and the sails flapped, but the lugger continued to plow through the water.

Yet another wave challenged the boat and bore it to its crest. At that moment Bryony feared they would never reach the coast of France. Would her life end before she had had a chance to avenge Reggie's death?

Holding on to a rope strung between two masts, she managed to reach the place where Jack was resting. A storm lantern swung wildly in the wind, throwing flickering light on his prostrate figure. He had pulled up the blankets to his chin; they were dripping with water. She thought he was asleep, but suddenly he emitted a heart-rending groan.

"What's wrong?" Bryony asked, and crouched beside him, her eyes wide with worry.

He twisted convulsively and turned his face away from her. He was panting hard, pressing a hand to his stomach.

She recognized the signs. Jack Newcomer was seasick. Seasick? But . . . She grasped his shoulders and cried out his name, shaken to the bone.

"You've lied to me! A sea captain would not be seasick."

He clutched his head and moaned. Without answering, he struggled to his feet and groped blindly for something to hold on to. She tried to stop him, but he shrugged off her hand and staggered headlong to the railing.

She had to talk to him. Ignoring the danger of the waves washing across the deck, she followed him. One of the sailors tried to warn her away with frantic gestures, but she refused to heed him.

Confusion and wrath mingled within her. And disappointment. She had given her love to a man who had betrayed her. She knew nothing about him, absolutely nothing. The realization infuriated her. Tasting bile, she wanted to strike him.

Whatever explanation he invented, she would never believe him now. Her heart constricted painfully, and she swallowed hard as the salty spray mixed with her tears.

As she reached out to grip his arm, a wave drowned him. In a moment of stark terror she thought he had fallen overboard, but as the wave receded, she saw he was hanging limp across the railing, his hands clutching desperately at the slick wood.

Another, smaller wave suckled at Bryony's feet, almost robbing her of her balance. Her hands touched Jack's cold fingers, and for a moment she recoiled. Something dark within her wanted to pry his fingers loose from the railing and see him swallowed by the greedy waves. She pummeled his back with all her strength. "You liar! You despicable liar! You've destroyed everything," she cried, tears streaming wildly down her cheeks.

She crushed the impulse to assist the waves in their endeavor to take him, and held on to him as another wave washed over them. It would take only one giant wave lifting his legs over the side and he would be no more. Grasping the railing on both sides of his body, she braced herself against him, pressing him desperately against the wood.

Every wave made her colder and stiffer, as cold and hopeless as the despair in her heart. Her hands were numb, and she would soon lose her grip.

Jack seemed powerless against the violent attack of seasickness. Wracked with convulsions, he trembled continuously. A small measure of compassion stirred in her, but mostly she wanted him to survive until she could vent the full extent of her wrath.

In frozen terror they rode through every wave that lashed them. If the waves grew any larger, it would be their last night alive. Bryony didn't want to die without finding the answers to her questions. And Jack should not get away with his lies that easily!

With renewed vigor, she tried to drag him toward the middle of the boat, but he held on to the railing for his life. Another wave choked her, and she felt Jack's grip slipping. On its return the wave squeezed them, trying to force them to surrender to its icy embrace.

Jack tilted farther and farther over the railing, and Bryony moaned. "No! Don't let go!" she screamed over the roar of the water. Momentarily she lost her foothold and clung to Jack's arms.

They would have gone overboard together had not a pair of strong arms grasped her from behind. Bryony felt herself being pulled back and almost torn apart, but still she refused to relinquish her grip on Jack. Someone looped a rope around her waist and another around Jack's arm. As a gigantic wave reared up, they were inexorably pulled toward the middle of the lugger. Blinded by the water and half drowned, Bryony struggled to free herself, but the burly sailor had arms of steel. He hauled her in and carried her to the relative safety of the rope coils under the canvas.

"Stupid landcrabs!" he shouted in her ears. And that they were, Bryony admitted to herself. "Stay here until the storm has abated," he warned.

She looked for Jack and saw that two men were busy hauling him in. He was beyond struggling and slid across the deck like a dead fish. They tied him in a sitting position against the mast so that he would not be a helpless victim of the sea.

His head tilted forward and his long hair was plastered to his neck. He coughed and retched, oblivious of his surroundings. The pitiful sight wrenched Bryony's heart, but she put up a barrier against her weakness.

Jack would have a lot to explain once the storm abated.

Snug within the confines of three sturdy coils of rope, she waited for the storm to subside, praying that it would soon. The ink-black sky and the sullen roar of the waves made her feel small and lonely, but the sturdy vessel rode the waves as effortlessly as a seagull. The only pinpoint of light was the swinging lantern attached to the mast.

She noticed that Jack's portmanteau was wedged between two coils of rope beside her. Desperate to find some answers about her mysterious lover, she opened it.

Water trickled into the shadowy interior as she sifted through his meager belongings. There were the pistols, horns of blackpowder, leather pouches bulging with lead balls, a tinderbox, the folded garments that she remembered, the documents, and, at last, what she had been instinctively looking for, the letters bound with a white satin ribbon.

As she pulled them out, a twinge of jealousy stabbed her heart. He had carried the love letters with him everywhere.

With cold, stiff fingers, she undid the ribbon. Her hands were shaking as she unfolded the first missive. Her eyes widened as she peered at the paper. The wind tried to whip it from her hands, but she clutched it convulsively against her chest. Shoving the other letters into the wet pocket of her cloak, she crawled toward the lonely lantern. Bracing her back against the mast, she tried to read the spidery scrawl. Glancing at the signature in the weak light, she knew that her fist impression had been right. It was signed "Oakfolly."

She knew only one person who had ever used that word before, and that person was Reggie. It was impossible to read the letters, but there was no mistaking her twin's

garbled handwriting. He had called himself Oakfolly after
the old oak behind the folly at Willow Hills. That oak
probably still guarded many of their childhood treasures.
The tree had been dead for many years, but her father had
refused to have it removed. He had claimed it was older
than history, and the trunk was certainly thicker than any
other tree that had grown on the estate.

A couple of owls had shared the hollow trunk with Reggie's treasures. They must be long gone by now, Bryony
thought without noticing that tears were streaming down
her cheeks. How could she have forgotten the oak?

Water trickled through a hole in the canvas and spat-
tered the paper in her hand, but she hardly noticed. The
message her brother had written to her via Uncle Butterball was clear now. They had once measured the steps
from the folly to the oak, made a map, and buried it in
the daffodil patch.

Everything fell into place. Reggie had hidden the French
map to the gold in the old oak at Willow Hills. The men
who were pursuing her probably wanted the map. Most
importantly, *Jack* believed she had it.

And if he was after the map, he must be a Jacobite, just
like Reggie.

She should have known.

The immensity of her discovery seeped slowly into her,
until she was unable to think of anything except the fact
that Jack had deceived her doubly from the very start. He
had never mentioned that he knew Reggie, and he had lied
about his occupation.

Deep sorrow flowed through her, numbing her every
nerve. How could Jack have done this? But most of all,
how could she have been so stupid as to fall in love with
him? She ought to have known better when he didn't tell
her anything about himself. He had totally blinded her
with his charm.

Her wild gaze dropped to the paper in her hands, and
she noticed that the ink had blurred into an illegible stain.
She was wet through to her skin and trembling so hard
she could barely keep her back straight.

She glanced at Jack, noticing that he lay curled around
the mast, oblivious to the world around her. He was suf-

fering, but it was only a small measure of what he deserved.

She wanted to rail at him, to shake him until he experienced the same intense desolation that was drowning her.

Chapter 23

Dawn arrived, with a sky invaded by roiling gray clouds. The waves had calmed, and the lugger was still afloat, but two of the sails were ripped, and everything on board was soaked with water, weighing the boat down. Listing slightly to starboard, the boat limped toward the uneven gray line at the horizon that was the shore.

But it wasn't France. According to the captain, the storm had fought their progress with such fury that they had never left English waters. Because of the battered sail, they would have to find shelter in some remote cove and make repairs. The captain was even considering dumping the ballast overboard to ease the strain on the remaining sail.

At a distance appeared the jagged outline of steep white cliffs. As far as Bryony could see, there was no trace of human dwellings, which was strange considering that small fishing hamlets usually dotted the small coves and inlets along the shoreline.

"We're south o' Worthin'," Clover said with an important air as he joined Bryony at the railing. "I could eat a whole pig," he added as an afterthought.

"How do you know we're south of Worthing?"

Clover slanted a glance at the captain. "Anyone would know that that 'igh point o' th' Downs is Cissbury Ring, m'lady." He pointed vaguely inland.

Bryony smiled. "I take it you know what Cissbury Ring is?"

He would not meet her gaze. "O' course I do! Ever'one does." His gaze swiveled to the cloth bag containing food that Jack had purchased the previous day. "When's breakfast? An' where's th' guv?"

Newcomer had remained by the mast throughout the storm. Now he was sitting with his forehead pressed against his updrawn knees. His skin had a greenish hue, and he shivered as if in the throes of a high fever. Bryony had to steel herself against the pitiful sight. She would not show him any mercy, no matter how much he suffered. She couldn't bear to look at him.

"Fella's a cully," Clover scoffed, and strutted across the deck.

"And you're a rude boy," Bryony admonished, pulling out a wedge of cheese and soggy bread from the bag.

Clover seemed to repent and walked over to Jack with a piece of cheese and a slice of bread. Bryony could not stop herself from throwing a furtive glance to see Jack's reaction.

He didn't even lift his head, didn't react at all. He was truly ill. When Clover returned, she ordered him to find some dry blankets—if there were any—and wrap them around their companion.

Clover was happy to comply and returned with word that Jack was mumbling in his sleep. "Th' guv is as 'ot as a brick," the boy said, taking an enormous bite of cheese.

For the longest time Bryony fought the impulse to make Jack comfortable, but her compassion won in the end. No matter what crime he had committed, he had the right to be cared for. Her heart thumped painfully in her chest as she neared the man whom she had loved with all her heart until yesterday.

Clover was right, Jack was shivering with fever. His eyes were dark hollows that saw only the frozen horrors of his dreams. "I'll kill him," he muttered, and flexed his hands.

"Jack?" Bryony whispered between stiff lips. He remained closed within his nightmare.

She spoke with the captain, who offered his own cabin set on the deck like a hut. When she explained that Jack was wet through, he even offered her a dry shirt and breeches.

"Madame Newcomer, when on shore you arrive, me think it best for you to leave, *non?* You must find another ship now, I will you set ashore outside of town. With *mon ami, le monsieur anglais,* and the little *fils.*" He rolled his eyes as he mentioned Clover, and Bryony smiled.

"Thank you for taking care of him last night," she said.

"I tie him to my desk, mademoiselle. He like storm."

With the help of some deckhands, Bryony managed to settle Jack on the captain's narrow cot in the cabin. They left her alone as she began peeling his wet clothes from his body. She dried his lean, muscular torso and legs with a flannel cloth, remembering every moment of pleasure that he had given her. To touch his flesh was bittersweet agony, this body that she had started to know so well. She blamed herself for not learning more of his secrets, of his life. Why had she been so careless?

Yet her heart had trusted him, which had been enough. Then.

He was mumbling and tossing from side to side, repeatedly wrestling with the blankets. It was time-consuming labor to dress him in the captain's clothes.

Bryony pried open his lips and dribbled some brandy into his mouth. To touch his feverish skin wrenched her heart. How was she ever to sever the bonds of love between them? She loved Jack so much she ached all over, and she found that his agony was hers as well.

As the brandy warmed him, he settled down somewhat. He opened his eyes, but was clearly having difficulty focusing. A fever fire burned in the onyx depths, and Bryony hastily averted her own gaze, which clouded with tears.

"Brye?" His voice was hoarse, and his fingers trembled as he reached out to her. "Why . . . are you . . . crying?" he forced out between cracked lips.

How could she accuse him now? She steeled herself against her weakness. Most likely the devious rascal had managed to make himself sick so as to inspire her pity!

But when she looked at him, she knew it wasn't true. He had caught a chill.

"Do you recall what we talked about last night?" she asked, struggling to keep her voice level.

He shook his head feebly and closed his eyes. "I'm burning up and I'm cold, so cold," he whispered.

She gave him more brandy and wrapped the blankets closely around him.

"Where are we?" he asked, once more directing his unfocused gaze at her.

"We're on the Channel, just outside Worthing. We'll land very soon. We'll have to leave the boat before it seeks a hidden cove to make repairs.

"Ah! My old friend Michel, the captain. He promised to take us safely to France." He clenched his fingers around the edge of the blanket until the knuckles whitened. "Even though I hate sailing."

"So I have found out," Bryony said dryly. "It's not very practical in a sea captain."

He was shocked into a sitting position, and two red spots glowed on his sunken cheeks. "You know the . . . truth." The words emerged as sounds of agony.

Bryony's eyes were infinitely sad. "I found Reggie's letters in your portmanteau. Why did you lie to me?"

He turned his face toward the wall without answering.

Forgetting his weakened state, she gripped his shoulders and shook him. "How could you! I trusted you." Her voice broke, and she had to hide her face in her hands.

He was silent for a long time. Finally, he said, "My feelings for you are true, lovely one, but my mission comes before everything. Many Scotsmen's lives hinge on its success."

She braced herself and looked into his eyes. She read the truth and the pain, yet she could not forgive him.

"I'll never be able to trust you again."

He had closed his eyes, and perspiration gave his forehead a sickly sheen. His few lucid moments were gone as the fever gripped him once more. A muscle worked in his jaw, and he groped blindly for her.

"I'll try to explain someday," he whispered.

"It'll never be enough," she responded, and heaved herself upright. She wanted to leave the cabin, walk away from him and her past. "You used me, thinking I would lead you to the map."

He didn't respond, and she saw that he had fallen asleep.

She could gain no solace watching his face, nor could she find peace looking at the captain's meager belongings. She wondered if she'd ever find peace again.

She could not stand to be in the same room as Jack. Ordering Clover to watch over him, she stood by the railing and stared with aching eyes toward shore.

She could easily discern the cliffs now and the grayish horizon. The narrow strip looked desolate except for a group of seagulls whose harsh cries filled the air.

Jack was unconscious when the sailors lifted him into the rowboat. Bryony and the other passengers watched in silence. She would be responsible for his well-being as soon as they landed on shore.

Perhaps she should leave him in the cold surf to die, but she knew she could never do that. The problem was, she still loved Jack. That love was an indelible stain on her heart, and no matter what horrors he had committed, he owned her heart. She despised herself for it.

And she would never admit her love to him. As soon as his health was on the mend, they would go their separate ways.

Staying in England in the first place had been a big mistake. Had she gone back to France immediately, none of this would have happened.

"Mademoiselle, I cannot help you further," the captain said beside her on deck, and shrugged apologetically. "I'm not—how say you it—welcome in this country." He laughed and spread his hands.

Bryony smiled. "Yes, I know. Thank you for trying to help us. I will return to France soon to confront—er—look for someone I know. Perhaps you'll sail me back to France then."

The captain promised to leave a message at The Star in Alfriston when he next returned to England. He bowed. "Good luck, Miss Shaw."

The rowboat brought them ashore. There were no one in sight. What was she going to do? Jack had regained consciousness, but he was very weak. He managed to walk across the sand while leaning heavily on Bryony's shoulders.

"What now?" she said aloud as she watched the sailors rowing through the surf and climbing into the lugger.

"We'll find an inn somewhere," Clover suggested. "Th' guv needs 'is rest."

Jack sank to his knees, his breath coming in shallow gasps.

"He cannot walk farther," Bryony said. She delved into her pocket and pulled out her purse. It contained only a few farthings. "Besides, we don't have funds to pay for a room." She sighed. "I never dreamed it would come to this." She sent Jack a glance and wished she could do something, or that a miracle would change their situation. Right now her first concern must be Jack's health. And then there was Clover. He seemed unharmed by their adventures, but she suspected that underneath his bravado hid a frightened boy. Her fate was inexorably linked with his as long as he needed her.

Clover waved at her. "Over 'ere's a cave, m'lady." "Th' guv can rest 'ere while we do some snoopin' round. I be very 'ungry."

Somehow Clover's words reached Jack's dazed mind, because he struggled to his feet and staggered toward the dark opening of the cave. "Clover's right," he said. "I'll be fine here with a flask of brandy and some blankets."

Bryony hesitated, but knew she would have to find food somewhere. Clover helped her make Jack as comfortable as possible, and since the French captain had not supplied them with anything except brandy, she spread her own cloak over Jack's trembling body. He didn't appear to know what they were doing to him. Clover formed a pillow of dry seaweed and propped it under Jack's head.

" 'E'll sleep like a wee babe until we return."

Bryony touched Jack's burning forehead. "He needs a warm bed with hot bricks all around him." Fear flurried along her spine. What if he succumbed to inflammation of the lungs and died? She hurriedly pushed away the thought.

"Come, let's find something to eat and some medicine for Jack."

Clover sneaked his hand into hers, and the warm, soft

touch comforted her greatly. "Scamp," she said, and smiled. "Let's hurry."

It was late in the afternoon before they returned, dressed in rough garments and laden with apples, milk, and a loaf of bread that a kindly farm woman had given them in exchange for Bryony's beautiful riding habit. Bryony's new wardrobe consisted of a gray wool skirt, bodice, white kerchief, and a huge mobcap. The farmer's wife had also offered to let them sleep in her barn, and Bryony felt lighter at heart. The hay would be warm for Jack, and she could get hot milk from the farm kitchen to feed him.

As they descended the narrow path leading to the beach, they heard voices. Bryony placed a warning hand on Clover's arm. They stopped and listened. There was no sign of the French boat. Bryony didn't recognize any of the voices. Cautiously, she moved closer to the cave. The voices were coming from inside.

She sucked in her breath, gave Clover a glance of warning, and stepped inside. Three soldiers were bending over Jack, pressing their swords against his chest. He was wide awake but remained silent as the soldiers questioned him.

"Minnie, you're back," he cried when he saw her. His voice trembled with the effort to sound normal.

She nodded curtly to the soldiers as they turned to her. "Who are you?"

"I just told th' good soldiers that ye went to buy some food, dearie," Jack said. "Ye didn't see any French boat, did ye?"

Bryony shook her head. "No, I 'aven't seen no boats 'ereabouts. Ye'll 'ave to go into Worthin' t'er find yerselves a boat, if that's what ye want."

"We don't want a boat," said the man who was obviously the leader. "I'm Sergeant Comstock," he added with a curt bow. "There was a rumor that a French vessel sailed from here but three hours ago."

Bryony eyed their scarlet uniforms with misgivings. They would not be easy to fool. "It wasn't from 'ere, no sir. What would we want wi' 'em Frogs?"

"That's what I'd like to know," the sergeant said ominously. "What are you doing here on the beach?"

Bryony sent Jack a veiled glance, trying to figure out what he had said already. He winked at her in encouragement. She plunged in. "Me 'usband took ill. A sailor 'e be. Th' fishin' boat, *The Minnow*, out o' Li'l'ampton, 'ad t' put 'im ashore, an' they sent this ere boy t' tell me."

The sergeant looked suspiciously from one to the other. "Smells very fishy to me."

Bryony let out what she hoped was a vulgar laugh. "Ye took th' words right outta me mouth, mister! Th' lad always smells o' fish."

The sergeant harrumphed. "I don't know what to believe."

"I don't 'ave time t' wait for ye t' make up yer mind. Me 'usband is dyin' wi' th' fever, an' I 've t' get im 'ome." She prayed that they would not offer her their assistance, because she had no home to take Jack to. She was grateful for the rough farm clothes. What would have happened had she been dressed in her elegant French riding habit?

"There are many Jacobies trying to get out of the country at this time, so we cannot be careful enough," explained the sergeant.

"We bain't no Jakkerbites, whatever they may be," said Bryony with a sniff. "We're law-abidin' citizens, I tells ye." She pinched Clover when he let out a nervous giggle.

"If ye as much as lay a 'and on me, I'll report ye t' yer superiors," she threatened, and drew herself up, hoping she resembled an outraged matron.

The sergeant looked uncomfortable. He exchanged glances with the other soldiers, who shrugged.

"Very well, I suppose you're what you claim to be."

Jack had struggled to his feet and stood swaying beside Bryony. "We'll go 'ome now, Minnie. I'll soon die if I don't git outta these clothes and into bed, wi' ye." He nuzzled her neck, and two of the soldiers sniggered.

She blushed furiously and wanted to jab Jack in the ribs, but the soldiers nodded knowingly, and she had to pretend to be the loving wife.

It was not the first time Jack had taken advantage of

such a situation. Yet she could feel his awful trembling as he forced himself to remain standing. He might faint at any second, and then there was no way she would get him up the cliffs.

The soldiers left, walking briskly along the shore. They obviously weren't going to give up their quest for the French vessel.

"I had no idea how to treat those men," Bryony murmured, weak-kneed now that the danger was over. "And how did you know—?"

"I remembered that time in the good doctor's gig, and I thought you might invent something similar, and you did—very aptly, too." He leaned heavily on her. "We'd better leave now just in case they come back to investigate the 'fishiness.' "

Clover hooted with laughter. "Ye pulled their legs good, not that I know eggsackly why."

"You don't need to know," Jack admonished sternly. "And don't you dare breathe a word about this to anyone, or I'll have your hide."

Clover pouted and fished an apple out of his pocket. "I picked it 'specially fer ye," he said, and gave Jack the fruit. " 'Twill set ye right as a trivet in jig time."

Jack hesitated before he accepted the fruit, and his hand hovered momentarily above the boy's head before he ruffled his hair. "Thank you. That was very kind of you."

Clover's face broke into a smile, and he clung to Jack's waist. "I don't like it when yer sick, an' I don't like it when m'lady looks so angry."

Jack scanned her face, worry flickering in the depths of his eyes. "Yes, she looks angry and sad. And she has every right to be." He sighed and grasped Clover's shoulder. "Now, scamp, you're going to be my walking stick."

To bring Jack up the steep cliff path was hard labor. The crashing of the surf and the screeching seagulls drowned their groans and curses. They were all tired and sweaty by the time they reached the barn, which was set somewhat apart from the small farmstead, giving them privacy from curious eyes.

Bryony knew it would be dangerous to stay in the barn

for more than one day, now that the soldiers were on the alert, but they had no other choice.

Now she truly was a fugitive, a traitor to England in the eyes of the law. Just as much as the traitorous Jack.

Chapter 24

Jack collapsed in the hay after drinking a mug of hot milk laced with honey that the kindly farm woman had brought. He was more feverish than ever, but no word of complaint rose from his lips.

On edge and unable to sleep, Bryony kept vigil all through the night. Clover rolled into a blanket and burrowed in the hay, and Jack slept peacefully for the first time since the storm, although he occasionally tossed and murmured as if haunted by a nightmare. He coughed in his sleep, too, a dry, wracking sound that alarmed her.

She had found a sturdy club and kept it beside her during the night. At the first light of dawn, she pulled out Reggie's letter with the cryptic message and studied it again: "Ask Bryony if she remembers one hundred steps to the north, five steps to the east, ten steps to the west. Tell her it's imperative that she remembers!"

She did remember the old oak behind the folly. She would have to return to Willow Hills and look for the map. Sighing, she pulled from her cloak pocket the other letters Reggie had sent Jack, but they were illegible, a sodden mass of salt water and ink. She would never know now what Reggie had written. Jack had a lot to explain, but would she ever be able to believe him again?

As long as she remained with Jack, she would be hunted by the militia and that unknown enemy, the man in the brown coat. He looked for someone, but who?

The man in the brown coat, Horace Watts, was at that very moment summoned into a dilapidated room in Craw-

ley. In his sleeve he had hidden a dagger that he knew he
might need for self-defense, since he had failed to accomplish his mission.

He met his employer's cold gaze and flinched. His life
wasn't worth a groat here. Keeping his arms pressed along
his sides to hide the bulge of the dagger handle, he bowed
stiffly.

"Well, Horace, where is she?"

"Gone, sir. I lost her trail."

The man nodded coldly. "So you failed. I should have
known. I have never had more incompetent help." He
sighed. "Miss Shaw will not give up her investigation. I'll
have to kill her now." He rose from the wing chair by the
fire and walked toward Horace Watts.

Slow heavy steps, steps of doom.

"I told you before what would happen if you failed."

Horace Watts shivered and stared at the thin wire in his
employer's hands. "I have served you well, and I wouldn't
dream of divulging—"

"I paid you extremely well to accomplish your mission,
and I suppose you have spent the money already. How are
you going to pay me back?" He flexed the wire between
his hands, wrapped it around his knuckles, and pulled it
taut.

"I-I have some funds left. I will gladly let you have
them." He retreated a step, then another as he read the
intent in the other man's eyes.

"It won't be enough. You'll soon join Reggie Shaw in
the grave. Say your last prayer."

Mr. Watts rubbed the sweat off his palms on to his
brown coat and ever so slowly let the dagger slide from
his sleeve. His hand closed around the cold handle.
Would he be able to whip it out fast enough and throw
it? At this moment he was glad he had written that letter
to Lord Bentworth, a powerful man and part of the Jacobite group. Just in case . . . he would know how to
stop this madness, before more lives were lost. "You
killed Reginald Shaw, didn't you?" Watts said to stall for
time.

"Shaw was nothing but a fool. He could have used

the map and found the gold in Scotland to finance his crumbling estate, but no! He was an idealist.''

''And you ordered me to kill Reverend Cleaves because he found out the truth.''

The man laughed. ''He snooped too much. Naturally there was a pretty penny involved with the map. I hope Charles Stuart will never see another *louis d'or.* '' He drew himself up and extended his arms. The wire glistened in the candlelight. ''As for the dear reverend, why don't you ask him when you meet him in hell.'' The powerful man's teeth gleamed in a sinister smile. ''Don't struggle. It will only take longer.''

Horace Watts's shirt soaked through with perspiration. It was now or never. He wished he didn't tremble so. His hands didn't want to obey, and they were so damp.

In a last desperate attempt to save his life, he whipped out the dagger and threw it at his adversary. But he was too late. The blade went wide. Already he could feel his head jerk back, the wire was cutting into his neck, severing his air intake. His flesh burned. Then there was a tearing pain, resignation, and blackness. . . .

The man dropped the wire to the floor, wiped his hands on his thighs, and contemptuously studied the corpse at his feet. He opened the door and beckoned to the man outside, the man with a head of bushy white hair. ''This is what will happen to you if you fail to locate Miss Shaw. Take him to Willow Hills and drop him in the graveyard. Miss Shaw might return. Perhaps finding another body there will be enough to scare her off.'' He pursed his lips. ''Once you've discarded the body, you'll have to stand sentinel at Willow Hills. Let me know if she returns.''

The man's eyes mirrored stark terror. But it was too late to back out now.

The next morning Bryony felt stiff after sitting in the same position all night. As she stretched, she noticed that Jack was awake. His face was ravaged with fever, but his eyes were clear. He looked infinitely sad.

She returned his glance coldly. ''Feeling better?''

He nodded almost imperceptibly.

''You should go back to sleep.'Tis very early.''

He grimaced and shook his head. "I need to explain a few things to you."

"I don't want more of your lies."

He patted the straw beside him, but she refused to move. She stood in the doorway, her rigid back turned toward him.

A gray mist covered the ground, and the trees shimmered with dew.

"Where's Clover?" he asked.

"He went down to the farm a few minutes ago. Wanted to watch the milking of the cows."

Jack sighed. "I love you," he said quietly.

Bryony was silent.

"I knew your brother well. We exchanged letters for six months. Reggie was supposed to deliver the map to me. My assignment is to bring it safely to Scotland."

Bryony spread her arms in a gesture of resignation. "But *why* didn't you tell me? You must have realized that *I* didn't have the map. We've been together long enough for you to know that." Her face contorted with despair. "That was all you ever wanted—the dratted map."

He tried to stand up, but collapsed against the straw with a groan exhausted. "That is not true. At first I only wanted the map, but when I came to know you, I fell in love with you."

"So much so that you trusted me enough to tell me the truth," she spat. "I cannot believe anything you say anymore."

"Let me explain." He hoisted himself onto his elbows and regarded her entreatingly. "That first night I went through your trunk looking for the map. And, yes, I was at the maze at Greymeadows. I have no excuses for those incidents."

Bryony's jaw fell. "The gall! You were the one who warned me that Reggie had been murdered. I should have known!"

"I truly believe Reggie was murdered, but I don't know by whom."

"Well, I do! By Lord Bentworth. All clues lead to him. He's powerful enough to get away scot-free. And what about the ambushes?"

"It's obvious that Reggie's murderer is after you now, probably because you're investigating your brother's death. The killer is afraid. That's the only possible explanation."

"Why did you come after me, Jack?"

"I was supposed to deliver the map to Charles Edward. Reggie was coming with me. He wrote to me, saying that if something happened to him, you would know where he had hidden the map. A precaution, since the mission was very important to him." Jack tensed and leaned forward. "Do you know where it is?"

She gave him a glance veiled in pain. "That is the only thing that is important now, isn't it? If I don't tell you, what are you going to do? Take apart my brain to find the truth?"

He heaved a sigh. "I know you're hurt. There is no way I can undo what I've done to you. I can only say that I'm sorry, from the bottom of my heart. But you have to understand that my happiness—and yours—is second to my mission. I will not stand by and watch more Scotsmen die from lack of food."

Bryony could find nothing to say. She sensed that he was telling the truth, and there was a fierce thrust to his jaw that told her he wouldn't stop until he had accomplished his goal.

"If you know where the map is, you ought to tell me," he went on inexorably. "Scottish soldiers are dying from starvation every day."

"And what if they had food and were strong and healthy? Wouldn't they kill British soldiers then?"

He shook his head in exasperation. "I don't know what they would do. Their ranks are greatly reduced. You would understand if you had been at the Battle of Culloden Moor. The English redcoats under the leadership of "Butcher" Cumberland slaughtered men lying helpless and bleeding on the battlefield. They killed innocent women and children—all in the name of a king who isn't even English!" He buried his face in his hands.

"I was there," he went on, "acting as a scout, or a spy, with my cousin Carey. I sided with the Scots, but I could not make myself join the battle. I could not fight my British brothers." He clutched his head in agony. "I feel so guilty—so cowardly. I can still hear the sullen thunder of the drums at Culloden Moor. It was freezing cold, sleeting and raining.''

Bryony felt the tug at her heart, and she could barely breathe, such was the tension he exuded. She sank down in the straw beside him and could barely keep from pulling him into her arms.

He continued. ''I saw the plaids of the tartans, the bonnets, the broadswords—too few swords—and I knew my Scottish brothers would be defeated. They were part of my family.'' He brushed the hair from his face. ''I will never forget the mournful sound of the bagpipes or the sight of the blood as the English cannon fire tore through the ranks of Scots, severing limbs from bodies.''

He clutched her hand and held it to his cheek. Tears glittered on his eyelashes, and a muscle worked in his jaw. ''The English ruthlessly cut down everyone in their path. Everyone. Looted and burned. I will never forget the sight of the blood, the bodies, the smell of burned flesh or the moans of agony.''

''And your family?'' Bryony asked softly.

''Two uncles fell dead on the field. I recognized their tartans—afterward. Three of my cousins were murdered in cold blood as they lay wounded.''

He took her hands between his own trembling palms. Struggling into a kneeling position before her, he said, ''I swear to you, I have never seen such blood thirst. The English acted like crazed animals. And I didn't take part in the fight. Don't you see? The only thing I can do to make amends is to deliver that gold. I cannot live with more lost lives on my conscience.''

''You cannot blame yourself for what happened.'' Bryony could not stop her own tears from wetting her cheeks. She rubbed the tense cords of Jack's neck as he sagged against her.

He groaned and hugged her close. He was dry and hot, the fever eating every inch of him. ''Reggie and I believed in the Stuart cause,'' he said, ''I want to make amends to my family, to all Scots, by delivering that gold. Can you ever understand?''

Bryony nodded. ''Yes, I understand. Guilt can be a de-

mon." Her voice broke, and she returned his embrace.
"Reggie was an idealist, and I would like to finish what
he started, to pay my last respects to him."

They sat together in silence for a while, each too moved
to speak. Then Bryony said, "Do you think I'm right to
think Lord Bentworth murdered my brother?"

Jack rolled away from her, beating the hay with his fists,
his face twisted with pain. "Why do you insist? Can't you
leave well enough alone? I don't know any more than you
do. Why torture yourself?"

"You don't have to fly into the boughs. You were the
one who suggested that Reggie was murdered."

He sighed in agony and regarded her through narrowed
eyes. His skin was damp and gray. "I believe any of those
men at the card game could have done Reggie in."

"But why?"

"Out of greed. There was a time when the French king
was willing to support the Stuarts. He has lost interest
now, but still French weapons, and dwindling French
funds, keep afloat the Scottish army—or what pitiful remains there are.

"Reggie's so-called friends might have wanted to line
their own coffers with French gold."

"I want to help you," Bryony said firmly.

He touched her cheek reverently. "Does that mean
you've forgiven me?"

She shook her head. "Forgiveness isn't everything. How
can I forget that you deceived me? You did it once, and
you'll do it again."

He groaned. "I was forced to because of my mission!
Anyone involved in the Jacobite cause must be extremely
careful so as not to find himself beheaded."

"I can understand your *words,* but don't you think you
could have trusted me? I haven't betrayed any of the Jacobite sympathizers who were at the card game."

He smiled wryly. "Yes, I know. I don't have much faith
in you, do I?" He leaned back against the hay and pulled
her with him so that her head rested on his chest. "All I
can say is, please forgive me. I find it very difficult to
place my trust in others, but I'll try to change. My life
was empty until I found you."

"As was mine. But lies are a weak foundation on which to build love."

He was silent, and she sensed his pain and indecision. "I'm probably the greatest fool that ever lived," he said forlornly.

Bryony laughed. "We'd better discuss that at another time."

"Will you really help me?"

"Yes, I'll do it for Reggie. Besides, you have been a great help to me."

He drew a deep breath, and his voice trembled when he asked, "Where is the map?"

Bryony hesitated only momentarily. "At Willow Hills." She felt his sharp breath of despair. "No, not burned," she explained. "It still exists. Reggie used to hide things in a certain oak tree when we were children." She paused, then said softly, "It looks as if we have to return to that sad place."

He stroked her hair. " 'Tisn't altogether sad. You gave me the most beautiful time of my life at Willow Hills. I'll always cherish our moments together in the folly."

"Yes, that was *before* I knew about the lies," Bryony replied.

"I'll spend the rest of my life proving just how much you mean to me," he promised, his voice husky with emotion.

Just as Bryony softened, Clover came rushing into the barn, shouting, "Th' militia is comin'! 'Urry! They'll find us 'ere, an' then—" He made a slashing motion across his throat. " 'Urry!"

Chapter 25

There was no time to lose. Bryony gathered their meager belongings and helped Jack stand up. He swayed alarmingly.

"Where shall we go? I don't want to be questioned again," she whispered, throwing fearful glances at the door.

"Into the woods, for now. They will not find us there."

"There aren't any woods here, only fields and cliffs," Bryony said, and peeped outside. The countryside was quiet. A cow stood chewing its cud in the farmyard, and the bell around the goat's neck tingled softly. The muffled roar of the Channel echoed in the distance.

Cold sweat pearled on Jack's forehead as he supported himself against the wall with an unsteady hand.

" 'Urry, then," Clover urged. "They'll be comin' any minute. I saw 'em wi' me bare eyes. Redcoats, an' they were arskin' questions o' th' farmer's marm."

"Were they the same men we met on the beach?"

Clover nodded. "I know a road behind th' chicken coop. I used it this morn."

Bryony trusted Clover's survival skills. He was quick and always alert to danger. She worried about Jack, but when he sensed her distress, he said, "I'll manage somehow. Don't you worry. I have absolutely no desire to get captured by the redcoats. If they recognize us, they'll realize that we lied to them down on the beach."

"Lies and more lies," Bryony said between her teeth as she followed Clover, laden with a basket of food and an extra blanket that the farm woman had given them the previous evening.

"We look more than ever like fugitives with hay sticking out of our hair and clothes," Jack said as he followed close behind. "But there's no time to fix that now."

Clover waved frantically from behind a hut made of flintstone and sod. Hens and chickens scratched in the dirt, fluttering away with loud squawks as Bryony and Jack hurried by.

Behind the coop was a thin strip of trees and scraggly bushes. Purposefully, Bryony braved the clutching brambles. The thorns clawed at her skirt and legs, but she pushed forward. The yellowing leaves soon concealed all three of them successfully, but for how long?

Jack had to stop repeatedly to regain his breath. Intermittent coughing wracked him, and Bryony fretted that the soldiers would hear him. Yet there was nothing he could do to stop the persistent cough.   .

He waved at them to continue, but Bryony would not consider leaving without him.

They heard a shot and running footsteps on the other side of the trees. Had their flight already been detected? Bryony didn't wait to find out. She urged Jack on, and he made a superhuman effort to run, all the while trying to subdue his cough.

She could not see Clover, but she heard him crashing through the thorny obstacles in front of them, leaving a neat path in his wake.

As suddenly as the trees had appeared, they ended. It had taken them less than three minutes to pass through. On the other side was a narrow road, two deep ruts of dried mud with an elevated strip of grass in the middle.

"Not exactly the London road," Jack panted, "but it'll lead somewhere. We'll have to leave this vicinity immediately."

They hurried after Clover's small figure as it disappeared around a curve in the lane.

"You should have thought about fleeing to the Continent like Mr. Forrester did, Jack," Bryony said between labored breaths. She was hot and tired. Because of Jack she had been drawn into a web of deceit that she must maintain if she wanted to save herself. By aiding him, she had become an enemy to her country.

But in the short time she had known him, he had changed her life, and she regretted only the lies that had passed between them.

A few cottages lined the lane, but Bryony didn't dare stop and ask for shelter. No one would risk hiding fugitives pursued by the militia. And the soldiers were close behind them, fighting their way through the brambles.

Winded, Jack staggered along, clasping his side. His face was perspiring, yet the gaze that he lifted to the trees along the lane was shrewd and alert. Still, he must be using the last of his strength.

All of a sudden he jumped across the ditch and said, "You go on. I will lead the soldiers on a diversionary chase."

She stood frozen in the middle of the lane, gazing at him in confusion. "No! You're in no condition to do it by yourself. We must stick together."

"Do as I say," he ordered. " 'Twill be for the best. I'll join you at The Gilded Goose posting inn at Worthing. Go!"

Running footsteps sounded behind her and suddenly there was no time to argue. She hastened to follow Clover, whom she could see ahead at the abutment of an old stone bridge that spanned a waterfall.

"Under 'ere, m'lady. They won't think o' lookin' 'ere," he urged, already sliding down the bank. "They'll think we rushed into th' village willy-nilly."

Bryony didn't know what to think. She slid down the bank, her feet landing in water just as two shots echoed among the trees some distance away. *Jack!*

In a moment of utter desolation, she pressed her fingertips to her heart and forced herself to suppress the moan that rose to her lips. Crawling among the reeds that grew at the base of the abutment under the bridge, she waited for the sounds of pursuit to come closer. But no one came. Jack had obviously succeeded in diverting their pursuers. More shots echoed still further away.

"They killed him," she whispered, forgetting the child beside her.

"Naw, 'e bain't no wee babe. 'E knows what 'e's doin'."
Clover snuggled close to her, his feet buried in the mud
of the riverbank. "Why are we runnin'?" he asked in-
nocently.

Oh, God, how am I going to explain this? Bryony wondered. "Do you know what the Jacobites are?"

"Crooks an' traitors," he said without hesitation.

"They support a losing cause. They want Prince Charles
Edward Stuart on the throne of England and Scotland. But
that doesn't make them less honorable. However, the present king of England, George, is afraid of another uprising
and wants the Jacobites rooted out."

Clover seemed to ponder her words, his young brow
furrowed in concentration. "Th' guv's a Jakkerbite, then?"

"Yes unfortunately. He's helping them even though he
never planned on becoming a Jacobite in the beginning."
The hand of dread squeezed her heart. "He must hide
until there is no more danger of detection. But he may
have to leave England in the end."

Clover's eyes were very round. "An' live wi' 'em Frogs
as talks queerly?"

"Exactly."

"Naw, 'twould be worse 'n death! We 'ave t' save 'im."

Bryony held him tight and pressed her eyes shut in agony. "It may be too late, but let's hope 'tisn't." She
sighed. "I believe 'tis safe to continue into Worthing now.
The soldiers must have pursued Jack."

She shook Clover's knobby shoulders gently. "You have
to promise not to breathe to a soul that Jack is involved
with the Jacobites. Do you understand?"

'O' course. I didn't tell anyone that Mr. Forrester was
one, did I? I brung 'im food in th' ol' ruins."

She hugged him once more, hiding the tears in her eyes.
"Yes, you're a good boy, Clover."

They scrambled up the steep bank and crossed the
bridge. The small waterfall glittered and gurgled in the
pale sunlight. It hurtled over stones and logs to form a
lazy stream below.

Guided by the sun, they headed north, away from the
quiet village. The lane was shaded by tall elms, a scene
out of a fairytale, but Bryony was in no mood to appre-

ciate her surroundings. She was full of worry for the man she loved, and she would know no peace until they were together again, at The Gilded Goose. Dear God, let him be there, she prayed as a kindly farmer stopped and offered them a lift in his wagon.

The Gilded Goose was a large, affluent posting house. Clover counted the horses aloud, and Bryony realized he could count no further than ten. There were at least twenty horses in the inn yard, and five or six carriages of different designs. The noise was deafening as travelers readied themselves for departure.

"If someone asks who we are, we'll pretend we're mother and son, farmers from the Hove area. That should be distant enough, so that no one will wonder why they've never seen us before."

Clover smiled sweetly. "I wouldn't mind if ye were me mudder fer real. I niver 'ad one."

Bryony was startled. She had never thought about that. Being a mother was a great responsibility, and she didn't know if she could shoulder it. "We'll see later."

"D'ye think th' guv's 'ere now?"

"I doubt he could have arrived before us. Let's find out." Cowering as if she expected a heavy hand to fall on her shoulder and a voice to denounce her as a traitor, she entered the taproom. Her gaze flitted from face to face, but there was no accusation in the eyes. No one even acknowledged her presence. Simple garb, and dirt streaks on one's face, worked wonders if one wished to remain incognito.

There was no sign of Jack, whose height alone would have set him apart. Remembering that she didn't have any money left in her purse, Bryony didn't dare approach one of the waiters for a table. The scent of roast meat and warm apple cider enticed her famished senses, but she would have to make do with the apples and the leftover bread and cheese in her basket.

Soldiers in splendid red or white jackets lined the bar, but as they raised their mugs of ale in cheers, they clearly weren't looking for Jacobite refugees.

"We'll have to wait outside. Let's eat something."

Clover agreed readily and found a peaceful spot away from the bustle on a grassy knoll, where they had a good view of the comings and goings of the inn yard.

They ate crisp, tangy apples and cheese. Bryony thought she had never eaten anything more delicious. Hunger was truly the best spice.

They waited until the sunlight slanted steeply over the roofs, Bryony growing increasingly convinced that Jack was not coming. Her worry escalated as the hours passed without a sign of him. Out of pure exhaustion she fell asleep leaning against a tree trunk.

Shots reverberated in her dreams, and faceless pursuers clawed at her with grotesque white fingers.

"There 'e is!" Clover exclaimed.

She bolted upright, staring sleep-dazed toward the inn. A man was entering the yard. She strained to see if it was really Jack, then disappointment washed over her.

" 'Tis not him. Jack is much taller than that. Besides, he was wearing a short peasant jacket. This man is wearing a black coat."

After that, she found it impossible to sleep. As the sun disappeared beyond the horizon, a cold draft crept over the ground. The night promised to be clear and cold. If they remained here, they would freeze.

"We'll have to find a place to sleep," Bryony said.

"Per'aps th' stables. We can sneak into an empty box when th' grooms ain't watchin'."

"No, too risky. We don't want to draw attention to ourselves." She stood and stretched her stiff limbs. "We'll find a barn somewhere."

Listless, she led Clover by the hand farther across the fields until they found a barn at a secluded farmstead. They waited until the sounds of the milking and the feeding of the calves and pigs had died down before they dared approach the dark building.

"Let's make sure we're gone before dawn. I don't want to be found here," Bryony said tiredly, and let herself fall into a soft mound of hay. Clover rolled up beside her, and five minutes later, they were both asleep.

* * *

The next morning they continued their vigil on the knoll. As soon as the inn had filled with people, Bryony sent Clover to look for Jack.

He returned without news. Bryony tried to keep up a cheerful attitude, but she was deeply distressed. There was nothing more lowering than spending the hours waiting for someone who might not even be alive. Yet, she refused to dwell on that horrifying thought. Jack had to be safe. He had to.

They spent the second night in the same barn, and as the third day was closing, still with no sign of Jack, Bryony began to accept that he wasn't coming.

"We'll have to return to Crawley without him," she explained to Clover. The boy was impatient and whined that he was hungry. They had eaten their last apples and chunk of bread that morning. Bryony could not bear to see Clover starve. Somewhere they would have to find some more apples until she could contact Uncle Butterball for more funds.

She accepted the stark truth that she might never see Jack again. Either the soldiers had shot him, or he had succumbed in inflammation of the lungs and was too sick to move. Guilt and worry nagged at her until her every nerve ending was raw and aching. She should not have left him to fend for himself.

"We'll go on tomorrow morning," she said. "You could go to the kitchen and beg for some old bread." She tweaked his nose. "If you turn on your charm, you might find yourself the owner of some other delicious food scraps."

Clover brightened at the prospect and promised to return with a pie.

"That is a bit too optimistic," Bryony said with a wry smile. "And I don't want you to steal." She gave him a stern stare, and he kicked a clump of grass rebelliously.

"Oh, daggers!"

"Then we'll starve until tomorrow, and I don't want to hear anything more about it!"

Clover set off and returned a short while later with some loaves of old bread. "Duck food," he said sullenly. "Ye shoulda seen th' meatpies th' cook was makin'. I drooled an' smiled, but no smile could make th' ol' sourpuss soften up.'' He shoved the bread into Bryony's hands.

"You did well," she praised him. "I promise you a dinner fit for a king very soon."

They had no difficulty finding a lift to Brighton. From there, they turned north, hitched lifts mostly with farmers going from one village to the other. It would have been too long a detour to collect Jules and the carriage outside Alfriston. They went through Pyecombe, Hurstpierpoint, Twineham, Bolney, Slaugham, and finally reached Crawley. Kindly farmers shared their food, and Bryony gathered apples that had fallen off the trees along the road.

She drew a sigh of relief upon seeing the familiar high street of Crawley and the benevolent view of Uncle Butterball's office.

But her depression returned when she discovered that the kindly Butterball had gone to London on business. Mr. Grimes explained that his employer had been awfully busy, traveling to various places.

Bryony was grateful when the friendly assistant advanced a small sum without asking any questions. She suggested to Clover that he stay overnight at the inn in Crawley while she visited Willow Hills. He refused. "I'm supposed t' protect ye," he said.

"Protect me? Why?"

"Th' guv told me not t' leave ye outta sight until 'e comes back."

Bryony knew this claim was Clover's invention. Jack had not had a chance to speak with the boy before their escape. She placed her hand on the boy's head and met his steady gaze. "He might never come back. We have to take care of ourselves."

But what would she do with the map if it really was hidden in the oak tree? She had no idea where to turn with it, unless . . . Of course! Why hadn't she thought of that before? Nigel would know what to do with the map. He was one of the Jacobites. It would surprise him if she managed to find the map that he insisted did not exist.

Bryony sighed in resignation. "Very well, Clover, you

may accompany me to my old home. Hopefully, this sad business will be over soon.''

In fact, she abhorred the thought of returning to Willow Hills, where last she had stared into the Reverend Cleaves's lifeless eyes. But the sooner she got it over with, the better.

It was afternoon before they finally set out in a carriage that Mr. Grimes rented for them. She didn't tell him her true errand, only that she needed to see Reggie's grave once more. He did not pry, only wished her good luck.

The day was cloudy, the cold air heavy with the threat of rain. Bryony shivered and swept the cloak closer around her. Depression weighed her down. How could she go on living without Jack? Their parting had come so abruptly that she hadn't had a chance to imprint her last look at him on her memory.

And she had never said good-bye.

After passing East Grinstead, the carriage turned south toward Willow Hills and bumped along a road covered with cinder that had rusted and fused into a hard, reddish surface. The slag came from the ironworks in the area.

"I don't like it," Clover said as they approached the gates of the ruined estate. "Shivers run up me spine, and th' skin on me neck prickles."

Bryony knew exactly what he meant. The charred remains of the house looked more sinister than ever. She stepped down from the carriage and wished she had not come with only Clover for protection. On top of everything else, it had started to drizzle, a fine, icy rain that crept between her collar and neck to freeze her very bones.

"You'd better wait here," Bryony said. "Talk with the coachman."

"At least 'e bain't no Frog, like Jules," Clover said, and climbed up on the box.

Bryony squared her shoulders and set out on her mission. Suddenly she hoped there would be no map in the tree. It would be best for everyone—except for the Scottish soldiers—if the map was gone forever.

As she walked up the littered drive, she felt as if eyes were following her movements from behind every tree and stone. Perhaps she should have asked Clover to come along, but it was too late now. If she turned around, she might never find the courage to brave the park again. At the folly, her memories would be happier, if bittersweet. All she had to do was pass the shed and the graveyard. . . .

Chapter 26

A thick mist shrouded the trees in an eerie light. Bryony
stumbled and almost fell on the debris in the drive. To her
surprise she noticed deep grooves freshly made by wagon
wheels, and she could not recall having seen them on her
previous visit. Three black ravens flapped from the ground
with harsh shrieks as she neared the shed where she had
found the reverend's body.

Cold shivers raced through her at the memory, and it
was with utmost difficulty that she forced herself past the
building. Clenching her hands in the folds of her cloak to
stop their trembling, she continued, keeping her eyes on
the ground, refusing to glance at the graveyard.

Where was Jack? What had happened to him? She had
never felt more alone, or with so little hope of future happiness. Just as there seemed little hope that the drizzle
would stop. In fact, as she neared the folly, the rain increased to a steady downpour. She could barely make out
the contours of the cone-shaped roof through the swirling
mists. But there it was, the gold-painted globe at its crest
gleaming dully.

Bryony heaved a shuddering sigh. So much had happened since she had shared that night with Jack in the
folly. It had been the happiest night of her life, even though
they had spent it in what was for her the saddest place on
earth.

"Oh, Jack, I wish you were here now," she whispered
as she stepped onto the narrow path leading to the entrance. The small, neglected building held a forlorn and
shuttered air.

Fear gripped her as she faced the closed door. Steadying herself with a deep breath, she tried the handle. It groaned, and water dribbled onto her hand from the ledge above the door. Holding her breath, she looked into the dim, musty interior. Leaves rattled across the floor in the draft from the open door.

Everything was as she and Jack had left it. Her old dolls still lay in their wooden box. The cushions were lined up properly on the seat around the perimeter of the folly. But even the silent emptiness was frightening.

She stifled a scream as a gust of wind tossed a loose branch against the wall. To calm her pounding heart, she sank down on the seat and stared out the window. She had to inspect the oak tree before she lost her courage.

The mist had thickened, billowing across the ground and swathing the daylight in a woolly veil. She walked around to the back of the folly, and there it was, the dead oak tree. The old trunk was dripping with water, and green moss grew on the rough bark. As in the old days, she measured the steps through the tall, wet grass. One, two, three . . .

The steps were exactly as Reggie had described. If the map was anywhere, it was hidden in the tree. There was the hole, halfway up the trunk, just as it had always been.

If she stood on her toes, she could easily reach it. The old wooden boards that Reggie had nailed to the trunk for steps had long ago rotted away.

"Let's see," she mused aloud, not knowing exactly what to expect when she stuck her hand in the hole.

But as she was about to explore the cavity, she heard steps, heavy uneven steps crushing the tall grass and crunching twigs, coming from the other side of the folly.

Bryony hid quickly behind the tree. Pressing herself close to the trunk, she wished she could disappear completely.

Though stiff with fear, she craned her neck to see who was approaching.

A male figure dressed in a tricorne hat and cloak approached like a vision in the mist. The body was hunched over as if he was suffering from a pain in the right side.

Moving clumsily he reached the folly and fumbled for support, found the wall, and leaned heavily against it.

Then came a cough that was absorbed by the dense silence of the mist.

"Jack!" Bryony's feet grew wings, and she rushed through the grass.

He turned awkwardly, then slumped back against the wall. "Brye," he croaked. "My lovely one."

Bryony halted before him, uncertain what to do. She wanted to embrace him, yet her wounded pride stopped her. He looked so pitiful that her heart ached. She wrung her hands in torment. "How did you get here?"

" 'Tis a long story," he forced out, barely able to speak. His face was ashen, with dark rings circling his sunken eyes. In their obsidian depths burned a consuming fever. His breath was labored, and he looked as if his last ounce of energy had been spent long ago.

"Did you find the map?" he demanded.

Anger ignited within her. "That's the only thing you can think about, isn't it? Always the mission. You're worn to a shade, but that cannot stop you!" She cried out in desperation.

"There is no time to lose," he whispered, closing his eyes. "Please tell me—"

"Are the soldiers still following you?"

He hung his head in weariness, and his hand clutching a decorative pillar on the folly's porch was white and thin. "I don't think so. The map—"

"I was just about to find out if the map is still there," she explained with a sigh of exasperation. She could not argue with him when his health was worn to its limits.

Perspiration trickled across his cheek and disappeared in his beard as he coughed wretchedly. "Please." He held out his hand entreatingly, but Bryony refused to take it. She turned on her heel, tears burning her eyes.

Once again she reached into the hollow oak. She touched the corner of a metal box. Straining to reach deeper, she got a good grip around the shallow box and hauled it out.

It was painted green with the initials "R.S." in gold on

the lid. It was the box in which Reggie had kept his coins and the other small gifts he had received while still a boy.

The box was rusty at the corners, and the lid didn't fit tightly.

Bryony slanted a glance toward Jack and noticed that his legs had given out. He sat slumped against the wall.

"I think the map is here," she said as she joined him. Worry nibbled at her as she eyed his trembling body. How had he managed to traverse Sussex in such poor health? And how had he eluded his pursuers? But he was in no condition to answer any questions.

He raised tired eyes to the box in her hands. She squatted before him and lifted the lid, her hands trembling with nervousness.

In the box were two stiff folded papers, one cream-colored, the other white and covered with official wax seals.

On the top paper was scrawled her name.

Heedless of the wet grass, she sank down on the ground beside Jack, unfolded the paper, and read:

Dearest Bryony,
It's with a heavy heart I write this, probably the most difficult letter I'll ever write, because when you read it, I will have departed this world. I hope it won't come to pass. As a precaution, I will hide this map in a place only you can find. You're the only person I trust in these unstable times. I fear there is a traitor in my circle of "friends."

The cause in which I strongly believe has proven to be ill-conceived from the very beginning, and doomed to failure.

You should know that I have always loved you, the second half of myself. Life has been lonely without you, and I would have asked you to come home had my affairs been in order. But mostly I wanted to protect you from any involvement in my dangerous commitments.

Please forgive me for any pain I might have caused you. I wish it could have ended differently.

Your loving brother,
Reggie
P.S Unless you can deliver the map to the prince,
burn it!

"How totally idiotic, and overbearing!" Bryony cried,
crumpling the letter and tossing it away. It disappeared
into the grass. "How dared he write such a terrible letter!
He must have known it would break my heart."

Sobbing uncontrollably, she pressed her fists to her
mouth in an effort to stifle the sobs. When she felt Jack's
hand on her shoulder, she shook it off with an irrational
need to hurt him. She wanted to run away and hide her
raw pain from his compassionate gaze.

"Your brother was young and foolish, rash in his actions and ideals," Jack said. "But he was honest to the
very end." He sighed. "And he was loyal. He might be
the only one of the men at the card game who was truly
loyal to the cause."

Bryony sent him a sharp glance. "What makes you think
that?"

"He hid the map. He put the mission before his own
life."

"You are just like him! Idiots cut from the same cloth."
She stood up, leaning over him in anger. "Look at you.
You're more dead than alive, but will that stop you? No!
You'd rather die than be overcome by guilt." She shook
her fist at him, her eyes flashing. "Your suffering is noble,
isn't it? Well, I don't give a fig for your suffering! A self-
centered martyr is what you are, not caring what others
think or feel. All that exists for you is the mission."

She yanked the box from the ground and upended it
over his lap. The map fluttered down. "Here! This is what
you've struggled to find all this time." Turning away, she
hurled the box as far as she could. It landed with a splash
in the stream.

"You will never ask my opinion, and I'm tired of being
a pawn in your political games," she shouted. Unable to
suppress her desperation, she ran away among the trees.
In solitude, and with her arms around the trunk of a sturdy
lime tree, she cried until every last tear was spent. Then

she swore she would never cry again. Especially not over a man!

When she returned, Jack was where she had left him. He hadn't even looked at the map. Perhaps he would never rise again.

She hardened her heart and walked slowly away.

"Wait," he croaked. "Dammit, I need to speak with you.'Tis my body that won't obey me."

"You should have thought about that before," she cried angrily. "I'm sick and tired of your mission."

At the end of the path, she discerned the outlines of the tombstones in the milky mist. As she approached, the gravel crunching under her shoes, large black birds exploded into the air.

In a daze, she heard Jack floundering along the path behind her. He took her by surprise when he advanced much faster than she thought possible and clamped a hand on her shoulder. His grip brooked no resistance. His breath rasped unevenly in an out of his lungs. His eyes were blazing, and she winced.

"I can understand your anger," he said, "but it's more than enough. You find it very easy to judge others, including me." He drew in a strangled breath. "I know I'm no saint, but I've done everything in my power to soften your difficulties." He flung out his arm, nearly losing his balance. "You don't know half the suffering that is behind this mission, so I beg of you not to resort to another of your tirades."

"Look at you! Almost dying, and still spouting your fanciful rhetoric."

He stared into the mist before him, and she saw that he was fighting to keep his temper under control. "If I weren't so damn weak, I would spank your lovely bottom," he breathed, and lost his voice in an attack of coughing.

Seething, her bearing regal, she said, "I suggest we end our liaison right here, right now. I cannot find a way to continue this charade. You have your map; you can continue to Scotland alone—if you don't die first."

She made as if to move away from him, but he grasped her arm in a grip that belied his weakness. "I won't let you leave. Not now."

"Ah! You want me to finish the mission for you so that
you can rest in peace, is that it?"

"Shrew." Swaying dangerously, his breath wheezing,
he pulled her into his arms. "My little shrew." He planted
a feverish kiss on her brow. "I can't bear to part with
you."

With her head pressed to his chest, his powerful body
hard against hers, his arms strong around her, her resolution weakened. Her heart twisted, and she could not
maintain her icy demeanor.

She gazed searchingly into his face. When he bent his
lips to hers and captured them in a kiss, she realized what
she had been missing. Though he was weak with fever,
his kiss was savage, possessive. Melting against him, she
did not want him to stop as he branded her with his tongue.
The sweet shock of him pressed so tightly against her was
intoxicating. The smell of fresh air in his skin, the crisp
feel of his hair under her fingertips, the contours of his
lean face, they all must be rediscovered until she knew
that his words were true.

They could not bear to be apart.

When he raised his head, she moaned in disappointment. He chuckled softly. "I pledged my love to you, and
I will not allow your dainty foot to trample that love to
dust."

She could only nod, still savoring his embrace, sweetness coursing through her body, sensations that his kiss
had reawakened.

A flock of ravens sat perched in the branches above the
graveyard, crowing and flapping their wings as if cheering
them on. Jack squinted up at the birds.

"I guess we interrupted their dinner," he mused, staring into the mist. He stiffened slightly and gently disentangled Bryony's arms. "I must go and have a look."

When Bryony offered to accompany him, he halted her
with a movement of his hand. "No, you'd better wait here
until I have investigated."

His breath rattled in his chest as he straightened and
took a few unsteady steps. He wound in and out among
the gravestones, the mist swallowing him, then momen-

tarily spitting him out again. He stopped abruptly and stared down at something. —

"What is it?" she called.

"Stay where you are," he said, the sound muffled in the mist. He retraced his steps with difficulty, his face set and grim. "We ought to take another path."

Bryony shivered. The tension she had felt when she arrived at Willow Hills had returned with double force.

"Another dead man?" she asked between stiff lips.

He nodded. "This one has a scarred face and is wearing a brown coat, but I don't think I've ever seen him before. Unless—"

"The man in the brown coat!" Bryony's gaze flew from tree to tree, as if she expected her mysterious tormentors to appear at any moment. "He's the man who was following me everywhere."

"Well, this time he left no calling card. His neck was—"

Bryony clutched his hand. "Come, let us hurry from this frightful place. I don't ever want to return here."

Jack did not protest, but their progress was slow and torturous, though he tried to make haste. They reached the drive and passed the crumbling front steps, the once-proud facade. Bryony could make out the contours of her coach, a horse tied to its back. Jack must have come on horseback.

Just as they began crossing the last few yards to the carriage, two shots roared through the air from behind. A musket ball buzzed past Bryony's head. Jack staggered and careened into her with a moan of rage on his lips. Then he crashed to the ground and was still.

Chapter 27

"Jack!" Bryony knelt beside his still form and felt the blood seeping through the coat beneath his right rib cage. His cloak lay like a shroud over his head.

Two more shots shattered the air, tearing through some bushes to her left. Where had her enemies come from, and who were they? Perhaps they had been watching the entire time she had been looking for the map. Tendrils of fear coiled through her, paralyzing her.

The coachman and Clover were rushing to her assistance. "Gor blimey, 'e's dead then," Clover said matter-of-factly, staring round-eyed at Jack's still form.

"No!" Bryony whimpered. "Help me lift him inside the carriage." The coachman grasped Jack by the shoulders, and Bryony and Clover each lifted a leg. With muscles straining to their limits, they managed to ease Jack onto one of the seats. "Make haste," Bryony ordered as she tore the kerchief from her neck, folded it, and held it against Jack's wound.

The whip cracked, and the horses jerked into motion. The carriage tilted dangerously as the horses turned in the drive. Another shot echoed, and the ball drilled into the side of the carriage. Splinters of wood rained past the window.

"Cor, did ye see that?" Clover said in awe, cowering in the corner.

"Yes, we're lucky to still be alive," Bryony said.

"Them villains are jest like angry 'ornets. I didn't know they was allowed t' shoot reg'lar people."

Jack moaned and tossed on the seat. Bryony truly worried for his life. Weak as he was, he could never survive this last blow. She clamped her hand harder over the wound and smoothed back his unruly curls.

If only they could outride their pursuers. She had never heard them, which meant that they had either just arrived or they had been waiting to ambush her, or Jack. She could not be sure of anything anymore.

Her kerchief was soon soaked through with blood. Swallowing hard to hold back her nausea, Bryony closed her eyes and pressed down even harder. She listened for sounds of pursuit, but could hear nothing.

As they approached East Grinstead, she dared to stick her head outside the window and take a quick look. She saw no one. Calculating quickly, she riffled through Jack's pockets and discovered a heap of coins in a leather pouch, even some golden guineas.

Leaning out of the window, she ordered the coachman to stop in town for bandages. At the sight of gold, he agreed readily. But just as he was about to pull up in the center of town, three men mounted on horses appeared at the crossing of two lanes a quarter of a mile behind the carriage. They rode unhurriedly, shoulder to shoulder, and Bryony sensed their menace, their intent.

"Drive on!" she cried, clutching the window frame so hard that it bit into her fingers. The road made a turn, and as the window gave her a vision of the road behind her, she forced herself to look at the men. One of them had a mop of white hair. They were unobtrusively dressed in simple coats and plain waistcoats. They could be bailiffs inspecting land, sports enthusiasts on their way to a horse race, or grooms exercising their masters'horses.

But she knew none of that was true. They were villains pursuing *her*.

"Clove, do you recognize any of the men riding behind us?" she asked, thoroughly shaken.

Clover pressed closer to her and peeped out the window. "Yep. Th' white-'aired fella in th' middle was at Potter 'Ouse once. I reckernize 'im, but I don't know 'is name."

"He-he was one of the men who shot at us then?" Bryony dreaded Clover's answer.

"Per'aps." Clover crept away from the window and crouched on the floor next to Jack's seat. "Looka 'ere. Th' guv's comin' round."

Jack was truly moving, struggling to sit up. The exertion made him wince and fall back. "Damn!" he swore under his breath. "They winged me." He clutched at his side and stared grimly at the blood-sodden coat.

"Lie still," Bryony urged him. "You'll only bleed more if you move. We'll take you to a doctor."

"Hollow as a sieve, am I?" he joked feebly. His face was ghastly white, with deep lines of pain etching his forehead. "Not much left of me, I'm afraid," he said, forcing out the words with superhuman effort.

"Don't spend your last strength talking," Bryony admonished. "You'll have good care soon." She knew those words might be an exaggeration, but she had to reassure him. He was shivering uncontrollably and could barely keep his eyes open. Bryony wanted to cry at the pitiful sight, but she smiled bravely and tucked her homespun shawl around his shoulders.

"I'm sorry," he whispered between cracked lips. "I'm not much help, am I?"

She said nothing, but the fear in her eyes must have betrayed her because he stared for a long time at her. "We're being pursued, aren't we?" he said.

She nodded. "We'll find a way to escape." She leaned forward. "I've been thinking what would happen if we stopped and confronted them."

He shook his head weakly and smiled, a crooked twist that was more a grimace. "They put the lead ball into me. If you're not careful, they won't hesitate doing the same to you."

"Did they follow you all the way from Worthing?"

He closed his eyes. "No." His voice was barely audible, and his head was gliding sideways toward the edge of the seat.

" 'E's 'dyin' now," Clover said gloomily. "Thass a fact."

Bryony kneeled on the floor of the coach and took Jack's hot, dry hand in her own. "No, but we have to find help soon." Where could she take Jack?

She had no close friends in East Grinstead since her old nurse had died five years ago. The vicar? No. The doctor? At least they had funds to pay for lodgings at some inn.

"What shall I do?" she whispered to herself while she continued to hold Jack's limp hand against her cheek.

He opened eyes glazed with fever, gathered his strength, and said, "Pay the coachman to head north. We have to try to fool our pursuers." He paused, recouping his strength. "Tell him to let us off in the woods somewhere. The trees will give us good over." His head collapsed over the edge of the seat. He had lost consciousness. Clover conveniently pushed it up onto the seat in a gesture on desperation.

"I've never seen a man die afore," he muttered, his bottom lip trembling.

"He's not going to die." Yet Bryony's words sounded hollow. She considered what Jack had said. He would never survive a night in the woods, especially a cold one. His plan would never work. Still, it was the only feasible plan. She had to get rid of their pursuers somehow. What would happen if they rode up and barred the coach's progress?

She looked out. The carriage was already passing the last cottages of East Grinstead. The men were still following, riding some distance behind but coming closer every second.

As another traveling chaise approached, Bryony decided to do something desperate. She called out to the coachman to turn around. "Right now! Block the road so that the other carriage is forced to stop."

The coachman swore and tried to argue, but when he saw her haunted eyes, he obeyed. As the other team approached at a fast clip, he drew sharply on the reins. The horses neighed and tried to rear, causing confusion in the approaching team. The collars of the two teams locked, and Bryony jumped down, screaming, "Highwaymen! We're being followed by highwaymen, over there." She pointed at the three men who had stopped further down the lane.

"They've tried to kill my—my husband," she blurted out

in desperation. She gesticulated wildly, and a fat matron with an enormous mobcap stuck her head outside.

"What's the to-do?" she complained. "McLendon, see what the tumult is all about."

A tall, extremely handsome man dressed in a mint-green satin coat heavily embossed with silver threads, and a wig that was a confection of exquisite curls and powder, stepped down. He stared down his long, thin nose and inquired, "What's the caterwauling about, miss?"

Bryony's jaw fell open in surprise at the vision, but she rapidly gained control of her thoughts. "The men—"

"The men?" The man furrowed his brow and stared at the three men on horseback standing farther down the lane. Then he hauled out a handkerchief and buffed his fingernails. "They don't look like highwaymen, m'dear."

Staring at her pursuers, she could have hugged the exquisite gentleman when she realized that the men were turning around. Her ruse had succeeded beyond her dreams.

The Exquisite waved her away with the handkerchief. "Tell your mistress not to panic. I see nothing untoward here."

Bryony realized that, in her simple clothes, she appeared to be a servant, someone the Exquisite would never have considered addressing under normal circumstances.

She bobbed and hurried back into the coach. "Thank ye kindly, sir." She watched the Exquisite's carriage head into East Grinstead. Knowing she had to return to town and get help for Jack, she told the coachman to stop at The Swan. There, she would send a message to Dr. Littleton, her family physician, if he was still practicing. If someone recognized her, she would just have to invent some story.

She smiled wryly. Jack had taught her well. She could tell any number of lies without blushing. She might be forced to tell the doctor the truth, but she trusted him.

As the carriage pulled up at the inn, Jack came to, his eyes unfocused. "Wha-what happened? Did we fall into a ditch?"

"No. We've returned to East Grinstead. I will send for the doctor."

"No! No!" He clutched her hand and shook it feebly. "We cannot stay in East Grinstead. We have to go on today."

"Why? Tell me why."

"We have to leave the villains behind as soon as possible."

"I know, but I'll think of something to protect us. The most important thing now is to cure you. A few days more or less won't make a difference."

"But they will find us." He groaned. "Don't you see? We have to take the map to Scotland."

"You'll die if you don't care for your wound. Then the map will fall into oblivion. Reggie asked me to burn it if I couldn't deliver it to the prince."

To find out the lay of the land, Bryony stepped into the silent inn yard, leaving Clover to watch over Jack. She pulled her large, plain mobcap deep over her ears, concealing most of her face. Praying that no one would recognize her, she advanced into the small building. The interior was much as she recalled from her childhood, dark with worn but clean floor planks, a hodgepodge of tables and chairs that did not match, a stone fireplace that took up one entire wall. Even the old wing chairs before the fire were the same, just as sagging as they had been when she was a girl. A crude homemade tapestry graced one wall. The landlord's lady, Mrs. Twiggs, had a passion for embroidery, though scant talent.

There he was now, Mr. Twiggs, pouring a tankard of ale for a customer. He looked to be the same small, rotund, and jolly man she remembered, but his hair was thinner and graying, his jowls heavier.

Bryony caught his attention by bobbing and saying, "Please, mister landlord, me employer's taken ill. 'E sent me t' bespeak a room." She rattled the pouch while holding her eyes shyly downcast. "Th' best room in th' 'ouse, an' we needs th' good doctor."

"Certainly, lass," the landlord said. "I'll send fer Dr. Littleton." He stared at her for along moment, and she pressed her chin further down. "Now then, 'aven't I seen ye afore?" he mused. Bryony counted five customers, who were all staring at her now. She shook her head miserably, and they all laughed. "A shy lass, ain't she?" commented a stranger.

Bryony was saved from closer scrutiny when the Exquisite with whom she had spoken in the road entered, leading on his arm a fat, tall matron dressed in a hideous purple gown. Bryony had never seen a more mismatched couple, and apparently neither had the other customers. Deep silence fell, and eyes widened, as the couple advanced into the room at a stately pace.

"I would have sent my groom to order a suite for the night, but I can't seem to locate him, and the coachman is deaf," the Exquisite drawled while studying the gold tip of his cane. He polished it against the flap of his enormous coat pocket. His head jerked up when no answer was forthcoming. The landlord's mouth was hanging wide open.

The Exquisite pointed with his cane. "Close that, or a bird might build a nest inside. I take it you have a spare suite?" he continued.

The landlord's head bobbed up and down, his chins trembling. "A suite I cannot offer ye, m'lord, but a nice room. 'Owever, this young person already bespoke it. There are other chambers, o' course."

Bryony had difficulty suppressing her mirth at the odd couple, but she pressed her lips into a thin line and took on a mien of innocence as the Exquisite favored her with a glance down his scimitar nose. The fat lady spoke. "McLendon! What's the delay? I need to lie down. Find me a room with a good bed."

"This young person will surely change her mind for the marchioness of Brambleberry."

"Ohs" and "ahs" rustled through the room, and Bryony looked suitably chastened. "O' course." She would have dearly liked to argue, but it was not her place. Besides, she didn't want to draw attention to herself. Yet she couldn't help saying, "But I'm not sure me employer will be satisfied wi' a lowly bedchamber."

The landlord drew himself up, all five feet of him. "I'll 'ave ye know that all me bedchambers are first-class."

Clover burst through the door. "Didya see th' cully wi' th' curly flash? I'd do anythin' to own a wig like it."

He stopped short, cringing under the icy stare of the Exquisite. " 'E's dead now," Clover said, his voice quavery. "Snuffed out like a candle."

"Oh, no!" Bryony rushed outside.

Chapter 28

Jack truly looked dead. His skin was cold and deathly pale, but Bryony felt a weak pulse at the side of his neck.

"Oh, I could strangle you, Clover, for frightening me half out of my wits." She tucked the shawl closer around Jack's chest. "Go find the doctor, and don't breathe a word about our business."

Several of the customers had followed them outside to view the dead man, but they retraced their steps in disappointment. Bryony called out before they had reached the door. "Please 'elp me carry me employer t' 'is room."

They agreed reluctantly. "In what capacity are ye workin' for th' likes o' 'im?" one asked insolently, with a leer.

"That's none o' yer bloomin' business," Bryony admonished with dignity.

The men muttered and carried Jack none too gently up the stairs, to what certainly wasn't the best chamber of the house. The marchioness's voice boomed from that fine room, which faced the street. The bedchamber allotted to Jack was small and dark, the window streaked with bird droppings. The bed was nothing but a cot, with heavy ropes forming a mattressless bottom.

The puffing landlord hurried inside with a pile of blankets which Bryony spread on the cot. The men laid Jack down and left.

"Couldn't put a peer o' th' realm in this chamber, now could I?" the landlord defended. "Yer employer'll be mighty comfortable in 'ere."

"Could ye kindly bring some 'ot water fer th' good

doctor? An' some 'ot broth?'' she asked, judging it wise not to complain about the room.

"Certainly." The host bustled away, leaving Bryony alone with Jack. He had not regained consciousness, and terror squeezed her heart. What if he really did die?''

She hastened to push the thought away. Stroking Jack's clammy brow, she prayed.

Ten minutes later, there was a knock on the door. Clover entered with the doctor in tow.

He was a man of medium height, thin and wiry. His white hair—what was left of it—was combed back and tied with a velvet bow. He wore a simple gray wool coat edged in black. The old man walked with a slight stoop, and his face was as wrinkled as the skin of a dry apple. His gray eyes were both severe and kindly.

Bryony realized she would never be able to fool him. His cheerful face had bent over her many a time when she was prostrate with ailments as a child. Taking off her mobcap, she let her dark hair fall freely down her back, almost to her waist. She had had no time to arrange it properly.

"Good afternoon, Dr. Littleton," she greeted, and watched his eyes widen in surprise.

"Miss Bryony! What are you doing here?"

"I'm in a pickle, and I don't have my brother to extract me this time." She pointed at Jack, and tears stood in her eyes. "I fear this man is dying."

The doctor gave her a long scrutiny, muttered, and bent over Jack's still form. "What's the matter with him?"

Bryony swept away the shawl, revealing the dark blood stain. "He was shot, and he probably has inflammation of the lungs. Besides, he has completely overexerted himself."

The doctor clucked and shook his head. "This is a severe case. I will need hot water and towels."

At a knock, Bryony hurriedly pulled the mobcap onto her head and stuffed her hair back into it. The host returned with a pitcher of hot water, lint, a bowl of broth, and several flannel cloths on a tray. When he saw the blood-stain on Jack's coat, he threw his gaze heavenward and muttered in aggravation. He placed his burden on a chair and advanced toward the bed. "Now, I cannot tolerate me linen—"

"Thank you," Bryony said, and maneuvered the curious man out of the room and closed the door. Since she desired to remove Clover from the gory spectacle that was bound to take place shortly, she ordered, "You guard the door, Clover. Don't let anyone inside."

"Not even that cully wi' th' powdered flash, if 'e arsks me?"

Bryony shook her head. "Go outside now."

"Will you be strong enough to assist me?" asked the doctor when she returned to the bed. With a knife he had already cut away Jack's coat and shirt.

"I'll try," she told him.

He worked quickly, and Jack's chest, which heaved in labored breaths, was soon bare. Blood oozed slowly from a gash in his side. The doctor probed gently, and Jack moaned, tossing his head back and forth on the pillow.

"The ball exited at the back, and I don't think anything vital was touched, but he has lost a great deal of blood."

Bryony could barely watch as the doctor removed pieces of fabric from the wound. He ordered her to place flannel cloths under Jack's body below the wound. Then he poured hot water onto it, making sure to remove the last traces of material. He clamped the two ragged edges together and barked at Bryony to hold them firmly. She was determined to obey.

" 'Tis good that he's out cold. This would hurt like the devil." The doctor swore under his breath, obviously forgetting that he had a gently bred lady beside him. Out of his bag he pulled something that looked like narrow leather thongs used to sew harnesses and saddles. Bryony commented on it, and the old man laughed. "It is. We have to sew the fellow up, or he'll bleed to death." He pushed the thread through an evil-looking curved needle.

As he set to work, Bryony closed her eyes, swallowing a threatening nausea. The doctor swore repeatedly and took a long time finishing his endeavor. "Tough as horseflesh," he commented.

She assisted him to the very last stitch, and he smiled as he put down the needle. "Good girl! Done at last.

There was always a lot of gumption behind that shy face of yours. You were an excellent horsewoman, if I remember correctly.''

Bryony smiled weakly. "I don't want to brag, but I am still rather good. Reggie was ten times better, of course. As he was at everything."

The doctor frowned. "Yes—that was a tragic accident. You're the only left of the family now."

Bryony nodded. As he wound bandages around Jack's middle, she wanted to ask him if he knew any details about the fire, but he was concentrating on his task once more. "We ought to keep hot fomentations on his chest until the cough has subsided." The doctor drenched a flannel cloth in steaming water, folded it, and applied it to Jack's bare chest. "You should make a fire and have a pot of water boiling at all times for the changing of fomentations. Can you do that?

"Yes, I'll see to it."

"I can send one of my maids to help you through the night."

Bryony shook her head. "No—no, that will not be necessary."

"Very well, but I will leave some coughing tincture for him."

At that moment Jack opened his eyes. "What—?"

"Ah! Returning from the dead, are you?" the doctor said bracingly. "Well, we will keep you from the devil's clutches a little while longer, eh?"

"Water," Jack croaked. "I'm damn thirsty." He blinked and stared at the doctor. "Who are you?"

Bryony stepped forward with the bowl of broth in her hands. "He's Dr. Littleton, an old friend of the family." She spooned some broth between Jack's lips while reading the warning in his fever-bright eyes. "Do not tell him," he whispered between gulps of broth. "We have to leave now."

"What is he mumbling?" asked the doctor.

Bryony smiled, thinking fast. "He wants to get up."

The old man guffawed and packed away his tools. "If he gets up, he'll fall down—never to rise again," he warned. "He has to remain prostrate for at least a week before he attempts another step."

Jack was tense, his face drawn, his eyes closing slowly. Bryony suspected he wasn't going to heed the doctor's advice. She would have to find a way to keep him abed.

"Besides he will hurt too much to move," Littleton added. "I'll have a brandy bottle sent up tomorrow. For now, I'll give him a laudanum draught so that he can sleep. Sleep's the best cure in cases like these."

Jack protested, but the doctor allowed no resistance. Frowning, Jack swallowed the tincture and obediently finished the broth. "I'm sorry about this," he said in an undertone to Bryony, and clutched her hand. "The men will be after us again." He tugged until she bent lower so that he could speak in her ear. "In my saddlebags are the pistols and some clean clothes. Perhaps you could have the stableboy collect the bags for you." He breathed deeply. "Don't go outside, and above all, be careful. Those men are after you, and they'll stop at nothing."

Bryony nodded, and Jack's grip slackened. His eyes were already veiling over with sleep. Before long his hand fell limply to the cot, and Bryony spread two blankets over him.

She would have to find the pistols.

Trembling with tension and fatigue, she trailed behind the doctor to the door. He turned his shrewd gaze upon her. "I don't like the smell of this, whatever it is you're involved in."

She clutched his arm entreatingly. "I can only beg of you not to breathe a word of what has passed here today. For Reggie's sake, and for mine."

He harrumphed and rubbed his chin. "Reggie was up to mischief, that much is clear, but I've turned a deaf ear to the whole sordid business."

"What have you heard?" asked Bryony in breathless tones.

He shrugged. "Oh, nothing much, but there have been some strange comings and goings at this very inn. Especially after the Reverend Cleaves was found dead in the shed at Willow Hills."

"I found the body."

He muttered something inaudible. "I'm better off not knowing more, but if you need my help or someone to confide in, I'll be here."

"Thank you."

He touched her shoulder in fatherly concern. "Will you be safe? It's unacceptable that a young, unwed lady travel alone across the country dressed as a servant, y'know. And in the company of a man, no less. If this comes out, you'll be ruined."

Bryony gave him a lopsided smile. "I know, but I'm trying to finish something that Reggie started."

He held up his hands to silence her. "I don't want to know what that hothead was up to." He shook his head. "And if my suspicions are correct, I don't want to know anything about the man on the bed. 'Twill be for the best, I'm sure."

Bryony nodded. "Thank you again. Next time we meet, I'll be the proper lady you'd expect."

"If there is a next time." He gripped her arm. "Remember what I said—be very careful. There is someone in the area that isn't—er—should we say, up to snuff. Someone murdered the reverend and might kill again."

Bryony blushed. "Yes, I know."

The doctor threw a last glance at his patient and another at Bryony. He looked as if he was about to say something further, then he clamped his lips into a grim line. "Good day, to you," he said and bowed, closing the door behind him.

"Did 'e save Jack's life?" Clover said, darting into the room before the door closed in his face.

"Yes, I hope so, but Jack is very sick. Only time will tell if he'll recover."

"I'm 'ungry," Clover stated.

"So am I," Bryony said, realizing she hadn't eaten for a long time. And she would have to find Jack's pistols. She recalled Littleton's warning, but this wasn't the time to turn craven.

Accompanied by Clover, she descended to the taproom below, where everything was quiet. After sending Clover to order their dinners on a tray, she ran out to the stables. The coachman was drinking ale and playing a board game with the ostlers. He stood as she approached, but did not doff his hat.

"I was jest about t' go back 'ome," he said, and wiped his lips with his sleeve. He was a short, bowlegged man with a surly countenance. How far could she trust him?

She drew him aside. "I'm very pleased with your services," she told him, and pressed a gold coin into his hand. "I hope this will help you keep silent about what you've seen today."

He stared with delight at the coin. " 'Twill, missy, 'twill."

He showed her Jack's horse, which had been well fed. The saddlebags were lying across one of the stall partitions. "This is what I came for," she explained, and hoisted the heavy bags.

"Need 'elp wi' those?"

She was going to say no, then gratefully accepted his offer. The driver would act as protection against the other men, if they were to appear. She had not seen any sign of them since the confusion of horses and carriages in the lane, and she knew she had done the right thing in returning to East Grinstead, though the silent menace of her pursuers still hung over her head.

Somehow she would have to deal with them. She would have to be strong for both Jack and herself—and Clover, who thought he was involved in a great lark.

She had never felt stronger, or weaker.

No one paid any attention to her and the coachman, as they passed through the taproom and climbed the stairs. Bryony thanked the man as he placed the saddlebags on a chair in the bedchamber, and left without so much as a glance at Jack.

Clover was already eating heartily, mutton chops and stewed cabbage in white sauce. Bryony's mouth watered as she watched him.

"Someone was arskin' fer ye downstairs when ye was out," Clover said between bites.

Bryony drew in her breath in fear. "Who?"

"I dunno. Some toff in a satin coat."

Who at the inn, beside the doctor, knew her identity?

"Was he alone, or was he part of the group that was following us earlier?"

"Naw, 'e came in alone, quiet-like. Tossed me a shillin'." He showed her the gleaming coin pressed into his fist. " 'E mentioned yer name, but I told 'im I've niver 'eard th' name in me life, even though ye've told me 'tis bad t' lie."

"Well, sometimes you just have to lie. It can't be helped. Was the man tall or short?"

" 'E was tall an' strong-lookin'."

Bryony took a bite of mutton and thought out loud. "Could have been Forrester or Bench. They're both tall."

"Naw, 'twasn't Forrester. I knows 'im."

As the invisible threat of the stranger seeped into her, Bryony lost her hunger. Who was the man? And how did he know where to find her? "Are you sure he wasn't one of the three men following us?" she asked again.

Clover nodded, his mouth full. When he could talk again, he said, "I saw 'em pass on th' road a long time ago, ridin' outta town."

"Why didn't you tell me immediately?" Bryony demanded, outraged. "It was very important for me to know."

Clover shrugged. "I jest told ye, didn't I?"

Bryony ruffled his hair in exasperation. "A good spanking is what you need, Master Clover."

She began pacing the floor, her body crackling with nerves. She tried to form some sort of logical explanation in her head. Besides Nigel, she knew three Jacobites—Mr. Forrester, Mr. Bench, and the late Reverend Cleaves. Then there was the elusive Lord Bentworth, whom she had never met, but who had recently returned to England—according to Mr. Bench.

"Have you ever seen Lord Bentworth?" she asked Clover. "At Potter House perhaps?"

"Would 'e be like th' toff wi' th' flash an' th' bile-green coat?"

Bryony nodded. "Yes, perhaps. The 'toff,' as you call him, is a marquess, and Lord Bentworth is an earl. They may dress alike."

"Naw, I niver saw 'un like th' marquess. This fella

spoke soft-like, but I didn't like 'im much, other than 'e
gave me a whole shillin'.''

"Why didn't you like him?" Bryony wished he would
give the stranger some feature that she recognized.

" 'Is eyes were cold, like those o' a fish.''

Bryony shivered. "Is he still downstairs?"

"Naw, 'e left, but I didn't 'ear 'im.'E 'as cat paws fer
feet.''

That detail frightened her more than if Clover had described the stranger as an angry giant. The boy was sur-
prisingly composed, despite their precarious situation.
Perhaps he was used to living on the edge of disaster.

While Bryony stared out the window at the falling dusk,
Clover studied Jack's drawn face, then curled up in the cot
beside him. Bryony smiled when she saw them together.
Clover's warmth would help Jack, even though she had
dreamed of being in Clover's place.

She would have to stand guard. Yet she had no idea how
she would manage to stay awake all night. She was already
exhausted. Folding the blankets back from Jack's chest,
she removed the fomentation and replaced it with a fresh
steaming one. He barely moved as the hot cloth smothered
his chest. Was she imagining things, or was his breathing
already coming easier?

Restless, she paced until darkness had fallen. She lit a
candle and pulled a chair up to the door. If someone tried
to break in, two pistol barrels would act as a welcoming
committee.

The sounds of the inn quieted down, and Bryony nodded in her chair. At the abrupt sound of a door slamming,
she jerked upright, her neck stiff and aching. But as soon
as silence prevailed once more, her head slowly tilted toward her chest.

Strange, frightening dreams disturbed her fitful slumber. Grotesque faces leered at her, skeletal fingers clawed
at her, harsh laughs reverberated in her mind. Toward
midnight, she was awakened by a sound outside the door.

At first she didn't know where she was or why she was
sleeping in a chair. Her hands were numb from cradling
the two heavy pistols. She had carefully loaded them, and
now she raised them toward the door. The candle was

guttering and would soon go out. Her heart was pounding harder every second as the movements outside continued. It sounded as if someone was dragging a large object across the floor, then halting in front of her door. Or had she dreamed it? She heard nothing else, and her hands were beginning to tremble with the effort of holding the heavy pistols in her outstretched hands.

Then the sound came again, and this time something slid across the door with a rasping sound.

Bryony gasped in horror. Swallowing convulsively to ease the dry taste of fear in her throat, she concentrated on aiming the pistols.

Behind her, Jack moaned in his sleep and fought the blankets and Clover's unyielding body in an effort to turn over. *Be quiet*, Bryony begged silently, wetting her lips.

Was the handle moving, or was it an illusion created by the flickering candlelight? Bryony stared until her eyes burned and her every muscle ached with fear.

Then came a crash. The door shook in its frame. To her intense relief, someone roared a ditty outside. A drunk patron struggling to find his room, she thought, and lowered the pistols to her lap. With her head hanging wearily, she drew in deep breaths to calm herself. All her strength was gone, and she had no idea how to get through the rest of the night.

When the nocturnal reveler had removed himself from her door, she checked the lock. Pacing, she tried to shake the frozen terror from her limbs. She lit a new candle and wished she had something to read. Images created by her fear would not leave her alone until the daylight came to sweep away the ghosts.

Her stomach growled, and she ate a piece of cold mutton chops, which tasted like sawdust. She wished she was a long way away, sleeping peacefully in a featherbed.

In Jack's saddlebags she found a watch on a chain. She snapped open the ornate lid and glanced at the dial. Three o'clock. Several hours to wait and brood before daylight.

Holding the watch above the candle, she read the inscription on the inside of the lid: "To J.N. with love from Mother, July 15, 1737." She counted the years. Perhaps this heavy silver watch had been a birthday gift to Jack.

His mother must have loved him very much and must have been a lady of funds, judging by the weight of the watch.

Bryony finally resumed her seat in the hard chair and faced the door once again, the pistols lying at the ready in her lap.

The next thing she knew, it was morning. She awakened with a start as someone pounded on the door. Cautiously placing the pistols on the floor, she slanted a glance at Jack and Clover on the cot. Jack had thrown off his blankets, and Clover had happily rolled himself into a cocoon.

"Who is it?" she asked, her voice sounding strangely weak. Still tired, she moved her leaden limbs to the door.

"Breakfast," came the host's brisk voice.

Bryony hesitated a moment before opening the door. "One moment." She rushed to the bed and pulled a blanket up to Jack's nose to conceal him from rude stares. Then she hid the pistols under the cot and opened the door.

"Thought a spot o' strong beer would do th' patient a world o' good," said the landlord cheerfully.

"Yes, I believe 'twould," Bryony said, peeping at him from under the rim of the mobcap that she had been careful to pull as far down over her face as she decently could.

" 'Ow long does yer employer expect t' stay 'ere?"

"A few days, more'n likely. Th' doctor said a week."

The landlord blinked and nudged her in the side. "Then ye'll 'ave some time by yerself. I'll be waitin' fer yer company, if ye knows what I means."

Bryony almost slapped him, but at the last minute remembered her "station." She lowered her smoldering gaze to the floor and said meekly, "Yer invitation is mighty kind, sir, but I'm loyal t' me employer."

"I see. Well, 'e could share 'is good fortune, couldn't 'e? It ain't as if 'e would know anythin' 'bout it." He pinched her breast insolently, and it was with utmost effort she stopped herself from crowning him with the beer jug.

" 'E wouldn't like it one bit. 'E would go arter ye wi' a broadsword, or me name ain't Molly!"

The landlord gave her an assessing glance. "Very well, if that's yer tune. Uppity, are ye? Takin' on airs even though yer naught but a whore."

Bryony flew at him with her fists. ''Get outta 'ere, or I'll claw yer eyes out.'' She pounded his face, his shoulders, and he retreated hurriedly to the landing outside. ''I'll remember this,'' he said ominously, and slammed the door.

Bryony braced both hands on the table and gritted her teeth. The beast! Furious, she wanted to push the tray onto the floor and awaken the entire inn, but instead she pounded the tabletop and groaned in wrath.

''What's 'at?'' Clover asked groggily, and rubbed his eyes. He climbed out of bed and eyed the breakfast tray avidly. '' 'Tis unhealthy t' be angry afore breakfast,'' he said matter-of-factly, and applied himself to the food with a hearty appetite.

Bryony took a few deep breaths to cool her anger. She glanced at Jack and noticed that he was awake, too, his dark gaze fastened upon her.

''How do you feel?'' she asked, her voice still unsteady with anger.

''You're right, y'know. I would go after the villain with a broadsword.'' He tried to rise but fell back against the lumpy pillow. ''That he would call you a—ahem—y'know what I mean, makes my blood boil. I will deal with him when my legs have solidified. They are as weak as water.'' He began to sit up. ''We're leaving after breakfast. I'd feel a lot better if there weren't hot tongs pinching my side.''

''The doctor stitched the wound for you, and I should change the bandages.''

''We had better leave before we're caught in an ambush. The longer we delay, the more we have to fear for our lives.'' With enormous effort, and grimacing wildly, he heaved himself upright.

Bryony gasped. ''No! The doctor said you have to stay prostrate for at least a week.''

Not answering, Jack advanced on her. Within seconds she found herself within the circle of his arms. In a bantering tone he spoke to Clover over her head. ''What you're about to witness will make you blush, Master Clover, but you might as well learn from an expert in these matters. This is how you deal with recalcitrant women.'' He bent toward her lips.

"Ye'll faint first," Clover warned." Besides, I've seen men maul women afore. Silly, thass what! I'd rather go watch th' ostlers." His cheeks bulging with bread and ham, Clover slammed the door behind him.

"Have you lost all decorum, Jack?" Bryony chided, but in his arms she felt safe for the first time in days.

"A desperate man doesn't worry about decorum." His gaze burned into her, and he clasped her face between his hot palms. Perspiration shone on his forehead, and Bryony knew that fever still raged within him. "I cannot get enough of you," he whispered. "Have you forgiven me for my deceit?"

She nodded. "But I haven't forgotten." She closed her eyes as he traced her face with his lips. His beard tickled her, and the sensation aroused other deeper, longings. She had almost forgotten. . . .

"Sweet little one with eyes the color of seawater, how I long for you. Last night in my dreams you did some very exciting things to me, and I would like to try them with the real you."

Though she found it increasingly difficult to think, she finally pushed him away. "That will never come to pass now. Not after all that's happened. The only reason I'm here today is because I want to finish the mission that Reggie began."

"Little liar," he said with a derisive laugh. His strength spent, he sank down on the chair by the table, and a veil of pain covered his face. "Once I get my strength back, I will show you how wrong you are."

"Your cough is better," she commented, and poured some beer into a glass. "Drink this. The landlord said it would give you solace."

He pinned her with a fierce stare. "The only thing that will give me solace is your promise of undying love."

Chapter 29

Jack ate his breakfast, stubbornly remaining at the table even though Bryony tried to coax him back to bed. She cold see that he was in great pain, yet not one word of complaint issued from his lips.

"Where is the map?" he asked between gulps of beer.

"In my pocket. I haven't had time to find a better hiding place."

"Let's take a look at it." He ate some bread and butter, washing it down with still more beer.

Bryony extracted the stiff document from her petticoat pocket. She smoothed the paper on top of the table, and they bent over it. Outlandish names sprang at her—Loch Morar, Loch nan Uamh, Glenfinnan, Sgurr na Ciche. They meant nothing to her, but Jack explained that Charles Edward had raised his standards at Glenfinnan in July the previous year when he had landed in Scotland.

Tiny dots in blue ink indicated a path that wound into the mountains.

"This area here"—Jack traced his fingertip around blue-painted slivers that marked two lakes, Lock Morar and Loch Nevis—"is mountainous and wild.'Twill be difficult to reach except by ship. That's why the French hid the gold here." He stabbed the two ornate letters "C" and "S," entwined to look like a rose stem with a full-blown flower at the end. Bryony had seen the rose design before, on Mr. Bench's wineglasses.

The gold was hidden in the mountains between the two lakes.

"I suppose the French sailors who delivered the gold

265

expected H.R.H. Charles Edward's aides to return to the coast at some point to collect shipments of weapons and funds," said Jack, "and Loch Nevis was easily accessible to the French. But King Louis has changed his mind; he refuses to send more help. Political reasons, of course. The Stuart cause is not profitable to the French, especially since Culloden." He sighed. "What are we doing here? There is no time to lose."

"How do you expect to travel across the entire length of England to the Scottish Highlands with a wound like yours?" Bryony demanded.

Jack's fingers clenched around the tankard, and his expression was grim. "This is not a time to complain. I'll manage somehow, and will do just fine once we have left this spot where we're surrounded by enemies."

He looked extremely pale, and the trembling in his limbs had returned, but Bryony knew there was no use arguing about his health.

"You should rest for a while first. Why, only yesterday you were on death's doorstep."

"Very well, I will rest for a while. In the meantime, you should see to hiring another horse so that we can leave as soon as possible." He staggered over to the cot and lowered himself gingerly. The wound must give him excruciating pain. His ground his teeth and could not quite suppress a groan. She spread blankets over him after arguing about the need to replace the hot fomentations on his chest. He finally surrendered and gazed at her in stoic suffering as she spread the hot cloth. After more cajoling, he reluctantly agreed to swallow the cough tincture.

"I should be the one taking care of you," he said with a snort of self-disgust.

"Even the strongest succumb to illnesses sometimes," Bryony said. " 'Tis nothing for it but rest."

Before his eyelids closed, Bryony glimpsed the tenderness in his gaze and her heart contracted with sorrow. Like the morning glory flower, a love like theirs was a short-lived blossom—destined to bloom for only one day. It was a fragile flower that was being crushed by the clumsy boot of political rebellion.

Grateful that Jack now slept peacefully, Bryony guarded

him for most of the day. To pass the time, she reorganized their few belongings, wishing that the French had never delivered any gold, and that the map had never been made. As a precaution she sat down and made a false copy of the map, which she stuffed into her cloak pocket. The real map she sewed into the lining of Clover's coat.

In another part of town, three men bowed in front of a fourth man who was sitting in a comfortable armchair. A white, curly wig framed the man's pale, angry face, and the black satin of his coat gleamed as he raised his fist in a threatening gesture.

"You let yourself be fooled," he stated. "I asked you not to lose their tracks."

The man with the mop of white hair spoke. "Sir, if I may be so bold, we knew we would 'ave no difficulty findin' 'em. We shot 'er protector, who's probably at this very instant breathin' 'is last."

His two cohorts—called in after the loss of the scar-faced man and the villain with the wooden leg, looked uncomfortable. Joe, a dark, uncouth blacksmith and a lover of strong drink, had been easily hired with the promise of ample payment, and Archie, a giant-sized, surly, red-haired Scot, owed the man with the wig a favor.

Their employer laughed, a soft, evil sound. "He is not breathing his last. *I* had to personally find Miss Shaw. She's at The Swan, and I saw the doctor descend from the sickroom. He told the proprietor that the guest would survive." He snorted in disgust. "Your marksmanship leaves a lot to be desired."

"We didn't expect 'er t' pull somethin' out o' a tree, some sort of box. We watched t' see if we could find out what th' papers said. She gave one of 'em t' 'er escort, th' bearded fella, an' tossed th' other into th' bushes." The white-haired man proudly extracted a crumpled paper from his pocket. "This is it." He handed it to the man in the wig, who leaned closer to the guttering candle.

"This is a letter from her brother." He read silently, then crushed the paper between his fingers. "By God! The map! The other document was the map."

He rose and took a few heavy steps across the floor.

"Unbelievable! My problems will be over if I can lay my hands on that map." He glared at the three men cowering before him. "You will help me. If you fail, you'll meet with the same fate as your predecessors." He shoved his fist into the chest of the man with the white hair, who cringed. "Had I but done this myself, I would have succeeded a long time ago. However, I hired you because the lady will recognize me. I don't want her to know that I will be the final benefactor of the gold. This time, threats will not be enough. We must get the man, then kill Miss Shaw."

After supper, Bryony stepped downstairs for a breath of air, and with a plan of purchasing a horse. Carefully concealed by her mobcap and voluminous cloak, she traversed the taproom floor, only to stop short when she recognized the three men sitting at the table closest to the fire. One had a mop of white hair, the other was swarthy, and the third had red curls. They had their backs turned and did not see her, but she knew it would be only a matter of seconds before they spotted her. Her hands trembled as she touched the pistols hidden under her cloak.

They had found out where she and Jack were hiding!

Swept by an overwhelming desire to escape, Bryony rushed outside. She could have used big Jules's strength now, but he was far away in Alfriston. Where was Clover? The air was light and clear, and all was quiet. A pale moon hung in the sky. She drew in a deep breath of refreshing air, aiming to calm her galloping heart.

The Swan was a posting inn, its stables filled with sturdy horseflesh. Bryony saw Clover carrying a saddle almost as big as he was. One of the ostlers was whistling as he placed a bridle over the head of a showy chestnut stallion.

"Did you see them?" Bryony whispered as soon as she had caught Clover's attention.

"No. Who?"

"The three men who were following us earlier are in the taproom."

The boy's gaze darted from building to building in the ever deepening darkness. Shadows crowded the yard, advancing closer every second.

They exchanged wary glances, and Bryony knew how much she had come to love the small boy. With the optimism of youth, he maintained that they could easily give their pursuers the slip.

"Why don't they confront us?" Bryony said.

Clover smirked. "They 'aven't seen ye. They can't eggsackly attack ye in public. 'Tis a great adventure, ain't it?"

She wanted to shake him, "Adventure, yes, but a dangerous one. I wish you weren't involved."

"I likes it," he said. "Niver 'ad such a lark."

Bryony shook her head. "You'd better come with me now so that I can keep an eye on you."

He complained so loudly that she finally gave in. "Ten minutes then, but not one second more."

She retraced her steps to the inn. Halting in the shadows of the vine growing next to the entrance, she glanced through the small window into the dimly lit taproom. The men had disappeared, and fear seeped through her veins. What if they had decided to attack Jack, lying helpless in his bed? Hastening around the corner of the building, she decided to look through the window closest to the fireside to make sure the men were really gone.

There were no signs of them, or of anyone else. The room was completely deserted, since the London stagecoach had left half an hour ago, carrying most of the customers.

Tension coiling within her, she headed toward the door, her pistols at the ready. Her arms numb with fear, she could barely support the weapons.

Rounding the corner, she whimpered in horror and surprise when she encountered two tall silhouettes that were darker than the shadows around them. As they advanced toward her, she automatically leveled the pistols. "Stay away from me," she warned, and cocked the hammer.

She screamed as a third man gripped her arm from behind, and rough fingers muffled her lips. The two pistols rattled to the ground. The hand smothering her was cold and clammy. Her arms were twisted back, and she cringed in pain. Another man pinched her nose shut, cutting off her breath. Her eyes grew wide with terror as the shadows hovered over her.

"Where is the map?" one voice demanded. "We'll strangle ye if ye don't tell us where th' map is. An' your lover will die a slow, painful death."

Bryony nodded, and the unkind fingers loosened from her nose. She gulped down a breath, filling her lungs to their limit.

"Well?" The word quivered in the air like the falling blade of a guillotine. One of the men bent and retrieved a pistol. Bryony glimpsed a bottle in his hand, and he chuckled as he poured liquid down the barrel, wetting the blackpowder. The pungent scent of beer filled the air. "Well?" The question cut anew into her dazed mind, and she winced.

"In my pocket," she forced out, trying to dislodge the hold of the man's relentless grip on her arms. Pain shot through her limbs until red lights danced in her vision. "If you don't let g-go of your hold, I will faint."

They only laughed, and two pairs of hands tore off her cloak and slid over her body in search of pockets on her skirt. "In the cloak," she explained. "Please let me go."

One of the men whistled through his teeth as he found the map in her pocket. "It's 'ere jest like she said." They let go of her arm, and the same man patted her on the head. "Good girl. I knew ye would be cooperative, just like th' master said."

"Who are you working for?" Bryony dared to ask, rubbing her aching arms. She suspected it was a futile question, but she had to try. "I'll pay you well to tell me."

"Wi' what?" another man said, and laughed evilly, jingling her brocade purse and Jack's money pouch, which he found in her cloak. He pocketed the money.

With mounting horror she witnessed the glitter of a knife in the weak light from the windows. The man with the knife shoved her in the chest, and she lost her balance, falling backward into a heap of leaves. Jarring her elbow on a sharp stone, she cried out. The man laughed. "Since ye were so 'elpful, we'll make it clean an' fast. Ye'll be dead afore ye know it."

"No," she pleaded. "No." Was that pitiful voice really

hers? He lifted the knife, and it was as if she could already feel it tearing into her tender flesh.

" 'Urry up, then. We don't 'ave all night," one of the others urged.

Before the knife fell, she rolled sideways, kicking out as she moved. The man roared in anger and lunged. He fell over her, and the knife dug into the earth beside her head. She flung out her arm to swipe at his head, but her fingers encountered cold metal. In a flicker of recognition, she reacted instantly. Gripping the second pistol they had failed to notice, she pointed it at his head.

"I'll shoot," she croaked, and stared into his wild eyes, only inches from hers. His wine-laden breath washed over her, and his weight was crushing her.

She cocked the hammer.

From the corner of her eye, she was aware of the gleam of metal in his hand level with her throat. The knife. But it didn't move. They eyed each other for along moment. Finally he crawled off her.

"What are ye waitin' fer?" called the others from some distance. " 'C'mon, Joe, get it over wi'."

Joe was crouching on all fours beside her, but her aim never faltered. "She 'as a pistol."

" 'Tisn't workin'," they chided.

"This one is." Joe inched away from her, and she sprang up. The others were advancing very quickly.

"Help!" she called out at the top of her lungs. "Help!"

Footsteps pounded in the yard. The three men swore and merged with the shadows. Suddenly Bryony was surrounded by the stablehands. The sound of rapid hoofbeats proved that the villains had slipped out of reach. She pointed into the darkness and said with a sob, "There were three men. They robbed me and tried to kill me."

Without losing a second, the stableboys ran after the fleeing ruffians, but Bryony knew it would be useless.

By the time the boys returned, she had found both pistols and tucked them into her voluminous pocket. Gradually shock set in. She began to tremble so violently that she could barely stand up. She didn't put it past the villains to return and enter the inn to murder them in their sleep. And this time they wouldn't fail. She had to warn Jack.

She rushed inside, up the steps, and along the corridor to their chamber. Cautiously she listened at the door, but there were no sounds of struggle. Everything was quiet except for the snores coming from the room across the hallway.

Very slowly she opened the door and slid inside. The room lay in total darkness. She gasped as the icy edge of metal dug into her neck.

"Don't move, or I'll slash your throat," wheezed a man's voice.

"Jack, 'tis me!" she said.

He sighed audibly, and cloth rustled against cloth as he lowered his arm. "Good God, you should have announced your arrival!" he exclaimed.

"I thought you were asleep." In a faltering voice she told him what had happened. She wrung her hands in despair, then fumbled with the tinderbox to light a candle. In the wavering light, she watched Jack stagger across the floor and sit down on the edge of the cot, his head hanging low from exhaustion.

"I told you not to leave the room," he said. "The mission is ruined now, and Stuart's enemies will have the gold."

"No, they won't!" Bryony knelt in front of him. "I made a false map. The real map is sewn into the lining of Clover's extra coat. Fast on his feet as he is, he's the one who could get away rapidly in an emergency. Better not tell him where the map is, though."

Jack gripped her hands between his own. "How very clever. I would never have thought of that myself." His eyes were dark with worry. "But they will find out that the map is false, if they haven't already. You couldn't possibly have falsified the seals."

Bryony shook her head. "No, I couldn't, but I poured some wax from the candle and pressed a coin into it. However, the wax isn't red like on the real map."

Jack stood, grimacing with pain. "I've slept the entire day when I should be on my way to Scotland. We have no time to lose."

She clung to his arm. "Are you really strong enough?"

"It's no use asking that now. We must go. Where is the money? We have to procure another horse."

"I'm afraid they stole the money. I was on my way to hire a horse when the villains waylaid me."

He swore under his breath. "Very well, we'll just have to steal a horse then." When he noticed her horrified expression, he smiled faintly. "We'll return someday and pay for it."

"I don't like it." Bryony hurriedly gathered their belongings. "We're acting like fugitive criminals."

"In the eyes of the law, we are." Jack suffered with every step as he crossed the chamber, clutching a hand to the aching wound in his side. White around the lips, he eased open the door and looked outside. Nothing there.

Bryony helped him don the vest, jacket, cloak, and tricorne. He had worn the cloak the first time she had met him. Now there were rips and burn holes in the fabric.

Jack tucked the pistols into the large pockets of his coat. "I'll not be taken unawares," he muttered, and slid into the corridor.

Bryony followed, holding her breath in fear. Jack's back was as tense as a washboard, and he moved with extreme difficulty. She feared he would fall into a faint at any moment.

The sound of voices, laughter and singing, floated up the stairs. The regular customers were trickling into the taproom. Had their enemies returned? Bryony prayed that Jack would not have to use his pistols.

As Jack struggled down the last step, the voices quieted, and all eyes turned in his direction. He looked impressive with his dark cloak swept around him and his tricorne pressed deeply over his eyes. As he slowly crossed the floor, he looked from one face to another, and the men's gazes flickered away. A hush of tension lay in the air.

Bryony stayed in the background, carrying Jack's saddlebags and Clover's jacket slung over one arm. She prayed that the boy was still at the stables.

"We're leaving, but will be back tomorrow morning," Jack lied brazenly to the proprietor, having no money to pay for room and board. "We will pay upon our return," he added, drawing himself up to his full height to discourage the landlord from arguing.

The landlord looked put out, but nodded curtly.

Jack advanced to the door. To Bryony's intense relief, she saw no sign of the three men who had stolen the false map and the money. Nevertheless, she knew they would soon arrive with vengeance on their minds.

She stepped outside, her gaze darting from one dark shadow to the next.

Jack was close behind her. "Hurry now. Every second counts."

The man in the white wig bent over the map spread out on the table before him. In the small chamber at The Golden Egg, the inn at the opposite end of East Grinstead, the only light came from the leaping flames of the fire. The man traced a fleshy finger over the clumsy wax seals. The pale candle wax mocked him, and he gripped the edge of the map and tore it in half with a savage twist of his hands.

"This is not the map!" he roared. "How could you be such idiots not to see that it's a badly executed false copy. Who would ever believe that the gold would be buried in The Grampians? No Frenchman has ever set foot in those mountains, especially no sailors carrying two heavy chests of gold."

He howled in fury, and the chambermaid paled as she carried in a wine bottle on a tray. She cowered as he took the bottle and hurled it with all his might against the wall.

"Since three men cannot succeed in the simple task of taking a map from one woman, I shall have to do it myself." He shrugged into his coat and stepped outside, followed by his three crestfallen cohorts. "Let's go before they slip away again."

Bryony watched as Jack negotiated with the ostler. What lies was he telling that poor man, who had so readily saddled an extra horse? She looked for Clover and found him watching two of the grooms play backgammon.

When she waved at him, he came running. "Where ye goin'?" Bryony hushed him and urged him to don his coat.

"We're leaving. Do you want to come or stay here?"

she asked, knowing full well he wouldn't want to miss a moment's excitement.

"Are ye daft? Comin', o' course," he scoffed, and swaggered across the yard to assist the ostler with the horses.

She was about to help Jack onto his horse, but he waved her off, led the animal to a mounting block, and managed to step into the stirrup. "There is no time to lose," he said in low tones as he wheeled the horse around. I can *smell* them. They are hot on our trail."

Bryony did not argue, just placed the saddlebags over the broad back of the horse. Jack looked as if he was having difficulty staying in the saddle. He was crouching forward, his head hanging wearily.

The ostler heaved Bryony into the saddle of the second horse, a calm roan mare, then lifted Clover up behind her. The boy clung to her waist with sturdy arms.

Jack led the way out of the yard. As soon as he had cleared the overhang at the inn's entrance, he urged the horse into a trot, heading west out of East Grinstead. Bryony heard the rapid *clip-clop* of more horses farther down the lane, and fear spurted through her limbs. Their pursuers weren't far behind. But they turned into the inn yard, giving Bryony and Jack a good lead.

Having heard the approaching horses, Jack clung to the pommel and brought his horse into a gallop.

As they left the town behind, darkness wrapped them in its silent shroud. In the pale moonlight, the trees cast long, thin shadows on the lane. A light breeze sighed in the branches, and nocturnal animals rustled in the grass bordering the ditches. The sound of their horses' hooves echoed along the lane.

Jack drew up in the middle of the road and gestured for Bryony to stop. He listened intently.

"What's afoot?" Clover whispered conspiratorially.

"Shh," Jack demanded testily, endeavoring to suppress a bout of coughing.

"There's nuffin' on th' road," Clover insisted. "I got ears t' 'ear wi'."

"And I will cut them off if you don't keep silent," Jack threatened. "Let's go. They'll soon be after us, but we'd best conserve our horses' strength for when 'tis really necessary.''

They rode abreast in silence. Bryony dared not admit that she was thirsty. There was no time to stop for water. Clover was chafing on her nerves, turning around repeatedly to see if he could spot their pursuers.

''The only chance we have now is to stay ahead of them,'' Jack said. '' 'Twill take all our ingenuity and all our strength.''

Chapter 30

They continued to ride almost the entire night without stopping. They headed northwest, passing through Guildford, aiming toward Reading in Berkshire, twenty miles away. Time and time again, Jack stopped and listened intently. The night seemed to listen with them, eerily silent and empty. The contours of the landscape changed from humpbacked ridges to flat fields bathed in gray moonlight. A distant waterfall gurgled faintly in the omnipresent silence.

The shadows were lengthening when Jack said, "I hear something."

He was right. From the far distance came the sound of hooves clear upon the wind.

"Could be someone else."

"Riding in the middle of the night? No. Except for highwaymen and other scoundrels, only us and our enemies are idiotic enough to be out." He patted Bryony's arm. "I understand that you're trying to ease my worries." He coughed into the crook of his elbow. Again she couldn't help thinking he ought to be stretched out in a bed with hot fomentations on his chest.

"We'll ride faster now," Jack told her. "We'll keep the lead as long as the horses last. It all depends on how strong their mounts are. Perhaps they are already tired."

But that hope was not to be fulfilled. Their pursuers gained rapidly. Bryony urged her mare to ever greater speeds to keep up with Jack's stallion. Still, he wouldn't let his horse have its head. Either the jolting was too painful, or he was mindful of her mare's lesser strength.

She threw a glance behind her. The lane was a gray ribbon fading among the trees. They pulled up at the crest of a hill to have a better view, and there, down below where the lane made a sharp turn, were the riders.

Bryony counted the black shadows streaking across the lane. There were four.

Fear made her skin prickle at the base of her neck. The riders neither slowed nor hesitated. She slanted a glance at Jack and discovered that he was slumped forward over the pommel in what looked like a swoon. He came to with a sudden jerk and raised himself with sluggish movements.

He was exhausted. They could not continue at this breakneck speed.

"Move on," he said. With a tired gesture he flicked the reins, and his horse started the descent.

Bryony followed while keeping an eye on his swaying body. As the lane ran down into the folds of the hills, the woods grew thicker. The shadows under the trees were coal-black where the washed-out moonlight could not reach.

Jack was tilting forward. As if finally aware of the desperate situation, he stopped. "We'd better . . . take shelter . . . and hope for . . . the best," he said with difficulty. Another coughing attack threatened, and he pressed a handkerchief against his lips and groaned. The cough apparently aggravated the pain in his wound.

Bryony's heart bled for him, and she slid down from her horse. Clover clung to the pommel, and Bryony took the reins of both horses, holding the stallion still as Jack swung out of the saddle.

Leaning momentarily against the solid strength of the horse, he regained his breath. Then he took the reins and said, "Let's go down here."

A narrow path was barely visible among the trees. They would not have noticed it had they remained on horseback. A shiver ran down Bryony's spine as she clearly heard the approaching horses. Their pursuers had reached the crest of the hill now. A pawing and a whinnying punctured the silence as the four men evidently stopped to scout the terrain.

The trees were dense, and the leaves on the path muffled their horses' steps. Bryony held her breath, as if fearing the men could hear her. Jack had halted. She could barely make out his body in the darkness. He exuded enormous tension, and Bryony shared the feeling.

Even Clover appeared to the tense and listening. Due to his youth, he would have the keenest hearing. Silence reigned once more under the sleeping skies. Clover gripped her arm and whispered, "They're sniffin' th' air, like th' curs they are. We could 'ave used that big Jules's protection now, but 'e's in Sussex."

Jack's horse pawed the ground, and Bryony saw him place a hand over its muzzle. Clearly, the animals, too, felt the brooding menace. Not a leaf stirred in the chill air.

The sound of hoofbeats resumed as the riders descended the steep slope of the hill. The sound increased in strength as they came closer, but the path would not be visible from the lane unless they stopped completely. Not many yards were separating them now. Bryony's hands curled tightly around the reins.

The horses had slowed to a walk, *clip-clop, clip-clop. Why weren't they racing ahead, as they had been before?*

Jack slid up beside her, and she felt the cold butt of a pistol being pressed into her hand. He stuffed pouches of powder and balls into her pocket. "Don't hesitate to use them," he whispered, then disappeared behind a bush.

A twig snapped, and leaves rattled under his boots. He paused.

Total silence embraced the world.

The horses in the lane had stopped, too, and it was as if everything was listening, Bryony imagined that the world had turned into one giant ear. Terror fizzled along her spine, paralyzing her limbs.

A bird catapulted out of a tree with a piercing screech, startling Bryony. One of the horses in the road neighed.

Bryony waited, then waited some more.

After what seemed an eternity, the horses in the lane continued, still walking.

Jack didn't move for another five minutes, and when he did, he crept forward cautiously and spoke only in a whisper. "Wait here. I will reconnoiter before we venture back onto the lane. Someone might be waiting for us."

"Let me go," she urged, but he said no.

She expected him to collapse at any moment, but he advanced slowly. When in danger he seemed to draw upon a deep reserve of strength, as if he refused to accept any kind of weakness in himself. She waited nervously until she could discern his dark silhouette returning.

"They're gone, but we'd better wait yet awhile."

They moved farther down the path and soon arrived at a clearing. Moonlight spilled onto the circle of grass, and Jack tied his mount to a tree.

"We can rest here. There is grass for the horses." Sighing deeply, he sank onto a tree stump and lowered his head. His hands hung limply between his knees.

Clover was talking softly to the horses as they inspected a clump of grass, but the animals would not let him caress their muzzles.

Bryony hastened to spread her cloak on the ground for Jack. "Please stretch out here until 'tis time to go on."

He opened his mouth to protest, but he was too tired to speak. He scarcely had the strength to lower himself to the ground. "I'll never be able to get up again," he said between clenched teeth.

"Nonsense."

He studied her in the gloom. "You'll be cold without your cloak."

She shrugged. "I've been cold many times before."

He reached out to her, but she ignored his hand. "I wish the closeness we once shared would return. You have given me so much."

Bryony sighed and wished that they could rediscover that intimacy, but it had fallen even further away with the latest events. The map had pulled them further apart.

" 'Tis perhaps too late," she said in a low voice so that

Clover could not hear. "I wish this was over so that I could return to my business of bringing Reggie's murderer to justice. This time I will travel to France without you, in case Bentworth is still to be found there."

Jack moved restlessly as if caught in the grip of a great agony. "You shouldn't—"

"Be still," she ordered. "Let me find your brandy."

He shook his head. "I don't want brandy now. Have to keep a clear head on my shoulders." A note of bitterness had crept into his voice.

"There is something else bothering you, isn't there?" she asked, and sat down on a mossy stone, pulling her knees to her chin.

At first, he didn't answer, then he said in dismissing tones, "No, nothing that I want to discuss. I only pray we'll come out of this adventure with our lives, and I wish you would forget your revenge. 'Twill ruin us both." He continued to brood, and Bryony felt he had cut that fragile tendril of intimacy that was trying to take root between them.

"You know I cannot do it," she said. "However, I'm not asking you to have a part of my revenge. Not anymore." She leaned her head against the tree trunk behind her and stared with dry, aching eyes into the night.

Some hours later she awakened, recognizing how exhausted she must have been to fall asleep with her head against a tree. Rigid with cold, she watched dawn's first light creep across the sky. The watery moon fought a losing battle against the advancing daylight. The air was silent, damp, and chilly.

Her limbs still tight and weary from the long ride, Bryony rose and stretched, finding that the clearing was covered in a heavy fog.

Through the dense white sea, she saw the outlines of Jack's body, with Clover's smaller one curled up beside him. They were trapped in a suffocating gray world.

Bryony knelt next to Jack and shook his shoulder. Close to the ground the fog was colder and damper. His clothes were wet.

"What?" he blurted out, and sprang up. He swore and clutched his side.

Clover sat up, rubbing his eyes. "Blimey, look at all th' milk," he said.

Jack's wavy hair clung damply to his forehead, and his expression was ghastly, one of excruciating pain.

"We need to change the bandages on your wound," Bryony said.

He sat obediently on a stone while Bryony extracted the necessary tools from the saddlebags.

"I'm hungry," announced Clover, watching wide-eyed as Bryony cut the soaked bandages with a knife. He squeaked in excitement as he viewed the roughly stitched wound. "Crikey! Yer tied up wi' a string."

Jack smiled grimly and eyed the grisly wound from which blood was still slowly seeping. Purple and yellow bruises had formed around the entire area. Bryony soaked a wad of lint in brandy and pressed it there.

"Aaarrgh!" Jack cried out in agony.

"We don't want the wound to turn foul. Here, hold steady." She made him press the wad in place while she wound several layers of bandages around his middle.

A powerful urge to bury her fingers in the curls on his chest came over her, but she immediately suppressed it.

"I wish I 'ad stitches like that," Clover said enviously.

Bryony glared at him. "No, you don't, silly boy! 'Tis extremely painful, and Jack is weak from the loss of blood."

Clover kicked a clump of bracken and murmured, "Oh, daggers!"

Bryony pulled a dry shirt from the saddlebags and helped Jack drag it over his head. His face was pale, his eyes still bright, but most of the fever was gone. The rest on the hard ground had served its purpose in spite of the cold air. But there was a grimness to his features that hadn't been there before. His beard softened the angry slash of his mouth.

Trying to deny the tenderness he evoked in her, Bryony extracted a comb and smoothed his tousled hair, then bound it into a queue. She liked the feel of his thick tresses slipping through her fingers.

He looked slightly less grim once she had finished. It

struck her anew how attractive he was, even with that bushy beard. She could not remember how he looked without it.

"Now, let us see if there is anything to eat." Bryony delved into the bags and handed them each a piece of dry bread and some cheese. "This is all that was left from supper, I'm afraid."

"Aw, an' we don't 'ave a groat t' our names," Clover piped in. "I'll find us a pie or two today," he bragged.

Bryony shivered at the thought that they might have to resort to stealing.

Jack cuffed the boy. "If you so much as steal a turnip, I'll whip your behind so that you cannot sit for ten days."

Clover's eyes grew enormous, and his lips trembled. To hide his devastation, he rushed in among the trees and stared at Jack from the cover of a bush.

"How dare you touch the boy?" Bryony demanded, seething with anger. "He's but a nipper, just like you were once." She gripped Jack's shoulders and shook him harshly. "Or have you already forgotten what it was like?"

He paled and got to his feet, towering above her in fury. "Don't tell me what to do."

"Demon!" she sputtered. "You were never young, always a curmudgeon eaten by hatred."

His eyes smoldered. "You have no idea what it was like."

"That doesn't give you the right to strike an innocent child." Placing her arms akimbo, she challenged him, "You'd better not repeat it, or I won't speak to you ever again."

"A relief that would be," he muttered, and turned his back on her. Hunching forward, he struggled over to where the horses were tied.

Bryony was so angry she couldn't speak. She stomped around the clearing, picking up their belongings and shoving them into the saddlebags. A bleak sun was crawling over the treetops, dissolving the fog into ragged tatters. But it couldn't chase away the chill.

Jack pushed himself onto a fallen tree trunk and managed to mount his horse. His gaze was disdainful. "Let's continue," he said.

Bryony resented his high-handed command. After hoisting the miserable boy into the saddle, she pulled her horse back onto the lane. Anger propelling her, she rode fast, leaving Jack some way behind her.

Chapter 31

An uncomfortable truce settled between them as they struggled onward. All through the following week, Jack drew on his immense stubbornness and his small reserve of strength. He adamantly refused to knuckle under to his increasing exhaustion. Bryony suspected that at any moment he would simply fall off his horse and die.

They were approaching Staffordshire without so much as a glimpse of their pursuers. They had paid careful attention to covering their tracks, zigzagging across meadows and open fields, climbing over hills, avoiding towns and villages. But Bryony still threw fearful glances over her shoulder. She did not underestimate their enemies. Only one thing puzzled her. Why had they not captured her or Jack before? There had been any number of opportunities in the past.

They ate what fallen fruit and berries they could find. Sometimes a farmer's wife showed them pity and supplied them with bread and cheese. One even gave them a fresh apple pie sprinkled with cinnamon and sugar.

That day they feasted, their backs turned to each other. Had that been three or five days ago? The days were blurring into a string of endless trials of patience. Their limbs were sore from the riding, their horses weary.

It was late afternoon when they crossed the border into Staffordshire. The orange disk of the sun hung low over the treetops, and the shadows were lengthening.

Clover sat in front of Bryony in the saddle, sleeping with his head against her bosom. He had been sleeping most of the day, exhausted and hungry.

One day he had brought a stolen meatpie and had found himself slapped on the backside. "Don't you know that you could hang for this?" Jack had ranted.

Ever since then, the boy had ignored the man. Bryony had tried to explain to Clover that Jack worried about him, that he cared enough not to want Clover to hang. The boy had stared at her suspiciously from under his fringe of dusty hair and remained sullen for the remainder of the day. His trust was easily broken, and she had tried to be extra loving during the days following the argument, but there was still a rift between her companions.

Early that evening they rode into the village of Tutbury and stopped at Ye Olde Dog, where Jack suggested they get a room for the night. He had earned a crown by assisting an elderly gentleman out of an overturned carriage, and now he wanted to buy provisions.

Bryony had noticed that ever since he had struggled with the burden of the old man, his last strength had been used up. His horse had wandered willy-nilly across the fields with his hands slack on the reins. Bryony had taken the reins and led the horse while Jack lay slumped over the pommel, either asleep or unconscious. Against all odds he had remained in the saddle.

"I can make the purchases," she offered as he leaned wearily against the horse. "You two can go to the inn for a meal and a bottle of ale."

The boy and the man stared at each other for along time. Jack reluctantly offered his hand to Clover. "What d'you say, old gaffer? Care for a meal?" The boy nodded, slid off the horse, clung to Jack's waist, and cried. The scene was so pathetic that Bryony wanted to cry as well. She brushed a hand across her face.

But before Jack and Clover could execute their plan, Jack collapsed on the ground. Bryony drew in her breath in terror and bent over him.

"Better fetch the doctor, Clover. Inquire at the inn for his address," she said, her voice shrill with fear.

Before Clover could enter the inn, the door opened and a stout man appeared on the threshold. "What's this?" he called out loudly. As he bent over Jack's prostrate form,

Bryony recognized the collar of a country parson. The old man had a jolly, kindly face.

"My fiancé has taken ill," Bryony explained, forgetting to contort her voice with dialect.

"Hmm, has he? That is most unfortunate. Where are you heading?"

"To the . . . the north."

He gave her a long, sharp glance as he pondered her words. It was as if he could see every lie she had ever told.

"Most unfortunate, indeed." He rose to his feet. "Happens that my wife is a nurse. She's familiar with every sort of illness and is often successful in curing them. A God-given gift." He smiled, and his round face creased into a myriad of wrinkles. "I often suffer from indigestion myself, but she always cures me. Do you know what ails this fellow?"

Bryony nodded. "Exhaustion, and he was—er—shot in the side several days ago. The wound is healing nicely, but he never had an opportunity to regain his strength."

Somehow she could not lie to this kindly person. There was something about him that demanded the truth, and she was relieved to speak it.

"Don't you worry, m'dear, we'll take him to the parsonage. Mrs. Partridge will set him right in jig time."

A load fell from Bryony's shoulders.

"I don't know how to thank you," she began as he hailed an ostler and ordered his carriage.

He patted her shoulder absentmindedly. "Don't mention it! One day I'll stand on your doorstep asking for help."

Bryony took Clover's hand and whispered that he should behave himself since they were going to a parsonage. He was staring in open fascination at the parson's three chins and at his belly, which wobbled every time he laughed. The man was one of the most cheerful people Bryony had ever met.

"And who's this little man?" Reverend Partridge asked once he had ordered his groom and one of the ostlers to lift Jack's limp body into the carriage. Chuckling, he bent and peered at Clover's grimy face.

"Clover, yer reverend, sir," the boy said, and shrank against the folds of Bryony's cloak.

"Clover? That is an odd name, but I believe cows have a great fondness for the flower, even though it gives them a terrible bellyache." He laughed heartily.

"Cows don't like me, and 'osses don't either," Clover stated from the folds.

"I see. A most unfortunate circumstance." The parson's laugh rumbled louder. "And what about you? Do you like them?" he asked, his eyes dancing.

Clover kicked the ground before finally giving an answer. "Better'n they like me."

"Jolly well! I promise you won't have to sleep in the stables." He ordered that their horses be tied to the back of the coach. After assisting Bryony and Clover, the parson heaved himself, puffing and blowing, into the coach.

" 'Tis unfortunate that your—er—fiancé didn't have a chance to try the ale at Ye Olde Dog. 'Tis the best in the Shires." He patted his ample stomach. "The very best."

"Perhaps before we leave . . ." Bryony said.

"Yes, of course. Besides, I have a hogshead at home, as well as plum brandy and geneva."

The carriage rattled through the village, past the town common and graveyard, and turned into the drive leading to the parsonage, located next to the church.

In the darkness Bryony could make out the forms of tall, swaying trees and a two-story brick building with a steep roof. Candlelight shone in every window. The carriage pulled up before the front steps, and after disposing of its passengers, continued around the corner of the house. Two grooms, Harry and Arnold, carried Jack into the house.

He had regained consciousness and was fighting their efforts to carry him to an upstairs bedchamber.

"Calm down," Bryony admonished, and pressed his hand in caution. "We're at the parsonage in Tutbury."

His face was weary, and he made a restless movement, but Harry and Arnold were strapping lads. They carried him up the stairs without ado and heaved him onto the bed. Bryony followed, clasping her hands in worry.

As Bryony saw Jack settled, Reverend Partridge appeared with a woman at his side. Small and almost as round as her husband, she was wearing a large mobcap edged with lace and a voluminous gown of fine moss-green wool cut in the French Watteau fashion. Holding out both her hands, she welcomed Bryony to their house.

Bryony glanced down at her own simple skirt, wrinkled jacket, and moth-eaten shawl. "I don't know how to thank you properly, Mrs. Partridge," she said.

"You have traveled far," the little lady said, and gazed deeply into Bryony's eyes.

"Yes, from Sussex." Bryony sensed it was wrong to pull these kind, innocent people into her and Jack's web of deception. What if they discovered that Jack was a Jacobite? This lovely couple might hang for sheltering him. Bryony's gaze flickered in fear, and she concentrated her attention on the floor.

"M-my fiancé is very tired." Bryony regretted saying that Jack was her betrothed, but now she had no choice but to keep up the charade. "And he has a serious wound. I believe the stitches should be removed."

"I see," the lady said, and peered at Jack's pale face. "A handsome fellow by all accounts," she judged, and clucked her tongue.

The parson laughed. "My lady has always had a weak spot for attractive young fellows," he said without an ounce of jealousy.

"I can see that," Bryony said. "She's very fortunate to have found you."

They both laughed, and the parson said, "Saucy miss! What's your name, by the way?"

"Bryony Shaw, and this is Jack Newcomer, sea captain." She lowered her eyes as she spoke the untruth.

The parson leaned over Jack, who had fallen into oblivion, and studied his lean, strong fingers. "A tender-skinned sea captain, I can see. Not like the salts of Southport."

Bryony knew he had seen through her deception, but he only patted her on the shoulder and said, "You must be hungry."

She nodded, but insisted that Jack be cared for first.

"Mrs. Partridge will see to him. I have every confidence that he will be a new man the next time you see him.'' The parson offered his arm, and she could not very well refuse it, though she was reluctant to leave Jack.

She didn't doubt that Jack would be stronger for the tender care of the parson's practical wife. Jack would not be able to refuse his host's hospitality even if he chafed at the inability to continue the journey. For the time being, they were safe.

The cold meal served to Bryony in the parlor was better than anything she had tasted since she had left her father's roof over two years ago. There was cold roast beef, mushrooms and peas in a hearty pie, buns baked with white flour, syrups and preserves in tiny glass bowls, plum pudding and tarts. Bryony wanted to cry at the sight of so much food. Never had she experienced a deeper gratitude.

"Where's Clover?" she asked breathlessly.

"I took him to the kitchen immediately,'' the parson said. "He needed a bath and a good dinner. Nice boy, that.'' The parson stirred the fire in the grate with a poker.

Bryony nodded. "Yes, a very good boy.''

"A servant, I take it?'' asked the parson, and sampled a piece of cheese.

Bryony had never thought of Clover as a servant, and she wasn't sure how to respond. Then she remembered Clover's uncouth tongue and realized she would have to call him some sort of servant. "An orphan from a workhouse in Sussex,'' she said. "I hired him as a page.'' Realizing at the last minute how incongruous it all sounded when she herself was dressed as a servant, she winced. Desperately seeking a way to extricate herself from the morass of lies, she opened her mouth to speak, but the parson interrupted her.

"You're a long way from home.'' He washed down the cheese with ale.

"Yes.'' Bryony timidly bit into a golden bun. It melted in her mouth, as did the wedge of cheese.

"I will look over my sermon for tomorrow, if you don't mind eating alone,'' the parson said, and popped a sugar plum between his lips. "We'll talk more tomorrow once you have rested.'' He offered her a dish of fried herring. "Our cook, Hattie Quinn, is awfully good, as you will

discover—almost too good." He patted his ample middle.
"You have to eat what she offers, or she'll be offended."

Bryony smiled gratefully. "You're very kind. You must
have noticed how very hungry I am."

He nodded vigorously, his three chins bouncing. "Yes,
I would be lying if I said I hadn't noticed your plight."

Bryony lowered her gaze to her plate. "One day I will
perhaps tell you about our adventures." Had it been only
a few weeks ago that she had listened to Aunt Hortense's
admonitions? Everything had changed since then. Bryony
had changed, grown into a woman. With Jack, she was
attempting to fulfill one of Reggie's dreams. But she was
doing it for herself as well, to test her own strength, to
find if she could accomplish such a demanding mission.

"Eat to your heart's content, my child," said the parson, and patted her shoulder before leaving the parlor.

Bryony obeyed him, sampling every dish the cook had
put on the table. After dinner she grew tired and wondered
how Jack was faring under Mrs. Partridge's care.

That lady arrived a few minutes later as Bryony's head
was tilting toward her chest. The firelight painted the walls
with leaping shadows while wrapping the room in warmth.
All Bryony could think of was a soft bed with blankets to
keep her warm.

"Mr. Newcomer is sleeping peacefully now," the good
lady said. "I removed the stitches, and he didn't issue one
word of complain, just kept biting his pillow. A brave
fellow, that." She sighed. "I can't believe he rode halfway across England with that wound."

"He did. Thank you for your help," Bryony said, turning her aching eyes on Jack's benefactor. "Jack is very
brave, but foolish."

"A nasty gash, but you kept it from going foul, which
is the most important thing." Mrs. Partridge nipped a
sugar plum from the bowl. "He'll be right as water as
soon as he has rested for a few days."

Bryony merely nodded. Jack was resting peacefully.
That was all that mattered. Then she remembered. "What
about his cough?"

" 'Tis almost cured. He must have had a difficult time,
but his breathing is easy tonight."

Bryony smiled dreamily, thinking of Jack's loving fingers on her body—before all the lies, before he fell ill. That was the man she wanted to remember, not the grim rebel.

"You'll be ill with the same complaint if you don't retire soon," Mrs. Partridge said, and swallowed another sugar plum. "Let me show you the guestroom."

Bryony slipped her arm through that of the parson's wife. "Why are you so nice to us? We have certainly not deser—"

"Nonsense! We're happy to help anyone in these difficult times."

Bryony considered the lady's words. Was she alluding to the Jacobite rebellion? Bryony shot a glance at the tiny woman at her side, but nothing except benevolence showed on her features. Perhaps Bryony was imagining the whole thing.

The parson's wife led her to a room lit by a cheerful fire. "If you need anything, I'll be across the hallway," she said.

Bryony could not think of anything more heavenly than a soft feather mattress and walls that fended off the cold air and the wind. "I don't know how to repay you for your charity."

The small woman patted Bryony's hand conspiratorially and laughed. "My husband loves people, especially strangers. In a small village like Tutbury we don't hear much news, and we see the same faces year after year." As she closed the door, she added, "Rest well, my dear."

"Thank you." Bryony took a dance step across the floor in pure delight. She discovered that there was hot water in the pitcher, and the towels were soft and smelled of lavender. It had been a long time since she had had a bath, even a sponge bath. She dragged off her clothes and poured water into the basin. It was sensual pleasure to lather her skin with sweet-smelling soap and rinse it off with warm water. Peace stole over her, along with the conviction that she had the strength to survive the ordeal ahead of her in Scotland.

Chapter 32

The next morning Bryony awakened late. She stretched luxuriously and yawned. She couldn't remember the last time she had slept so peacefully. When she pulled aside the curtains of the four-poster bed, she found that her simple clothes were gone. In their place lay a wool gown of the same design as the one Mrs. Partridge had worn the day before.

This gown was deep blue with light blue bows in a row down the front of the loose-fitting bodice. On a chair were clean stockings, a shift, two starched petticoats, and a starched cap. The cap, a small square of lace and muslin, did not offer much protection against curious eyes, Bryony reflected, missing her voluminous mobcap. But she could not turn down Mrs. Partridge's kindness by refusing to wear the clothes.

She dressed hurriedly, finding that Mrs. Partridge's gown was very wide and rather short at the ankles. She must look ridiculous, but no worse than when wearing her old, tattered clothes.

She brushed her hair until it shone and crackled, then wound it into a chignon high on her head. Leaving a few ringlets curling around her face, she pinned the cap to the chignon. Glancing at the arrangement in the mirror, she noticed that her eyes were clear, and the fatigue that had been lining her face was smoothed away. She would never be able to repay her kind hosts for their generosity.

Scents of breakfast floated up to her, but before going down, she wanted to know how her ''fiancé'' was faring. Due to the impropriety of the situation, she suspected Mrs.

Partridge wouldn't allow her into Jack's bedchamber. Besides, he probably didn't want to see her. Their relationship had been so strained lately.

As she hesitated outside his door, it opened, and Mrs. Partridge stepped out. Carrying a tray piled with bandages and bowls, she was dressed in a flowered cotton gown that parted over quilted petticoats.

"A good morning to you," she greeted cheerfully.

"How is he?"

"Oh, still exhausted, but he had a peaceful night. He's very resilient and will soon be chafing to get to his feet, I wager."

"I-I would like to see him, if possible. I know it's not conventional—"

"The parson's man is helping him wash. Perhaps later, after he has rested some more. Come with me. Breakfast calls. I hope you will like a dish of tea."

They descended the stairs together and entered the dining room. The master of the house was already sampling crisp bacon and a wedge of meatpie. He chewed convulsively as he stood to make his bow. When he had swallowed his food, he apologized for his rudeness and held out a chair for Bryony.

"I can tell that you slept well. There is some color in your cheeks today, Miss Shaw."

Mrs. Partridge filled Bryony's plate with food, then her own. Bryony dreaded the questions that would surely follow the meal, but she decided to answer them as truthfully as she could without further endangering her hosts.

To her surprise the couple only asked her about her family, questions that she could answer without bad conscience. She explained about Reggie's death and discovered that talking about it didn't hurt quite as much as it once had. In fact, she was eager to talk about Reggie, and told them scraps of childhood memories. They were good listeners, and she could not help but blurt out that she feared her brother had been murdered.

"Oh, how dreadful!" Mrs. Partridge exclaimed, clasping her hand to her heart. "Why?"

"Well . . . he had something valuable that someone else wanted. But I'm almost certain of the murderer's identity.

He's on a diplomatic mission to France, negotiating possible peace, they say."

"And such an important man would be a murderer?" Mrs. Partridge shook her head in bewilderment.

"I have no proof, but I will continue my investigation until I find some. The villain should be suitably punished for his crime."

The little lady fluttered he hand before her face. "Such vehemence in such a young person!"

Bryony looked down at her plate. "I won't rest until I know the truth. Several facts and witnesses' accounts point to the man's guilt." She squared her shoulders defiantly. "I'll find a way to prove it."

There was a movement by the door, and Bryony turned. "You're frightening these kindly people with your gruesome plans for revenge, my sweet," Jack drawled as he stepped into the room.

"Jack!" Bryony rose abruptly, her chair scraping on the floor. "What are you doing up?"

"I smelled breakfast." He smiled his old roguish grin and sauntered to the table. His gait was stiff as he favored his right side, but that did not diminish his commanding presence which was rapidly returning with his recovery.

Bryony's heart raced, and she could not find her tongue. One fact glared at her: she loved Jack more than ever. The relentless persecution, their quarrel, and her constant worry about Jack's illness had overshadowed her feelings, had numbed her. In this temporary haven, her emotions were returning with full force. The floor seemed to tilt toward her.

"What's the matter?" Jack's hand came around her elbow and steadied her, but all she was aware of was his burning touch through the fabric of her gown. Only when Jack gently eased her back onto the chair did she snap out of the spell.

As the maid bustled in to ask Mrs. Partridge if she wanted more tea and to remove the plates, Jack sat down beside Bryony. "Are you feeling faint?" he murmured for her ears alone.

She shook her head, gathering her scattered wits. "You should be resting."

"And go wild with worry about you? And about our plight? No, my lovely." He appeared to scrutinize the ale in his glass as he continued in an undertone, "Remember, our enemy has not given up, only lost our tracks momentarily. But they will be back." Aloud, he said, "I say, this is splendid beer."

The parson rose and immediately offered him another bottle. "There isn't a better cure for all sorts of ailments. My own recipe, y'know. You shall have it before you leave."

Bryony could not believe that Jack was sitting at the table carrying on a casual conversation. It was as if he had risen from the dead. He looked pale and gaunt, but made no sign of suffering much pain. He was wearing a pair of the parson's breeches and one of his coats, both much too large. The sleeves were too short, the lace of the shirt cuffs barely reaching his wrists. He would have made a comical figure were it not for his overwhelming masculinity.

Running footsteps reverberated along the hallway, and Clover put his head around the edge of the door and giggled. Jack's frown chased him away.

"A very young manservant you have there," said Mrs. Partridge.

"And a very saucy one." Jack said dryly. "I'm afraid there is no way to tame the little scamp without the rod. Clover has quite turned our world upside down with his tricks. I've never met a more precocious child."

The parson guffawed. "He will be teaching our errand boy all his tricks then. By tonight, the pair will be a handful."

They all laughed, except Jack.

"I'm so glad you're feeling strong enough to join us, Mr. Newcomer," said Mrs. Partridge. "Your fiancée has been telling us some of her sorrows."

Jack glanced at Bryony with a question burning in his eyes. Then his expression softened. "I hope I will always be a shield between her and her sorrows."

A shiver rippled through Bryony's body as his words echoed in her ears. She blushed, but said nothing. There was a time when she would have loved to hear those words, but a sharp sliver of doubt was still imbedded in her. Could she ever again wholly believe him? He was a master at twining words into lovely garlands, but would there be more worms hidden among the innocent petals? She could not read his mind.

"If you think you're strong enough, perhaps a short walk in the garden would do you good," the parson suggested to Jack. "After you've finished your breakfast, of course. You young people should spend some time together to discuss your plans." He glanced from one to the other in a meaningful way, and Bryony grew puzzled.

Mrs. Partridge laughed. "What the parson means is that two young people who are betrothed should solidify their relationship before they travel together without a chaperone. Especially since the young lady is alone in the world." She glanced at her husband and pursed her lips. "Since Alastair is a parson, 'twould be convenient. . . ."

Jack slanted an amused glance at Bryony. "There is the little problem of a license."

"Pshaw. By the time you have recovered fully, we'll have procured a special license for you," said Partridge.

How would they get out of this? Bryony wondered, and stared at the bacon rind on her plate as if she expected it to answer. The thought of marrying Jack was dizzying.

He stood with some difficulty and held out his hand. "Shall we take that walk, my lovely, and discuss the good parson's suggestion?"

Bryony could not very well say no. Besides, she had landed herself in this predicament. She took a last sip of tea and patted her lips with the starched linen napkin.

Arm in arm, they walked into the hallway and through the tall French doors at the back. The trees were sunbursts of red, yellow, and orange, and the flagstones were covered with leaves. The sky was brilliant blue, as sharp as crystal.

Jack gazed at Bryony for a long moment. "Your eyes are the color of the sky today, so cool, so brilliant, and so aloof."

Saying nothing she directed her gaze at the leaves on the ground.

"You involved us in this imbroglio. What in the world made you say that we were betrothed?" he asked.

Bryony shook off the arm he had placed around her shoulders. "I know it was exceedingly stupid, but that was the first thing that came into my mind. We'll tell them we want to wait. There is nothing they can do about it."

He laughed. "Only make you, lovely one, feel uncomfortable while we're here."

"And what about you? Do they make you feel uncomfortable?" She glanced at his inscrutable face. "Apparently not!" she spat. "Nothing can disturb your equilibrium." She instantly regretted her anger.

His dark eyes were filled with pain. "Don't put words in my mouth. I do have a conscience."

"You hide it well, just as you hide your face behind that beard."

He chuckled. "I thought you liked my beard." When she didn't respond, he continued. "Well, it gives a good disguise for now."

She halted in the middle of the path and stepped back as if distance from him would give her security. "I don't know a single thing about you, other than that you lied to me about your identity."

He looked guilty and turned a shade whiter. "I will tell you something of my dull life," he said. "This may well be the perfect time." He bowed and offered the support of his arm once more. Bryony accepted it out of pure curiosity. She could not wait to find out more about him. Unless he was telling her more lies . . .

"I was born thirty years ago in East Sussex, to a father and mother—"

"I believe we were all born to fathers and mothers," Bryony commented dryly.

Unperturbed, he continued. "We lived in a small manor house called Thornhollow, a house that I call my own today. I had no brothers or sisters, and I had the usual schooling—tutors, Eton, and Oxford." He gazed into the distance and sighed. "Thornhollow is the loveliest house in the world, and I hope to show it to you one day." His voice turned dreamy. " 'Tis quite small and simple, brick covered with ivy, and has deep latticed windows. My mother was happy there until Father died. She was a gentle soul and quite helpless. That's why she remarried; she could not care for us alone. I've told you what happened next. She married my stepfather, and he ruined her life, bit by bit.''

"And yours?"

He shrugged. "I could have killed him for hurting Mother, but naturally I didn't. Those were the worst years of my life. I was shy and innocent in those days, and my hatred festered in me." He laughed mirthlessly. "The hatred in my heart had to be confronted one day, and you forced me to do just that. Since I've met you and Clover, I'm beginning to see a way out of the past. Clover touches a sore spot in me. He's as brave and strong as I wish I had been at his age, and he has had a worse childhood than I ever had." Jack caressed Bryony's hair. "You have given me a new reason to live."

He placed his hands on her shoulders. "I've finally found the lady with whom I want to spend the rest of my life."

Her eyes were huge and vulnerable. "Are you saying you'd like to marry me . . . here?"

He let his hands drop, and a veil clouded his eyes. "I wish it was that simple."

"If you have doubts, then we shouldn't marry. Why should we if you don't know what you want?" Bryony stepped away from him to conceal the tears in her eyes. He didn't love her enough to marry her. Her common sense had been so clouded with passion that she had given her dearest gift to him—her innocence. But he refused to give her the gift of marriage in return.

"We should talk about this later, lovely one." He grabbed her shoulders from behind and pulled her against him. "Don't cry. I know I compromised you dreadfully. I will not take back the promise I made to you at Reggie's grave. I pledged you my undying love. Someday I'll give you my name as well." His low voice trembled with emotion. "It's just that this isn't the right time."

When? her heart silently cried, but she wiped her tears, angry with herself for her watery display. "The whole thing is silly. Once we've left the parsonage, no one will know the truth."

He said nothing.

She would rather die than show the full extent of her desolation. "We'd better go back inside. You must be chilled and exhausted." Bryony forced out a smile. "Come."

He obeyed, and together they returned to the house. Just as they traversed the hallway, the knocker sounded on the front door.

One of the servants appeared as Jack and Bryony entered the dining room and closed the door. They heard voices, a loud male voice and that of a female servant. The loud voice rose to a pitch, and the dining room door flew open. The servant's frightened face appeared in the opening.

"There's an officer t' see ye, parson. Says 'e's business wi' ye."

The parson rose and tossed his napkin on the table. "Very well, show him into the parlor. I will join him in a moment." The door closed, and the parson gave Jack a meaningful stare. "I hope there is nothing you have concealed from me. Are you wanted for some crime?"

"No. Nothing at all."

The parson pondered Jack's words. "I suppose they're still looking for Jacobite sympathizers. The militia has been to every house in the village, looking for escapees in every cellar and attic."

Jack nodded but kept silent. As if nothing was amiss, he sat down at the table and drank more beer. "I'm not a Scottish lord, if that's what worries you, Reverend Partridge," he added before the parson left the room.

Tension vibrated in the air. Mrs. Partridge fiddled with the centerpiece, an arrangement of autumn leaves in a Meissen vase. Jack's back was as stiff as a board. Bryony, barely able to breathe, sank down on a chair.

Conversation resumed in the hallway, and the parson's voice boomed louder than anyone's. The door opened again, and Bryony drew a sharp breath of fear.

Two men in scarlet uniforms stepped into the room. They bowed politely to the ladies and gave Jack a thorough scrutiny. He did not move a muscle. They introduced themselves as Sergeant Hornsby and Corporal Simms. Hornsby was tall and wiry, his sandy hair bushy and tied back with a black ribbon. His face was dominated by a beaky nose that twitched unbecomingly. Simms was short and stocky, with a vague light in his blue eyes and soft, pudgy hands that constantly tried to pry loose the tight cravat around his neck.

"We're looking for refugees, dangerous Jacobites who are believed to be heading this way." He paused. "Could you please identify yourselves with papers. The parson vows you're only visiting."

"We are," Jack said, and rose. "I will fetch my papers directly, but first, what makes you look in Tutbury?"

"We're searching every village."

"I see." Jack turned to Bryony, "Come, dear, help me search for my papers."

Bryony's legs trembled so that she could hardly walk. She took Jack's outstretched hand and drew on his strength as he led her into the hallway. They could hear the officers' voices all the way up the stairs.

"What now?" Bryony whispered. "How did they find out? Do we have to flee through the window?"

Jack looked grim, his face closed and determined. "No, we'll brazen it out. Don't worry. How are they going to prove that we're not who we say we are?" He halted her and stared. "Good God! What's the name on your papers?"

"Brienne Descroix. I used my aunt's married name, and Brienne is for Bryony. I traveled under a French name in France and under my real name here." Her eyes widened in fear. "What about yours?"

He smiled wickedly. "You think I would travel under my own name?"

"This is only a lark to you, isn't it? You're nothing but a big boy!" she scoffed, and pushed away his hand. "Does nothing ever frighten you?"

"The sea. My knees turn to jelly when I sail, as do my insides, and I pray I never have to repeat our trip across the Channel. Wait here." He turned and hurried to his room at the opposite end of the corridor.

Jack rejoined her a few minutes later. "If they think you're French, they might consider you a prisoner of war.

Don't say anything. I'll tell them you're my sister. 'Twas a mistake pulling the Partridges into this.''

"What should I have done, let you die on the doorstep of the inn? Once the parson saw you, there was no stopping him from meddling.'' She gave Jack a fulminating stare. "And I'm glad he did.''

They entered the dining room, and Bryony took a deep breath to steady her nerves.

"My sister forgot her documents at home,'' Jack explained, and handed the sergeant his papers. "But I can vouch for her.'' Bryony noticed that the parson started, glaring suspiciously at Jack. She could barely breathe from suspense as the officer scrutinized the document. It was heavily embossed with seals, and she wondered where Jack had managed to procure them.

The silence was dense, smothering.

To Bryony's amazement, the officer bowed deeply and said, "I understand fully. Your papers are in excellent order, sir. I'm honored to meet you. You must forgive us for being suspicious.''

Sergeant Hornsby looked almost disappointed as he handed back the papers. Had he been sure he would catch Jacobites at Parson Partridge's house today? Bryony wondered. Her heart pounded and her limbs shivered as she willed the officers to leave. Every moment they lingered was a trial, and every moment posed the possibility that someone would utter facts that would betray them.

But the parson's wife was calmly drinking her tea, and the parson was pacing the floor, his face red with indignation. "If you're quite finished here, mayhap you could let us continue our breakfast.'' He accompanied the redcoats to the door and slammed it behind them.

"Impudent young puppies,'' he grumbled as he returned. "Disturbing our meal in such a brash way.''

He sat down at the table and pinned his gaze on Jack. "Now, jackanapes, perhaps you can tell us the whole truth. Sheltering Jacobites, are we?''

Bryony and Jack exchanged glances. There was no escape. They would have to tell the truth.

"Yes—er—'twasn't our intention to stay here,'' Jack explained but before he could continue, the parson interrupted him.

"Say no more! We don't want to know the details." He seemed calmer as he rose and went to a finely carved oak cabinet in a corner of the room and unlocked the door with a key on a chain. Bryony glimpsed glasses and decanters. He solemnly carried the tray to the table.

Bryony gasped as she recognized the rose design. The Jacobite glasses! Without saying another word, they made a silent toast to the young prince.

"Now I'm truly glad you took us in," said Jack with great relief. "But, tell me, you're not of the Romish persuasion. Why—?"

"In my opinion," said the parson, "religion has nothing to do with my sympathies in this case. Charles Edward may be a Catholic, but he seems reasonable about leaving things as they are, were he to gain the throne of England. Now, his father is another kettle of fish entirely. A fanatical Catholic." He refilled their glasses. "The Stuarts are the true kings of England, always have been. There is no doubt about it. That German blockhead who calls himself king should go back to Hanover. It's as simple as that." He shook his head in despair. " 'Tis perhaps too late now. Stuart was badly beaten at Culloden, and it's not likely that his forces will recover."

"You can't predict the future," Jack replied. "Stuart is still there, and his supporters remain loyal."

The fact that Jack felt a need to atone for the bloodshed of the Scots made him a Jacobite, even though he had never been a direct part of the rebellion. Bryony realized there were many unexplained twists in the tapestry of his character. Obviously he had been very attached to his family—on his mother's side.

Trying to make some sense of his actions, she suddenly felt weary and low, not wanting to hear another word about the Jacobites. Desiring to be alone to sort out her thoughts, she excused herself, saying she had a headache.

"Reverend Partridge, I'm sorry I deceived you at the inn," she said as she was about to leave. "But we were in desperate circumstances. We still are."

Before she had a chance to close the door, the Partridges' boy servant came running down the hallway. '' 'Urry,'' he panted. "Clover's fallen in th' pond!''

Bryony gasped, and Jack pushed his chair back violently. Without hesitating a second, he followed the boy, tearing open the front door. Bryony followed suit, her heart lodged in her throat.

"What happened?" Jack shouted as he ran.

"Clover tried t' ride yer 'oss, but 'e tossed 'im orf into th' pond. 'E was sinkin' like a stone when I left.''

Jack swore and increased his speed, heedless of his own weakness.

They ran down the slope toward the pond located close to the stables.

Bryony moaned when she saw Clover flailing his arms pathetically and sinking below the surface once more. Jack tore off his coat and waistcoat as he ran and hurled himself into the water. It didn't look deep, but it was deep enough to drown one little boy.

Jack swam to the spot where Clover had disappeared and dove. Bryony waded halfway out herself, but her heavy skirts hampered her movements.

Jack surfaced without the boy and dove again.

The Partridges had reached the weedy rim of the pond, and Mrs. Partridge was praying aloud. Bryony joined in the prayer and could have cried in relief when Jack came up with Clover in his arms. The boy lay limply against his chest, a small, thin figure.

Jack waded out of the water, his face ghastly pale. Pain etched lines on his forehead, and he was shaking the boy gently. "We might be too late," he said, holding the boy upside down.

Bryony whimpered and slapped Clover on the back. At first nothing happened, then the boy convulsed in a coughing spasm. When he had emptied his lungs of water, he cried pitifully. Jack held him close to his chest, his head bent in sorrow as he waited for the boy to calm down.

Clover rubbed his eyes and pulled a wet sleeve under his nose. He drew a deep, shuddering sigh. "Are ye goin' t' spank me now?" he asked between coughs.

Jack did not answer at once. His shoulders were shaking. Bryony knelt beside them, caressing Clover's wet curls, and felt an irresible urge to cry. Jack's face was contorted in sadness, and several moments passed before he could control his emotions.

"No, scamp, I will not spank you, not ever again."

Raising his eyes, he looked straight at Bryony. "It's a promise."

Bryony's heart filled with warmth and wonder, as if she had just witnessed a miracle. Tears shimmered in Jack's eyes, and he was struggling to contain himself.

"You were naughty, Clover. You should not have mounted that big horse," she admonished gently, wiping the water from his face.

"I wish th' dumb 'osses would like me," the boy said, his eyes huge and filled with resignation.

"If you're gentle with them, they'll like you," Jack explained, his voice still gravelly with emotion. "You must speak to them kindly instead of rushing up and scaring them as you're wont to do." He smiled, and the boy's lips curved weakly in response. "They don't understand your jokes, y'see."

Clover clung to Jack's neck and said into his shoulder, "Oh, I likes ye, guv."

Jack pressed the small boy close. "And I like you."

Bryony blinked against the sun. The Partridges were standing some distance away. She was alone with the two people who meant most to her in the world. Believing that Clover had drowned, she had learned how much she cared for him. And Jack had risked his precarious health to save the boy. In doing so, he had gained something of even more value, the healing of an age-old wound.

After drying Clover and giving him some warm clothes, Bryony ordered him to bed. Jack had returned to his chamber, explaining that he needed to change clothes, too, but Bryony knew he wanted to be alone to sort out his feelings. She had some thinking to do herself.

Chapter 33

Trying to rest, Bryony lay down atop the bedclothes and tried to push thoughts of Jack from her mind, but it was a losing battle.

Above all things, she wanted to study his identification papers. What was written in them that had made the sergeant bow and scrape? She had to find out. She sensed that those papers would tell the truth about Jack, much more so than any of his glib evasions. When the perfect moment arose, she would slink into his room and search for them. Justifying her sneaky plan because of her need to know the truth, she finally fell asleep.

When she awakened, it was late afternoon. Still tired, she didn't want to go downstairs and face her host and hostess. The sooner they completed the mission to Scotland, the sooner she could go on with her investigation. At this point the very thought exhausted her. Their mad flight across England had taken much of her strength, and the anger that fueled her in her quest for revenge had been diluted by other emotions.

She got off the bed and righted the quilted cotton bedspread. Every detail in this house had been planned with care and love. She wondered if she would ever experience as solid a happiness as that which the parson and his wife shared. Surely they had no secrets between them.

She rearranged her hair and smoothed her gown before going downstairs. The house was silent. Was everyone still napping?

She found the lady of the house in the kitchen making preserves. Jars filled with the orange, blue, and green of rowanberries, plums, and gooseberries cluttered the table. The air was warm and redolent with the sweet aroma of summer and sunshine that the fruit had soaked up during the flowering season. Apples shone rosy in baskets on the floor.

"There you are, my dear. Feeling better now?" asked Mrs. Partridge, her arms covered with soap. She was washing jars, and one of the maids was drying them.

"Can I help?" Bryony asked. "Time would pass more quickly if I had something to do."

With a few words, Mrs. Partridge sent the maid to another part of the house and told Bryony, "You may help me dry the jars, and there are still gallons of berries to be sifted through and the leaves removed."

Bryony smiled and put on an apron hanging on a peg behind the door. "I would be delighted. You remind me of my mother, who used to stay in the kitchen for days preserving the summer harvest. The scent is exactly the same. I'll never forget it."

Mrs. Partridge shook her head in sorrow. " 'Tis a pity your mother is not alive."

"I barely remember her." Bryony stared dreamily out the window. Clouds were gathering in the sky, and a cascade of leaves whirled in the ferocious wind.

"My memories of childhood home are vague, except for those of my brother. He became the focus of my life when Mother died. Father wasn't easy to live with, a man of stony silences or violent rages," she sighed. " 'Tis only during these last few weeks that I have really started to live."

Mrs. Partridge smiled. "Love does that to you. And I don't blame you for being attracted to Mr. Newcomer. By all means he's a fine fellow, if perhaps a bit difficult to fathom. He's a fierce sort of man who gives all or nothing."

Bryony knew Mrs. Partridge was right. "He's helped me discover an inner strength that I had no idea I possessed." As the words left her mouth, Bryony realized their importance. During this autumn she had found that she could shape her own destiny by facing and solving the difficulties in her path. She had discovered the strength to do what she had to do. The knowledge sent goose bumps of pleasure down her spine.

By facing her own weakness she had found her strength.

All of a sudden she wanted to skip around the room, but she restrained the urge. Nevertheless, she couldn't stop the laughter bubbling from her lips.

"I say, that was a good little rest you had," said Mrs. Partridge with a chuckle. "Let's pray that your fiancé will behave in a similar fashion when he comes down. He was awfully fatigued when he stepped upstairs for his rest. Had I had my say, he would never have left the bed."

"You cannot tell Jack anything," Bryony said ruefully. "He makes his own laws."

"And is all the stronger for it," said Mrs. Partridge, drying her hands on a towel. "Now for the really arduous part, snipping the tops of the fruit and removing the debris. My least favorite task." She leaned closer with an air of conspiracy. "One that I often delegate to my husband," she added with a twinkle in her eye.

The kitchen door creaked open. "I heard that," said the parson as he stepped inside. "But she's right. A very good way to get a glimpse of my wife is to join her in the kitchen. Besides that, she makes the best gooseberry tarts in Staffordshire."

"Your happiness makes me envious," Bryony said wistfully.

The parson's wife patted her on the arm as she fetched the decanter to serve her husband a glass of wine. "You will find equal happiness, you'll see."

"Perhaps I already have, but it's not of the lasting kind," she said with a sigh, tearing the stem off a plum with unnecessary force.

Just as she was saying those words, Jack appeared in the doorway.

"I wish you would take my advice and marry," said Reverend Partridge.

Bryony challenged Jack with her eyes, and he met her gaze squarely. "This is not the right time, but I hope that very soon 'twill be," he said, unsuccessfully hiding the doubt and worry at the depths of his eyes. If there was something he was unsure about, it was the matter of their future. Still, there was a part of him that sounded so certain.

Bryony sensed his fear and it was contagious. She had no idea what a future with Jack would bring.

"Well, 'tis settled then. I will not push you further," said the good parson, and fired up a long-stemmed clay pipe. "It was foolish of me to get involved in the first place, but Elvira would so very much like to arrange a wedding party." He winked at his wife.

"You have done quite enough for us as it is," Bryony said as she handed Jack a bowl of gooseberries.

He joined them at the table, and his nimble fingers flew over the berries as he kept up the conversation with the parson.

This might be the perfect moment to search Jack's room, Bryony thought. With the excuse of wanting to fetch her handkerchief, she left the kitchen and darted up the stairs.

She hoped none of the servants was around to watch her. The corridor was quiet. Giggles and snippets of conversation came from the parson's bedchamber, indicating that two of the maids were cleaning the room.

There was no sign of any other servants. Bryony paused momentarily before the closed door to Jack's room, then tried to handle. It didn't make a sound, and to her relief, the door did not creak as she opened it.

Since the curtains were still drawn halfway across the windows, the room was gloomy. Jack's elusive scent of virility and fresh forest air wafted around her. His old clothes were hanging over a chair. An intense longing to bury her face in his clothes and remember the brief moments she had lain in his arms assaulted her. But the poisoned dart of doubt was still lodged in her heart. She was determined to resist his charm.

She searched his pockets, but found nothing other than some string and a handkerchief. His saddlebags were slung over the back of an armchair. They contained a shirt, a cravat, a folded waistcoat, and pouches of blackpowder and balls. The pistols were lying on the nightstand.

Her gaze flew from object to object in the room. Where had he hidden the documents? They had to be somewhere.

Sliding her hand under the mattress, she hoped to run across them, but found nothing. She pulled out the drawers of the tallboy, but they were empty except for some tablecloths that Mrs. Partridge had stored there.

Jack's wardrobe was meager at best. She peeped into jars and under statuettes dotting the surfaces of tables and chests. Nothing. The papers were not hidden under the pillow. Finally she went down on her hands and knees to look under the carpet.

So intent was she on her search, she didn't hear the door opening behind her.

"If you tell me what you're looking for, I'll be happy to assist you," drawled Jack.

She catapulted to her feet, a guilty flush blossoming on her cheeks. Clasping her hands to her scarlet face, she tried to invent a feasible explanation.

There wasn't one.

"I take it you're here because you wanted to spend some time in my presence—alone," he suggested in seductive tones. He advanced warily, a predator stalking its prey.

"I've lain in my bed dreaming about what I would do to you if I had you in my arms." He released an exaggerated sigh. "Such wicked dreams were fruitless between these walls of kindness and righteousness—until now." He captured her face between his hands, pushing his fingers through her hair until the pins scattered across the floor and her midnight-dark tresses tumbled down her back.

She was mesmerized, her reason scattering into a mishmash of meaningless thoughts. She stepped away, but he followed. The edge of the desk bit into the back on her thighs, and she was trapped. He pushed her relentlessly against it.

He cupped her neck and pulled her face closer. "You must have longed for me terribly to dare entering my room in the middle of the day. But I like your bold spirit. Let us use this time to its best advantage."

His breath wafted over her face as he bent to kiss her lips. At first his touch was light, like moth wings, stirring her desire until her lips throbbed with longing. Hungrily, she parted her mouth and gave him access to the sweet recesses. His tongue made love to hers, whipping her desire into a frenzy. It had been so long. She had almost forgotten.

She dug her fingertips into his shoulders, then caressed the broad span and finally explored the tantalizing column of his neck. Every moment in his arms became a greater agony because of the barrier of clothing that separated them. But how could they take off their clothes without being shamelessly wanton, without desecrating the trust of their kind hosts?

Jack moaned deep in his throat and released her lips to cover her throat with fervent kisses. He held her at the small of her back, pressing her against himself until she thought she would burst with need.

"This is what you came for, isn't it?" he murmured. He gently released one of her small breasts from the confines of the loose bodice and suckled the rosy tip. "Oh, my sweet wanton. I want to see and touch every inch of you. Your skin drives me insane." He rotated his tongue around her turgid nipple and the sensation was excruciatingly sweet. Then he managed to kiss her all the way down to her stomach as the bodice threatened to rip at her shoulders. She would have collapsed had it not been for his steadying hand on her back.

He lifted her skirts and slid one hand along the length of her leg. His caresses sent a thrill along her skin that lodged and swelled in the center of her being. She whimpered against his lips as he touched her secret places.

"Oh, this is it," he whispered, and took her lips. His kiss was almost violent in its force, but she reveled in the rough treatment, wanting more. He touched her more intimately, almost lifting her off her feet in his yearning. He let go of her lips and gazed into her eyes, his own darkened by desire. The raw longing in his eyes found a response deep within her. When he continued to caress her, she closed her eyes in ecstasy and was vaguely aware that a warm flush of pleasure had spread over her body. If she was ever to have the strength to stop, this was the time.

"This is a parsonage," she whispered against his lips.

He stiffened. "I'm sure the parson is, and has been, a lusty man."

She pushed against him, though her entire body cried out for him. "That doesn't mean we can misuse their trust. They let us be together because they believe that we will behave with decorum."

Jack was busy covering her face with kisses. "I never did behave with decorum. 'Tis very simple—I love you, and I want to make love to you." He slipped his fingers into her, and it was almost her undoing. He sighed. "I could die for the chance to burrow between your thighs one more time. I have dreamed of nothing else since that night in the barn."

She pushed him away at last, feeling immediately bereft. But she knew she had done the right thing. "Nonsense! All you've thought of is the map and the gold in Scotland."

He took her roughly by the shoulders. "That's not true, and you know it! How very unfair of you."

She righted her clothes. Still overcome with longing for more, she found it an agony to be in the same room with him without touching him.

But she had no desire to further cross swords with Jack. She had too many unanswered questions, and he was never going to tell her the truth if she asked point-blank. Besides, her search had not unearthed any answers. She was glad she had not succumbed to her desires. Shaking off his hands, she went to the door.

"I will go downstairs and continue washing the fruit."

He smiled with curious tenderness. "Your cheeks are very red. Perhaps you ought to wait—"

"Oh! You!" she said, and stomped out of the bedchamber.

But the closed door could not erase the yearnings of her body, and she berated herself for ever letting him touch her.

As she paced the length of her room, the flush of her desire slowly subsided, but her longing sat like a dull ache in her stomach.

Returning downstairs, she was relieved to find that Jack had stayed in his room to rest for the remainder of the day. Mrs. Partridge praised Bryony for her industriousness, and she was doubly glad she had not given in to Jack's bold caresses. If she had, she could never have returned the good lady's glance again.

Time moved at a snail's pace. As a volcano of desire seethed within her, Bryony chafed against the stillness and serenity of the parsonage.

Evening came, and Jack had supper on a tray in his room. Bryony ate her own meal in silence, boiled tench in caper sauce, topped off with Mrs. Partridge's famous gooseberry tarts. Bryony started as a thump sounded outside the window, then a low whistle.

"Who is it?" she asked, her eyes wide with fear.

"Don't you worry, girl," said the parson, who peered outside. "If I'm right, this should be a delivery of a hogshead containing rum." He went into the hallway and unbolted the door.

Sure enough, on the steps sat one dripping wet hogshead. "That's the free trader's customary delivery."

Bryony gaped, and the parson laughed at her expression of surprise. "Hogsheads of spirits are a common sight in the village. Besides, my delivery man sends vital messages for the cause." He counted up some gold coins and placed them under the mat outside the door. Then he called the servants, Harry and Arnold, who rolled the barrel away.

The parson closed the door, and a few minutes later there was a scuffle by the door and three timid knocks. Then silence reigned once again.

"No message tonight." The parson stretched and yawned. "Time to rest. Let us end this glorious day with a glass of the missus's best elderberry wine."

As he served the wine in the Jacobite glasses, Bryony studied the design. On one side was the rose and on the other an etched portrait of a young man who must be the prince. He looked nothing like the man she had once seen at Versailles, but that seemed such along time ago. Besides, she had been standing very far away from him during the one ball Aunt Hortense had allowed her to attend.

" 'Twill be another night of peaceful rest," said the parson, and yawned.

Plagued by thoughts about Jack and their heated embrace, Bryony didn't fall asleep until the clock in the hallway chimed midnight. She slept for about an hour until someone gently shook her shoulder.

"Bryony, my sweet, awaken!"

Struggling with the cobwebs of oblivion, Bryony recognized Jack's urgent voice.

"Pssst, Bryony!"

She bolted upright, pulling the covers to her chin. "What are you doing here?"

"You have to dress now. We must leave. I went down to the village for a glass of ale, and I saw our four friends again. They were just riding up to Ye Olde Dog as I left. I spied them from the cover of the trees, and they were very tired." He caressed her bare shoulder. "Five minutes. Don't take longer."

"Clover? The map?" she inquired.

"I've already spoken with Clover and fetched the map from his coat. He's happy here playing with the errand boy. The parson has promised to care for him until we return."

Bryony was already dressing in the weak moonlight that filtered through the windows. This time she pulled on her old peasant clothes. "I will miss him."

"He'll be much safer here. I wish you would stay here, too, until the mission is accomplished, but I assume that's a futile request."

"Yes," she said. "I won't rest until I do this for Reggie. That's why I came with you in the first place."

She had finished dressing and threw a shawl across her shoulders, then her cloak. "Are you carrying the map?" she asked.

"Yes, inside my shirt." He led her out of the room and down the dark stairs. One puny taper burned in the hallway below. Their hosts were there, dressed in voluminous night robes and nightcaps. Mrs. Partridge handed the saddlebags to Jack. "These are filled with provisions which should last a day or two," she said.

The parson gave Jack a heavy purse. "This is only a trifle, but if you see the prince, tell him he has staunch followers here."

"For the cause," Jack said, and pocketed the money. "I will give him whatever we don't use on the trip."

They sneaked through the door and waited in the darkness until the parson had bolted the entrance from the inside. The wind was up, chasing ragged clouds across the sky.

Bryony pressed closer to Jack as they hurried to the stables. Their horses were ready and waiting, the saddles clean and the harnesses mended.

Bryony's eyes smarted from the lack of sleep, but she clamped her teeth together in determination. She wasn't going to complain on the very first night. This time she would not have to worry about Jack, who appeared much stronger. One of the grooms hoisted her into the saddle, then assisted Jack, since his wound still would not permit any sudden movement.

The wind rushed through the branches above, and leaves rattled across the yard as they rode from their temporary haven. Once again they were on their own. The lane wound through the village, passing cottages that were silent and dark. Everything was covered by a silver haze. Although she knew their pursuers were settled at an inn and could not be following yet, Bryony nevertheless threw a cautious glance over her shoulder. The lane was empty except for a cat that streaked across it. On the hill above the Dove Valley towered the dark, crumbling walls and turrets of Tutbury Castle.

A sensation of imminent danger fluttered through Bryony. Behind them waited their faceless enemies; at the other end of their journey they might very well face death.

But Bryony did not regret her decision to accompany Jack. She never had. This adventure was her last act of homage to Reggie. It would put his soul to rest—more so, she was beginning to believe, than would bringing his murderer to justice.

The wind was cold, and she shivered. Jack urged his mount to greater a speed, and so did she. He had an air of purpose now that he had lacked during his bout of ill health. The farther they rode from the village, the stronger his aim grew.

"Now that we have funds again, we can ride faster and change horses often," he said as they rode abreast. "We will stop at a village outside Carlisle, and leave—or take—

a message from one of my contacts. We should have met
him at East Grinstead, but he never arrived. Besides, I
was too tired and sick to find out what really happened
there.''

''From what I know, no one asked for Mr. Newcomer
or left a message at the inn.''

He chuckled. ''My contact would not be that obvious.
He comes straight from Stuart, and I'm very eager to hear
the latest news.''

''Reverend Partridge said Charles Edward is still fleeing
for his life.''

''The parson doesn't have the latest news,'' said Jack.
'' 'Tis possible that Stuart has been able to raise another
army, and if that's the case, he needs funds desperately.''
He glanced at her and added, ''Do you think you're strong
enough to ride night and day for a few days?''

Bryony raised her chin. ''Of course I am. The faster we
can get this business over with, the better.''

They stared at each other, although the darkness of the
night partially concealed their expressions. ''And what will
happen after the mission?'' Jack asked.

''I don't know,'' Bryony replied in low tones.

''When we've succeeded, we will celebrate. And perhaps resume where we left off this afternoon.''

She was glad he could not see her blushing face.

They rode in silence for the reminder of the night. As
the gray light of dawn appeared in the east, they found a
cave in a hillside covered with brush. A fast-flowing stream
gurgled below, and there they stopped to eat breakfast.
Jack fetched water in a tin mug, and it tasted like ambrosia
to Bryony's parched throat. The gooseberry tarts were delicious and chewy since the crust had soaked up the flavor
and moistness of the berries.

''This is the best meal you'll have until the mission is
completed,'' Jack said, leaning against a tree trunk at the
opening of the cave. ''The cured ham is heavenly—and
the bread!''

Bryony laughed. ''Your cheeks are bulging most unbecomingly.''

''Something else is bulging every time I look at you,''

he said with a mischievous grin. "Come here," he held out his hand toward her, and when she took it, he drew her closer. "I do not think God will be desecrated here, do you? I admit the parson's house was too holy for my wicked thoughts.," He sighed. "Thoughts that plagued me night and day."

He set down the rest of the meal and pulled her into his arms so that she lay facing the endless sky and fading stars. "You do want me as much as I want you, don't you?" he asked, suddenly concerned.

Since his maneuver had taken her by surprise, she could only nod in response. He *had* chosen the right moment, and their longing overshadowed everything else on their minds. Bryony wanted to taste his passion, his love, one more time, a memory to cherish forever. Yet she was sharply aware that their lovemaking would solve nothing between them.

Watching him detach the blanket from the saddle and spread it on the mossy ground in the cave, she started to shed her clothes. The wind was cold, but she never noticed the goose bumps on her skin. All she wanted was to be close to Jack.

He gazed at her as her skirt slipped from her hips into a heap on the ground. He groaned as she unbuttoned her simple jacket and pulled the peasant blouse over her head. Her breasts strained against the plain shift, and she shivered in anticipation.

Jack had doffed his coat, vest, stockings, and breeches. Bryony's gaze followed the taut lines of his thighs to the hard buttocks, and her breath was arrested in her throat as he pulled his shirt over his head. Weak light slanted into the cave, and she could clearly savor the view of his flat, muscled stomach, lean hips, and broad chest.

She loved every inch of him.

Holding her breath, she glided across the ground and nestled her head against his chest, curled her arms around his flat middle. She was strongly aware of every nuance of his desire as he pressed himself against her. He was hot, and the scent of his arousal touched a chord within her.

Lifting her lips to his, she gave herself up to their intimate pleasure. She clung to him as his hands slid over every pore of her body. Unable to get enough of him, she let her hands explore him until they came to rest on the core of his desire.

"Sweetest woman," he moaned into her ear as she gently massaged him. "I'm wild for you."

He showed her just how wild as he lowered her to the blanket and tasted every mound and crevice of her body with his tongue. She cried out in pleasure, again and again, and he finally heeded her whispered pleading and entered her. She moaned as a tempest of rapture swept through her, bringing her to crest after crest. She was one with him as he effortlessly played the instrument that was her body. And when at last he joined her in ecstatic fulfillment, they clung together, tears of joy streaking their faces.

Chapter 34

They slept until the morning was old. The wind had risen to a blustery force outside the cave, but Jack and Bryony were protected from its cold bite. Curled up under their cloaks, they rediscovered the bliss of their passion once more.

Later, Jack rose and stretched his powerful body. "It's high time we left, my lovely one. Our pursuers cannot be far behind, even though they will have to stop at times."

"We could stay here for the rest of our lives," Bryony suggested with a sunny smile. Happiness soared through her. Jack had given her his all, never once hesitating to show her his innermost feelings. And she had opened up to him as never before.

Yet he remained an enigma.

She scrambled to her feet and danced a little jig of happiness. He caught her to him, a strange light glittering in his eyes. "My sweet fairytale princess, my sweet elf," he whispered into her hair.

"I'm real!" she reminded him, and pinched the flesh of her upper arm. "See? A fairytale princess sits on a high pedestal and is untouchable."

"I thought you were that, at first. I thought that I would have to adore you at a distance."

She punched him in the chest. "You did not! I recall distinctly that you told me I would have to *beg* for your favors. Who was high and mighty then? And who said he didn't believe in love?"

"You *did* beg, didn't you?" he said with a lopsided grin.

She blushed. "Yes, I did, but that was after you promised me your undying love, remember?"

He nodded and bent to retrieve his breeches. As he looked up, his face grew serious, his eyes cloudy. "Yes, I remember, and I still mean it, but—"

She placed her finger over his lips. "Please, say no more. 'Twould only ruin my happiness."

He hesitated, then put on the rest of his clothes. It was as if every garment he donned brought another layer of separation between them. The sunlight seemed to have dimmed, and Bryony wished she had never brought up the subject of his past promises. Her euphoria was crushed like a rose petal under a boot. For a few hours, she had wanted to pretend that the other side of him, the lies and secrets, did not exist.

Jack slung the saddlebags onto his horse. Then he brushed his hair and bound it back. Bryony watched him walk down to the stream as she brushed her own hair and piled it on top of her head. After pulling on her old voluminous mobcap, she was ready.

They drank from the stream and splashed water on their faces, then left their haven of bliss behind them, knowing that their enemies lurked nearby, that further hardships awaited them.

During the following days, they established a pattern. When their food supply was gone, Jack rode to the nearest farm and bought more. They avoided villages and towns as much as possible, and slept in snatches of two or three hours. Bryony grew more and more weary as the days wore on, but she refused to complain.

As one day flowed into the next, she could not remember how many had passed since they had left the parsonage. The landscape had changed, turned mountainous and gray, unforgiving yet majestic. The ground was covered with scree, coarse grass, and clumps of heather. The trees were different, more windbeaten and scraggly compared to those of the more gentle south. To the west rose the Cumbrian Mountains.

When Bryony's horse lost a shoe, their schedule was disrupted. Far from a road, they had to lead the horse for hours to the nearest village. The hamlet had no posting house, but it did have a blacksmith who willingly set to work after Jack urged him on with the glitter of gold. But the man was a slow worker, and the shoe had to be refitted several times. Even then, the fit was poor.

Jack was pacing the dusty yard in front of the smithy, staring at the road from whence they had come. Did he really expect their pursuers to ride up? Bryony wondered. His restlessness was contagious, and Bryony wanted to pace as well, but she remained seated on the overturned wooden pail that the blacksmith had offered her as the only chair available.

Exhaustion crept up on her, and before she knew it, she was nodding. She wanted to lie down and sleep for the rest of the day.

The next thing she knew, Jack was shaking her. "They are coming," he said hoarsely.

She blinked as his words sank in. "Wh-where?" Glancing down the lane, she saw nothing.

"A great cloud of dust about half a mile away." He inspected the roan's new shoe and swore. "This'll have to do for now." Without wasting time, he aided Bryony into the saddle.

"It could be a hunting party," she protested.

"No, it's them. Hunting parties usually ride across the fields, not along the road. They must have ridden without break for at least two days." He cursed as he swung himself into the saddle, momentarily clutching his side. "Let's get out of the village." He tossed the blacksmith another coin after muttering something to the man.

"What did you tell him?" Bryony asked as they galloped side by side.

"I told him to keep his mouth shut." The grimness that Bryony remembered from their last flight had returned to Jack's features.

"We need to reach the village of Wetheral before they do," he said, and urged his mount onward. "We should be there this afternoon."

The lane wound up the top of a knoll, and Jack pulled in the reins to take a look at the village behind them. "There they are! Just riding into the village now." His horse danced nervously at the sound of his irate voice. "We're going to need our wits today," he added, and set off down the other side of the hill. "Thank God the road is dry. We can ride faster."

Bryony looked over her shoulder but saw nothing as trees concealed the curve in the road. The next hours were harrowing. She feared that their enemies would catch up with them at any moment. The suspense chafed on her nerves, and exhaustion made her reckless. She had a sudden wild desire to stop this mad chase and confront their enemies, if only to connect faces to their bodies. She suggested it to Jack. "We could set a trap for them," she said.

He shook his head. "No, 'twill make no difference. We cannot accuse them of any crime, and if we did, we would only draw attention to ourselves."

The mad pace tired the horses, and finally they had to stop. They rode in among the trees along the lane and down a slope, reaching a dry streambed. They walked the winded horses and wiped the foam off their coats with handfuls of dry grass.

Bryony tensed and listened for the sound of hooves thundering along the road. The threat was painfully real. Someone wanted the map badly enough to follow them clear across England!

"We'll stay behind them from now on," said Jack, his gaze calculating. "That they will not expect."

After resting for a few hours, they continued their journey. Bryony was jittery with apprehension, suspecting that they might ride into an ambush. Every shape that wasn't a tree or a boulder became the barrel of a musket or the sweep of a cloak.

They inquired at inns along the road and discovered that their enemies had passed through only hours before them. However, at the last inn where Jack asked, the proprietor said he had seen no men of that description pass by or stop for refreshments.

"They have figured out that we're behind them," Jack said, his lips a grim slash of determination. "We'll have to ride across the moor at night. 'Twill take longer, but the stars will guide us." He absentmindedly fingered his chest where the map was concealed, and Bryony sensed his mounting tension.

If they were caught, everything would be lost, their reckless ride across the country all in vain.

"Let's go." Jack lifted Bryony into the saddle with a grimace. His side still pained him, and his eyes were ringed with dark circles. He never complained or sought additional rest. Bryony suspected she would never have been able to keep up with him had he been in peak condition.

An owl hooted at the distance as night enfolded the earth. Bats swirled and danced soundlessly in the darkening black sky. The wind was cold, slithering along the ground and whipping up flurries of dust. Weak moonlight cast a feeble light, and Bryony's horse stumbled several times on stones imbedded in the heather.

Jack led the way across the fields but tried to avoid the open spaces as much as possible. Their progress was very slow, and Bryony wanted to rest as they passed a copse of trees dense enough to give their horses shelter from prying eyes.

Jack halted his own horse and waited for her to draw abreast. He placed a hand on the roan's neck and pointed silently at the copse. The only sound was the wind in the heather. Bryony strained her eyes to see.

Then she heard it, an unmistakable jingle of harnesses. A horse whickered among the trees. She froze in terror, could almost feel the cold gaze of their pursuers pierce the night.

"What shall we do?" she whispered between stiff lips.

"We cannot fight them. They are four men, and most likely armed." He drew his pistols from his saddlebags and primed them even as he turned his steed around. "Let's go back. We have to find the road—and pray that the horses don't stumble and fall."

Bryony set off, Jack close behind. Instantly came the sounds of horses crashing through the trees in hot pursuit. Bryony whimpered in fear as she threw a glance over her shoulder. A shot sliced through the darkness and whistled past her head. Several more shots shattered the silence, and Bryony leaned closely over the roan's neck. Her horse

would have bolted had not the difficult terrain hampered
the animal's movements. As it was, the mare plunged
ahead at heart-stopping speed, every step threatening to
be its last.

Jack was close behind Bryony, and his answering shots
rang in her dazed ears. She heard a cry in the distance.
One of Jack's lead balls had found its target.

Bryony's senses were assaulted by the pungent odor of
her mount's fear. Every breath was painful in her parched
throat, and her tongue cleaved to the roof of her mouth.
As another round of shots reverberated in the darkness she
fully expected every breath to be her last.

Jack loudly urged her to head for the nearest trees. Her
horse seemed to aim instinctively for shelter, and she let
it have its head. Closing her eyes, she clung to the mane
and prayed fervently that they would reach shelter in time.

"Miss Shaw!" Her name echoed in the night. The fact
that one of the men knew her name sent chills down her
spine. But, of course, he knew her name! Hadn't they
always been there, waiting in the shadows at Willow Hills
and on the roads across Britain?

"If you want to help your brother, stop your mad flight
and listen to me. I can help you."

She stiffened in the saddle, her mind dissolving into
fragments of confusion. She had heard that voice before.
Now it was muffled, distant.

"Hear me!" the voice taunted her, sounding closer. Fear
constricted her throat, and Bryony willed her horse to move
faster.

Jack was beside her, so close she could feel his knee
bumping her own. "Don't listen to them," he urged, his
words punctuated by labored breaths. "They want to confuse you, nothing else."

Bryony bit her teeth together in determination as the
first trees approached. Branches clutched at her, and she
bent lower in the saddle. The roan stumbled once, and
Bryony cried out in alarm. As the horse quickly regained
its foothold, Bryony tried to calm her staccato pulse, but
to no avail.

Both horses slowed automatically as the ground grew
more treacherous. Jack gripped the roan's bridle and gave

it a tug. Bryony could feel the horse shiver under her as it turned sharply, obeying Jack's command.

The men behind them were still in close pursuit, but their horses were experiencing the same difficulty with the terrain. The men cursed and slashed at the bushes with their swords. Jack's stallion, followed closely by Bryony's roan, had turned at a ninety-degree angle away from the pursuers, confusing them, putting distance between them. Jack made another ninety-degree turn, actually steering the horses toward the approaching men.

At one point he stopped, and Bryony's horse trampled the ground nervously behind him. He stroked the muzzle gently, and the horse calmed.

The men passed very close to them. Bryony could clearly head their progress, only twenty feet away. She was so frightened she was frozen to the saddle, her hands riveted painfully to the pommel. Her heart hammered heavily in her chest, almost dully, as if it was about to stop, and her every muscle contracted in terror.

Through the vegetation she could make out the horsemen's dark shapes as they struggled forward. But since they didn't expect her to be off to the side twenty feet away, they were intent on gaining speed.

The danger wasn't over, just temporarily assuaged as the men disappeared from sight and their voices faded.

"Let's go," Jack whispered. He led both horses out of the trees and back toward a road they had crossed earlier that evening. The stars were hidden by a bank of clouds. Still, Jack seemed to know his way. When they had left the trees at a safe distance, they rode at a trot, grateful for the heather's muffling effect on the hoofbeats.

When they reached the road, they stopped and scanned the wide expanse of moor, dotted with granite outcropping and a few groves of trees. There was no sign of their pursuers.

Because of the exhaustion of their horses, they had to ride very slowly and finally stop in a clearing beside the road. Bryony was so tired, she felt permanently fused to the saddle. She could barely move her fingertips.

Jack lifted her off, but his arms trembled with fatigue. They sank down, back to back, against a tree and let the horses wander by themselves, tearing up the turf with their strong teeth.

"Why did the man imply that he wanted to help me? What does he know that I don't know?" Bryony asked suspiciously.

Jack laughed, a harsh, weary sound. "He was merely trying to unsettle you and perhaps capture you." He rubbed his beard thoughtfully. "I would do just about anything to get you back if they managed to catch you."

Bryony brightened. "Would you? Even give them the map?" She peered at him in the darkness, fearing the truth.

"Even the map."

She heaved a sigh of relief. Cradling her tired arms around his neck, she whispered, "Thank you. That was the most wonderful compliment you have given me. Before, it was always the mission first."

Yet there was still a tiny seed of doubt in her mind. He could easily *say* the words without really meaning them. But she pushed away her doubt. She'd rather believe him than not.

They dozed against the tree, and Bryony's body was stiff with discomfort when Jack shook her gently half an hour later. "We'd better continue now. The sun will soon be up, and the cover of darkness gone." He whistled for their horses.

They mounted their animals and looked in both directions of the lane, but saw nothing except the night.

"I want to reach Wetheral before daybreak. I do hope my contact has arrived. He will take us into Scotland on safe routes," Jack explained, and urged his horse into a canter.

"Do you mean the war is still going on?"

"Not exactly, but the redcoats are everywhere, looking for Scottish soldiers. They are trying to uproot every trace of the rebellion by hunting down the remaining faithful. Everyone who is not a member of the British army is looked upon with suspicion."

"I see. Your friend must be very good at eluding the British army then if he expects to lead us through half of Scotland without being captured."

"He is. You'll soon find out for yourself."

They rode on in silence. When rosy sunlight first spread across the sky, they entered the sleeping village of Wetheral, four miles east of Carlisle.

"We'd better leave the horses here and continue on foot. That will draw less attention."

They tied the horses where grass grew in abundance next to the river that flowed past the village. Jack explained that it was the River Eden, and he pointed to a peel tower on the other side. "That's Corby Castle. It was used in defense against the Scots two hundred years ago."

"You do know a lot." Bryony followed him, grateful to stretch her legs after the endless hours of riding.

"Towers like those are a common sight in these parts."

Large stone houses bordered the village's triangular green. The dominant color was gray—gray slate roofs, graystone walls, and gray cobblestones. The small garden patches were orderly and surrounded by walls of piled stones, but they lacked the sense of abundance of the gardens in the south. Even the fruit trees were smaller.

Still, vines clung on walls here just as abundantly as they did in the south, and the stark grandeur of this village could never be found at home. The cottages had dignity, like the mountains below which they had been erected.

No one was up this early, and the main street was deserted.

THE TROUT INN said a peeling sign above one of the larger buildings close to the church.

"This is our meeting place," Jack explained. "Better hide for now until we can find out if our contact has arrived."

"How will you know?"

"He always stays in the same room, the one with the window at the corner. He'll keep a lighted candle on the sill all night if he's here. I don't see one now."

Jack led her behind the inn to the stables. They were modest since this was no posting inn. "This is a perfect time to sleep. Who knows when we'll get another chance."

Glancing once more toward the inn, Jack cautiously opened the door and stepped inside. They found the hay in the loft soft and sweet smelling, and there was a glassless window facing the room on the corner. As soon as the lighted candle appeared, they would know.

They burrowed deep into the hay and fell asleep, Bryony's head cradled on Jack's shoulder.

Chapter 35

Bryony had no idea how long she had slept, but it was dark again when she opened her eyes. Jack was still resting peacefully beside her. Crawling to the window, she looked outside and breathed deeply of the clear night air.

There was a light in the window.

Excited, she crawled back to Jack and awakened him with a kiss. "He's here," she whispered.

"Wha— Who?" Jack rubbed the sleep from his eyes.

"Your contact."

Jack came slowly out of his slumber, resting his head against his knees. His shoulders slumped wearily, and Bryony realized how this long trip had worn his already exhausted body.

"I'm hungry," he said, and raised his head. "How long has it been since we last ate?"

Bryony could not remember, but her stomach was clenched into a grumpy fist.

"First things first," Jack said. "We have to contact my friend."

They brushed off their clothes, even though the creases could not be smoothed out. Bryony would have paid a golden guinea for a simple bath.

A stableboy was snoring on a chair in the stables below, but he did not awaken as they passed. The door stood wide open, and Jack glanced around the corner before announcing that the backyard was empty.

They slunk like thieves along the walls to the main building. Jack sidled up to a window and looked inside.

Judging from the sounds of laughter and song, Bryony decided this was the taproom.

She heard Jack's sharp, indrawn breath and clutched his arm. "What is it? What are you seeing?"

"Our 'friends' from the road."

"How do you recognize them?"

"They look like they have ridden across England." Jack prevented her from looking inside. "Careful! They might see us," he replied, dragging her around the corner of the house. "I didn't spot my contact. Let's see if he's in his room."

He scooped up a fistful of gravel and tossed it against the window. Bryony's gaze flew nervously toward the taproom as the gravel clattered against the pane, but no one appeared to investigate the sound.

A shadow rose in the room above, wavered and vanished as a figure appeared in the window. He swung the casement open and peered outside. "Who's there?" he asked in a baritone edged with anger.

Bryony saw an elegant powdered wig, but the facial features were a blur.

"Pssst, 'tis me," hissed Jack.

The bewigged head swiveled downward. "Jack, you snail! Is that really you at last? I've been waiting in this godforsaken hole for two days. I'm about to die of boredom."

"Shhh, you idiot! Do you want to inform the entire world of our presence? Our enemies are downstairs, by the way."

Fingertips rapped on the windowsill, and a low whistle pierced the air. "Not the four men drinking downstairs? One of them was shot in the shoulder by a Scot—or so he claims. I won twenty guineas at quadrille."

"The very same men, and I'm only half Scottish. Come down here, you joker."

Bryony stared in wonder as one elegant leg swung over the windowsill and a pair of boots found foothold among the stones supporting the ivy. The man's descent was so rapid, Bryony had no idea how he managed it. The next second he stood there, a glorious vision in a red satin coat trimmed in gold and the immaculate sugar confection of a wig. He brushed his jacket carefully.

"It's you!" was all that Bryony could choke out.

"Who? What?" breathed Jack.

" 'Tis the man who entangled his horses with mine at East Grinstead. You were unconscious in the carriage, Jack."

The Exquisite stared at her down his scimitar of a nose. "I say! You're the servant—"

He found his jaw battered by Jack's flying fist. "Watch what you say! Miss Bryony Shaw is a gently bred lady."

The Exquisite whistled under his breath. "By thunder! Reggie's sister." He wafted off an imaginary speck of dust from shirt cuffs made of spiderweb-thin lace. "I never knew that old peg had such a lovely sister." He made an exaggerated leg, and Bryony fought a desire to laugh hysterically. "The marquess of Brambleberry at your service, fair lady."

"Brambleberry? Now, that's rich!" Jack said with a snort of laughter. "What's next? The duke of Pig's Hoof? Carey, you fool, don't you ever take anything seriously? I'm surprised you're still alive, the way you defied the cannon fire at Culloden."

"All that mud on the battlefield ruined the sheen on my boots," the mysterious Carey said in bored tones, and yawned. "It took my man two hours of furious polishing to remove the last traces. However, I think they are a lost cause. The leather will never be the same.

Bryony stared from one man to the other. Was she losing her mind or was this man losing his?

Suddenly the two men embraced. "I'm glad you've come," said Carey.

Jack whispered something in his ear, then said to Bryony, "This is my cousin Carey McLendon. He has but lately been in France to plead the prince's case with King Louis."

Bryony could hardly believe that this fop was someone whom Prince Charles Edward Stuart would trust to plead his case with the French king. "My—er—pleasure," she said with a small curtsy.

The Exquisite tilted his head back and laughed.

"Shhh, you idiot! Do you want us to be discovered?"

Mr. Carey McLendon wiped his eyes with a lace-edged handkerchief, not in the slightest perturbed by the threat in the taproom. "Very well, we might as well set out. But I cannot leave without my cane. The gold tip alone is worth a fortune."

Jack rolled his eyes as the Exquisite climbed back up the wall and disappeared inside the room.

"Is he—er—always like this?" Bryony ventured.

Jack nodded. "Yes, he is the most exasperating man I know. Yet he has a brilliant mind and has embarked on some of the most dangerous missions that ever existed."

"For the prince?"

Jack shrugged. "For him, and for others."

"I don't understand."

"Well, he's sort of a mercenary, if you must know. Always was the black sheep of the family."

Bryony pondered his words as she watched McLendon descend once more, this time carrying a cane under his arm. He swirled it in front of Jack. "Handsome, isn't it? Bought it for a small fortune in Paris."

He bowed once more to Bryony and offered his arm. "Shall we go?"

"Where is your carriage?" Jack asked.

"Outside the village."

"And your wife?" queried Bryony.

"Ah! You mean my fat companion in East Grinstead. Our roads parted after I won five hundred pounds from her at cards one night."

Bryony glanced at Jack and saw that he was laughing. "I wish I had been well enough to see that spectacle," he said with regret.

As they walked along, Bryony told him every detail of her previous meeting with McLendon.

Jack groaned. "So you were there!" he told Carey.

"And took the only good chamber in the house," added Bryony ruefully. She presented her escort with a scorching glance.

"Alas! Had I but known . . ." the rogue defended himself with a glint of humor in his eyes.

Jack pounded him in the back so that he had to take a

double step. "You would rather have let me perish from
my wound than turn over your room, wouldn't you?"

McLendon harrumphed and changed the subject.
"Where is that blasted coach?"

It was soon visible in a farmyard. The horses were graz-
ing in the farmer's backyard, and the coachman was
stretched out asleep on the seat inside the coach, his employer's cloak wrapped around him. His snore was abruptly cut off as McLendon grabbed him by the jabot and
shook him awake.

Ten minutes later the horses were harnessed. Jack went
to collect his and Bryony's mounts. When the horses were
hitched to the back, the party left the sleepy village of
Wetheral.

The carriage crossed the border into Scotland the following morning. Using the drove roads along which herds
of sheep and cattle were driven, they would travel by coach
as far as Glasgow and from there, on horseback into the
mountains.

Carey seemed tireless as they journeyed night and day.
Bryony was grateful for the well-sprung carriage, and she
slept as much as possible. Jack was clearly happy to be in
his Scottish cousin's company, though Bryony doubted
their professed relationship. The Scot did not have any
trace of a burr.

Accustomed to Jack's reluctance to reveal anything about
himself, Bryony did not pry into Carey's past. Yet she
could not have had more delightful traveling companions,
a sharp contrast to the dangerous days she had just passed.
Protected by the two men, she felt safe.

One morning, south of Glasgow, the carriage was
stopped by a troop of British soldiers. Jack signaled to
Bryony that she should keep silent. She handed him her
papers and pretended to be asleep.

Carey adopted a haughty tone of voice, playing the role
of the marquess of Brambleberry to perfection. After the
soldier in charge had read their papers, he left with a salute
and an apology.

Bryony dearly wanted to see Jack's papers, but at the
same time she was reluctant to do so. She didn't know if

she could bear to discover that the identity under which he traveled was yet another deception.

Carey McLendon was a handsome man of broad shoulders, slim hips, and long legs. But his eyes, the color of a rain-spattered sea, lacked the fire of Jack's obsidian gaze. Yet Bryony suspected that a volatile temper existed beneath the smooth facade. She had seen glimpses of it as he dealt with the soldiers.

The other irritating, if comical, side of Carey was his constant fiddling with his attire. He appeared every morning without a hair askew on his wig. What color was his real hair? Bryony pondered, and tried to think of a way to push off his wig as if by accident. The man rarely slept, and there was never a wrinkle in his clothes, never a mud spatter on his stockings.

To Bryony's eyes, Jack was infinitely more appealing, with his rough beard and plain clothes. There was such an earthy liveliness in his laughter, in his being. She knew that if he left her, she could never forget him. He had spoiled her for any other man's love.

But there was no guarantee that he would want her by his side after the mission was completed.

Chapter 36

The four villains debated in the yard of The Trout Inn in Wetheral. The bewigged leader was dressed in a blue satin coat with braid ornament. Over his shoulders hung a dark cloak, and the gold scrolls on the scabbard of his sword gleamed. His eyes flashed in anger, his fury formidable to behold.

"They were here last night! The stableboy saw them leave with the fop. He must be a Jacobite contact. He had a carriage that he kept at a farm outside the village." He angrily fingered the hilt of his sword. "We could have caught them! They left together. The boy saw two horses tied to the back of the coach as they drove north."

He cursed them long and hard. "I cannot forgive your stupidity—or my own. Nevertheless, the fop will be easy to follow, and they are with him." He turned to Archie, the Scot with the red hair. "You've always prided yourself on being a good scout. Now is the time to prove it."

Archie sneered. "This is me 'ome country. I know it as thoroughly as me own pocket."

"What shall we do when we find 'em?" asked Joe, the swarthy blacksmith.

The man in the wig stared contemptously. "We will confiscate the gold, of course. Then they'll die, all three of them. We don't want any witnesses to survive, and I'm tired of Miss Shaw dipping her nose into matters best left alone."

Leaving behind the wounded man—the one with the mop of white hair—the three set out on the northbound road. The tracks made by the coach were still fresh. One of the horses had an ill-fitting shoe that made a very distinct print in the dust.

One day later, Jack, Bryony, and their foppish companion had left their carriage and the Scottish Lowlands behind and were riding along the shore of Gare Loch toward Arrochar. The water was ruffled with diamond-crested waves, and the brilliant blue sky lent its color to the water. North and slightly east loomed the peak of Ben Vorlich, its crevices glazed with snow, its sides shadowed by clouds. To the east lay a sweep of mountains topped by Ben Lomond. In the inlets along the loch huddled sod-roofed crofts, clawing a foothold on the rocky shores. Wind-beaten birches clung defiantly to the thin soil, their golden leaves fluttering in unison with the water lapping at their roots.

"I'm surprised you had the circumspection to select good horseflesh, my friend," Carey said to Jack, and readjusted one of his shirt cuffs.

Jack, riding between Carey and Bryony, laughed and shook his fist playfully. "If you're trying to get my goat, you'll have to try harder."

"Goat, me?" said the other man with an air of deceptive innocence. "I was talking about horses, surely."

Jack's lips quirked. "I'm sure you were. Well, it's important to ride strong mounts—our only chance to stay ahead of the men pursuing us. They will not give up at the border, but follow us all the way." He grew serious, rubbing his beard. "I can only pray that they don't know the mountains as well as you do."

"They will, rest assured of that. If not, they would not venture into Scotland at all, but send someone to do their villainous deeds for them." Carey polished the gold top of his cane with a spotless handkerchief. "You should have rid yourselves of them long ago."

Jack shot a glance at Bryony, and a tingle of fear slipped along her spine. "Yes, I wish I had," he said. "But since I was out of commission for several days, I could not get rid of them."

Carey turned to Bryony. "Are you the only one who believes your brother was murdered?" he asked her.

"No, I do, too," interrupted Jack. "And I'll prove it someday—hopefully soon."

They pondered his words, and a sweet softness stole into Bryony's heart. Jack might be a rascal, but he had always supported her in her efforts to find Reggie's murderer. In fact, he had spent an inordinate amount of time helping her.

The following three nights, they slept in scree-filled crevices and in caves that had preserved the cold of a hundred winters. Bryony was cold all the time, but the men appeared unaffected. Jack swept an extra blanket around her and patted her back, evidently aware of her discomfort. There was no sign of their enemies, but Bryony sensed their threat.

As they rode deeper into the Highlands, traversing the forbidding glens at the foothills of the mighty Ben Nevis, the formidable beauty captured their full attention. The mountains were splintered by deep silver blue fjords. Bryony knew the sights would have impressed her coachman, Jules, had he been present, but it would have been impossible to travel by carriage among the crags.

She smiled when she thought of Clover, imagining what his comment would have been had he seen the splendor: "Crikey, m'lady, 'ave ye seen th' likes!"

It was hard to imagine that the Highland heather had soaked up the blood of Scots and Brits alike.

The farther north they rode, the more signs of recent battles did they see. Sod-roofed crofts were scarred with fire, and the peasants stared at the riders with suspicion and anger.

The inhabitants of the Highlands looked as if they had grown straight out of the dark rock itself.

Bryony tried to involve them in conversation, but they ignored her. Here and there they encountered British camps, the red uniforms incongruous spatters of color in a world of grays, browns, mellow purples, and dark greens.

They traversed a pass in the mountains that led down to Loch Linnhe on the other side. A ferry brought them and their horses across the water. The wind smelled fresh and sweet, like well water, filling Bryony with a sense of euphoria. The skies were as clear as a polished globe, but a mass of blue-gray clouds was swelling in the northwest. The water of the loch rippled and slapped against the flat sides of the ferry.

Jack placed his arms across Bryony's shoulders and asked if she had seen a grander view.

"No," she responded truthfully, "this is true splendor."

"Where we're heading, there's a serenity that will soothe and heal you." He bent and planted a kiss on her cheek. "I will always remember the color of your eyes as they are today, soaked in the clarity of the sky and painted with the blue of the lochs."

She smiled and traced his cheek with one finger. "You sound almost sad."

Carey cleared his throat. "Don't look too deeply into each other's eyes or you'll lose your balance and fall into the water."

"Nonsense!" chided Jack. "You're just envious."

Bryony slanted a glance at Carey. Not a hair was out of place on his wig, though a breeze ruffled her own tresses. The sugar-confection curls must be held in place by pomade, she reflected.

Carey's gaze traveled over her with deliberate slowness. "Hmm, perhaps I am a trifle jealous," he admitted with a roguish twinkle.

Jack touched his sword hilt. "Don't even finish that thought," he warned, fire glowing at the depths of his eyes.

Carey chuckled. "It never took much to rile your temper," he said. "I don't have any designs on your lady."

Bryony blushed at his words and looked away. Jack placed a protective arm around her back. "He's but a grumpy old bachelor. Never had a love to call his own, not after a certain Lady D dropped him."

There was a flash of fury in Carey's eyes, and his face whitened. He turned away abruptly and looked toward shore, which was almost upon them.

By evening, Bryony was weak with hunger and fatigue. She wanted to sleep in a bed and eat a hot meal at a table,

but all she got was a bale of peat moss, two slices
bread and ham, and a bottle of strong beer.

Having finished the beer, she grew heavy with slee
knew no more.

The next afternoon, after an arduous ride through the
craggy mountains where the air was thin and mist swirled
around the horses' legs, they reached their goal, a tiny
glen between two jagged mountain ridges. The cloud-
covered and ominous peak, Sgurr na Ciche, loomed behind
them, as if desiring to smother them with its stony mass.

These mountains were the most inhospitable Bryony had
seen so far. The ground was treacherous with loose scree,
and only moss and tufts of heather clung to the rocky
surface.

At the very bottom of the sloping glen a deeper pocket
of earth allowed a thin belt of trees to grow. The riders
headed for the trees.

Bryony remembered that the map had indicated such a
thicket. But she soon realized that the trees gave no shelter, and the ground was strewn with rocks of all sizes,
scabby with lichen and covered with fierce bumps and fissures.

At the end of her endurance, Bryony found the most
comfortable boulder and sat down. She watched as Jack
and Carey spread out the map and studied it. They were
clearly arguing, turning the map this way and that. They
gesticulated and shouted at each other until Bryony decided she had had enough.

Her voice weak with weariness, she asked for the map.
They glowered at her and reluctantly handed it over. "See
what you think," said Jack.

The signs were confusing; the entwined letters "C"
and "S" were located some way up the side of the mountain, but an arrow pointed toward the middle of the glen,
in among a clump of trees. "Well, it's either here"—she
touched the area indicated by the arrow—"or up on the
hillside."

"Let's scout the area." Carey aimed his steps toward
where the arrow pointed and bent down—but only to wipe
off some earth clinging to his boot.

Bryony rolled her eyes as she followed closely behind him. The sun, which cast a strong light through the glen, was about to disappear beyond the mountains. Long purple shadows already stretched across the land.

Bryony knelt on the ground and studied the moss. Digging into the soft carpet, she found that below it was noting but granite. "There is no chance that they could have dug here," she stated, and wiped the dirt off her hands.

Jack was scanning the ridge of the mountain, his hand shielding his eyes from the glare of the sun. "Do you hear something?" he asked, alert and poised for action.

"No, nothing," Bryony replied. "What do you hear?"

"I thought I heard horses."

They all listened intently, but nothing stirred. Bryony had never encountered a more profound silence than among these mountains. Every noise their feet made on the rock echoed repeatedly.

An eerie sensation crept along Bryony's back as she stared at the pass from whence they had descended into the glen. But she saw no movement, and no sounds reached her ears.

"Imagination, old fellow. Relax," said Carey, but his hand was already on the gilded sword hilt at his side.

Their faces grim, the two men studied the map once again. "We have to find the gold. His Royal Highness Charles Edward is expected at Glenfinnan at midnight," murmured Carey.

Bryony started in surprise. The prince! They would deliver the gold directly to the prince!

"The message I received yesterday said that the French ship *L'Heureaux* is waiting at anchor to give him passage to France."

Jack sighed. "I wish the news had been more positive. Do you think all our effort has been in vain?"

"No, not at all. In fact, the gold is most needed now. The men are starving. If the prince sails tonight, he'll return later with reinforcements. His soldiers have to eat now to be ready for battle later."

"But the cause is over for now, isn't it?"

Silence fraught with tension hung in the air.

Carey nodded slowly. "The battle is over. The prince

will fight no more at this juncture. There is a re
thirty thousand pounds on his head. Besides the re
bounty hunters are after him.''

"The Highlanders would never betray him," Jack stated.

"Perhaps not, but Charles Edward is tired of running.
Sooner or later, he would be captured.''

They stared at each other in misery, and at that moment, Bryony shared their sentiment. She had never thought much about the political reasons for their arduous trip, but there was something infinitely sad about Carey's statement. The Highlanders would not see their dream come true.

To soften the blow of defeat, they had to find the gold and deliver it. Only then would Jack be able to forget. Bryony took the dog-eared map from his tense fingers. She stood on the spot indicated by the arrow and stared up at the mountainside. As the sunlight angled deeper, she noticed a darker spot on the rock.

Pointing, she said, "What's that? Looks like some sort of cave or crevice.''

They stared toward the mountain, and Jack whistled. "You might be right, Brye," he said. "Let's explore.''

Bryony was about to reject the invitation, but excitement took hold of her and she scrambled through the scree at the bottom of the mountain. The going was difficult, but once she reached the first ragged platform, the climbing became easier. By zigzagging from one plateau to the next, she soon reached the dark hollow. Jack was already there, Carey not far behind, a peacock against the rough granite surface. He swung his cane as if he was walking in Hyde Park.

She gazed at their horses below. Darkness was falling rapidly now.

Jack gave a shout as she joined him. He stood over two small wooden chests in a shallow corrie, dusting off a layer of dry moss. "I've found them! Look!" Iron bands surrounded the chests, and the hinges looked sturdy.

As soon as Carey arrived, they turned their attention to opening the lids. To Bryony's surprise, Carey produced two keys that perfectly fit the crude iron locks. He must have come directly from France with the keys.

"Who are you?" she asked, unable to stifle her curiosity.

Jack replied in his place. "He's one of Charles Edward's *aides-de-camp*. After Culloden, he sailed to France to negotiate for more arms and soldiers." He indicated the chests. "This is what he got—nothing more, nothing less."

Bryony gasped and stared at the exotic man before her. Then giggles bubbled unbidden to her lips. "Tell me, did you really fight in all the battles?"

Carey snorted. "Of course!"

"But what about your beautiful clothes?" Bryony felt compelled to inquire.

Carey studied one perfectly manicured fingernail. "My man never managed to remove the stains. I had to purchase an entire new wardrobe while I was in France."

Bryony wanted to laugh, but she bit down hard on her tongue to still the impulse, since she didn't want to offend him. Turning her attention to the treasure, she managed to calm down.

There were ten heavy leather pouches stacked in each chest. Jack lifted one and pulled the drawstring open. He poured the coins into the chest and sifted them through his fingers. The *louis d'ors* gleamed richly in the fading light. They upended two more pouches, adding more gold to the heap.

" 'Tis all there. Let's carry it down the hill," Jack suggested. With utmost effort, he hefted one of the chests but cried out in pain. Dropping it, he held his side. "Blast and confound, you would think the pouches were filled with lead. You'll have to assist me," he said between gritted teeth. "Else you'll have my corpse on your hands."

Carey cheerfully grabbed one leather handle, and together they bore the first chest down to the bottom of the hill, Bryony following. She remained there as they walked back uphill for the other chest.

The evening sky was streaked with veils of purple and a scarf of red. A halo of gold capped the mountains. The glen already lay in darkness, and Bryony shuddered from the frosty bite of the night air.

For a moment she thought she saw a faint light in the

pass through the mountains. Then she decided she must have imagined it. The slash between the mountains was now darker than night, and nothing stirred.

Impatiently she awaited her escorts' return as a sense of foreboding brushed through her.

Jack and Carey were two dark dots on the mountainside as they descended with the second chest. Suddenly losing their balance in the scree, they cursed and rolled down the remainder of the hill. The chest lay stuck behind.

Bryony scrambled up the slope and helped them locate the chest in the darkness. She was so intent on the gold that she did not notice the slow procession of horses through the pass. Not until she straightened her back did she see the torchlights. Three of them.

"Look!" she whispered, pointing at the advancing procession.

"Could be Charles Edward's men," said Carey.

"No! They're not," Bryony said in a strangled voice. "What shall we do?"

Jack touched her arm. "Don't be afraid. Take cover behind some large boulder and don't come forward until we're finished." He pulled his sword from its scabbard.

Carey did the same, and they both shed their cloaks and coats. Jack's pistols protruded from his coat pockets, and Bryony scrambled for their icy handles and the heavy pouches of powder and balls. Taking shelter behind a boulder, she began priming the weapons. They would be ready if Jack needed them, she vowed, her lips pinched into a thin line. Her hands trembled, and her fingers grew numb. She spilled more powder outside the barrel than inside, and she accidentally upended the pouch of balls, though they didn't roll far in the moss.

Taking aim, she stared at the approaching menace. She shivered as she pictured the agonized face of the highwayman she had shot on the way to Cuckfield, and she suspected she would never dare to fire at a man again. The three riders were almost upon them, the torchlight creating an eerie glow around them. The men were dressed simply as far as Bryony could tell, except for one man who was wearing a wig and an elegant coat.

They said nothing until they reached the spot where

Jack and Carey waited, their swords glittering in the torch-light.

"Halt!" Jack's voice rang out. "Who are you, and what is your business?"

The man with the wig chuckled evilly and rode closer until the light fell on Jack's face. He stared in shock, and the torch began to shake in his hand. "You! I should have known it! Who else could have foiled my every effort?" His voice trembled. "I will spear your traitorous heart at last!"

Bryony gasped, unable to believe what she was hearing. It was a voice she recognized all too well.

"Get off your horse and fight, Lippett. You have many things to explain," Jack replied.

Nigel Farnham, Lord Lippett!

He had been following her across England, had aimed to kill her ever since she had first stepped over his threshold and begged for his help.

A blinding fury took hold in the pit of Bryony's stomach and grew until every inch of her was roaring with wrath. She stumbled forward, waving both pistols. Tears of anger streaked her face.

"You—you *cur!* I'll shoot you, I promise."

Nigel stiffened as she burst upon the scene and raised a hand as if to ward her off. "Bryony! Listen to me."

"I'll never listen to you again. I cannot tell you the loathing I feel for you." She waved a pistol dangerously, shouting in anger. "You deserve to die. You have made my life a hell since I returned to England. I've never been more afraid in my life, and you're to blame! I never thought you capable of such villainy."

Jack's hand closed around her elbow, bringing a sense of reality to her. He gently coaxed one of the pistols from her frozen hand and placed it on the ground.

Nigel's eyes shown triumphantly in the flickering torch-light, and Bryony felt an overpowering urge to squeeze the trigger of the other pistol. Her finger moved of its own volition, but at the last moment, something held her back.

She couldn't do it.

Surrendering the pistol to Jack, she cried softly into his shoulder.

"Do you know on whose shoulder you're crying, dearest Bryony?" came Nigel's taunting voice.

Through the blur of her tears she glared at him. 'Shut your snake lips," she spat.

Nigel went on relentlessly. "The man at your side is Lord Bentworth, Reggie's murderer."

The world reeled and tilted, then began to swirl. She had fallen into a vortex of horror that had no end. Arms clutched at her, trying to strangle her, and she fought. She was caught in a void.

"No, no, no! Don't!" Was that hysterical voice really hers?

Carey's command cut through her anguish. "Take hold of yourself." He tried to pull her upright, but she clung to the resilient heather.

Then the sounds of clashing swords sliced through her mind like shards of glass. Stunned, she looked up. The fighting was interspersed with groans and loud shouts.

Booted feet tore apart the moss close to her head, but she didn't move. Numb from the blow of betrayal, Bryony didn't care if she lived or died. She wished they would penetrate each other's black hearts with the swords.

"Give me that gold, and I'll let you all go free," came Nigel's voice above the clash of swords.

"Over my dead body," Jack ground out.

"Sooner or later, you'll be beheaded like all the other Jacobites," Nigel threatened between great gulps of air.

"Then you'll share the same fate." The force of Jack's attack pressed Nigel back, away from Bryony. Jack lunged forward, thrusting furiously at Nigel, who managed to deflect the sword aimed at his chest. The metal clanged in a series of feints and parries. Jack's sprang forward again, his sword glancing off Nigel's shoulder. His left foot caught in the heather, and he fell to one knee. Instantly Nigel closed on him, and his boot clomped down upon Jack's blade.

With both arms, he raised his sword as if it were a dagger, ready to drive it into Jack's body. Furious, Jack flung himself backward, disengaged his weapon, and rolled away. Nigel's blade broke as it connected with the hard ground. At the same moment, Jack jumped to his feet, and lunged forward, his sword slicing into Nigel's shoulder.

"You—foulness!" Nigel swore, clutching his shoulder. He stumbled back, away from the circle of light.

Behind him, the fight between Carey and the other villains escalated, and voices rose in dispute. Jack threw himself into the mêlée as Nigel sank to his knees, groaning.

The sound of scores of thundering feet echoed on the rocks, and Bryony slowly turned her head. In the wildly wavering torchlight, she viewed hairy legs and whirling tartans.

Claymores slashed the air. Scottish war cries rose in the night. Help had arrived. As if watching a Greek tragedy, Bryony saw one of the three villains, a swarthy man, writhe on the ground, a broadsword buried in his chest. The red-haired giant's legs buckled as a huge Highlander bore down on him, ramming a claymore through his flesh. He howled in agony, then lay quiet in the heather.

The fight ended abruptly. Silence fell. The sound of fast-receding hoofbeats echoed in the darkness.

"Where's Lippett? He got away!" Carey called out.

Swearing, Jack sank down on a rock, his chest heaving in labored breaths.

Bryony struggled to her feet, wrapping her arms around her stomach. Jack rose slowly and leaned on Carey's shoulder, their swords hanging limply at their sides. Carey had lost his wig, and Bryony vaguely noticed that his hair was as black as Jack's.

Her heart twisted as she remembered Nigel's revelation. Jack had deceived her once again. No, not again! Always. Ever since the moment she had first laid eyes on him, he had deceived her. Lord Bentworth. No wonder he never wanted to talk about himself or travel to Paris!

Unable to stop her shivering, she wiped her tears with the back of her hand. There was no sign of Nigel. His horse was gone, and the torches scattered on the ground were about to go out. Smoke wreathed ghostlike among the men.

The Highlanders were talking animatedly, bending over the gold. A glittering waterfall of coins flowed through their fingers. Bryony saw an imposing figure join the circle of Scots around the chests. They stopped talking abruptly. Reverently, they whipped off their bonnets and stood at attention, their broad backs straight and unyielding.

Carey rushed forward and fell to his knees before the blond stranger.

"Your Majesty," he said.

Chapter 37

The tall, fair man stood in the center of the ring of highlanders. He was dressed in a tartan plaid, leather sporran, bonnet, and cockade. Broadsword and dirk gleamed at his side. His face was round and cheerful, and he exuded energy and optimism.

"Your Majesty," Carey continued, "I have heard the worst news. Say that it's not true!"

"Aye, I'm afraid it is," responded Charles Edward Stuart. "Time for me to go. I will sail tonight with the French ship anchored at Loch nan Uamh." He touched Carey's shoulder gently. "But I will return, and this gold gives me much hope of a more successful landing in the future. You have been a clever and loyal servant."

"I could not have done anything without the help of my cousin and his brave friend." Carey waved at Jack and Bryony, who stepped forward. Bryony blushed and made an awkward curtsy. Stuart laid his hand on her shoulder. "You have done me a great service," he said softly.

Bryony glanced into a pair of blue eyes that shone with simple gratitude, and she could not help but like the young prince. "My brother wanted to serve you," she said, and dragged a deep breath into her lungs. "But he's dead now." She instantly regretted her words, as she didn't want to burden Charles Edward with her sorrow, but it was too late.

"I will forever be grateful for his support. You shall tell me all about him. I'm sure he was as brave as any of my soldiers." His kindness aroused more misery within her. She could only nod.

Charles Edward turned to Jack, who was on his knees beside Bryony. "And you, my friend, without you there would be no hope for the Stuarts. You have acted admirably."

Jack hung his head. "I could not watch the slaughter of my kinsmen without doing something to atone."

"You have endangered your proud name and everything you own for the cause, and I'm eternally grateful. Once I return to Scotland, I will be honored to call you to my court."

"I shall come," Jack said simply. "There is as much Scottish blood in me as there is British."

Stuart laughed and walked away, whistling a tune. There was purpose in his step, and he swung his bonnet in the air. "Will you come with me to France, McLendon, old fellow?" he shouted over his shoulder.

Carey's sword clattered to the ground, and he sprang forward. "I'd be honored." His face alight with emotion, he turned to Jack. "Will you come and wave me off?"

Jack shrugged, his movements sluggish as he went to fetch the horses. The Scots helped him pile the dead villains onto one of the horses, and they formed a slowly moving procession out of the glen.

Jack looked as if he had lost everything.

Bryony refused to return his entreating glances, rejected his efforts to speak. She stayed far away from him as they rode through a mountain pass to Morar and from there to Arisaig. The hours passed, the horses plodded on, keeping pace with the briskly marching Highlanders. At last they reached the shore of a wide loch, Loch nan Uamh, bordered by high mountains on both sides and lined with a rocky beach.

Here the proud prince had landed little more than a year ago, and here he would end his adventures. Bryony gazed across water reflecting the silver moonlight. The loch widened into the Sound of Arisaig, where a French man-of-war rode at anchor.

Bryony slid from her horse and approached Carey McLendon. Jack followed her closely, trying to stop her, but she shook off his hands.

"May I come with you to France?" she pleaded.

Carey furrowed his brow and stared from Jack to Bryony. He addressed Jack. "Do you mean to say you never told her the truth?" His voice held a tinge of incredulity.

Jack shook his head miserably. "How could I? She believed I killed her brother. I wanted to clear my name before I told her."

"You did kill him!" Bryony wailed. "And I will find a way to prove it."

"Shhh," Carey urged in pained tones. "You're worrying the king." He looked long and hard at Jack. "You didn't kill young Shaw, did you?"

"Of course I didn't," Jack said in disgust. "But make *her* understand that." His eyes were deep fissures of hurt. "I have given her my heart, yet she doesn't believe me."

She wanted to shake him until he felt as much pain as she did. "This is the second time you have deceived me on a grand scale," she cried. "You had weeks in which to clear your conscience, but you never made one effort. I can never forgive you for this."

His face was stark and ghostly in the moonlight. "And would you have believed me if I had told you the truth?"

"You could have trusted me enough to tell me. This is a good measuring stick against the depth of your love. You never trusted me enough to tell me the truth."

"I could not imperil the mission. I told you so before."

Bryony shoved him in the chest in a renewed fit of fury. "You could have told me *after* we secured the map. Perhaps I would have given you the benefit of the doubt, but now I never will. You used me the entire time, and I have struggled through hardships for a cause I was never part of."

Carey clamped a hand over her mouth and shot a furtive glance over his shoulder. "Watch your tongue, firebrand!"

Bryony slumped against him. "I'm sorry. I *did* want to finish the mission for Reggie's sake. He would have been very proud tonight."

Jack moved closer to Bryony. He stood so close, she could feel his agitated breath wafting across her hair. "I'll tell you who murdered your brother," he spat. "That holy friend of yours, Lippett."

She wanted to slap his face, but he caught her fist in an unyielding grip. "Lippett was a greedy cur," she agreed. "He wanted the gold for himself, but as for killing Reggie? No. Impossible," she said. "They were old friends."

Jack shrugged and dropped his hand. "Whatever you say, lovely one. But the fact remains, Lord Lippett turned against Reggie at some point." He brooded for a moment. "And he made sure he was the one who buried your brother's remains—probably to keep anyone from detecting evidence of murder."

She glared at Jack, and his shoulders sagged. "I will not argue further. You're blind to the truth, Bryony."

"Your theory is nothing but wishful thinking, Jack."

They glowered at each other for an interminable moment, then Jack turned away, his steps leaden.

"Will you come with us?" Carey called after his cousin.

Jack shook his head. "I'm weary. Too long have I neglected my estate. I will return to Bentworth Court posthaste. Hard work may well help to mend my broken heart."

Bryony's own heart contracted. She took a tentative step toward him. "I will sail to France, but I'll be back in Sussex to collect Jules and Clover."

His eyes burned into her. "If you plan to rub in my defeat, you might as well not bother to come. I'll send Jules and Clover to you."

"You can't do that. There is a war going on!"

"As if you cared about anyone but yourself and your precious brother," he chided.

Bryony wrung her hands. "That's not fair, Jack."

A sigh trembled on his lips, but he remained motionless. There was no way to bridge the chasm between them. "Godspeed, Bryony."

Tears flowed into her eyes, and it was with heavy steps and a heavier heart that she climbed into the waiting dinghy. As the man at the oars pushed away from the shore, she wanted to rush back, but she remained motionless.

Jack's white shirt was a pale blur on the shore as he waved good-bye to Carey.

"I will miss him," Carey said with sigh.

Bryony's lips quivered. Her world had fallen apart, but she still loved Jack. It was a fact she could not deny.

Dazed, she did not resist when Carey assisted her aboard the ship. She could not feel any excitement about being on a ship with Charles Edward Stuart, heading for France.

"You should not mourn so," Carey said as he showed her to her cabin.

"I thought he planned to marry me," she whispered, clutching Carey's handkerchief to her cheeks. "He pledged me his heart. But that was just another one of his deceptions." Not wanting to exhibit her devastation in front of her escort, she forced back her tears and schooled her features.

"Marriage?" Carey said in dazed tones. "He wanted to marry you?"

Bryony shot a glance at him, noticing the surprise that he couldn't quite conceal. "Yes, I know you must have thought that I was his—er—lightskirt—and I suppose I was in view of what happened." She sighed deeply. "A man can discard a lightskirt, but he can not discard a wife."

"Well, you—er—discarded him, and since you were traveling with him alone, I thought—"

"Yes, yes, I know!" Bryony could not hide the edge in her voice. "I was an utter fool to stay with him. I blindly believed in him." She sighed. "However, I don't want to return to my Aunt Hortense in Paris."

"You managed passage from France all alone and in the middle of a war?"

She gave him a watery smile. "My coachman, Jules LeBijou, has many contacts, some of them not so law-abiding. He arranged false papers and off we went." Her shoulders slumped as she entered the cabin. Carey remained at the door, holding her cloak over one arm.

"I wish I had never fallen in love with the man who killed my brother."

Carey snorted. "I'm certain my cousin did not kill Reggie Shaw. It must be as he said, that Lord Lippett was behind the murder and all the other atrocities you've experienced since your return.''

She smiled again, but her eyes were sad. ''Yes, I admire your loyalty, and I pray every moment that you're right, but that doesn't change the fact that Jack lied to me.''

Carey gazed at her for a long time, then said, ''I believe you would be very good for him. Give him a chance to explain, Miss Shaw. I implore you. After all, Jack saved your life. He told me about your adventures in Sussex.'' He placed her cloak on a cot attached to the wall and left, closing the door softly behind him.

Bryony was numb, every inch of her body stiff. Her heart throbbed, as if a wolf had torn into her chest and clawed that tender organ.

The ship swayed gently as it set sail, and the movement intensified as the wind bore them farther out in the sound. Every second took her farther from the man she loved. Lying on the cot, she stared at the timbers that formed the ceiling and deck. The thick air in the tiny cabin was suffocating her, and she wished it would finish her off. Anything to escape the relentless pain.

For the next two days she barely stirred, and refused to eat the food on the trays that Carey offered her. He was deeply concerned and hovered over her like a mother hen. Once more he was as impeccably attired; he had brought his style to dazzling grandeur without being tasteless. Somehow the elegance did not detract from his manliness, only accentuated it. It also had a comical effect and was the only thing that cheered Bryony.

She teased him, and he responded with a shrug of supreme indifference.

At night sleep would not bless her, and finally she decided to go topside for some air. The proud sails of *L'Heureaux* billowed in the wind. Bryony wished for a storm that would swallow the ship, but her prayer was not answered. Every morning brought pale sunlight and clear skies.

She leaned over the railing, thinking how easy it would be to hoist one leg over the side and let herself fall into the sizzling froth below the ship.

But something held her back.

Reggie's murder had not been explained, so her purpose in going to England had not been fulfilled.

She was trying to make up her mind as to what her next step should be when she sensed Carey's presence at her side. He spoke, slowly and earnestly. "I never thought Jack would find someone to love. He's been a curmudgeon and a recluse ever since the old rumors that he was involved in his stepfather's death."

Bryony shot him a probing glance and opened her mouth to speak, but he continued. "When we were children, Jack was the most good-natured and thoughtful boy anyone could meet. His stepfather treated him badly, and the effect on his mother when his stepfather took a mistress was a hard blow to Jack. I don't blame him for hating the man, but the hatred was slowly destroying him." Carey placed his hand in brotherly concern over Bryony's white knuckles on the railing. "You have worked wonders with him, m'dear. Jack is a changed man. I don't know what you did to him, but when I climbed out of that window at the inn, it was the first time in ten years I had seen him truly happy."

"He simply faced his hatred, and it began to evaporate," Bryony said thoughtfully. "But he still has a long way to go. And now he has lost my trust. Deception ruins the best relationships."

Carey bent eagerly toward her. "Don't you see? He needs your help. You're the only one who can bring him out of himself." He squeezed her fingers. "I beg of you, go back to England. I will personally escort you across the Channel in my yacht. At Seaford we'll find a boat to take you up to Alfriston."

Bryony smiled and hope grew out of the ashes of her heart. "Your're a very persistent fellow. I'm not surprised that Charles Edward wanted you for his aide. You could probably wring money out of a rock."

"Don't change the subject. Go back to my cousin. Jack needs you, and I'm sure he'll help you find the truth about Reggie."

Hope swelled in her chest. "Very well. I will give him one more chance to explain. Besides, I have to collect Jules and Clover."

Chapter 38

A week after landing in France, Bryony and Carey McLendon returned to Sussex. Filled with trepidation, Bryony stepped onto British soil. If the authorities found out that she had spent several days on a French ship with Charles Stuart, they would gladly place her in fetters and take her to the nearest ax block.

Yet the immediate danger was past. Having grown used to the constant threat to her life, she found her new freedom strange. She still threw glances over her shoulder, but always heaved a sigh of relief when she remembered that the nightmare was over.

One ordeal remained. She would have to face Jack. Her longing to see him was almost painful, but her anger overshadowed everything. She prayed he would explain his actions without more evasions and lies. If he gave her one more lie, she would leave and never return.

Alfriston looked unchanged. The town was basking in the bleak evening sunshine of this chilly October day. The road winding past the The Star was dusty and quiet. In fact, the entire village seemed to be asleep as the two riders passed through. Just to the north of Alfriston, they turned onto the road that would end at the gates of Bentworth Court.

"Sussex is lovely, isn't it?" Bryony commented to her gallant escort. Carey had decided to accompany her all the way, just to make sure her confrontation with Jack went well.

"Yes, 'tis indeed," he replied with a wink. "You'll be very happy at Bentworth, and you'll like Thornhollow, the small house Jack loves so well. 'Tis but a short distance from Bentworth.''

She pulled her imperious eyebrows together. ''Yes, he told me about Thornhollow. I only wish he had told me he was the master of Bentworth Court as well.''

''Jack deceived you because he was afraid of losing you. I might have done the same thing,'' Carey told her. ''Yet by concealing the truth, he did lose you. You must give him another chance.''

She flashed him a rueful smile. ''Jack is fortunate to have a friend like you.''

They continued in silence, and soon the tall, wrought-iron gates appeared. There it was, the glittering gem of an estate whose owner was no longer faceless. Her brother's murderer had a name. *Oh, God, let it not be true.* Jack could not have murdered Reggie.

To their surprise, the wide drive was dotted with carriages, and fear clutched at Bryony's heart. *Had something happened to Jack?*

As soon as her horse stopped at the entrance, she slid off and rushed up to apply the knocker. The door stood ajar, and she pushed it open. The hallway was empty, but she could hear the sound of voices coming from the back of the house.

''Ma'am, may I help you?'' said a voice beside her. She turned and came eye to eye with the haughty butler with whom she had spoken once before. He glanced at her elegant, lace-trimmed gown of deep blue velvet, which Carey had purchased for her in France.

''Yes, I would like to see Lord Bentworth,'' she said.

''Whom do I announce?'' The butler turned to look at Carey, who had just entered. ''Ah! Mr. McLendon.'' He bowed and steered his steps toward the sound of voices. There was a movement by the arched doorway at the back, behind the wide, curving staircase. A man swept into the hallway, his steps echoing purposefully over the black-and-white checkered marble floor.

It was Jack. Bryony barely recognized him. Dressed in a pearl-gray satin coat with wide embroidered cuffs and a matching waistcoat, he was the epitome of elegance.

Yet what astonished her most was the transformation of

his face. Without the beard, his jaw was more aggressive than she remembered, and there was an adorable cleft in the middle of the rock-hard chin. His cheeks were gaunter than ever, and there were dark smudges of fatigue under his eyes. His hair was brushed to a shiny ripple of waves and tied back with a velvet bow.

Her heart lurched, and her blood shot through her veins. God, she loved this man! Though her love battled with suspicion and anger, she wanted nothing more than to throw herself into his arms.

Their eyes locked, and Bryony noticed his sharp intake of breath. The fatigue in his face vanished at the sight of her, and his eyes kindled with tenderness.

"Hello, my love, thank you for coming," he greeted her simply. "I've waited in agony for this moment—almost lost hope." He turned to Carey, and they slapped each other's backs. "I knew you would bring her back to me," Jack said with a grateful smile.

"What is happening here?" Carey asked.

"The neighbors, Lord and Lady Dalrymple, their numerous offspring, the squire, and the vicar arrived, wanting to welcome me back home. They desired to hear all about France," he added with a wink at Bryony.

"You must have traveled night and day," said Nigel, studying Jack's face.

He nodded. "I finally got passage with a south-going sloop in Saltcoats. But it was a tedious and lonely journey."

He placed his arm around Bryony's shoulders, and she could not bear to pull away. He led them toward the voices in the back, along a carpeted corridor which ended in a solarium that stretched the length of the main building. The sun made the room pleasantly warm and light. There was a splendid view of the park in the back, and evergreen plants of every size and shape gave the impression of a forest.

Jack introduced Bryony and Carey to his guests. Bryony smiled automatically to the plump Lady Dalrymple and evaded her pointed questions. Lord Dalrymple looked like a strutting peacock in a scarlet coat and waistcoat stretched across his paunch. Their sons resembled their brash father.

Bryony was so dazed by Jack's presence and all the new impressions that she could not follow the small talk with ease. She pulled away and stared across the park, sorting through her thoughts. As she stared at the copse of beeches, she noticed a shadow moving under the trees. Her curiosity awakened, she kept her gaze trained on the spot. The shadow moved forward, and she saw a black cloak and the gleam of a scabbard. It was a man with his hat pulled low over his eyes.

She caught Jack's gaze and beckoned to him.

"I'm anxious to speak with you, darling Brye," he whispered in her ear as he joined her. "There are so many things to explain."

She pointed to the man among the trees. "Who is that?"

Jack stared for a long moment, and when the man stepped out on the lawn, Jack's breath hissed between his teeth. "Some unfinished business. Please go into my study and wait for me. Carey will escort you." He strode over to his cousin and said a few words, then opened one of the tall French doors and stepped onto the terrace. As Carey took Bryony's arm, she saw a last glimpse of Jack sprinting across the park toward the man.

Waiting for Jack to return, she paced the floor of his study. The parquet floor was covered by a soft, jewel-toned Oriental carpet. The cherry wood panels gleamed with polish, and the books lining all the walls stood in military precision behind glass-fronted doors. The room was cozy and warm. A fire rustled in the marble fireplace topped by a frieze of elaborate wood carvings.

The door shot open, and Jack ushered a man swathed in a cloak into the room. The man stood in the light by the fire and doffed his tricorne.

Bryony gasped. It was Lord Lippett. "Nigel," she breathed. "How dare you—"

"I'm glad you have come today, Lippett," said Jack, "so that we can settle our business. This time perhaps we can contrive to keep a civilized conversation." Jack stepped briskly across the floor and stood next to Bryony, who had halted beside the wide desk. He placed a protective arm around her shoulders. "I'm happy that Miss Shaw arrived in time to hear your explanation."

Nigel's lips parted in a contemptuous smile.

"Explanation? I have come to challenge you to a duel."

"But your shoulder must be hurting," Jack said breezily, and riffled through a stack of papers on the desk.

"I will not find peace until I have pierced your rotten heart, Bentworth."

"But why? What have I done? Besides, you could send your seconds to me," he explained patiently, as if talking to a recalcitrant child.

"There is no reason to wait. You've been a thorn in my side ever since Reggie invited you to join our group."

"It was all for a good cause, don't forget that," Jack said. He waved a stiff paper in his hands. "The widow of a Horace Watts forwarded a letter from her husband. According to her, Mr. Watts was in your employ. The gamekeeper, if I'm not mistaken."

Silence fell, heavy and ominous.

"Where is he now?" Jack continued inexorably.

"He left," Nigel said sullenly. He stared from one face to the other with lowered eyebrows. "What does that have to do with our quarrel?"

Carey McLendon laughed. "Have patience, old fellow. I'm sure Jack will explain everything." He sat down on a chair and crossed his legs.

Jack sauntered over to Nigel. He seemed to have grown, and there was vigor in his steps. "This letter proves that you killed Reggie Shaw and Mr. Watts. Mr. Watts killed the Reverend Cleaves on your orders."

Bryony gasped and pressed fingertips to her lips. She had to lean against the desk for support. The air was so thick with tension it was hardly fit to breathe.

"That is preposterous!" Nigel's face paled, and he tried to snatch the paper from Jack's fingers, but Jack held it high in the air, out of reach.

"I will read it aloud." Jack cleared his throat, and Nigel licked his lips nervously, his eyes trained on the letter. "It's no use planning to confiscate it. I know all the words by heart." Jack recited:

I have been struggling with my conscience and my sense of duty toward my employer, Lord Lippett of

Greymeadows. But since he threw me out of the cottage I have shared with my wife for many years, I must clear my conscience. I served my employer with devotion, and I'm embarrassed to confess that I went to any lengths—including murder. I killed a Reverend Cleaves from Battle when he came one night to confront Lord Lippett about a fight with Mr. Reginald Shaw at an earlier date. Mr. Shaw was never seen again after that fight.

I fear for my life since I have failed to locate Miss Bryony Shaw and force her to return immediately to France. Lord Lippett might try to kill me because I know too much. He's afraid Miss Shaw will find out the truth about her brother—This letter is my revenge on my ungrateful employer.

"No!" Nigel lunged for the letter, but Jack stepped neatly out of reach.

"Miss Shaw is entitled to hear the rest, don't you think?" Jack directed at Carey.

"Of course," Carey said, and brushed a speck of dust off his knee.

Nigel tore off his coat, and then there came a sound of metal grinding against metal.

"Jack, beware!" Bryony cried as Nigel held his sword high.

Jack sprang back and ripped out his own sword. The blades met with a bone-grinding clash. Jack wrenched free and took his position in the middle of the floor. Carey McLendon had jumped up, drawing his sword, but Jack waved him back.

"This is between Lippett and me." He glared at Nigel, taunting him with his sword. "You deserve to die for the pain you caused Miss Shaw. We shall finish the fight we started in Scotland. I should have penetrated your heart then"

He delivered a series of fast jabs at Nigel, who struggled to deflect them. He was heavier than Jack, and slower.

Bryony moaned as Nigel managed to evade Jack's attack and get into position. He plunged forward, sword's point aimed at Jack's heart. But Jack's footwork was quick and light across the floor, and he easily parried Nigel's thrusts.

"Give up now and I'll spare your life," he panted as their swords locked at the hilts. They stood eye to eye, only inches apart.

"Never! I will not stand by and take more insults," Nigel ground out. He wrenched free and leaped back.

"You buried nothing but a heap of ashes in that grave at Willow Hills. Isn't that so, Lippett? I know now that Reggie was really buried at your estate Greymeadows, and I have had the body exhumed. It's here in the Bentworth vault now."

Nigel snarled, his sword shooting forward. "Liar!"

Bryony thought she was going to faint. Swirls of blackness were gathering at the edges of her vision.

Jack was standing with his back to the door. He reached behind him and turned the knob. The door swung wide and he jumped into the corridor. He answered a series of passes from Nigel's sword.

Jack's guests must have heard the commotion and crowded into the other end of the passage. "Ohs" and "ahs" came from their shocked mouths, and the other gentlemen drew their swords.

"Stand back," Carey called out as he followed the duelists out of the study.

Bryony's legs barely carried her across the room. She prayed that Jack would emerge from the fight unharmed.

Jack waved the letter in his hand. "The proof is right here," he taunted. "Mr. Watts says you killed Reggie."

Nigel growled and made vicious slashes with his sword. Jack parried his thrusts. With a sharp twist of his wrist, he broke Nigel's offense and forced him back into the study. The deadly dance continued, back and forth over the carpet. Hatred gleamed in Nigel's eyes, and desperate determination tightened his features. "You're a lying fool, Bentworth, trying to push the blame away from yourself," he spat. Making a mad stab with his sword, he managed to spear the letter in Jack's hand. Springing back, he trust his sword into the fire. The paper went up in flames.

Gasps filled the air, and Jack swung his sword, slashing

through Nigel's sleeve. The wounded man howled and dropped his weapon. He sprinted across the floor, shoved Bryony out of the way, and headed for the French doors on the opposite wall.

Carey made a movement as if to pursue him, but Jack held him back. "Let him go," he ordered curtly, his chest heaving. He wiped the blood off his blade with a hand-kerchief before he pushed the sword back into the scab-bard.

"Let him go?" Carey stared at him in disbelief. The guests exclaimed their outrage in high, excited voices.

"That paper was the proof that he killed Shaw!" Carey cried. "How can you prove his guilt now?"

Jack smiled. "Mr. Watts's original letter is in the hand of the magistrate in Cuckfield, the good Squire Hopkins. Soon we'll bring Lord Lippett before him, but not until we have some physical evidence to put before the law." He sighed. "Lippett is too powerful a man to arrest on the grounds of a letter from a dissatisfied employee."

Bryony hurried to Jack's side. "Is it true that Reggie's body is here in the vault?"

Jack cradled her close, and Lady Dalrymple tut-tutted in the background.

"No. I don't know exactly where Reggie is buried, but he's somewhere on Greymeadows land. Magistrate Hop-kins has set two constables to watch Lippett's every move."

"So this play today was to set Lippett up and force him to investigate Reggie's grave?" Carey said thoughtfully. He slapped Jack's back. "You devious devil! How did you know Lippett would be here today?"

"I invited him. Said I had matters concerning Reggie's death to discuss."

"What about the guests?" Bryony murmured, her head resting against his shoulder.

"They will be good witnesses when the time comes. They saw Nigel throw the letter into the fire, after all, and observed the fight."

"What shall we do now?" Carey asked sotto voce.

"Get rid of the guests and ride to Greymeadows. I have

a feeling that Lippett cannot stand the pressure much longer. He'll be forced to investigate the grave. When we find Reggie, we'll have proof that Lippett murdered him.''

Chapter 39

Bryony insisted on riding with Jack and Carey to Grey-meadows, although they warned her that it might be an ugly scene.

"It might be a long wait before he acts," Jack argued.

"I have to find out the truth," she insisted as they rode across the moonlit landscape. It had grown dark before they had managed to extricate themselves from Jack's curious guests.

"How can you be so sure that Reggie didn't burn in the fire?" she prodded.

"You might as well hear the whole story, lovely one." He inhaled deeply. "After the card game, I followed Reggie into his study to discuss the ridiculous gambling debt. I wanted to assure him he had nothing to worry about concerning the debt. Besides, I wanted to ask him why he had gambled so recklessly in the first place. As you know, Reggie was hard up, and I certainly had not joined the gathering with the intention of fleecing him further.

"He told me about Lippett's financial difficulties. Reggie—charitable man that he was—tried to win a lot of money at the card game to help Lippett." He sighed heavily. "But Reggie's luck turned against him. The only reason I can think of to explain why Lippett fought with Reggie later is that he wanted the map . . . for himself. Reggie must have been furious and challenged him. It fits, y'know. Lippett came after us to Scotland when he realized that we had the map."

" 'Tis awful," Bryony said. "But you don't know it was Nigel who struggled with Reggie." Bryony relived the nightmare she had experienced when she had first learned that Reggie was dead. A black cloud was descending over her. She groped for Jack's hand.

"It must have been Lippett who later entered the study at Willow Hills to confront Reggie, but no one saw him. I had just left the estate and was on my way to East Grinstead. I turned in the saddle and saw flames coming from the windows of the study." Jack patted Bryony's knee, sensing her sorrow. "I tried to get inside to save Reggie, but the fire had invaded the other rooms. I was there as the fire consumed the estate."

"But Reggie—"

Jack silenced her with a gesture, his face grim in the moonlight. "There were about twenty people battling the flames with a bucket brigade between the pond and the house. Since there was no sign of Reggie, we took it for granted that he must have died in the fire. The butler said he had heard sounds of a struggle. During the fight, a candelabra must have overturned, accidentally setting fire to the house."

"Why are you so sure Reggie didn't die there?" Carey asked.

"Mr. Watts's letter says he later witnessed Lord Lippett's murder of Reggie in cold blood—he stabbed Reggie from behind when Reggie didn't want to give him the map. He saw Lippett bury Reggie at Greymeadows." Jack hesitated momentarily. "I deduced that Reggie must have revived and crawled out the window. The fire had spread everywhere. I don't know why Reggie didn't stay to fight the flames, but perhaps he was too dazed to realize what was happening."

"You mean he confronted Lippett later?" Carey sounded incredulous.

"Yes. I believe that Reggie—with vengeance on his mind—rode to Greymeadows to take Lippett to task for wanting the map for himself."

"It makes sense—if Reggie is buried at Greymeadows as the letter indicated," Bryony said.

Concentrating on their own thoughts, the three friends continued to ride in silence the fifteen miles to Greymeadows. At the boundaries of the estate, they dismounted.

Since Bryony had visited here many times in the past, she knew the way through the woods. They entered the extensive park behind the mansion and, protected by darkness, sneaked across the lawns, skirted the dry fountains, and chose a path, shaded by tall trees, that led to the terrace. The house was dark, the silence deep.

Jack whistled softly, and a return whistle came a moment later from behind a hedge of cone-shaped bushes.

Jack gripped Bryony's hand and led her from one bush to another until they had reached the hedge.

There, two men were crouched on the ground. "Lord Bentworth," said the first, a thickset man with a deep voice. "Lord Lippett just came home and went straight to his bedchamber, as far as we could tell."

"These men are the Constables Hines and Perkins," Jack explained to Bryony. "They have been keeping watch on Lord Lippett ever since I contacted the magistrate."

The two men doffed their hats. "Evening, Miss Shaw. Fancy that Lord Lippett is a murderer," they said, shaking their heads.

"I only wish he would make his move," Jack replied, brushing a hand through his hair.

"The letter could be wrong, governor," said the thickset Constable Perkins. "That Mr. Watts was sort of a strange bird." He scratched his head. "And a cold one. It wouldn't surprise me if he killed a man."

"He did," Jack said in clipped tones. "In the letter, he confessed everything. I found his corpse at Willow Hills."

"Did Mr. Watts's letter say exactly where Reggie was buried?" Bryony asked. So many things had been revealed that she felt dizzy.

"No."

"We'll find out where," muttered Constable Perkins. "Soon, I hope."

The hours dragged on until there was a faint line of gray on the horizon.

"He's not coming out tonight," Bryony whispered, and stretched her stiff limbs. "The wound in his arm may be too painful."

"I only nicked the skin," Jack explained. "I doubt if he had a minute's worth of sleep tonight. Not if he believes

I moved Reggie's body. He won't have any peace until he finds out for sure.''

Bryony knew he was right, but the waiting chafed on her nerves.

Jack clasped her hands. "You came back to me, gave me another chance. I will always be grateful for that,'' he whispered. "And if I can only prove—''

"Shhh,'' Bryony said, placing her fingertips on his lips. "I do believe you're telling the truth.''

"I deceived you, and I hate myself for it. But I was afraid you would leave me if you knew my identity. You were so set on your pursuit of Lord Bentworth.'' He hung his head. "I couldn't take the risk of losing the only woman I truly love. And I was afraid of what might happen to you, alone and defenseless.''

Tears streaked her cheeks, and she dashed them away. "I pray that your suspicions are right, that Nigel is guilty.''

He looked so worried that she had to reach out and smooth the lines on his forehead. "What if we don't find the body? Will you still trust me?'' he asked.

She sighed and smiled weakly. "We do know one thing—you did not pocket the French gold. Your motives were pure, so even though I hate to admit that I might have been wrong in my accusations, you're probably innocent.'' She thought for a moment, concentrating on the first pink glow over the treetops. "Reggie would have fought anyone who was trying to steal the map. Only that person had a reason to kill him.''

A smile dawned on Jack's face. "You're too clever by far, lovely one.'' Throwing a furtive glance among the bushes to see if the constables were watching, he leaned closer to kiss her. But before their lips could meet, a *pssst* reached their ears.

Carey was crawling toward them. He had been keeping watch on the opposite side of the house. "Lippett crept out of the house a minute ago. No servants are up, so I think this is the moment we've been waiting for.''

As they followed Carey, Jack asked, "Where was he heading?''

"Toward the shed by the stables. To get a shovel, I'll wager.''

They looked cautiously around the corner of the house, and there he was, a shovel sticking under the hem of his cloak. He threw a furtive glance over his shoulder before heading toward the spinney at the farthest end of the park.

Jack squeezed Bryony's hand in excitement. They smiled at each other, and Bryony realized how close she was to putting Reggie's soul to rest. Peace stole over her, and a heavy burden left her shoulders.

One of the constables had left, and the other explained that he had gone to fetch the magistrate in Cuckfield. Afraid to reveal their presence to Nigel, they stayed far behind him, barely keeping him in sight. Carey, at the front, waved them forward once Nigel was out of sight.

Darkness still hung heavy in the spinney. The moss on the ground muted their footsteps. Nigel had stopped in a clearing. Hauling a flask from his pocket, he took a deep draught and swayed slightly. Bryony realized he was inebriated. He swept his gaze along the trees bordering the glade, then went down on his knees. Peering closely at the ground, he swept his hand back and forth over the earth. A gray light filtered through the trees, barely revealing the cloaked figure. Bryony held her breath. The seconds dragged on. There was a slight movement behind her, and she turned her head. The constable was returning accompanied by a tall, lanky man with a sleep-heavy face who must be Magistrate Hopkins. He halted without a sound, his eyes widening at the sight of Nigel.

Suddenly Nigel swore and jumped to his feet. He stared at the ground, perplexed, then he raised his head and howled in rage. "Bentworth tricked me!" he cried, and flung the shovel away. He stomped around the clearing, spewing out invectives. "That devil tricked me!"

"Reggie's body must be here," Bryony whispered to Jack. "You were right."

She rose, her legs numb. Jack tried to stop her, but she pushed his hand away. No one halted her progress as she walked into the glade. "You killed Reggie, Nigel," she said, her voice breaking. "You buried him here."

He whirled around, his eyes boring into her. "What—? Bryony!" His gaze darted past her, and his shoulders slumped. "The law, is it?" he said with a sneer as the men approached. His face grew hard and cold. "Yes! Yes, by God, I killed Reggie!" He pointed to where he had been kneeling. "You'll find him there."

Bryony averted her eyes, unable to bear to look at her brother's grave. She scarcely noticed when Nigel walked up to her and whispered softly, "Do you want to join him, little Bryony?"

She jerked her head up, staring into his bloodshot eyes. "How dare you! Why did you do it?"

"I told you about my financial difficulties. They have worsened this last year. I needed the gold, don't you see? Reggie didn't want to give it to me. My beautiful estate was on the brink of ruin, and he wouldn't help me."

"You could have sold some of your art collection."

He stared at her as if she was insane and laughed hollowly. "Sell my art? Impossible! Don't you understand anything? It belongs to me. Its rightful place is at Greymeadows. Don't you see? The others would hold me in contempt if I let it go." He sneered with haughty disdain. "Besides, who are you to tell me what to do with my art? It is my true passion, my only pleasure." He glanced at the lawmen who were now digging up the grave. Jack stood close behind him to prevent any attempt to escape.

Nigel's arrogance suddenly broke, and he croaked, "Reggie could have used part of that gold to rescue Willow Hills from ruin. But he could see nothing except the cause—the damn cause! He sold everything he had and gave the money to Stuart."

Bryony felt a twinge of compassion for Nigel then, but only a twinge. "So all that Mr. Watts wrote in his letter is true?"

Nigel looked deathly pale in the strengthening dawn. "I suppose it's no use denying it." Abruptly his manner charged once again. "Don't you want to look at your brother?" he taunted with a last show of defiance.

Bryony shook her head. She felt cold and utterly sad. "You and I and Reggie were all friends once."

Nigel's eyes glittered and he seemed to shrink away, as if life was draining from his limbs. "I do remember our times together when we were children. But Reggie changed. He became my enemy when he refused to help me.''

''*You* changed, Nigel,'' Bryony cried. ''You became calculating and evil. Reggie tried to help you by staking all he had left at the card game. Doesn't that count for anything?''

''Farthings and pennies,'' Nigel whined. ''A few pounds. It would not have saved me.''

''That isn't true,'' said Jack. ''Hundreds of pounds were wagered that night.''

''I needed more, much more!''

Bryony slapped his face. ''You killed Reggie because he wouldn't give up his high principles to save your skin.''

The lawmen put aside their shovels, waded through the weeds, and surrounded Nigel. Jack pulled Bryony close and held her as if he never wanted to let go. Tears shimmered in her eyes as she glanced up at him. ''We'll have to bury Reggie properly,'' she whispered.

He nodded. They clung to each other as Squire Hopkins placed manacles around Nigel's wrists, and led him away. Nigel lifted his head once and looked straight at Bryony, his eyes red with tears. ''I never meant it to end like this.''

Bryony cried until she was empty inside.

After the confrontation with Nigel, Bryony returned to Bentworth Court with Jack and Carey. Exhausted, she had slept through the rest of the day and the next night.

Rising early, she dressed in a simple gown and walked downstairs. No one seemed to be up this glorious autumn morning. She was still tired and sad, but a feeling of relief was beginning to raise her spirits. Hope glowed in her heart. The nightmare was over at last, and Reggie would be at peace. She smiled and ran into the sunshine outside.

Bentworth Court was lovely even during the leafless season. The gardens were laid out formally in a pattern of box hedges and fountains. The borders would be blazing with color in summer, but now they were covered with mulch. The gravel paths were raked, and not one weed had taken root to mar the perfection. Every inch of the gardens had been designed to create beauty and harmony.

Steering her steps toward the back of the mansion,

Bryony happened upon a greenhouse partially shielded by a tall hedge. The garden beyond the greenhouse was wild and unkempt, the uneven patches of earth cluttered with spindly rosebushes.

There was a movement in the greenhouse, and Bryony looked through the fogged-up windows. She instantly recognized Jules's hulking shape, and beside him, Clover. As she stepped inside, the boy rushed forward and threw himself into her arms. His face lit with a wide grin, he shouted, "M'lady, yer 'ome at last! I 'ave waited by th' gates ev'ry day."

Delight curled within her, and she had to cover her face against his tiny shoulder lest he saw her tears. "I have missed you, too," she said. She glanced at Jules and smiled. The tall Frenchman laughed so that his round middle shuddered alarmingly.

"Mademoiselle, 'tis a pleasure," he said with a sigh, and folded his hands reverently.

Holding Clover by the hand, she advanced into the greenhouse and let Jules kiss her fingers. "What are you two doing in here?" she asked.

Jules showed her his grimy hands. He gripped a shovel in one hand and a wooden pail in the other. "I'm a gardener here now. The estate, Thornhollow, where Lord Bentworth sent me when you went to France, is close by. Le Comte owns that estate and this one. He lets me pick as many roses as I want. Le Comte has a passion for roses and lets me help him in his experiments."

Bryony's heart fluttered. They shared an interest in roses, and Jack had never told her. Walking from one large raised bed to another, she studied the plants. Each was marked with a tag with a name written on it.

Jules led her to one plant that was nothing but a stem and two tiny branches. "This is his favorite," explained Jules. "He has invented it and cannot wait to plant it in the garden."

Bryony read the label, and her heart lurched. It read BRYONY, MY LOVELY.

"It's a very pale yellow rose, almost white. But it—how d'you say—it glows with an inner light, just like you, mademoiselle.'' Jules's face was wreathed in a simple smile, and the radiance of his kindness wrapped around her.

She placed her hand lightly on his arm. ''You like it here, don't you?''

Jules nodded vigorously. '' 'Tis heaven.''

''And you? How did you get here?'' Bryony asked Clover.

''Th' master came an' fetched me at th' parson's place in Tutbury. 'E says as 'e wants t' make me like 'is own son. I can't remember th' word.''

''Adoption,'' Bryony explained. ''He wants to adopt you.'' She caressed the small blond head. ''And how do you like that idea?''

''I likes it! 'E 'as already let me ride 'is 'oss, even though th' 'oss tried t' toss me off agin. An' 'e says I'll 'ave to learn readin' and writin'.'' He pouted. ''I don't like that idea.''

''You will, once you find out what 'tis like to know your letters,'' Bryony promised him.

''Th' Frog is teachin' me French. 'E's a big looby, but I likes him. 'E's always kind t' me.''

''Then you should be kind to him.''

''Miss Shaw is right, you know, scamp,'' Jack said from the doorway. He was leaning against the doorframe, and his expression was tender. Looking more attractive and dangerous than Bryony remembered, he sauntered forward and placed his arm around her shoulders. ''Miss Shaw has brought me two very nice friends, and now I need to convince her to stay with us here.''

''Ye mean t' say 'e 'aven't arsked 'er t' marry ye yet?'' Clover asked in disgust.

''No, I haven't, but I will very soon.'' He looked deeply into Bryony's eyes. ''Would you like to come with me for a walk?''

She nodded, drowning in his smile. As they left arm in arm, Jack glanced back over his shoulder. ''And don't you dare spy on us, Clover!'' he admonished.

''I promise,'' Clover chimed, but Bryony and Jack exchanged knowing glances.

Jack led her along a narrow path bordered by tall elms. ''This is the Thornhollow spinney,'' he explained.

Bryony sighed. "I wish you had been honest with me from the first day we met. How easily you could have told me that Thornhollow bordered on Bentworth Court, one of the largest seats in the south country. You could have told me everything. I had a right to know. But you kept it all from me."

Taking hold of her shoulders, he gazed into her eyes. "I know. But Mr. Watts's letter didn't arrive until I returned from Scotland." He flicked the tip of her nose. "I planned on clearing my name, and if you hadn't arrived when you did, I would have come looking for you. To the ends of the earth, if necessary." He brushed away an unruly curl from her brow. "You mean everything to me."

Bryony's lips trembled in joy. "Do you think we could bury Reggie's body here?"

"Of course. It's a great honor that you would even consider Bentworth as Reggie's last resting place."

"He would have approved." She felt as if she had reached her haven in a stormy sea. "Oh, Jack, I forgot to ask you one thing," she said. "You might think that I'm prying."

"Ask me."

"Explain your paper that opened every barrier as we rode to Scotland."

He smiled enigmatically and delved into his pocket. "I happen to still carry it around. I don't know when I'll need it." He handed her the document. Heavy seals embossed the bottom, and she studied the signature: George II.

She gasped. "How did you come by this? You're one of George's advisers?"

He shrugged and smiled enigmatically.

Bryony's eyes widened in understanding. "No!"

"No . . . Let's just say that the smugglers in Alfriston have contacts in the underworld.'

A smile grew at the corners of Bryony's lips. "You—you *rogue*. Your document was forged."

He chuckled, and they continued their walk, clinging to each other. At the end of the path, Bryony glimpsed a white trellis shaped like an arch. Red vine twined around it.

"I hated to witness all the pain Lord Lippett caused you," Jack murmured.

"I confess I never was very good at judging character," Bryony said with a sigh. "He seemed so sincere."

Jack smiled. "Well, your *heart* obviously has no difficulty judging people. The only thing that worries me now is that you will shun my offer of marriage because of my deception. But, remember, I was desperate." He tilted up her face, and she read the love in his eyes. "Can you live with me and share everything with me, even if I'm far from perfect?"

"If you can live with me, a woman who is also far from perfect," Bryony stated with a mischievous smile. "I love you."

He shouted his joy and lifted her high in the air, then reverently pulled a paper from his pocket. Unfolding it, he ordered her to read.

"Special license for marriage?" she asked.

"Why wait, eh? Reverend Partridge helped me procure one, and he and his wife will be delighted to travel here and marry us in the family chapel at Thornhollow. What do you say? Will you become my darling wife?"

She gazed at the two-story brickhouse in front of her. Thornhollow. It was an enchanged place, or was it their love that infused everything with magic? Toward the back, wholly covered with rose branches, stood the chapel. It was the perfect place to seal their love. Bryony gazed into Jack's eyes for a long moment, and he grew restless for her answer.

"Yes, I will," She finally said. "And let's not wait."

"Hurray!" came Carey's and Jules's baritones and Clover's shrill voice from behind the hedge as Lord Bentworth gathered his lady into his arms and gave her a kiss that left her breathless and longing for more.

AUTHOR'S NOTE

Charles Edward Stuart—Bonnie Prince Charlie—left Scotland with the French man-of-war *L'Heureaux* at the end of September 1746, and returned to France. Although he still had loyal sympathizers in both England and Scotland, he was never to stand on Scottish soil again.

When the war between England and France ended, Stuart was ultimately barred from France since Louis XV was forced to recognize the Hanoverian king, George II, as the only king of England—unless he wanted another war on his hands.

Stuart's every attempt in Europe to raise weapons and funds for his cause failed. The treasure I describe in *Desperate Deception*, which was intended to support another Stuart uprising, was my own invention.

MARIA GREENE

A native of Sweden, MARIA GREENE is a blonde, blue-eyed echo of her long-ago ancestors the Vikings. Like them, she roamed the world looking for adventure until she settled down with her American husband, Ray, in New York State's beautiful Finger Lakes region.

Maria likes to read books by Susan Howatch, Jennifer Wilde, Patricia Veryan, James Herriot, Sidney Sheldon, Barbara Pym, and Charlotte Vale Allen. When she is not writing, she does needlepoint, gardens, plays with her cat, Max, and sometimes goes fishing for lake trout and salmon with Ray, an avid fisherman.

Maria, the author of the Avon Romance *Reckless Splendor*, loves to hear from her readers!

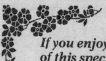 

*If you enjoyed this book, take advantage
of this special offer. Subscribe now and . . .*

GET A *FREE*
HISTORICAL ROMANCE
—— NO OBLIGATION(a $3.95 value) ——

Each month the editors of True Value will select the four best historical
romance novels from America's leading publishers. Preview them in
your home Free for 10 days. And we'll send you a FREE book as our
introductory gift. No obligation. If for any reason you decide not to keep
them, just return them and owe nothing. But if you like them you'll pay
just $3.50 each and save at least $.45 each off the cover price. (Your
savings are a minimum of $1.80 a month.) There is no shipping and
handling or other hidden charges. There are no minimum number of
books to buy and you may cancel at any time.

send in the coupon below

Mail to:
True Value Home Subscription Services, Inc.
P.O. Box 5235
120 Brighton Road
Clifton, New Jersey 07015-1234

**YES! I want to start previewing the very best historical romances being published today. Send
me my FREE book along with the first month's selections. I understand that I may look them
over FREE for 10 days. If I'm not absolutely delighted I may return them and owe nothing.
Otherwise I will pay the low price of just $3.50 each; a total of $14.00 (at least a $15.80 value)
and save at least $1.80. Then each month I will receive four brand new novels to preview as
soon as they are published for the same low price. I can always return a shipment and I may
cancel this subscription at any time with no obligation to buy even a single book. In any event
the FREE book is mine to keep regardless.**

Name _____

Address _____ Apt. _____

City _____ State _____ Zip _____

Signature _____
(if under 18 parent or guardian must sign)
Terms and prices subject to change.

75562-9A